iii
third eye

an imprint of Skywriter Books

SKYWRITER

Also by Holly Payne

The Virgin's Knot

The Sound of Blue

Praise for Holly Payne's *Kingdom of Simplicity*

"Payne takes us into the exotic, strange world of the Amish to explore the universal nature of forgiveness. Eli Yoder is a young man born with a disfigurement common to his community—webbed hands—but who carries a deeper disfigurement in his heart—an inability to come to terms with a tragic accident and the unknown man who caused it. I found myself rooting for Eli, and I was taken to the place where the best books take us—into my own heart, wondering what on earth I would do if I was in his shoes."
-Caroline Paul, author of *East, Wind Rain* and *Fighting Fire*
www.carolinepaul.com

"Holly Payne's KINGDOM OF SIMPLICITY is a classic tale of the redemptive power of forgiveness. Eli Yoder will capture both the reader's heart and their compassion as he struggles to come to terms with the trauma of his past. Payne's skill as a writer makes KINGDOM OF SIMPLICITY irresistible and Eli's story will remain with her readers for years to come."
- Kathleen Caldwell, owner of A Great Good Place for Books

"I loved this story. It so moved me that I sat in the middle of the Philadelphia airport reading the end of this book in tears. My heart broke for Eli Yoder page after page. How misguided we are in our youth, or even as adults, when we make assumptions about our identities and the way others perceive us. Holly Payne's KINGDOM OF SIMPLICITY is a gift to be shared with abundance."
- Rosanne Selfon, President of Women of Reform Judaism

"An unforgettable tale of loss, hope, and redemption that establishes Holly Payne as one of our finest literary fiction writers . . . Eli's journey resonates with our human need to find meaning in an often incomprehensible world."
- C.W. Gortner, author of *The Last Queen*

kingdom of simplicity

◇

a novel by
holly payne

Skywriter Books
Sausalito

Published in the United States by Third Eye, an imprint of Skywriter Books, Sausalito, California
www.skywriterbooks.com

Skywriter Books, SkyMountain design and Third Eye are registered trademarks of One Pink Hat Corp.

LIBRARY OF CONGRESS CATALOGING-IN-PUBLICATION DATA

Payne, Holly
Kingdom of Simplicity: a novel / Holly Payne
p. cm.
ISBN 978-0-9822797-7-9
LCCN: 2009900693
1. Amish—Social Life and Customs—Rumspringa—Fiction. 2. Teeange boys—Fiction.
3. Religion—Christianity—Anabaptist History—Fiction. 4. Pennsylvania—Lancaster County—Fiction. 5.
Spirituality of Forgiveness—Fiction. I. Title.
PS3616.A97 K5 2009
813'.6—dc22   2009900693

Printed in the United States of America on FSC (Forest Stewardship Council) paper
First Printing, July 2009

Design and art direction by Leslie Iorillo, lesle i. design

Grateful acknowledgement is made for permission to reprint the following:
Diesel Fitter joke used with permission from the compilation CD "J2K: As Told by Jackey Budderschnip" created by Mel Horst, Witmer, PA ©2000. Dirty limerick used by permission from The Book of Bob by Paul Chasman, Dancing Moon Press, ©2005. Amish pluckets recipe printed with permission from Bear Wallow Books, Indianapolis, Indiana 46240, Bear Wallow Books Imprint, 2002 edition ©1980 by J. S. Collester

For more information, please contact the publisher at
Skywriter Books, 180 Harbor Drive, Suite 204B, Sausalito, CA 94965
info@skywriterbooks.com

For my father
Ellis P. Payne

and Patrick Pash

Note to the Reader:

When I set out to write this book, I did not know I was embarking on a journey of forgiveness. I was simply inspired by the 18 years I spent living near the Old Order Amish of Lancaster County, Pennsylvania, and wanted to capture the essence of their culture. However, as the story progressed and I was led deeper into the journey of Eli Yoder, I realized that I had created him as a way to forgive a drunk driver who struck me in 1994 and left me unable to walk for nearly a year. I have written nothing about this accident other than what is in my journals. For many years, it was too tender of a subject for me to write about, so I didn't. Perhaps I needed the protection of fiction to give me the safety and freedom to express how 'the accident' impacted me, and to realize that maybe it was no accident at all. I have never met the driver, yet he continues to be a great influence on my life. Although I would not wish it upon anyone, the accident was a gift because it set me on a course that forced me to reckon with my own mortality at a very young age, and to use the gift of writing while I'm alive. In many ways, this novel is the first experience I have had as a writer where I was aware of the journey it was taking me on toward my own healing. Usually, that comes later, in retrospect.

It is my intention as a storyteller to illuminate the endangered people and places of this world. I hope the world I have created in this story reflects the Amish in the most authentic light. Although they value simplicity, they are by no means a simple people but a complex and complicated subculture that I have done my best to research and to understand. It is perhaps the Amish practice of forgiveness for which I am most grateful to have learned from them, and to see during the writing of this book, when on Monday morning, October 2, 2006, a young man shot ten Amish girls in a one-room school house in Lancaster County, killing five girls and himself. Over the course of the same week, I watched in awe, along with the rest of the world, how the Amish community reached out to the shooter's family and attended his funeral while they were also burying their own daughters. During the next six months, the Amish razed the old school, rebuilt and relocated a new school, and established a fund to help the shooter's widow and three children recover from the tragic school shooting. It was no wonder that a group of Lancaster County Amish traveled to Virginia Tech University to support the grieving families and friends of the 32 students and teachers shot in April 2007. Although the Amish wish to remain separate from our world for many reasons that I have hopefully brought to light in this story, their compassion and forgiveness remain boundless.

-Holly Payne
Sausalito, California

"Forgiveness is the fragrance a violet sheds on the heel that has crushed it."

- Mark Twain

PART ONE

◆

Lancaster County, Pennsylvania

ONE

IN THE THICK BARK of a walnut tree that grows on the road at the edge of our farm is a scar that has haunted me for most of my life. Though the mark resembles a lightning strike, it is less visible to the unpracticed eye. Those of faith say it was the hand of God that put it there, but it's taken me a long time to see the imprint of anything holy.

They say an accident happens by chance, with no planning or deliberate intent. And people who knew my sisters would have said just that. *It was an accident.* But I would like to tell them there are no accidents. There are only opportunities.

Yes, in a perfect world, I'd like to tell them that, and most people who pass our farm consider it to be a sort of paradise. But my message would be misleading if I didn't tell them that by telling my story, I am rebuilding that paradise, word by word.

Like the old walnut tree, I, too, was struck. Not by lightning, not by a horse, and not by anything man-made. I was struck one year ago by the lot, an occasion more solemn and sobering to an Amish male than the day we choose to be baptized after years running around in *rumspringa*.

Nothing scares an Amish man more than knowing his entire life might change because he is asked to serve the church. It's not like we can prepare. There are no courses to study, no tests to take. Even when a man is chosen, the Amish traditionally offer condolences, not congratulations. It is not a moment to celebrate.

No boy I ever knew dreamed of growing up to be a minister. He dreams that the lot passes over him, for an appointment lasts not a few years, but for the rest of his life.

I was that terrified boy, even at the age of 45, head down, eyes closed, smelling the cracked leather hymnals as they were passed around the ten of us who had been named by our family, friends and neighbors as candidates for ordination. Not one of us had a dry shirt. We sat at the table and sweated together, looking at those hymnals with such intensity, I swear we could have started a collective fire with our fear. Inside one of them was a slip of paper with two verses, one from Proverbs and one from Acts, that basically said whoever finds the slip of paper in their hymnal was chosen by God. There wasn't a man among us whose fingers didn't shake, whose legs didn't bounce under the cover of the table and who, given the choice, would have run like mad to avoid the burden of living life as a chosen servant. I'm not sure any of us thought we possessed the traits of a qualified minister as iterated by Timothy. A man must be "vigilant, sober, of good behavior, given to hospitality, apt to teach." Who among us could qualify for that? Who among us would ever be ready to serve *for the rest of our lives*?

I know I wasn't. I had a wife, children and a job, having inherited my father's auctioneering business and five acres of paradise to preserve. I had no more juice for my vocal chords after a busy night calling auctions than I had for a Sunday morning sermon. Of all the men sitting with me at the table, I was the least likely candidate.

Didn't they know? I was no servant. I had been a thief. I wanted to tell them after all these years of secrets and shame that I had stolen a camera when I was nine years old. The Amish don't like to have their photos taken, though I have seen a few Amish gladly lift their eyes from the shadows of bonnets and black brims to smile for the camera and share the joy of our simple living. We believe in graven images. We believe that a single photograph has the power to steal our souls, though the photos don't reveal the secrets behind the smiles, all that we hold back with our eyes and all that we choose not to see. I never wanted the camera. Not really. I wanted what it held.

TWO

THOUGH IT HAS BEEN nearly forty years, I remember the day that lead to the accident. July 6, 1976. Tuesday. Market day. A tourist family had left the camera behind with their change, a few dimes that I scraped into the cigar box behind my grandfather's candy stand, one of many side-by-side stands inside the market tent. My sisters had left me in charge of the counter while they snuck outside to watch local teenagers set off fireworks in the parking lot. I couldn't see them through the huge tent, but I knew what they would do. My oldest sister Hanna had been known to exchange our grandfather's confections for multi-colored smoke bombs that the girls would set off behind the barn, where they could dance unseen by our father. After every Fourth of July, when the fireworks went on sale, she'd make an extra block of fudge to barter with the local boys who supplied half the county with explosives from the Carolinas. She was bold. And although she did not see the harm in colored smoke, Hanna knew the damage of a photograph.

She had returned for more fudge and paused, seeing the family's teenage son had returned, too, with a camera, to take pictures of me. Hanna asked him to stop. She was nineteen and not afraid to ask for what she wanted. Her tone was warm and friendly at first, but the boy continued to snap at me.

And I let him.

Nobody had ever wanted to take my photo. Not that it mattered. We weren't allowed to pose for the tourists. My parents had lectured us countless times, but my oldest sister preached best. Hanna pulled Sarah and me aside one day when she was walking us home from school after a tour bus stopped to see us. "If they insist, close your eyes," she said. "Eyes are the door of the soul. Whatever you do, keep it locked. Look down. Look away." I wanted to know what happened to our souls if our photos were taken anyway. Hanna said as long as we didn't look directly into the camera, God would know we hadn't intended to give away our souls.

Tourists loved Hanna and my sisters, and had no qualms about shoving their way out of rental cars to gather at the edge of our farm, watching us work the earth between our bare hands and feet. We were used to the cameras in the same way we grew accustomed to the welts on our arms from spider bites and poison ivy. Cameras were like cars. We avoided them when we could. I don't think the tourists meant any harm though. My sisters possessed a universal beauty and for this, they became the darlings of all who laid eyes on them.

They shared my mother's blue eyes and fair Swiss skin, faces framed by walnut colored hair spun with copper and gold at the temples, twisted into a bun and pinned at the nape of their necks. I shared only the color of their hair. I was a boy, and nothing about me matched their beauty or grace.

At nine, I was half their size, skinny, and barely able to reach over the counter. I usually hid behind my sisters and scooped candy from the cases, but something about the boy with the camera made me want to be seen by him. I held the spade that I used to shovel candy and stepped away from the counter so that he could have a better look at me. I pulled the brim of my straw hat over my eyes and bit my lip, chewing away the smile. It felt good to hear the click of the camera, and the click of his tongue when he got excited about whatever he saw through the lens. I felt his eyes on me and I liked the attention. The boy moved closer, his red belly pressed against the counter. He was sunburned and sweaty and left round prints that looked like glazed donuts on the glass.

I flashed a toothless grin. I figured he wanted to see the gap in my teeth. I liked how it made me whistle when I spoke. "Sweet corn," I said and pointed to the gap.

"You get any money?"

"For what?"

"Your tooth."

"No." You get money for losing your tooth?

"Just hold your hands still," he said.

The boy snapped more photos. I watched his fingers press the button, bearing down with precision and purpose, like he was hunting. Suddenly, a pair of scissors and a hairy knuckled hand with thick gold rings covered my face.

"Please don't take his photo."

I recognized the voice. An authoritative boom, sharpened by a childhood lived in North Philadelphia. Unmistakably Leroy Fischer, an old family friend who had worked for us as a driver when we needed to travel long distances. We'd spent many hours with him in his big white van, a side business he'd started to help pay for the barbershop he wanted to buy in Strasburg. My family gifted him pipe tobacco during inclement weather when he made special trips to drive at night to my father's auctions. He took care of us, and we returned the favor by taking care of him. He was the only Outsider my parents had ever invited into our house. We never called him English either. He was Leroy. We loved him. And he was the only black man we knew.

He waved his hand in front of my face. His fingers smelled of talcum powder and Lebanon bologna, which he rolled with thin slices of white American cheese and called "lunch". I could see bits of cheese caught in his nails. He held a pair of scissors, blades stuck with quarter-inch pieces of silver nose hair from an Amish man who watched from Leroy's make-shift barbershop: a stool, drop cloth, and hand-held mirror, catty-corner to us. Besides grand-datt's candy stand, Leroy Fischer was a fixture in the market for locals and tourists. He had a way of imitating the Amish like nobody we knew, affecting a Pennsylvania Dutch accent so precise with its attenuated and lilting phrases that when I closed my eyes and listened behind the candy stand, I swore that Leroy was Amish.

"Auch chust listen," he'd say, swapping a hard "ch" for j and a p for b. "It's my chop to make you laugh. Did chu know that Beter, Baul and Mary got a lot of choy from beanut putter and chelly? It's no choke. They did!"

I wondered how he learned all that and I asked him once. "God whispers the words into my dreams at night," he said, which confused me because I thought that sometimes Leroy might have been God. I asked the bishop once if God was a black man and he told me, "God has no face." I figured the color of his face didn't matter. There were no black men I knew about in Switzerland during the Reformation. Leroy's roots extended into the sidewalks of North Philadelphia.

Despite all the evidence that Leroy could have been God or at least a good substitute, he was not a religious man. He never spoke of Jesus like many of the English did. He didn't hang wooden crosses on the walls of his house, or the stand, and he didn't carry those strings of "rosy beads" that I'd seen draped around the necks of nuns who stalked the market for sticky buns and a pulled-pork sandwich. He offered his services every Tuesday in the summer, and I had watched for years, with awe and envy, the way his dark fingers maneu-vered the scissors. But that day I didn't want him around.

"Go away, Leroy," I said.

"Suit yourself."

"Leroy's not going away and neither am I until this boy leaves you alone."

Hanna stepped between us. Leroy withdrew his hand. My ears burned and I crinkled my nose. I shifted my eyes to the purple smoke bomb she dropped on the floor then stared at her clenched fists. Her voice quivered.

"Step away, Eli."

"I'm not finished," the boy said.

"Eli Emanuel Yoder."

"He's not finished," I said.

I pressed my heels into the floor, refusing to leave, feeling the cool concrete. The boy took more photos, and the more photos he took, the more I liked it even though I knew it was wrong. I liked the attention of the camera more than I feared losing my soul. For the first time in my life, somebody from the outside wanted to see me.

"If you don't stop, I'll take your camera," Hanna said. My sisters had now trickled in one by one and smelled of smoke bombs and firecrackers, pieces of frayed paper caught in their prayer caps. They paused at Beiler's bread stand across from us, arrested by the threat in Hanna's voice. They whispered to the vendor and her daughter, Emma, who watched with flour-dusted hands clasped over their mouths. Emma and I had been friends since we were toddlers. Her father was the bishop of our district and she was like another sister to me. She stared, dumbfounded, and shook her head.

The boy lifted the glass case, inching toward me, near the licorice wheels.

"Give me five," he said, knocking the spade from my grip, offering his palms in the gesture I had come to understand even though I hardly spoke English then. Even our dogs knew what "give me five" meant. I had seen older boys in rumspringa slap each other, strutting to and from their buggies with transistor radios, trying to be cool.

I held out my hands, expecting him to give me five, but he took a photo instead. He laughed then groaned.

"Woah. Those are some big ugly hands," he said.

"What did you say?" Leroy asked.

"Big Ugly," he said, slowly, winking at me.

It took me a few moments to translate. At home we spoke Pennsylvania Dutch, a dialect of Swiss-German, and we read almost everything, including the Bible, in German. Like most Amish kids, I'd been speaking English since I turned six and could understand more than I could express. Big. Ugly. Easy words that felt hard in my stomach, lumpy in my throat. I looked up at the boy's parents, who had returned to squabble over the change my sisters had made from a fifty-dollar bill for two dollars and twenty-three cents of candy. I expected them to say something, anything, to their son.

"Please don't make us angry," Hanna said.

The boy laughed again and turned to his mother.

"Mom, the Amish don't get angry, do they?"

"They can't," she said and snapped her purse shut.

Hanna reached out and slapped the camera with her hand, pressing the palm tight against the lens. The boy looked up, startled. Hanna held his gaze, waiting patiently for the boy to leave. Her cheeks burned and red splotches bloomed on her neck. I had never seen her so upset but we all knew why. That's when Leroy turned and walked away. He knew there was only so much he could to do help me that day.

The boy lifted Hanna's hand off the lens and stepped away from her, toward me, to fire one last shot.

"Smile, Big Ugly."

But I didn't. I withdrew my hands and thrust my fists behind my back, pinching my fingers like Hanna. I could feel my own face flushed now and the burning in my neck. My lips flattened and the smile vanished. I stared at the floor watching the passing shoes pause, open-toed sandals shifting nervously, the white heels of a nurse itching an ankle. Nobody moved, but I wished they had. I felt a burning in my back work its way through my kidneys, into my lungs. It hurt to breathe. I had watched with awe a Vietnam vet play an accordion in the parking lot of the marketplace, squeezing music through the folds in the instrument. My lungs felt like the accordion then, squeezed and suffocated, kicked with the brutality of reality. Nobody had ever told me that my hands were ugly. I knew they were different. A doctor had diagnosed me with syndactyl, a genetic disorder common among the Amish. He also said I'd be fine. "Make a good swimmer," he joked, "just like a Golden Retriever!"

The webbing began at the first knuckle and climbed up to the third knuckle, the skin translucent and waxy. I curled the webbing into fists and buried my face in them, suddenly and inextricably aware of myself. The boy was right. My hands were big and ugly. It was as if God had lit an oil lamp and said, "Eli, this is you," and I no longer wanted the attention of anyone.

I stood there, eyes pinned to the licorice wheels, unable to move, when an explosion of sorts scattered everyone but me outside. All frantic. One of the local teenagers had launched a M-80 through the tent arched over the market. The boy had left the camera on the counter when he ran outside and it sat there, waiting.

I'm gonna take it, I said to myself without apology or regret.

I knew it was wrong and I didn't care.

I scanned the empty market, spotting a row of faceless Amish dolls at the stall beside grandfather's candy stand. There were six of them, five girls and one boy just like my sisters and me, but without eyes to see. I bowed my head and whispered, asking the dolls for permission to take the camera. I dug a hole in the bin of licorice wheels and buried it, then closed my eyes and prayed the boy with the red belly would never return. When I looked up, beyond the dolls, I caught Leroy Fischer staring at me in his mirror.

◇

I remember not wanting to go to bed that night because I didn't want to think about how I'd spent the day. During dinner, I imagined the bishop asking me, "In what ways have you contributed to good or evil?" I got the shivers thinking about my answer even though it was hot in our kitchen. How could I ever tell the bishop or anyone in my family that I'd stolen the camera? I had been quiet, and every time I tried to eat, I kept seeing that puzzled look on Leroy's face and I'd drop my fork and stare at my own reflection in the plate. The table felt crowded with my cousins, Uncle Isaac and Bishop Beiler visiting. The meal was supposed to have been a celebration of sorts. The week before, the twins, Katie and Ella, 18, had announced their decision to get baptized and join the church that fall. My parents thought they'd invite the bishop for dinner to offer our barn for the ceremony, since they figured, and hoped, that finally Hanna, their oldest child, would get baptized, too. But nobody talked about baptism. Instead, they stared at me, concerned.

Uncle Isaac was the only one at the table who asked if I was okay.

"Emma told me you had a big day at the market," he said.

I swallowed but said nothing and stared at the lump of Chow Chow, marinated carrots, cauliflower, yellow and green wax beans in my bowl. My mother paused behind me with a basket of rolls, then pressed the back of her wrist against my forehead. I held my breath, hoping any diagnosis would be better than being scared sick. She only sighed and stared at my sisters for more clues to my odd behavior, why I hadn't eaten anything and why I was sitting on my hands.

After the first few minutes, I didn't feel much of anything at all, just a numbing, tingling sensation in my fingertips—the only place where the webbing wasn't. If it had been winter, my posture would not have caused concern. But it was early July and 90 percent humidity, the air thick and buttered with heat. I wouldn't have cared if it had been a hundred degrees. I intended to sit on my hands all night. Maybe for the rest of my life.

There were other ways to eat, I figured. I didn't need a fork and spoon. I didn't need a table. I could eat alone. This idea cheered me up a bit. I think I even smiled. Sitting on a hard wooden bench, hiding my hands from my family, I was suddenly hopeful. If I had pockets, I'd never have to show my hands to anyone.

Just then my mother set the spoon back and said, as if she'd read my mind,

"Then tell me what I can get for you."

"Pockets," I said, without a moment's hesitation.

My mother drew in a breath. My father raised an eyebrow as did the bishop. My sisters lay down their forks.

"Pockets?"

"Yep."

"Why do you want pockets?" my mother asked, casting a knowing glance at my sisters. They looked up from their plates but remained silent.

"I want pockets because it's time," I said, even though we consider pockets worldly. We wear mostly broadfall pants that button on each side, but most Amish boys get pockets in their pants when they turn six. I was overdue by three years.

"I'll see what I can do. But you're a growing boy. And you need to eat if you want your pants to stay on."

Sarah, who sat to my right, giggled. She was two years older than me, and at 11, the spitting image of Hanna, but shorter and more talkative. Ruth, who at 14, could hit a home-run with her left hand, reached across my lap and squeezed Sarah's leg until she said ouch. I looked up at my mother.

"Can you sew them tomorrow?"

My mother locked eyes with my father. He shook his head.

"Your mother has to work. There's been twenty births this week alone. Her hands will be sore."

I didn't believe him. She rarely complained about her work, a hobby called *Fraktur*, a form of calligraphy that looks like needlepoint on decorative paper. Since the Amish keep no photographs of the living, the only history we have of our existence is in the form of these family tree *Frakturs*, used mostly for family records. The Amish who'd heard of my mother's beautiful calligraphy hired her from places as far away as Montana.

"My hands will be fine, Reuben. I don't mind."

"I don't have pockets," my father said. "And I'm 45."

"You don't have my hands either," I whispered, feeling the blood flush my cheeks, wanting to believe that pockets would be enough to hide who I was from the world.

The sound of tires crushing gravel and the backfire of Leroy Fischer's 1962 Austin Healey broke our silence. In addition to the van, the Healey was the only other car that frequented our farm on a regular basis. A door opened, then closed. We heard the clap of heels on the flagstone sidewalk; the clink of our dog's collar when she got up to greet Leroy and the thwap of her tail against his leg. Leroy scratched the screened door.

"Sorry to interrupt," he said in his jagged North Philly accent, "but I wanted to drop this off for Eli."

I clutched my stomach and groaned.

"A gift? Eli's birthday isn't until September," Mamm said, getting up.

"Wouldn't forget that, Rachel. Does a boy need a birthday to get a gift?"

My mother grinned. "Oh, Leroy. Stay for dessert."

My father stood and pulled out a chair at the table, between himself and the bishop, granting Leroy the respect and the right to join him and a holy man.

"Thanks, Reuben, but Ruthanne and I are off to catch the fireworks."

My mother protested.

"We've got corn fritters. And deviled eggs."

"Ruthanne packed us a picnic."

My mother nodded. Nobody, not even she, could compete with Ruthanne's cooking even though she had tried. The Amish women didn't win all the contests.

"Won't you stay for some root beer?" she persisted, "The children would love you to tell them some new jokes."

That got my sisters excited and they scrambled to make space between them, bickering over who got to sit beside Leroy, whose face was the color and sweetness of a Shoofly Pie.

Leroy stood at the door with a shoebox tucked under his arm, the lid bulging and secured with duct tape. He flashed a smile, his big teeth bright against his dark face.

"Let me at least cut you a piece of pie."

"Okay, but just a small slice," he said and patted his bulging belly.

Leroy took off his hat, a white straw fedora he wore in the summer to keep the heat off his head, and hung it beside my own straw hat on the rack by the door. He wore a pair of red and blue plaid trousers, a red golf shirt, and white patent leather shoes, all honoring the spirit of the holiday and his own independence. Our cousins had never seen him or anybody dressed in such an array of patterns and colors. We were used to black pants, skirts, and plain, solid shirts of blue, green or purple. Leroy's clothes fascinated us.

He stepped into our kitchen, the shoebox cradled awkwardly under his arm. When he shifted his large dark eyes to me, the pronouncement in them made me nervous. He bowed his head reverent, fingers tracing the fraying tape on the lid of the shoebox, perhaps uncertain if he wanted to give it in the first place. Leroy dabbed at the beads across his temples, feeling the curious glances of my family, our dog included. I felt the prickle of heat on my neck, imaging the camera. I was so nervous I peed my pants.

"I need to use the bathroom," I announced, standing.

My father nodded and struck the table with the side of his fist, the way an auctioneer said yes at his own table. "Hurry back," he said. "Don't keep Leroy waiting."

Leroy looked over at me and smiled. I spit him a look of disdain before I slipped into the hallway and disappeared into the bathroom where our cats were curled up in the window sill, catching the cross breeze on a humid night. I took a wad of toilet paper and dabbed at my pants, trying to dry what I could. I opened the window wider hoping the cross breeze would help, then facing the door with my backside to the draft, I peered out the key hole to watch Leroy, my heart pounding.

My father pushed himself away from the table and slid across the long kitchen floor in his roller chair, the customary furniture piece in almost every Amish kitchen and, in this case, acquired through one of his auctions. My father sat like a judge in it, the fleshy gavel of his fists planted on the metal arm rests, granting him the power to make important decisions, often deferring the most difficult to my mother. The wheels spun smoothly on the linoleum, then rumbled when they hit the wood floor in the hallway. They rattled to a stop outside the bathroom door. He knocked hard, and the loose door handle jiggled itself free and fell off. He peeked through the hole, trying to find me.

"Eli?"

"Yeah?"

"Are you okay?"

"I don't feel so good."

"Uncle Isaac will rub your belly."

"No," I said. Uncle Isaac was the last person anyone wanted touching their stomach. He tickle-tortured until his own sons peed their pants. I couldn't take that kind of humiliation twice in one day. I looked over at the kittens in the window and thought about pushing in the screen and climbing out to the yard where I could disappear by the pond behind our barn. My father whispered through the keyhole.

"Eli, this is no way to receive a gift."

"It's not a gift, Datt."

"How do you know if you don't open it?"

I slowly pushed open the door. One of the kittens leapt down from the window and followed me back to the kitchen, where I stood beside my father's roller chair. "Hi, Leroy," I grumbled.

"Why hello, Eli. This is for you."

He leaned into my mother and whispered something in her ear, passing the box into her hands. She nodded, then patted Leroy on the shoulder. He turned, took his hat and slid a wink into the split second he looked at me. Then he waved and walked out the door as quickly as he had come.

I waited until I heard the click of his heels on the flagstone and the opening of the car door, hoping it would be the last time I'd have to see him.

"What did he say?" I demanded, blurting out the words in Pennsylvania Dutch. Everyone at the table turned to me. My words were icy and hard despite the soft dialect.

"He said you ought to open this in your room."

My mother cocked her head but said nothing. It was my father who turned to me and I could feel the shame in his voice rub against the fear in my own.

"What's wrong with you? You didn't say thank you."

"I don't think it's a gift," I said.

The Amish don't use polite language on most occasions. Please and thank you are not part of the every day speech of the Amish, although we will use these words when we speak to Englishers. Polite language was the talk of officials and nobility who had tried to kill us long ago during the Reformation. The only time we say thank you, *Denki*, is when we are receiving a gift.

"I got confused," I said and threw my eyes on the kitchen floor, following the skid marks of my father's roller chair.

My father flicked the point of his beard. Nobody spoke until he bowed his head, concluding the meal with a silent prayer of thanksgiving. When he lifted his head, he fixed his eyes on my mother, who handed me the box.

"You're excused from the table, Eli," she said.

I pressed the box against my chest and ran past my family up the stairs, to my bedroom, and closed the door as the first fireworks bled the sky over our farm.

I changed my pants, then sat on my bed and held the damp cardboard box. I lifted the lid slowly and found to my surprise a stack of brightly colored mini-magazines with pictures of characters and captions in tiny boxes. I had never seen a comic book before and all I could do was sound out the name of the title: CAPTAIN COURAGEOUS. I thumbed through the box and pulled out one of the comic books, flipping through the pages, amused and entertained by the heroic man drawn in the squares. Leroy left a hand-written note, which I could not understand but sounded out in English:

COURAGE IS THE HERO THAT HELPS A BOY LAUGH.

I didn't get it, but I was so relieved that it wasn't the camera that I laughed and kicked the box under my bed when I heard the stairs squeak outside my door. My mother opened it without knocking and stood with a plate of watermelon.

"Are you feeling better?"

"A bit."

She crossed the room in the dark and sat on the edge of my bed, eyes reflecting the lights from the fireworks. She lay her wrist on my forehead then brushed the hair out of my eyes. Her skin was warm and sticky in the humid air and her sleeves carried the smell of fried corn fritters. She offered me the plate.

"I picked the seeds out."

My stomach growled. I was suddenly hungry and wished I had eaten her potato salad. I sat up and took the slice, devouring the melon, slurping the juice from the rind. I ran my tongue back and forth over the grooves. My mother watched me with the kind of quiet satisfaction I had seen her express over her own simple pleasures, but I could tell there was something else on her mind the way she pulled a loose strand of hair over her lips, pinching the urge to scream or cry. I didn't know which, but I wanted to stop her.

"You know the English get money for losing a tooth?" I asked, glimpsing the dimple in her left cheek. She wiped the juice from my chin.

"Is that so?"

"Yep. An English boy told me."

"Hanna said he told you a lot."

"She did?"

I was surprised Hanna, with her hands full of smoke bombs, had said anything. I suddenly wondered if she and Leroy had conspired in any way. It was just like them to figure things out without asking me.

"I'm so sorry, Eli. Did he hurt your feelings?"

I looked up at her, watching the dimple disappear. I put the rind on the plate and glanced at the quilt, following the white stitching. "Yes, Mamm."

My mother gently lifted my hands to her mouth and kissed them once at the base of the knuckles. Then she lay them over my chest and pressed them gently against my heart and whispered in our Pennsylvania Dutch dialect. *Vass-evvah es diah havva vellet es leit doon zu eich, so Emma diah du zu eena.* The Golden Rule. Do to others what you want them to do to you. It is the first lesson we learn as children.

"You must find a way to forgive him, Eli."

"I'll try, Mamm."

"Try? What if he was God?"

"God made my hands," I said.

"Yes, he did."

"Would God say what he made was ugly?"

My mother turned her eyes from me and set the plate on the wooden night stand beside my bed. She pressed her lips together and straightened.

"You're old enough to understand what I'm saying."

I nodded and swallowed the lump in my throat. She spoke in English only when she was upset. This time, my belly ached for real, but it wasn't the watermelon that made the knot. My mother stood, smoothing the wrinkles in her apron. She turned toward the shadow of the door, her face in silhouette.

"What did Leroy give you?"

I pointed under the bed, rolled over and pulled out the box, lifting the lid.

"Comic books," she said, surprised, almost pleased.

"You've read them?"

"Once," she said. "Everyone loves a comic book."

"I can't read Leroy's note."

I handed her the paper. She paused, thoughtful, reading it. She was good at English and often sounded like there was another woman inside her when she spoke it.

"Courage is the hero that helps a boy to laugh."

I listened, holding on to the word laugh.

"What is a laf?"

My mother reached out and brushed the bangs out of my eyes. She smiled and spoke to me in Pennsylvania Dutch.

"A laugh," she said, "is the sound God makes when he forgives us for making mistakes."

"Oh," I said, but I didn't understand her.

"Forgive the boy," she said.

"So God will laugh?"

"No, Eli. So one day you will, too."

My mother lifted her eyes to the fireworks framed by the window and I could see the glitter of red and gold reflected in her skin. She pulled the sheet over me and kissed my cheeks, her own already wet when she touched me. She stepped into the hallway and closed the door but did not leave. I saw the heels of her shoes under the door and every few seconds I'd hear her catch her breath, choking back a sob.

I didn't want her to cry for me. I wanted to forgive the boy for violating the Golden Rule, but I wanted God to forgive me more for stealing his camera. I lay in bed listening to the pop of fireworks, turning my hands around in the red light reflected from the window, wishing I had never gone to the market that day, praying that the next time I did, I'd have pockets. Over the next three days, I'd hear my sisters through the wall at night, praying for the patience to forgive the boy. I knew I should forgive the boy, too, but I left my sisters in charge. I was too busy asking God for other things.

THREE

NO AMISH I KNOW would ever admit it, but I have always believed that our choice to forgive is more an act of survival than virtue. We were persecuted people after we started protesting the practice of infant baptism in 1525. We believed that adults, not children, should choose their faith, and so we initiated an *anabaptism*, a second baptism. During the Reformation, we fled our homes and villages in Alsace, Switzerland, finding refuge in Rotterdam, Holland for a hundred years before we sailed to Philadelphia, Pennsylvania, October 2, 1727, nearly two hundred years after the protests began.

We are descendents of Mennonites, the first Anabaptist separatists, formed in 1563 by the Catholic priest Menno Simmons. Like Simmons, we were persecuted by the Catholics and Lutherans. Although they tried to kill us many times and occasionally succeeded, we survived. We recall those who perished in the pursuit of their faith through the stories printed in the *Martyr's Mirror*, a compilation of letters and songs written by Anabaptist prisoners during the Reformation. Our way of living is a reaction to that struggle.

For four hundred years, we've held secret services in barns or houses to avoid further persecution. We tend to avoid people dressed in uniform like the soldiers who tortured, imprisoned and burned us. At our core, we are peaceful protestors, and I had believed that stealing the camera was a form of quiet dissent.

My sisters never spoke of the red-bellied boy again, but I know they thought about him whenever they offered to hold my hands or help me do what my hands could not. I found myself reluctant to reach out to them over the following weeks. I crossed the road by myself, tried to cut my own meat, learned how to button my shirt using the tips of my fingers and the edge of my palms. At market, I began to take my lunch breaks alone in the parking lot. I would realize later that my independence offended not only my sisters and my parents, but my cousins, schoolmates, teachers, and Bishop Beiler, who had derived a certain sense of goodness from helping me cope with my condition. Short of slicing through the skin, there was little they could do to separate my fingers in 1976.

At night, I'd lay on my bedroom floor, pressing my ear against the wood, hearing my parents argue about it after they thought I had gone to sleep. My mother had always argued for an operation, but my father said it was not God's will. Every day, I'd pester them for pockets. I'd even been bold enough to pray for them, making my requests public in the grace we said before meals. There was never a shortage of nail biters or napkin shredders at the Yoder table, especially when the topic of pockets arose; and I made sure to ask about it before the conclusion of every meal. My mother would offer the same answer, "Let's wait and see how you feel tomorrow," as if tomorrow I'd wake up and my hands would be normal.

I felt angry and frustrated that nobody seemed to want to help me hide them. I had always been told that my defect was one of the more common genetic disorders among the Amish, but I had never seen anyone else with hands that looked like mine. I would notice more and more people at the market staring, but I figured they'd been staring that way for years. I hated the pity in their eyes. I didn't want pity. Just pockets.

I had no intention of returning the camera to the red-bellied boy. I wanted to rescue it from the bin of licorice wheels, then destroy it somewhere in the safety of our farm. Light it on fire, run it over with my scooter, or toss it in the pond behind our barn. Or, I could have simply put it behind the wheel of a car and watch it flatten, like we did with pennies on the railroad tracks. I didn't sleep well with these thoughts in my head, trying to figure out how I'd get the camera without being seen by my sisters. I'm not sure they expected me to come the following Tuesday after everything that had happened, but I was the first one up that morning and had already hitched the horse to the buggy in the dark. Had I been old enough to drive, I would have done so and set up our candy stand alone.

I didn't speak on the way to the market that day, rehearsing over and over how I'd explain myself if I got caught, but nothing I could have said would have prepared me for what I'd find when we arrived. Posted outside the bathrooms and on all the tent poles were flyers that depicted a sad looking boy and a reward for making him happy.

LOST CAMERA. Valuable property.
1963 Leica M3. My (dead) grandpa's gift to me.
$100 Reward. Last seen July 3.
Marcus Paoni   717 - 555 - 2791

We saw the flyers everywhere we walked, though my sisters didn't seem to pay much attention to them. Hanna turned to me and said, "God's will." I nodded, but when it was my turn to take a bathroom break, I walked around the market and tore off every last flyer in sight, then tossed them in the trash cans outside the bathrooms, not caring who saw me. It never occurred to me that I could have ended my misery by turning the camera in and collecting the hundred dollars. I didn't see anything related to the red-bellied boy as an opportunity then.

As I was walking back to our candy stand, I passed Leroy at the deli counter next to his stand, assessing the damage from the M-80 with a bunch of men in suits. One of the men's sons had purchased the firework and another had set it off. They were confused as to who was responsible. Leroy claimed none of this would have happened if those boys had had real jobs like the Amish kids. He pointed down at me and winked.

"Right, Eli? You all stay out of trouble."

"I guess," I said, stepping out of their way, feeling my face and neck burning.

"There's no guessing with trouble," Leroy said and thumbed an empty Tic-Tac box. He continued to take photos of the shattered glass door of the deli counter.

"Is it yours?" I asked, and pointed to the camera.

Leroy paused and looked down at me.

"Yes."

"How's it do that?"

"This?" he asked and aimed the camera at a group of passing tourists. They paused, flattered, and smiled, then Leroy pressed a button. The camera screeched like a scared crow and spat out a small square card the size of my hand. Leroy handed it to me.

"Wave it around. Let it breathe."

I flicked it back and forth, wondering how a picture could breathe, but that made sense, in a way, when the people started to come to life inside it.

"Will you show me how to use it?" I asked, surprising us both.

Leroy drew his head back and stared at me.

"You want to know how to use a camera—after last week?"

I shrugged. My voice cracked. "Why not? I've never taken a photo," I said.

Leroy nodded. "Why not? Your daddy might never speak to me again is why not. Your mama might kill me. You aiming to get me into trouble?"

"No, Leroy. I just thought… you could help me understand."

Leroy pressed a fist to his mouth. "Help you. Shit. You know that boy's come looking for his camera this morning? Posted signs all over creation here. They even had one of the cops following, taking notes here and there. Seems that boy's daddy is some kind of fancy-pants lawyer. Now you don't want to get involved in all that, do you?"

Lawyer? I felt my heart pound and my throat tighten. "Did you tell him?"

Leroy shook his head, disgusted. "You think I'd ever tell on you?"

"Maybe. If I was bad."

"Bad. What's bad?"

"If I broke the rules."

"You did do that. You stole something that wasn't yours."

"I know. So does that make me bad?"

"In comparison to what that boy took from you?"

I stared at him, confused.

"He didn't take anything," I said, feeling even worse.

I felt a lump in my throat. I knew stealing was wrong. I didn't have to be Amish to know that. Stealing was stealing. A person wasn't supposed to take what wasn't theirs to keep. I expected to hear a lecture from Leroy, but he laughed instead, and I caught the glimmer of the gold filling in his upper tooth.

"Some rules are meant for breaking, son, but you're too young for that. Between you and me, that's why those bishops of yours invented rumspringa. Let all you run around and let off some steam. Sheesh. Rules. Rules. Too many rules out there."

My gut told me that now was the time to ask him. It's not like I heard any voice or words. I just felt an urge in my whole body to know how the camera worked.

"Show me," I said and held my hand out to receive the camera from Leroy. He paused, seeing my hands shake.

"Aw, Eli. I knew it."

"What?"

"Don't tell me you're afraid of it like all the rest of you people."

"Nope," I said, fish-lipped, squeezing back the lie.

"You sure? You swear?"

"I don't swear," I said.

"You know what I mean. What about Deuteronomy?"

"What about him?"

"He's no champion of the camera."

"I never read anything about cameras in the Bible," I said. It was true.

"Graven images, Eli. You understand."

"Yes."

Leroy paused, studying me. I straightened my back.

"And you're not gonna freak out that you stole someone's soul or anything?"

I nodded so hard that my hat fell off. Leroy reached down and lifted it off the floor, then put it back on my head, straightening it with the flick of his finger. "Just look through the lens, find something you like. When you're ready, push the button. It's easy."

I held the view finder up to my eye and looked through the lens, overwhelmed by the world inside the frame. The market looked different. I expected it to shrink, but it seemed to get bigger. The simplest of objects took on greater significance, even shoes.

"How do I choose?"

"You don't. The object chooses you. That's when you take the photo."

I looked up at Leroy, unable to understand.

"Cameras have a heart of their own, Eli. They get stirred up by the moments that matter. That's what a photograph is."

"A stirred up moment?"

Leroy nodded. "A moment that matters. Surely you've had one of those."

I nodded, considering what he meant. I had never seen God but had always believed he visited my mother's garden when she was working in it. "But I got no photos." I said, suddenly concerned that if one day I did see God in Mamm's garden, nobody would believe me without a photograph.

"Then you have a lot of catching up to do."

I held the camera in my hands, considering all the moments from my short life that seemed to matter to me and my family. We had no record of them. No Amish families ever have had any kind of photographic record, only pen and ink drawings from the days of the Reformation; and nobody seemed to look any different in those drawings. Only the Outside World seemed to change. I shoved the camera back into Leroy's hands, then bounded down the aisle, my heart pounding.

"Where you going?"

I didn't stop to turn and explain. I ran back to the candy stand, grabbed the box of licorice wheels, and left before my sisters could stop me. I ran past Leroy and Emma's baked goods, past the clock maker and the old man who built bird houses from coconuts, past the candle lady at the corner, then through my father's auction, in the middle of a bid, sending a flock of chickens into a frenzy, feathers and fowl dust flying. I pushed open the back doors and ran across the parking lot, past the street vendors and fireworks and snow cones and funnel cakes, following the ravine between the corn fields and the hot black ribbon of road that tied Paradise to Providence in Southern Lancaster County. I ran past the roadside flea markets, fruit stands and antique shops and candle barns cluttered with billboards for buggy rides, quilts and Shoofly Pies. In the distance were one room schools and covered bridges, green valleys, hillsides and hundreds of farms, but I didn't stop to photograph them because they didn't matter to me like that. I ran instead to Strasburg with an instinct and urgency to capture what mattered most before it was too late.

I stopped in my mother's garden, panting. My arms were sore from carrying the box and I set it down on the earth, exhausted. I was disappointed that Mamm wasn't tending to her herbs or flowers, or reading in the shade of the hazel tree. The garden was not enough to photograph. It was the joy that beamed from Mamm's whole being when she was there.

Though no Amish would proclaim to be artists and set apart from the group, the garden served as a canvas for my mother's creative expression. For years, tour buses parked on the side of the road and visitors from all over the world walked down our gravel driveway to see my mother's work, often featured in the brochures printed by the Chamber of Commerce and Visitor's Bureau, who supplied my mother with plenty of seeds for annuals or any flower she wanted. There was never any money involved.

The garden gave my mother a freedom that she could not experience elsewhere. It was more than a labor of love. It was where my mother thrived, hands digging in the rich soils of Lancaster County, planting, weeding, shaping the landscape around her to reflect the beauty she saw in the world, and to create more where it was lacking. Though my mother never said so, I believe she felt closest to God when she worked with the earth.

I never considered that my mother might have taken great offense to my plan, and standing there alone, I realized that taking a photo of the moments that mattered would be a challenge. How would I capture Ella's and Katie's laughter (which was so distinct that everyone knew them by it, even if they still couldn't tell them apart after eighteen years)? How would I capture the blazing speed at which Ruth could speak English at the age of 14, or the secret achievement she possessed when she demonstrated, at the dinner table, that she was faster than Datt? How would I show the passion Sarah had for teaching, even if she seemed bossy to me? How could a photograph convey her patience and earnest in helping others learn? I was stumped, most of all, by how I would capture my oldest sister Hanna, who always seemed to be living in a secret world inside her head. How could a photo express her dreams? I wondered, too, if my sisters would ever let me photograph them with their hair wet and hanging loose over their shoulders on the one day they all took baths. These were all moments that mattered, and I would have to find a way to capture them without anyone knowing I had a camera.

FOUR

ALTHOUGH I STILL HAD no pockets by the following week, I had taken liberties with the camera. Small things at first. I had pried up the floorboard beneath my bed, and had hidden it, taking it out only when I knew everyone was asleep. I'd sit on the edge of the bed, holding the camera in my hands, thinking it nearly impossible that such a tiny mechanism had the power to steal a soul. I wondered how much of me was inside it, or how much of anybody it had the power to hold. But the longer I kept it hidden under the floorboard, the more I ached to use it, and the more afraid I became that I'd lose it if my father found it first. What he had found were the wadded up flyers by the bathrooms and a note on his auction stand from Marcus Paoni's mother. Seeking justice and some flavor of retribution, she had taken matters into her own hands and contacted our local bishop.

Of course, there had been a lot of talk—the activity the Amish like best. Our neighbors and closest friends refused to believe either scenario spreading like apple butter on a slice of raisin bread: I had stolen the camera and Marcus's father was trying to drum up business for himself and use the incident as a public relations tactic. I didn't know what public relations was or that you could make money from it, but I did know that I didn't like the sight of the bishop and a few deacons gathered at our kitchen table for a Monday meeting in mid-July. Eating slices of my mother's warm rhubarb pie, they discussed, between quiet burps and root beer refills, the possibility of my father's help in diverting the public's attention on the Amish. By the very nature of the auction business, my father was the most public man in our district and they needed him to mediate.

Only the ticking of the wall clock answered them while my father bowed his head in prayer, assuming my innocence. I watched him through the banister from the stairs where my sisters had also convened, feet bare and blackened with earth. Though they had told our parents about my strange behavior and the missing box of licorice wheels, they had not asked me if I had taken the camera, as if they didn't want to know the truth. They gathered the corners of their aprons in their fists, wondering what Datt would decide, if he would risk speaking out against Marcus Paoni in defense of his only son.

We sat in the sticky cross breeze of my mother's oven and the windows that offered no escape for the heat, but we were taken by the suspense. Usually Datt asked Mamm for help with these kind of things since she was unwavering in her choices. It was Mamm who convinced Datt to get an air-compressor for milking the cows. She knew she didn't need an invitation to offer her suggestions, but she respected her place among the elders and kept to herself, quietly wiping the already white counters. Even when there was nothing to clean, Mamm would find a way to ease her mind by meditating with a dusting cloth. Eventually she would speak. It was the moments of quiet consideration that defined her most, and I often wondered (and still do) if the landscape of her mind matched that of her gardens. Everything had its purpose. Everything had its place. Every choice a seed. Whether or not it resulted in a flower or a weed was the risk she took in thinking for herself, rather than having somebody think for her. She had the uncanny ability to make her voice heard without saying a word.

She knew Datt was watching, waiting for her to reveal her leanings. She served the last slice of rhubarb pie to the oldest deacon, wiped the counter twice again, tossed the sponge in the sink and crossed the kitchen to let herself out the back door to her gardens. She paused at the hazel tree. With a gesture as discreet as an Amish woman's smile, she placed her right hand on the lowest limb and imperceptibly raised her thumb, keeping herself in full view through the kitchen window. It was all my father needed in order to speak. Datt cleared his throat. The deacons set down their forks, swallowed the last gulp of root beer.

"I'll do it," he grumbled. "But only this time, okay?"

The deacons exhaled, exultant, picking crumbs of rhubarb pie from their beards. "Thank you, Reuben."

"Now don't get so excited. Didn't do nothing yet."

Datt swatted the air, buzzing with his own reputation as an auctioneer. My father could find anything, even when he wasn't looking. Rare books. Antique steamer trunks. Miter saws, shark jaws, Civil War muskets and stuffed moose heads. He had the rare ability to understand the English better than they understood themselves. He studied their buying habits. It was emotion that trumped the real value of most things for them. If the item promised status, he was sure to make a sale, whereas with the Amish, every item that came across his block had to be presented as a pragmatic purchase, which is why he would never understand in a billion years why I had stolen the camera. And why I lied when he asked me if I did. I should have been happy that my father had agreed to help our community. He was a good man doing a good deed. Instead, I felt a wrenching in my stomach when he stood from the table that night in July and looked at me like *he'd* bought a stuffed moose.

It was only a few hours after the deacons had left that night that I felt compelled to use the camera for the first time. I took it out from under the floorboard and stuffed it down my pants, then as quietly as I could tip-toe past my sisters' rooms, I snuck downstairs and took it outside, following the cool, slate trail behind our barn to the edge of the pond where I dug my toes into the mud. I pressed the camera against my chest, trying to stop my heart from exploding—because it felt like it would at any moment.

I blinked twice. Then again, arrested by this vision: washed by the light of the moon was Hanna, her long pale neck flecked by the shadows of barn swallows flying through the willow trees. Pressed against her, oblivious to me or the moon, was a rather tall boy with broad shoulders, dressed in denim and short sleeves. Even though it was dark, he wore sunglasses and a baseball hat that fell off when he leaned in to kiss her neck. I held my breath, feeling the urge to gasp. I had never seen my sister with any boy. I had never seen anyone kiss, not even my parents. I didn't need Leroy to tell me that this was a moment that mattered, and just as I raised the camera to my eye, Hanna bent down to pick up the boy's hat, and turned, finding me at the edge of the pond. She shoved a silver horseshoe into the boy's hand, then leapt across the yard, away from me, the flap flap of her skirt mocking my heart.

I found my father the next morning, with a rolled up newspaper in hand, waiting for me in his roller chair. Behind him, in the window, the sun was rising, the sky streaked with silver and pink. To anyone but Datt, it might have been a beautiful morning. He drummed the table with tar-blackened thumbs and snapped the pink rubber band around the newspaper. "Sit down, Eli."

I sat. Datt rolled across the linoleum to set in the sink his coffee mug, stained with the dark ring of his only addiction, then rolled back to the table and stared at me with outstretched hands. They were twice the size of mine and completely opposite in their form, full grown and competent. I had never seen my father lose his temper, although I knew of other fathers who had seen the blistered backs of boys whose skin had endured their lashings of cracked leather.

My father, a notoriously impatient man, had never hit me but I wondered then if I had given him a reason to try. "Give me your hand."

I felt myself shaking and reluctantly extended my left hand, then closed my eyes, wondering how much it would sting when he struck me.

"Stand up."

I stood with my eyes closed. My father placed my hand upon a crumpled up piece of paper. I didn't have to see it to know what it was. In a voice tinged with distress and disgrace, he simply said, "Look."

I squeezed my eyes shut tighter and my father roared. "Open your eyes, Eli."

The boom of his voice rolled through my body and my chin quivered when he spoke again. "There's only one set of hands on this earth that match these."

That's all he needed to say. I snapped my eyes wide open and saw the crumpled flyers, smudged with grease and ketchup from the trash cans. I'm sure the horror he read on my face was enough to confirm his suspicions. He sat in his chair, chin propped on a fist. He shifted his heavy gaze from me to the wall and said, "Do you know when a man breaks the law, the police often use fingerprints to know who the bad man is?"

"Maybe it was a bad man here," I said and pulled my hands away and threw them behind my back.

My mother came in from the garden just then; seeing the two of us at the table, she turned on her bare heels and headed outside again to occupy my sisters. My father saved his voice for auction and rarely used more than one breath, one line of communication at home. Grunts, really, the codes of which only Mamm could decipher. To hear him utter full phrases indicated something was very wrong.

"Did you take these and stuff them in the trash?"

I closed my eyes, knowing that if I lied again, I might never be forgiven. The pressure built up like the gases in a barn stuffed with hay bales, and I feared that I would explode with the secret inside me. I hadn't realized I'd been holding my breath and sounded like a leaky balloon when I finally spoke. I pointed to the handprints.

"Those are mine. I took the flyers."

My father leaned back in his chair. He dug his elbows into the table and propped his chin in his hands, scrutinizing the grain in the wood for the right words.

"It is not your turn to determine the value of things," he said even though I had never imagined he would teach me. We had never spoken about me learning how to assess things for market and I had never expressed any interest in it, hoping he would never ask. It seemed scary to have so many people depending on you to sell their junk. I had hoped he would teach Ruth instead. She liked auctions and could speak English well, and fast. No girls in our family had been auctioneers. Ruth had wanted to be the first.

"Did you ever stop to think about what that boy lost?"

I shrugged and picked a scab on my knee while he continued.

"The camera meant a lot to him. It was his granddatt's."

I stared at him, confused, unable to understand why that mattered.

"See, the English like their sentimental things. The Amish do, too."

"What's a semi-mental-thing?" I asked, sounding out the new word.

My father laughed, but his smile looked sad. "Why did you do it?"

I swallowed, feeling as if my throat had already been stuffed with his fist.

I paused, trying to find the truth. "I didn't want Marcus to find his camera," I said, waiting for him to ask me if I'd taken it, too, or worse, that Hanna had told him herself.

He only sighed and said, "Okay, Eli. Okay. That's understandable."

My father nodded, then slowly, quietly, began to hum a song from the *Ausbund*. I knew the song but didn't like the melody and only moved my lips to the words about an ancestor who survived a near drowning in the Danube. It was an awful story and I chose my own words, recalling the lyrics of Jim Croce that I had heard on Leroy's car radio, thinking I'd heard "Bad, Bad Eli Brown." It would have been about right.

I could not concentrate on my chores the rest of the day. I needed to talk to Hanna and I knew the perfect place. I found her sitting in a small row boat on the edge of our pond where she stored and painted the horseshoes she sold at the market. Years ago my grandfather had stocked the dark waters with trout and taught us to fish, but it wasn't the prospect of catching anything that lured Hanna as much as everything she could let go of there. I had caught her circling it more than ever that summer, at sunrise and sunset, absorbed by the silo reflected inside its waters. She talked to herself, quickly, of many things I could not understand then. The pond seemed to be the place to toss the thoughts that troubled her, and I, too, sought its confidentiality.

It was deep, more than twenty feet in its center, and slippery all around with dark green mosses clinging to its sides, slimy and cool on our feet during the hottest days of summer. In the winter, it would freeze, and we'd spend entire slate-sky afternoons playing hockey or skating; and in the summer, we'd dive into the pond from the dock.

The pond was both the source of pleasure and peril, which is why Hanna designated it the official site to procure good luck. She liked to listen to the humbelch of bullfrogs which she insisted were God's symphony, and to watch the reflection of the clouds and see if maybe she'd catch God looking down on us.

I walked behind her and tugged the black apron strap that had slid off her arm while she painted. "Did you see Him?" I asked.

Hanna turned to me, startled, and dropped her paintbrush into the boat. A cloud of mosquitoes buzzed around her prayer cap and I flicked them away with my wrist.

"Did I see who?"

She was frustrated with me and cast her gaze into the boat and the heap of rusted horseshoes that remained.

"You know," I said, palming the sky with my hand.

"No, E. I don't know who you're talking about."

"HIM," I said.

Hanna clenched her jaw and blew the wisp of hair that escaped her prayer cap and grazed her neck.

"I'm not looking for him anymore."

"He's looking for you and for me," I said, shocked to hear the disdain in her voice.

"He doesn't even know you, Eli."

"Why would you say that?"

"He's never even seen you. Not up close anyway."

"He hasn't?"

I looked up at the sky and waved, then climbed into the boat and faced her, refusing to believe that God hadn't seen me in the nine years that I had been alive.

"Is it because of my hands?"

Hanna looked up, locking her large blue eyes with mine.

"What?"

"Maybe he made a mistake making my hands. Like when you and Mamm burn cookies and have to throw them away."

Hanna straightened. A sad smile worked its way across her face, but I had not intended to tell a joke. I couldn't understand what was funny. My voice was small. Our knees touched and I reached down and grabbed hold of a horseshoe.

"Maybe I'm supposed to throw them away, too," I said.

"Eli, come here."

Hanna set aside her paintbrush and stepped out of the boat, offering her hand. I refused and clung to the sides of the boat, feeling safer with the horseshoes at my feet.

"That's why he doesn't want to see me," I said.

"God sees you. And he didn't make a mistake."

"How do you know?"

Hanna rubbed her fingers around her forehead.

"Listen, Eli. I'm not talking about God. I'm talking about somebody else. The boy you saw with me last night."

"Oh, him. Right. The English kid."

"What? No. No, Eli. His name is Levi Esh and he's not English."

I was confused.

"But he had a baseball hat."

Hanna nodded, and I followed her gaze into a lily pad floating in the middle of the pond. Whatever it was that delivered her there consumed her, and this bothered me because I didn't know where she was when I looked in her eyes.

"The one who kissed—"

"He didn't, Eli. I don't know what you saw last night."

"He kissed your neck. Right there. Below your chin."

Hanna paced the edge of the pond in her bare feet. She walked five steps then turned, then walked three, then turned again, the mud making sucking sounds at her heels. Every few seconds she would close her eyes and purse her lips, wiping them with the side of her fists, holding the small of her back with her hand as if somebody had kicked her there. She scratched at her neck then wound a wisp of hair around her pinky, coiling and uncoiling as if it were the very secret she contemplated sharing with me.

"Okay, Eli. You're right. You saw us."

She hitched up her dress and climbed back into the boat. She sat there staring at me, just as my father had, but for different reasons. His look was accusatory, but Hanna's face twisted with the frustration of having accused herself of something she could not undo.

"You understand what *rumspringa* means?"

"Yes," I said delighted to change the subject. *Rumspringa* was the time for running around as the bishops put it. It was a time to engage in the Outside World, own a car, drive it, live among the English, maybe even date one. The point was to give Amish kids a chance to see what it was like to live a different kind of life; then choose one to follow. I had heard that a lot of kids had parties with kegs and bands, and I often wondered if this was where Hanna had been late at night. I perked up and smiled, thinking she might take me. "Katie and Ella say you get to drive a car. I hope Leroy lets me drive the Healey."

"Forget it. *Rumspringa* is not about driving a car. It's about making the most important decision of your life," she said and tossed a big stone into the pond.

I felt my brows bunch up.

"What decision is that?"

"To live the life that Mamm and Datt want us to. Join the church."

I was suddenly disappointed. I had visions of spending a few years driving around in that red convertible, listening to the radio, learning the words of songs that contained my name, or making up ones that did. I'd take my buddies in *rumspringa* to the movies. We'd change out of our broadfall pants into jeans (with zippers! and pockets!) and wear T-shirts and baseball caps like the Englishers. Nobody would stare at us. And nobody would laugh. And maybe we'd drive to the airport and stop at the Foster's Freeze for a soft-serve twist and watch planes take off to places whose names didn't translate into Pennsylvania Dutch like Los Angeles. Las Vegas. New Orleans.

"It doesn't sound all that bad," I said.

"Do you know you can leave?"

I turned to Hanna, startled.

"Leave? Why would you want to do that?"

Hanna pressed her lips together, looking as if the stone she had tossed into the pond had somehow lodged itself in her throat. She closed her eyes when she spoke, but it didn't sound like she was speaking to me, rather like she was recalling the words of somebody else.

"Sometimes you just need to go and you don't know why."

"I'd never leave," I said, hardly understanding her.

"Even if Datt found your camera?"

She reached out and closed my mouth. I could barely breathe and I suddenly didn't feel safe at all with the horseshoes pointed down and the luck running every which way but mine. "You told him?"

Hanna cocked her head and jabbed her index finger into the humid air. She spoke clearly, deliberately, with an air of conspiracy.

"I didn't see the camera. And you didn't see the kiss."

I said nothing, listening instead to the crescendo of cicadas and the first belching of bullfrogs at noon. Hanna looked at me until I nodded, slowly understanding. I shifted my eyes to the black waters of the pond and spoke to Hanna's reflection.

"I'll give it back someday," I said.

"That's up to you. You'll know when."

Hanna's lips parted and a smile emerged wider than I had ever seen in my life. Her teeth glowed in that summer haze as white as our mother's kitchen counters. Her joy was so carefree and innocent. Looking back, I wonder if she knew the trouble she'd begun by protecting me.

I held her shoulder, feeling the heat through her sleeve, watching the muscles in her forearms twitch with life. The heat was good and light and felt like love in all its forms combined; and I knew then there was no reason, now or ever, to leave our farm.

"Is this a moment that matters?" I asked.

Hanna tapped her finger against her bottom lip.

"Every moment matters," she said.

"But this feels different," I said. "It's special. Like God would want to see it."

I wished I had had my camera then, and I knew instantly why it was necessary and why Deuteronomy was wrong. Cameras were like another set of eyes that could see the moments that mattered, in case God had forgotten to look.

FIVE

OUR CONSPIRACY OF CAMERAS and kisses collided with each other the next day. Saturday morning, August 14. One of the hottest, haziest days of the summer, the air thick and humid carrying the promise of rain. The heat forced my mother and sisters to move their entire canning operation into the summer kitchen, even then, with the windows open and a spring-operated ceiling fan, they found little relief and moved everything back into the main house, where the kitchen offered more room and a surprise. Caught between the door and screen door was a worn pink satin shoe.

"*Vas es das*?" Sarah asked, startled, although I think Ruth knew, because she kept biting her lip and casting her eyes every which way but at my mother.

Mamm, her dress already soaked through from the heat, set down the crate of peaches on the floor and picked up the shoe, turning it in the wedge of light pushing its way through the window. She ran her finger along the arch of the sole, then wound and unwound one of the pink ribbons around her wrist, considering the second surprise.

A copy of the *Ausbund* lay open on the kitchen table as if it were a newspaper that the reader had been too busy to finish. My mother walked over to it and read the name plate inside the cover: HANNA.

Sarah stiffened. Ruth cleared her throat.

"Maybe she just forgot it," Ruth said in her quiet voice, even though she meant the shoe more than the hymnal. We all believed the twins and Hanna were at the bishop's house, enrolled in a course to prepare them for baptism.

My mother wiped the sweat running along the edge of her prayer cap. Wisps of dark hair had curled inside the hollow of her cheek and made her look wet and matted, trampled not from the heat, but from the deviance of her first child.

"She's been forgetting a lot of things. Just last week she forgot to add soap powder to the wash. And sugar to the pies," Sarah said, giggling, nervous, embarrassed.

Ruth shot Sarah a look that told her to keep her mouth shut, which she did and threw her gaze on the black and white squares of linoleum where Mamm paced. She turned and looked at me. "Take it to your sister," she said handing me the *Ausbund*.

"What about that?" I asked, pointing to the shoe.

"That's not required for baptism."

But I knew it might be, reading Ruth and Sarah's smiles. I also knew that when my mother walked out the door to resume her canning, I could slip it under my hat.

I parked the scooter by the front porch of the bishop's house and walked over to Katie and Ella who sat in a small group of teenagers on the grass. They drank lemonade and recited the Seventeen Articles of Faith but stopped talking when they saw me.

"Eli?"

"Hanna left this at home."

I dropped the *Ausbund* on the lawn and hid my hands behind my back, aware of the other girls and the silence that overcame them.

The twins got up and walked over to me in bare feet.

"Thank you, Eli. We'll be sure she gets it."

I looked around. None of the other girls spoke.

"Where is Hanna?" I asked.

"She's coming," Ella said and Katie covered her own mouth with her hand, eyes shifting to the other girls whose faces were pronounced with judgment.

"You can go on home now," Ella said.

"I have to pee," I said. "Where's the outhouse?"

"He can take you, right?" Katie said and pointed to the one boy in the group.

He got out and walked over, seemingly pleased to meet me, and extended his hand.

"You must be Eli."

I stepped back. He wasn't wearing a hat, and his hair had been cut real short, like shingles in the back, which made me think he was English. He looked like one of the guys on the billboards we'd seen on Route 30 with the big smiles and perfect teeth. His eyes glimmered like the waters in our pond. He had large hands, working hands, and a network of rivers and veins in his arms. His hair looked like oiled straw and he had a few pimples on his neck. He was broad shouldered and barrel-chested with a small waist and hips, and I marveled at the way he silenced the girls when he walked past them. I didn't know then that beauty could be as disarming as the grotesque. We were completely the opposite, which is why this boy could intimidate me as much as intrigue me. Nothing about his posture suggested he was Amish. We don't swagger. And we don't assert cockiness. At least we're not supposed to. He wore jeans and had a baseball cap in his back pocket. If it weren't for his suspenders, I would've believed he was from the Outside, but he spoke in our dialect.

"*Nohch-machah*," he said. Follow my example.

We peed behind the bishop's barn, between a broken down hay loader and an overturned wheelbarrow. It was a strange place to pee and even stranger to learn what the boy had to share with me.

"Those girls your sisters?" he asked, zipping up his fly.

"The twins," I said, fascinated by his zipper, trying hard not to stare too long. "But I was looking for Hanna."

"Gabe's Daniel's Hanna?"

"No," I said, confused. Zippers seemed a lot easier to maneuver than buttons, and I didn't know why Mamm hadn't used a zipper on the sides of my broadfall pants.

"Bitterroot Betty is my aunt."

"Bitterroot Betty works with my Uncle Isaac," I said, wondering why we had to play this genealogy game. It's not meant to sound funny but it did. Since most of the Amish shared limited last names, we had devised other ways to identify ourselves because on any given day there might be more than a dozen Hanna Mae Yoders or Eli Emanuel Yoders or any other combination of common Amish names. I found it odd that he would ask me all this when he already acted like he knew me, or knew of me when he said "You must be looking for Redbeet Reuben's Hanna."

"Redbeet Reuben's my father," I said, even though my father never warmed up to the nickname given to him for the color he turned when he called too long at the auctions.

"My sister is Horseshoe Hanna."

The boy extended his hand, then withdrew when he saw me pull mine behind my back again.

"Redbeet Reuben's Horseshoe Hanna is your sister?"

I nodded and I got the feeling he knew this all along but wanted to play.

"So you're Horseshoe Hanna's Eli?" he asked. I nodded again. "I have a secret about Horseshoe Hanna and I'll share it with you if you promise to keep it to yourself."

He was tall and I had to crane my neck to get a good look at his face in the bright light. I thought at first he was trying to tell me a joke the way he laughed before he spoke, but there was anger in his voice and he lowered it so that the other girls couldn't hear.

"Hanna studies with her feet," he said, then got real quiet as if he wasn't sure what or how much he wanted to tell me next. Instead, he offered to take me to Hanna's "classroom" under two conditions. First, that she didn't know he had done so. Second, that I never let her know that we had met.

It seemed like a simple trade-off. My silence for her secret. I wasn't even allowed to tell the twins, and managed to sneak across the lawn and take back the *Ausbund* when they had gone into the bishop's house. In case they did see me, I waved goodbye from my scooter at the end of the bishop's driveway, where the boy told me to meet him. I stared at him dumbstruck, when he said his name was Levi Esh. "You're the guy who kissed my sister?"

"Tried to," he said, and he dug his hands into his jeans pocket. "Hanna wants nothing to do with me."

"That's 'cause you look like an Englisher."

"No more trying to be English than your sister."

Levi pushed up the sunglasses that had slid down his nose. He would wear those gold rimmed sunglasses with the big black lenses long before they were worn by the Amish. I didn't like that I could see myself in the lenses.

"Hanna's not English," I insisted.

"Not yet," he said. "I'll show you. You'll see."

I agreed to let him ride on my scooter, but no sooner did we leave the bishop's farm, did we turn down a narrow, winding country road and a rutted dirt driveway that led to a sad looking dairy farm with a handful of sickly cows milling about the fields.

"I thought we were going to Hanna's school."

"We are. But it's too far to scoot."

The boy told me to wait by the barn. He stepped off the scooter and walked up to the barn door, sliding it open to reveal a large black truck inside. I felt my eyes grow wide because what I was seeing struck me as both beautiful and scary, like I was staring at a monster on wheels, all that chrome catching the morning light, the black paint gleaming under layers of wax, buffed and polished like a saddle. I'd seen cars, of course, but I'd never seen one in a barn.

"Wow. Is that yours?"

"Most of it. Figure a few more months working with your dad and I'll pay it all off."

"You work for my dad?"

"Apprentice for now," he said.

"Does my father know you drive a car?"

Levi smiled.

"That's why he hired me. He needs to get around."

"Oh," I said, wondering why Datt didn't hire Leroy to take him to the auctions. "But he already has a driver."

He picked sap off the hood. "Who? That Fischer man?"

I shook my head. "He's a barber, too."

"Yeah. No. I get it. He cut my hair like this," he said and ran his hands up the shelf of golden shingles. "I was the last one he ever cut at the market."

"He's gone?" I asked, feeling the lump in my throat.

"Took down the barbershop at the market. There's a new guy selling sweaters now. Some kind of acrylic made in Taiwan."

I stared at him. I didn't know what Taiwan was. I only knew that I couldn't imagine the market without Leroy.

"Why?" I asked.

"His wife is sick. She needs him at home now."

He reached into the truck and turned on the radio real loud, then picked up the diaper on the hood and stood stooped over the front bumper, running the cloth over the chrome, rubbing out the rust caught in his own reflection.

"She's a real beauty, huh?" he said and turned up the radio.

"What's that?" I asked, wondering why Leroy hadn't told us about Ruthanne.

"I SAID DID YOU EVER SEE A CAR SO BEAUTIFUL?"

I shrugged. The only car I considered beautiful was Leroy's Austin Healey.

"NO," I shouted. "CAN YOU TURN IT DOWN?"

He did, but only for a second.

"I don't want my mom to hear me start up the engine."

He turned up the volume again. The station was crackly but I could make out the words. He sang along. *Can you see the real me, preacher? Can you see? Can you see? Can you see? Can you see the real me?*

I doubted he wanted Bishop Beiler to see the real him. Not wearing blue jeans and a baseball cap to baptism classes. It occurred to me that kissing was probably not part of the lesson plan and I doubted how serious he could be about joining the Amish.

"Hop in," he said, but I just stood there, staring at myself in the bumper.

"I'm not supposed to ride in any car but Leroy's."

"Bet you never been in a '69 Dodge. Hop in. I'll teach you to drive it."

I looked up at him, trying to see beyond the dark lenses.

"My feet won't reach the pedals."

"When you're older. You can drive it when you start *rumspringa*."

I stared at him a moment, taking in this tall, fair-haired guy who had tried to kiss my sister. He opened the door of the passenger's side. I lay the scooter on the ground and walked toward it with my sister's copy of the *Ausbund*, but before I climbed into the monster, Levi took the book from me and lay it on the hay bale outside his door.

"Don't bother with this. Hanna won't need it."

"But how's she gonna know what to sing?"

Levi jammed the keys into the ignition and looked over at me. "Who said Hanna was singing anything?" Then he stomped on the gas. The engine sputtered and spit and made me wonder if a monster should ever be driven.

There were no seat belts in the truck. I slid across the seat whenever the road turned, and it turned a lot. We passed dark green fields of tobacco and corn, our one-room school house and the cemetery at Bunker Hill where a flock of ravens peppered the sky when the truck backfired.

"What was that?"

"Hole in the pipe," Levi said but I didn't believe him because he gripped the steering wheel tighter than he did when he learned I'd never heard of him until yesterday.

"Hanna never mentioned my name?"

"Only once," I said, clarifying.

Levi laughed, but with the same sadness in his voice that I had detected at the bishop's house. I didn't know it then because I didn't have all the pieces of their story, but Levi had found Hanna in the wrong place that summer and his mind was working overtime trying to find a way to put her back to where he thought she belonged.

Levi had been right. Hanna didn't need the *Ausbund*. She needed the shoe that she'd left behind at our house. Even more than the *Ausbund*, Hanna needed the prayer cap we spotted in the parking lot of an old stone mill, where girls in pink and black leotards leapt past the windows. A large wooden wheel turned in the creek beside the mill and beyond its limestone walls, a piano played Mozart and Brahms above a clap of summer thunder. I got out of the truck and climbed down, crossing the parking lot to pick up the fallen prayer cap, then followed Levi into the studio.

We joined a group of mothers in a dark waiting room. I moved beside Levi, behind a one-way mirror, focused on my sister who stood in the corner of the studio with bare feet, winding and unwinding the wisp of hair that had slid out of her bun.

My first reaction was anger, not awe, when I saw her. The Amish do not encourage or practice performance of any kind. We consider it as high-minded and vain as high school or any formal education beyond the eighth grade. We believe it takes our focus off God. It didn't feel right to see her so exposed in the short-sleeved pink leotard. I wanted her to put her black dress back on, to tie the apron tight around her waist and cover her head with the prayer cap. I reached out and put my hands on the window, trying to block her from everyone in that room. I was shocked that my sister showed signs of being *Hochmut*, proud of her dancing, clamoring for attention from the English.

Hanna had fooled us all. We'd believed she was memorizing the Seventeen Articles of Faith every Saturday, but my oldest sister had memorized the classical positions of ballet. *Battement jet, battement fondu, battement frappe, gliesse, lent, tendu, petit, grande, en cloche. Dessous, Brise, chasse, pas de basgue, pas de bourree, port de pras, pirouette, plie.* A whole new language. A whole new life. I had thought the words were the names of plants because she mumbled them whenever she watered our gardens, stretching her arms this way and that, lifting a leg, twisting her long body beneath the arch of the garden hose, leaping boldly like a stag across the slates. I thought she loved the garden. What she loved was practicing the names of the dance positions where the plants would not betray her secret.

The mothers looked up from their magazines and smiled at me.

"Is she your sister? She's very gifted."

I shook my head. I did not want to be associated with Hanna's false pride. The piano stopped and everyone turned to Hanna, waiting for her to dance, but she stood there staring out at the floor, looking lost, and that made me feel worse than being mad at her.

I quickly pulled my hand out of my pocket and tapped the glass with my fist. Levi pulled it back. "What are you doing?"

"She needs her shoe," I said.

It got quiet in the waiting room and the mothers lay the magazines in their laps and stopped cutting recipes. I negotiated my way between them, walking toward the door, then opened it and stepped onto the dance floor. Frozen on the opposite side of the studio was Hanna watching me walk toward her. When I got close enough to her, I whispered in our dialect. "You didn't tell me you were leaving," I said.

Hanna covered her mouth with her hands. Her neck and cheeks burned bright. I lifted off my hat and flipped it over to reveal the ballet shoe. "You'll need this."

Hanna reached out and took it. "I love you," she whispered.

I felt the eyes of everyone, including her teacher watching us. I turned and started back for the door but Hanna called to me, in English, so everyone could understand us.

"Will you stay there and watch me?"

I paused in the middle of the dance floor, shifting my eyes to the girls who sat curiously watching, legs crossed, backs against the mirrors.

"Here?" I asked and pointed to the floor at my feet.

"Yes. Sit right there. Is that okay?"

Hanna looked over at her teacher, a young woman not much taller than she was, with spiky dark hair She stood by the piano, smiling.

"Break a leg," she said.

Hanna smiled. Break a leg? Breaking a leg was nothing to smile about. Hanna knew this more than anybody because she had watched me fall out of the old walnut tree when I was four. It took my arm six weeks to heal. Broken bones weren't things that made a kid happy like ice cream and puppies and purple smoke bombs. I looked over at Hanna and called out in desperation, in our dialect, trying to stop her.

"You can't dance with your leg broke!"

Hanna laughed. She was crouched over, wrapping her ankles with the worn ribbon. "It means good luck, E."

"A broke leg is good luck?"

"Means break a legacy," she said. "Break a tradition."

She tied a double knot into the ribbons then rubbed a chunk of resin on the tips of her shoes and stood. The piano started to play, but Hanna held out her hand and the room fell silent. She lowered her head and closed her eyes, tuning into the music inside her, then began to dance. The grace she possessed made her appear to float above the floor when she moved. Her cheeks were flushed and the tops of her shoulders glowed pink. Everything about the way she looked suggested she was not Amish or English, but of some other world entirely, of heaven it seemed, with wings spun of light. What I was seeing, what all of us were seeing when Hanna danced, was God. That was her glory, and the reason I'd have to find a way to forgive her for leaving.

SIX

HANNA MADE GOOD ON her promise. And I made good on mine. We told no one about the pond or the dance studio, and for three days, I felt as if Hanna and I had become best friends. I'd never had a best friend and would not have one again any time soon, but for three days, I felt as if everything was right in the world. My parents, however, were not so joyous. They sat us down at the table one night to tell us that Ruthanne had gone blind and that Leroy wouldn't be driving us anywhere anymore or coming to dinner.

"Blind?" I asked, dumbfounded to hear the news confirmed.

"Diabetes," Datt said and shook his head.

I had heard of this disease. My granddatt had warned us about eating too much candy, but he never told us we could go blind from it.

"Too much candy?" I asked.

My mother shrugged and dabbed the corner of her eye.

"Leroy won't accept any help."

"Why not?"

"Sometimes it's too hard for people to accept."

"Is Leroy *hochmut*?" I asked, wondering how proud a person could be.

"*Hochmut*? No. Just a stubborn old goat."

I had never heard my parents speak ill of Leroy. They usually had only good things to say. I looked over at my father. He yanked his shirt collar, airing his neck.

"What are you going to do about your auctions?" Ruth had asked, more concerned about my father's business than Ruthanne and Leroy's situation.

"We'll find another driver," he said. "That's the least of our concerns. Really."

The discussion turned back to me. Apparently, my father had disappointed the clergy when he refused to meet Marcus Paoni's parents in person. Rumor had it that Datt had begun a search to find the camera, having contacted almost every camera dealer or pawn shop in the area—as far east as Gap and as far west as Mount Joy. Apparently, he had had no luck locating it, which was one of the first times in his life that he would have had to admit defeat. I don't think it was this admission that stopped him from meeting Mr. Paoni. I believe that he couldn't bear to tell them, or anyone else in our district, that his son had tossed the flyers into the trash—and that he wasn't all that sorry about it based on everything that I had lost since Marcus had taken my picture.

Sensing Datt's defeat, Hanna had offered him a horseshoe.

"Why don't you use this in your search?"

"I don't believe in horseshoes," he said but took it anyway. Nobody was foolish enough to refuse my sister's horseshoes, which had proved quite profitable since she had started to sell them in the market as decorations to hang over doorways for non-believers, and for the believers, u-shaped declarations that defied darker fates.

Hanna believed in luck, but she never professed it would be on her side, or that of anyone. Hanna said luck was like the weather and you had to pay attention to the signs to determine the forecast. Just as there was fire and rain, there was good and bad luck, which is why Hanna had made it her business to protect herself and the people she knew.

I needed luck the day we were to pick up my pants. I worried the pockets wouldn't be big enough to hide my hands, or they'd be too small and I'd get stuck. Hanna said not to worry. She had hired one of the girls from Twirly Top to sew them. When I asked her what the girl knew about pockets, Hanna said, "Everything. She's English."

She had finished loading the boxes of hand-painted horseshoes in the back of the buggy when my mother walked out the door to meet us, carrying my hat.

"You going to the market?" she asked.

"Yes, Mamm," I said.

She looked back at the yard and frowned. "But you haven't finished your weeding."

I felt the lump in my throat and all the disappointment pressing down on me. I'd waited six weeks for pockets. "I'll help him when we get back," Hanna offered and slid the real panel of the buggy shut. Mamm reached inside the window to put on my hat. "Tomorrow then. And not a day later."

"Tomorrow," I promised, "your weeds will be gone."

She stared, eyes narrowed, looking back at my sisters who had come outside to join us. Whatever voices spoke to her then, she did not share with us. She looked at the sky instead, reading the dark bands that had already gathered that morning.

"It calls for rain. Drive safely."

"We will," Katie and Ella said, climbing into the back. Sarah followed. I sat in the middle, up front, between Hanna and Ruth with a smile as wide as the whole world. My troubles were over. By the end of the day, I'd have pants with pockets and nobody would ever have to see my hands again.

I should have paid better attention to the sky that night, like Hanna would have done, but I was too young to glean its meaning. We were warned about the storm, but we were determined to spend a small portion of the money we'd earned selling horseshoes. We wanted ice cream, the perfect ploy to get us to Twirly Top where my new pants awaited. My father protested, reminding us that Mamm was waiting at home with peach pies. He forbid driving in the dark, or the rain, even with gray tops and battery operated headlights. He was overly cautious even though we had already installed orange triangles on the rear panel as required by state law. We used three carriages in our family; a standard carriage pictured in most postcards, a spring wagon for hauling heavy supplies and a market wagon, which is an enclosed buggy that functions like an Amish station wagon with heavy suspension and a removable back seat. Whenever we went to market, we drove the carriage buggy and we fought for the window seats to avoid being squeezed in the middle of either the front or back bench, especially in the heat of the summer. My sisters wanted the views that night and I let them. I rode between the twins and Ruth, and Sarah rode up front between Datt and Hanna, all of us on crushed blue velvet.

We were unusually quiet on the ride. Even if we had had the courage to tell

Datt that we were picking up my new pants at Twirly Top, he wasn't listening. He had other things on his mind. He had done his best to stave off the bishop and deacons who believed that he had faced Marcus Paoni's parents and put an end to their incessant finger-pointing at the Amish. They flogged him with unwarranted and extraneous praise and it was all he could do to escape them. Like us, he kept his eyes on the road, its stillness amplifying the struts and squeaks of our buggy. We watched the first splatter of rain drops in the dying light. I turned to look out the back window, searching the sky to see if perhaps God was watching, feeling like he was, like he knew to watch this time.

We pulled into Twirly Top, parking in front of the two hitching posts reserved for the Amish. Two teenage girls, the Twirly Top Twins, dressed in white mini skirts and ruffled pink halter tops, sat on the posts, smoking Marlboros. Red-faced, they quickly tossed the cigarettes onto the ground and stamped them out, then disappeared behind the building and reappeared at the window. One of them had turned up the outdoor speakers. We were not strangers to Jackie and Leanne, the fair-skinned, feather-haired bleached blondes who went out of their way to make us feel welcome. They respected our loyalty, which was never about the ice cream, but the radio station they favored. We made plenty of ice cream on the farm whenever it was our turn to host services in the barn, but besides Leroy's car radio, we rarely heard modern music. Jackie and Leanne had good taste. We liked FM 97, a local station that played the top rock 'n roll and Motown. Ice cream was our code for feeling the backbeats of Gladys Knight and Marvin Gaye that reverberated across the parking lot, pumping us with the kind of excitement reserved for fireworks.

Our trick worked like this. Jackie made it a point to lift me up to the counter to sample the latest batch of soft serve, while my father waited patiently behind the counter for the verdict. I'd take my good old time tasting the latest flavors while my sisters sat in the buggy and listened to the music that played from the stereo speakers outside. They had excellent memories and often translated the lyrics to our dialect, hoping my parents wouldn't catch on if the words were in Pennsylvania Dutch. My sisters insisted they had learned them from the Sunday song groups popular among Amish youth, passing them off as revival tunes from 19th century gospels. My parents, like most Amish parents, frowned upon the radio, but I would often catch my mother humming "Let's Get it On" while she cooked.

The weather foiled our plan that night. Lightning flashed over the neon sign where the R was missing, and the Y blinked like a stutter. My father pointed to the sky.

"There's no time for tasting, E."

I looked back at my sisters through the window. Hanna winked. Katie, Ruth and Ella poked their heads out of the buggy and gave me the thumbs up. Even Sarah raised her hands in prayer, all of them excited that I'd soon have pants with pockets.

"But what if they changed the flavor?" I asked, more worried about my new pants. We hadn't talked about how I'd actually receive them—definitely not in front of Datt.

"We don't change what's worked for two hundred years," he said. "They're not gonna change what's worked for ten."

I rubbed my nose, unconvinced. Jackie had already prepared the first sample. "Double Dutch," she said, holding out the cone. She knew better than to give me a cup. Cones were easier to maneuver. I smiled. She leaned close to my face and whispered.

"Your pants are in the milk box outside."

I nodded. My father cleared his voice.

"Eli, the light. We must hurry."

"Okay, then. Double Dutch."

My father sighed. "We'll take six Double Dutch cones please, and one twist, for me. Can you hurry now?"

Another clap of thunder and the crackle of electricity. The lights flickered and the freezers clicked on and off.

"We want to avoid the storm, you know."

"Sure thing, Mr. Yoder."

Leanne set aside the mop she had used to clean up a bottle of Coke that had exploded and shattered on the floor. She took the cones from Jackie and set them into what looked like an overturned egg carton. She flinched, startled by a honk. A group of Little Leaguers stuffed inside a Ford Country Squire station wagon had pulled up to the window. A bunch of boys wearing baseball caps and grass stained jerseys, waved through the windshield at Jackie. They looked familiar and I squinted, trying to make out the face of the boy in the rear, behind the weary driver. He was rounder than the others with full red cheeks and a belly I couldn't see, but remembered all too well. Marcus Paoni seemed to remember me, too, and waved through the window, his fingers purposely stiff and without separation.

"Hey Big Ugly!"

"I'll be right there," Jackie barked. "My god. You guys act like you own this place. You're Little League. Little!"

"That's the kid who stole my camera!"

"What?"

Marcus shot his hand out the window and pointed at me. A woman who might have been his mother rolled down the driver's window.

"Him? How do you know? They all look the same," she said, pointing at me.

I pulled the brim of my hat over my eyes.

"No, Mom. It's him! Look at his hands."

"Let's go, Datt," I said and reached for the tray of ice cream cones that Jackie had just then slid over the counter. My father pulled out his wallet. Jackie waved him away, motioning toward the brewing storm. Lightning crackled outside the window and left silver threads in the sky. Jackie looked concerned.

"It's on the house, Mr. Yoder."

"We can't accept this without paying."

"Come on, Datt, they're melting," I pleaded, eyes glued to the station wagon. Jackie turned her back to us, opening the window wider to take the Little Leagues' order.

I hopped off the counter as fast as I could. I didn't want to risk another second with Marcus, but that very second might have changed everything for us. I took the cones and walked toward the door, turned and pushed it open with my seat, holding it for my father just as the sky opened and the rain blew hard into the store. He did not move and stood there under the oscillating ceiling fan, looking lost. I had never seen my father frozen like that, staring up at the blades in the fan as if each were a sign he was supposed to read.

I looked back through the window, seeing that Marcus had gotten out of the station wagon and was charging toward the door. My heart raced. The cones were dripping on the floor and I decided to run into the rain, risking their ruin over mine. I didn't stop at the milk box, and to this day, I don't know if my new pants were ever inside it.

"Take them," I said and shoved the tray into Hanna's hands. I pulled myself into the buggy and climbed into the back seat, between the twins who were too consumed by the Double Dutch cones to notice how wet and scared I was. I crouched on the floor between them, trembling. Hanna handed me the last Double Dutch cone, already half-melted.

"What are you doing down there?"

I took the cone but said nothing.

"Did you get your pants?"

"Not yet."

"Why not? Jackie said they'd be ready. You sure stayed in there a long time."

Ruth leaned down and squeezed my shoulder.

"Yeah. We learned the last verse to 'You're So Vain.'"

My sisters chimed in together, mimicking Carly Simon's voice. They giggled, amused that the English would write a song that poked fun of themselves.

I didn't laugh or join in the fun. I didn't even eat the ice cream, hoping my father would take us home. My stomach ached and my heart raced. I watched my father through the window in what seemed like a heated exchange between him and Jackie. He pointed a finger to the buggy and Jackie pointed a finger at my father. She flung her hands in the air, then slapped her arms across her chest, shaking her head.

"You think she told him about the pants?" I asked.

"No. It's not about the pants," Hanna said, watching them with a hand clasped tightly over her mouth. "Jackie wouldn't blow it for you."

"Then what's wrong?" I asked. I wanted to crawl up on the seat and take a look myself but didn't want Marcus to see me on his way out the door.

"Nothing, Eli. It's nothing."

"Jackie said the ice cream was on the house."

"She did?"

I nodded. I couldn't imagine why my father would put up such a fuss over free ice cream. But that was the point. Nothing's free. Nothing comes without a price.

My father unhitched the reins from the post and climbed into the buggy, his shirt soaked and sticking to his arms, defining the hills of muscle. Hanna held out his cone.

"You eat it," he said, his voice hoarse, ground down from more than calling at the auction that night.

"But you're the only one who likes vanilla, Datt."

He turned to my oldest sister whose face had grown red.

"We will talk when we get home."

My father took the cone and held it in his left hand then jerked the reins with the right, trying to control our horse who had already been spooked by the thunder. Rain blew into the buggy then suddenly turned to hail, thrashing the windshield and bouncing off the roof. My father tried to turn on the headlights but they didn't work. Hanna turned to him, concerned. He sighed and lowered his head, staring at the windshield through fogged glasses.

"Thought I asked you girls to change the batteries."

Hanna bit her lip. Katie nudged her. My father looked like the parent in the station wagon, weary, exhausted, desperate for the simplicity and solace of his kingdom. We paused at the edge of the Twirly Top parking lot, waiting for the station wagon of Little Leaguers to pass. We pulled onto the road behind them, following the soft red glow of tail lights, extinguished too soon by the storm and the flash in our minds that told us to wait until it passed. We were only one mile from home. Less than six minutes, even in a storm. We were close to safety and only drove faster into the darkness to get home.

It was my mother who found us first. I stared up at her through the crook of an arm that had bent backward like a doll in the crash. She remained kneeling at the base of the walnut tree, barefoot and strangely calm, studying us with the scrutiny she imposed when we received her instructions in the garden, although nothing about our arrangement that night suggested order. I worked my fingers through a tangle of hair and seized her hand. She flinched. My hands were covered in blood and my thumb had smashed the ice cream cone. It was soggy, now, like wet tissue. I lay on my back, squeezing her wrist, watching the clouds move across the moon. The air humid, sticky. Too still.

"Eli?

"I'm stuck," I cried, pierced by the pain in my back. My hands were bloody, my mouth, too. I had bitten through my top lip and spit when I tasted it. I felt the weight of the arm slung over my chest, and another wrapped around my neck. The blade of a shin bone dug into my own, pinning me to the floor of what had been our buggy. I turned my head, feeling the soft cotton dress of the lap cradling me, the body still warm. I shifted my eyes, seeing the tip of my father's peppered beard grazing the hand of a body I did not want to identify. I reached over to nudge his shoulder and saw that one of his shoes had come off and lay by the tree. His right foot had twisted backwards and bled on the bark.

"Datt?" I cried. "Datt?"

My mother rolled Hanna off my legs and pushed the twins aside, Katie and Ella entangled, arms clasped, as they had once been in her womb. Their mouths did not move.

"They're not talking," I said. "Why aren't they talking? Mamm! Make them talk."

My mother said nothing and grabbed me firmly by the wrist. Her other hand under my neck, fingers cold and wet.

"Please do not move," she said, exploring my body for injuries, pressing firmly on my hip and pelvis, arms and legs, my feet, too, and my hands. I felt nothing more than the piercing in my lower back, like a horse had kicked me.

"I want to get up," I said, feeling frightened of the silence first, then the whirl of sirens in the distance.

"I have to pee," I said, my voice shaking. It was too late. A warm stream worked its way down my leg. My mother wrapped her arms beneath me and pulled me out of the tangle of bodies and what remained of the buggy.

I steadied myself on her shoulder and stood, staring at the mess before us and the sight of my mother. Her face held the color of twilight and her flour-dusted hands left white prints on the shoulder straps of my sisters' black aprons. She followed with her eyes the wheels of the over-turned buggy that wobbled from a twisted iron axle, crushed against the great trunk of the tree. In her lap lay a plastic triangle reflector from the tailgate that flashed orange in her eyes. She was perhaps more lost than me, searching for angels in the blackness. I buried my mouth into her prayer cap. "Make them talk," I pleaded.

"I can't, Eli."

"Please, Mamm. Say something," I said and knelt down beside her again, poking my sisters shoulders.

My mother reached out and pressed her hand on mine.

"Eli," she said with her eyes closed, as if she had the power to soften the pronouncement. "They're dead."

I paused. "All of them?"

My mother nodded stiffly, then lifted her chin as if to adjust the distance between her own tears and the ground. She had not looked up from the girls. She had not moved nor blinked. She sat there, neither hunched nor slumped, but shrunken. The sight of her five daughters dead had reduced her instantly, leeching her skin, leaving her white and ghostly and small. She had not sifted through the bodies to find my father. She had not asked about him, yet. I looked over at his limp form and presumed he was dead, too. My mother had not reached out to check his pulse.

The sirens of an ambulance wailed in the distance, red and blue lights glowing beyond our silo. To this day, we have no idea who called but I've always believed it was the driver who hit us.

"I want you to go inside and get me the scissors."

Scissors. I thought I had heard her wrong.

"Get me the scissors now."

My mother repeated herself without looking at me, each word pumped with the burden of her order. She spoke in a voice I could barely make out as if it had been pushed deep inside her throat and slipped behind her heart, like a lost penny in the back of a junk drawer. I didn't like what I suspected she might do with the scissors, and my eyes filled with tears.

"You sure, Mamm?"

My mother nodded, methodically removing the white prayer caps from my sisters' heads with the precision and purpose reserved for when she cooked or had nursed us. She lay each of the bloody cloths across her lap in the order she had given birth. First Hanna's. Then Katie. Ella. When she took the tassel of Ruth's bonnet, her fingers shook, fighting to untie the small cross it formed beneath her chin. Sarah lay across my father's chest and for a moment when he breathed, I thought she had lifted her head.

"Datt's alive," I said.

My mother didn't hear me. She was too lost in the ritual, removing the prayer caps, preparing to part. The horse that had come unhitched from the buggy ran through the cornfields and crossed the road, trampling my mother's garden in its hysteria. She remained calm and silent, waiting for me to help, her arm outstretched beside her, palms up, waiting for the scissors.

"Go to the house," she said in a voice so low I thought the words had swallowed her. I did not know that my mother had already disappeared and whatever voice spoke through her now was an echo of my own.

"What for?" I whispered, my bottom lip trembling with the truth. She lifted her chin and her gaze slid into mine.

"THE SCISSORS."

I swallowed the blood dripping down my throat.

I knew nothing of redemption then, but I believe now that my mother's rage burned through her beauty that night. She would be haunted by the bright lights, the pop of the hood she'd heard through the kitchen, the crumpling of iron, the tear of leather, the whinny of a spooked horse running wild and lost through the fields, and the memory of a driver who had never stopped to see if her family had lived or died.

I wanted to shake her back into herself. I did not recognize the kneeling woman. Her silence scared me and I ran from it and from her and from my dead sisters whose eyes looked up at the sky as if they were counting fireflies or waiting for the moon to rise. I wanted them to blink as much as I wanted them to close. Any movement would have been enough to assure me there was no truth to the accident.

I kicked off my shoes in the walkway and stood staring at the great white house, trying to hold it all in my eyes. It seemed so huge to me then, imposing its false sense of safety. My father's Kingdom of Simplicity had suddenly and erroneously been complicated by circumstances beyond my control or comprehension. Lightning flashed, illuminating our house, luring me to go inside. But I refused to enter through the front door, believing, like my mother did, that it was bad luck. I ran to the back of the house instead, seeing my mother's red geraniums overturned, the flagstones covered with potting soil and black footprints. The screen door to the kitchen was open and two white kittens lay curled in the threshold, relieved by the cross breeze. I shooed them away with a stone, clearing the doorway, bracing myself against the frame, knowing that everything had already changed no matter what my mother decided to do with the scissors.

The porch door swung back and forth in the breeze inviting flies to gather around the pies that she had spent the evening baking, the smell of peaches and cinnamon-rubbed rhubarb wafting over the table. An apron lay crumpled on the floor and the unattended flame of a hurricane lamp breathed soot onto the glass. I blew it out on my way to the drawer where I knew my mother kept the scissors, hoping God would not see what I was about to do, or blame me for being an accomplice to my mother's crime.

I reached for the knob of the drawer, praying the scissors would not be there, wishing that for once my mother had misplaced something besides the bobby-pins for her prayer cap. I opened it slowly, hating the soft sound of the rubber rollers, the rumble of loose marbles among loose coins. The scissors, made by a local blacksmith, lay in their black velvet casing, handles glistening in the flashes of lightning that continued to brighten the white walls of our kitchen.

I stood on my tiptoes and reached into the drawer, taking the scissors out of their case. I could see half my face, distorted by the bend in the metal, cheeks streaked with blood. I dragged my pinky slowly against the cut above my right eyebrow, watching the skin bounce back, sponge-like, bearing the convenience of a scar that would, years later, remind me why my rage still lingered.

I left the kitchen and carried the scissors to my mother. Policemen and paramedics blocked the road, lighting it with flares for traffic that crawled along, seduced by the horror. I remember hearing a car door open and a horn honk. A walkie-talkie. More sirens. The lights blazing from the squad car. I handed my mother the scissors and took my place beside her, knowing full well what she wanted to do.

"Thank you, Eli. Now close your eyes."

The paramedics stopped working and stared at both of us. My father opened his eyes and coughed, clearing his throat, trying to gesture to my mother to stop. She didn't see him. She didn't need to ask for his permission.

Her right hand shook and her wrist went limp, defying the strength in her fingers that forced the blades to part. She had braided each of my sisters' hair while I was in the house. Then one by one, she cut the braids off at the crown of their heads, working swiftly, furiously, forehead wet, veins throbbing and threaded with the kind of worry that would never unravel in one lifetime. She snipped off the tassels of the prayer caps, and with her fingers still shaking, managed to secure each braid with a double knot. Lightning flashed and everything went silent. The paramedics turned down the squelching walkie-talkies. The crackle of electricity reminded us that the storm still lingered. My mother kept shaking her head, as if the conversation inside her conflicted with the silence that remained outside. She collected the braids, then steadying herself on my shoulder, stood and walked back across the yard to the house and shut the door.

My mother never looked back at the bodies. But I did. I stood there standing in my mother's place, beside the paramedics who tried to close my sisters' eyes.

"Keep them open," I shouted, feeling my voice crack.

My nose burned and my lips trembled and I bit through the bottom until it bled to keep from crying. But the tears still came, crawling down my cheek with nothing to stop them but the slap of my hand. Tears, Hanna had said, were the raindrops in your heart, and I let them drip over my sisters' faces, hoping to wake them.

"Hey, hey. Maybe you should go inside."

The paramedics exchanged glances. I felt their eyes on me even though I had not lifted my own off my sisters, trying to memorize the lips, the noses, the eyes. I was overwhelmed by the intricacies, having never counted the freckles on my sisters' faces or noticed the depth of the dimple in Ruth's chin or the way Kate and Ella's cheekbones looked like the polished halves of sliced pears. I stared at them, trying to make sense of their mangled bodies. Sarah's neck had snapped in the crash. She looked like a broken doll. I reached down and covered her with my hand, but one of the paramedics pulled it away.

"Son, please."

"You didn't fix her. You need to fix them," I pleaded.

The paramedic swallowed and quickly dabbed his neck with his sleeve. His supervisor, a small, square man wearing yellow gaiters stepped toward me. I shuddered, seeing the blood smeared down his legs, knowing it wasn't the man's blood and that rubber didn't bleed.

"We can't fix them," he said. "They're gone."

I slapped my hands over my ears to minimize what felt like a bee stinger piercing my eardrum, the high-pitched frequency of truth digging its way into my head. A prick, a pierce, a jab. *They're gone.*

The words did not register when my mother first said them, but now, I realized I would never see them again. The Amish have no photos of the living.

I screamed. Then everything went dark.

When I woke up, I remember the paramedics stepping toward me, lifting me off my sisters' bodies, trying to pry my hands off their arms and legs. I didn't know that I possessed that much strength at nine years old. It would take three paramedics and a policeman to pull me away. I held on to whatever I could. A sleeve, a neck, an arm, a face. I worked my body beneath my sisters again, to hide myself or to take back the moment, to deliver me to the buggy, to the storm, to Twirly Top, the auction and the wagon full of horseshoes. The paramedics waved something that smelled like salt under my nose and I blinked, seeing them hover over me.

"You've got to let go, son."

I felt my hands being pried from an arm, but I looked up and managed to focus through the tears. "Stop," I said. "I need to get something."

The paramedic in gaiters hesitated but it was a young cop who told them to give me a minute. He pulled me to my feet, tapped my shoulder and nudged me to move.

I ran back to the house, through the kitchen, past my mother's pies, up the back stairs, taking two at a time, flinging open the door of my bedroom so hard it left a dent in the wall and brought down the hat rack.

I moved across the floor in the dark and dropped on one knee beside my bed, fishing beneath it, feeling a few scattered watermelon seeds, a broken pencil, a penny, and the loose floorboard where I had hidden the camera. I pried it open, unaware of the nail that went through the webbing. I'm not sure if I was feeling anything at all that night but the piercing in my ear and my heart. I took the camera and pressed it against my chest, trying to release the tightness in my lungs, already sticky with the dust motes that drifted through the darkness. I stood and walked to the window seeing the paramedics looking back at the house. In my absence, large black bags had been set on the ground beside my sisters. A Bloodhound had been released, running through the cornfield, trying to follow the scent of the driver. My father, who had suffered a shattered femur, struggled in the gurney, trying to release himself from the buckle that pinned him in place. His flailing suggested that he would be alright. He called out to no one in particular, his voice exploding the stillness after the storm. "It's only broken bones. It's only broken bones." But we all knew that bones were the least of our injuries.

I walked back across the room with the camera, leaving the door open and made my way down the stairs, walking past my mother. She sat at the table in the dark, staring at an empty cigar box where she had placed my sisters' braids. She looked up at me but said nothing about the camera. I will never know whether or not she recognized the shame we shared or wanted me to join her on the flip side of her crime: Amish women are forbidden to cut their hair. The Bible tells them it is their only glory, and to cut it is to disgrace themselves. Maybe she knew that what I had to do was beyond her control, but a part of me wanted her to get up out of the chair and take the camera. In my dream, she does and I am a different person with a different kind of story. But she didn't. I do not blame her. She knew that her will and my own could not be broken or tamed through dogma or scripture, although I'm sure at times we have both wished it could. My mother knew the force of a rolling stone and she let me go. I paused at the door, scooping up the kittens in the doorway, burying my face in their fur. Then I set them on the flagstones and crossed the threshold with the camera in my hands.

I don't remember walking back across the yard to the bodies. My feet seemed to glide over the wet grass and the blades glittered with light as if I had slid into the space between heaven and earth. Everything about our farm began to glow and split and sparkle and I saw the faint forms of my sisters silhouettes in the cornfields, then the sky. They had climbed the trunk of the walnut tree and sat in the highest limbs, looking down, waving, beckoning me to join them. They knew I loved to climb trees despite my hands but it wasn't play they intended. I blinked. Rubbed my eyes. I turned to the paramedics and asked them what they saw in the tree.

"Nothing," they said.

They were right. I looked back up at the tree. The branches were empty. Then a flash in the cornfield. I turned, seeing my sisters flying above the stalks, hair free and unbridled, blowing back black as raven's wings. I wanted to chase them but I wanted to take their photo more.

I waited until the paramedics lifted my father into the ambulance and closed the door. Then I stepped closer to the bodies and raised the camera to my eye. I drew in a sharp breath, holding the camera still as Leroy instructed, and focused on my sisters' faces. I had kept their eyes open, knowing full well what I was doing even though it was wrong. This time I didn't ask for permission to make it right. I snapped five photos, one for each of them.

All I remember next was a surge of heat in the camera, as if it had been charged by the storm. It grew unbearably heavy and hot in my hands and I dropped it on the ground. The grass sizzled. The paramedics swore. "Jesus Christ."

I picked up the camera and turned my back when they zipped up my sisters into long black bags and loaded them into the ambulances. They asked me if I wanted to ride with my father and I told them no.

I climbed into the walnut tree instead and watched the ambulances disappear between the hills connecting Paradise to Providence, trying to make sense of what little I could. Everything had been scrambled. I felt disconnected and far away from myself, floating somewhere above the cornfields, chasing fragments of my sisters' forms that had, to my dismay, dissolved into the husks like black ink. I clutched the camera and clenched my teeth, then opened my mouth and screamed, pushing my apology into the darkness.

Sorry, but I want to keep you with me, not God.

I was a true thief now. I had stolen more than a camera that summer. I had stolen my sisters' souls. My mother had stolen their glory by cutting their hair and together we tried to bury our secrets with the bodies. I had thought the photos might be enough to cope with our loss. But as much as a photograph could remind me of the dead, it would not contain a strategy for living, which I needed most of all.

PART TWO

◆

ONE

A PART OF ME REMAINED in the old walnut tree, looking down, trying to make sense of the edge of our farm where my sisters were last seen. On the anniversary of their death, I'd climb into the tree and watch the sun rise over our farm to understand better my role in the accident, hoping that one day, when I climbed down and let go of the limbs, I would also let go of the need to know why it had happened. If I had been a true Amish man, I would have believed it was God's plan. But I couldn't when I was that young.

Everyone in Lancaster had heard of "Eli and the Yoder Sisters" even though my parents had never granted an interview with reporters, chasing the vans of WGAL TV 8 off our property. The story had made headlines across national, state and local media, including both weekly Amish newspapers, *The Budget* and *Die Botschaft*, as well as the monthly magazine, *The Diary*.

The accident catalyzed a statewide prayer group, which flooded our roadside mailbox with letters, cards, gifts, prayers, and, much to my father's chagrin, money. In the first year, more than one hundred thousand arrived in the form of a check or money order, or, for those who didn't know we used bank accounts, cash. At first, my father accepted the money graciously; it helped us pay his medical bills for a fractured femur, hip, pelvis and shoulder. To this day, he has never seen the extent of his injuries in any x-ray, even though my mother had, telling me "it looks just like smashed Saltines." Datt's recovery did not deplete the Amish medical aid, our form of health insurance, which he refused to tap into in case another person needed it more.

By the time the media barrage ended, which lasted until the day my father graduated from crutches to a cane, his auction business had tripled. My father was busy almost every day of the week, which hurt our tobacco crop and the men who depended on it for their cigars, Leroy Fischer included. In a way, I think my father appreciated the business so that he'd never have to stop to think, and despite my mother's pleading to sit and rest when he began to show signs of limping, my father never stopped moving. Once he began to walk, he was on a mission to forget. He focused on honing his craft, gaining an intimate knowledge of the value of things. He loathed the money filling our mailbox every month, because no sum could ever replace his five daughters.

It's a funny thing to know that money sometimes was the means by which the Englishers communicated their connection to each other, and to us. Don't get me wrong. I know that their money was a way to show their love, but our wealth was measured in the depth of our experiences with the land and in our relationship to God and each other. However, money affected us, just the same.

For many months after his recovery, my father's nightly ritual consisted of counting the bills and smoking his cigars, pushing the heap of money to my mother, who would count the bills again with teary-eyed disbelief, then push it back across the table to Datt, uncertain as to what to do with it. The volley continued for years. In fact, every summer, usually not exactly on the anniversary but within two weeks of it, we'd receive a check for ten thousand dollars from an anonymous donor. The third time it happened, in 1979, my father counted the zeros a few times, tapped the ash of his cigar onto the check, then looked up and said, "That's it. Who do they think they are? They need to move on." The very next day he painted a sign and hung it along the fence line (where it would remain, misspellings and all, until the day he died):

Where Doing Fine, Thank Ye. NO Need to Stup.

The next year, when the check arrived in our mailbox, always a money order with no return address, my father wrote in the huge jagged print known only to belong to his palsied right hand:

We Need Less Money, More God.

My mother opposed him. She wanted to keep the money and set up a fund for Amish children with special needs like me and find a doctor who could help mitigate the backlash of the less than desirable genetic traits we suffered, from webbed hands and webbed feet to Maple Syrup Urine disease. After all, we are the descendents of only two hundred Swiss Anabaptists, a considerably small gene pool. Mamm suggested surgery for my hands, to slice through the webbing and separate my fingers. My father protested, believing it was God's will, to which my mother would look at the money and say that was God's will, too. My father drowned in the flood of care and concern, not so much from the Amish, but from the English. Something in him couldn't accept their help, and he distanced himself from their gifts, and from my mother in the process. Each year, his signs grew larger, the writing bolder and more barbed.

For the first two years, we could hardly keep up with the fudge orders, which my mother was making exclusively. She hadn't touched the recipe but received an award for the best fudge in the county, beating our competitor Meise's Candy, who, in my grandfather's opinion, made fudge far smoother than ours. Still, tour groups rushed the stand, loading up boxes and backpacks with bricks of maple fudge and an empty jar they decided was appropriate for 'tips.' Week after week, they stuffed it full not with one dollar bills, but tens and twenties. They would pay for the fudge and dump the change into the jar, but never coins, as if coins were offensive and cheap. The only time I saw coins in that jar was when a small girl, a few years younger than me at the time, with a bushel of gold curls and strawberry stains on her lips, dug into the front pocket of her overall dress and pulled out two silver dollars as big as her blue eyes. Her father caught me and smiled. "It's Madison's birthday money."

People wanted to give to us. And they wanted to share our grief. They wanted to reach out across the counter and through the barrier to our world to say they cared. There was an odd connection I felt to these people who, like me, struggled to forgive the driver; and so they filled the tip jar, driven not by the confections they might find, but by the guilt of their association they could relieve instead. I heard them often say "They should hang the bastard" or "I'd kill him myself." Everyone assumed the driver was a man, but none of us knew for sure. We didn't dwell on it. The driver remained faceless, not because the police had failed to find him, but because we never focused on humanizing him by giving him eyes, lips, a nose, ears. Or a heart. If he had had these things, we would wonder why he never came to meet us.

I was reminded day after day from my teachers, classmates, cousins and neighbors to forgive the sinner but not the sin, but no matter how many times I repeated this adage, I failed to practice what I preached. I couldn't comprehend anybody living with the fact that they had killed my sisters. There were other people who felt like me but they were not Amish. I would not find them at the school house, or in the fields or working behind the stands at the market. I found them instead, in the 1,251 letters they wrote in 1976.

There was a certain freshness to the letters that I'd never heard expressed openly among the Amish, and this raw and curt honesty compelled me to read them over and over, even though my father had tried to get rid of them by throwing them in the trash. I was careful to wait until he fell asleep to dig out the crumpled pages that infuriated him but consoled me. Never before had I read such expressions of rage, disgust, injustice, pain and hate. The English language suited me. There were more ways to say how I felt in it, and a certain freedom of feeling that came with a cost in our Deitsh dialect. Perhaps it was my insatiable curiosity with other people's anger that compelled me to learn how to read and write English quicker than most Amish boys my age. I wanted to feel this rage expressed in a voice that was not my own. The more I read, the more indebted I was to the writer for relieving me of the exact same thoughts. There were even doodles included in the cards sent by school age children—pictures of long blue swimming pools and swing sets, invitations for me to visit and enjoy them. I liked the rainbows they drew arched over pots of gold with me and the child artist holding hands between it, stick figure friendships extended beyond purple crayon fence posts.

I wanted to thank these writers for the gift of their letters and for making me feel less alone. Over the years I have been tempted to travel to the destinations I'd tracked through the many postmarks. It didn't matter where the letters came from: Kansas, Kentucky, Louisiana, North Dakota. Almost everyone said the same thing. They were praying for me and my family. They were sorry, sad and angry we had lost my sisters. Some even went on to call the driver a coward for never coming forth. I felt understood by the English and was frustrated that I could not write back to them at the time because of my hands. Day after day, cobbling the message inside their pages, I realized that in many ways I was more like them than the Amish.

There were countless stories in the *Martyr's Mirror* about the Amish forgiving their transgressors, but no story intrigued me more than that of the Dutch Anabaptist Dirk Willems. I had first heard this story on my tenth birthday at school, a rainy afternoon barely a month after the funeral. I had sat on the floor, cross-legged, while my teacher explained that Dirk had been chased by a "thief catcher." Not because Dirk was a thief, but because he didn't believe in infant baptism. In the midst of his escape, Dirk turned back to rescue his pursuer who had fallen through an icy lake that he had just crossed outside his village. Dirk was captured and burned at the stake on a windy day, which only delayed his death when the winds lifted the fire away from his upper body. According to villagers, he cried "Oh my Lord, my God!" seventy times during the fire.

When my teacher read over Dirk's story, she emphasized not the crying or the torture of the fire, but the significance of the seventy times Dirk cried. It was Jesus, she reminded us (but looked at me when she spoke), who told Peter that he should forgive those who sinned against him not just seven times, like he asked, but seventy. The point, she said, was that being Amish meant embracing the fundamental practice of forgiveness, which was the very tool of our survival over the last four hundred years. We had forgiven our enemies during the Reformation, and we had learned to love them.

I remember thinking how long it'd take to forgive the driver seventy times when I hadn't even made it to one. When the teacher asked us if we had anyone in our hearts we needed to forgive, I raised my hand, but asked to go to the bathroom. I used the outhouse but did not come back inside. I ran home instead, hoping that my mother would mistake the source of my wet eyes and cheeks as the rain.

She found me in the barn, beating the hay bales I draped with my father's black capes. My parents were no more willing to talk about the driver than my teacher, and the more they refused to bring him up, the more prone I was to address him directly. Not him exactly, but the hay bales that I shouted, spit at, and whacked with a baseball bat so frequently that I had blisters on my hands more often than not that autumn. I don't know if my mother thought this to be destructive. She never said anything that day and left me alone, returning later with an aloe plant and a bandage. When my father asked about my hands, I told him I had climbed a tree. I did not have the courage to tell either parent that if I had been Dirk Willems and had seen the thief catcher fall through the ice, I doubted I'd ever have the courage to save him. I wanted to end the questions that plagued us all, my teacher included. I wanted to know why the driver never said he was sorry. Back then, that would have been enough for me to move on.

◇

I learned to seek comfort from Captain Courageous. Rather than play with my friends at the school house, I sat by myself at recess and read. I had found more instruction in the comic books Leroy had given me than in any lesson my teacher had planned. I called them my buddy books and I read them more than the *Ausbund*. They would become my friends over the year as I had ignored my own and let them slip away that autumn. Just as I didn't want pity from the people who saw my hands as ugly, I didn't want the canned comfort of anyone who believed I should be moving on faster. The more they tried to turn my focus away from my grief, the more I resisted, and the more time I spent with my nose inside the buddy books. I'd sneak them into class and hide them inside my notebooks, translating the English words and phrases, becoming fluent in its sordid slang. I'd unwittingly drawn attention to myself once by letting out a good howl during class.

My teacher asked in high German, "What's so funny, Eli?".

I'd look out the window as another tour bus stopped to take pictures of the Amish kids playing softball in the school yard, tossing them pennies for their photo, as if their souls cost as much as a large gumdrop. "The English," I'd say and she'd bite her lip and nod, then turn to the vocabulary list she'd been writing on the blackboard. I didn't have to lie. She knew what I had been reading, and although Captain Courageous had not been part of her lesson plan, she responded well, touched to hear me laugh. I did not talk much, rarely in school, and it surprised her as much as my classmates to hear my voice.

I'd come to rely on the comfort of those buddy books. I'd take the magazines with me and climb the hill above our farm to lose myself in the blurbs and balloons hovering over Captain Courageous, a prophet of quests and conquests. I marveled at his supernatural powers to come to the aid of people in distress, mostly frightened soldiers during World War II. It made sense to me that somebody would do that, but I often wondered if Captain Courageous, in his mask and special suit, was God in disguise. In later issues, I liked that he later formed the Super-Mystery Men, a group of heroes that banned together to help free themselves and everyone else captured by a wayward soldier. Although he was not an Anabaptist, he still interested me, and I respected him. I often wondered if Leroy had given me the comic books to make me believe that I could rescue myself.

◇

Emma Beiler was the only person I knew who wasn't bothered by my sadness, and oddly enough, in her presence, I was able to feel joy. We were used to seeing each other every week at the market, but now that my sisters were gone, neither of us could ignore the huge space between us. Though I had grown used to eating lunch by myself, Emma began to bring me turkey subs from Mr. Brubaker's deli, or a paper cone filled with Fink's Fries, so that I wouldn't leave. I managed to grunt a thank you, because it was, after all, a gift; and there we'd stand at our stalls facing each other while we ate in silence, the English in the aisle between us. Over time, she had found ways to engage me in pleasant conversation about things that had nothing to do with forgiveness. Eventually, we sat together to eat lunch, though she was the one who came to join me. She even stayed to help at the candy stand when things got busy and she had sold out of bread. We soon passed the slow times at market talking about fishing rods and scooters and dogs, and when I didn't feel like talking, I gave her a copy of Captain Courageous to read.

Years later, she would confess that she never liked the comic books, but she liked the smile they brought to my face. Of course, she was quicker to understand, explaining to me the courage of Captain Courageous, as if she hoped it would be mine some day. Ever since my sisters had died, she'd kept an eye on me at school, especially at recess, and she did not dare let the tourists have their way when a camera dangled from their rubbery necks. I had seen her on more than one occasion scoop up gravel into her fists when the tourists got too close, then she'd let it go and wave her empty hand, skin pocked from the tiny stones. "If you take a picture of his hands," she said. "I'll break your camera."

Emma was my only friend then, and we spent every Sunday by the pond behind our barn, fishing even when there was nothing to catch or when the reeds had turned to glass with ice. In the summer, we spent hours floating on inner tubes, staring up at the humid sky of Lancaster County, daring it to open up with rain. I liked sharing those summer rain storms with Emma. Something about the rain soothed me, and I appreciated the unapologetic sadness of it. Emma taught me to take my shoes off and walk through the mud, then lie on the ground and let it absorb my grief.

"Don't you feel it dripping off your ankles?"

I rolled my head, feeling the mud in my ear.

"Like what?"

"I don't know. I suppose like candle wax."

"Are you making a joke?"

Emma shook her head, then cracked her lips and smiled. We both laughed. Lying there on the ground, we howled, mouths open, tongues sticking out to taste the rain.

"This is malarkey, isn't it?" I asked, getting up, feeling silly.

"No," she said. And she was serious.

Emma understood that my mourning would only last as long as I needed to process everything. She never tried to talk me out of the way I was feeling, and for this I grew indebted to her. I found ways to show my gratitude— bringing her flowers from Mamm's garden every so often, or a packet of seeds, though it was not always easy for her to deal with my moodiness.

I'm sure I tested her patience, given the fact that she was two years older and far more mature than me. I know I saw the frustration in her face when, even on a sunny day floating on the pond, I hadn't smiled once. It was as if my mind, and my heart, were working through a long thaw that none of us knew how long would take. The only thing Emma ever told me, which was not advice but a simple understanding of the way of things, "Time heals everything, Eli, if you let it," she said, then added. "If you want it."

TWO

IT DIDN'T SEEM RIGHT to celebrate Christmas without my sisters that year. We hadn't spoken of the holiday after the accident but I knew my mother was worried she would make too much food. I stood in the doorway of the kitchen the day she gave away half of her cake and cookie tins to neighbors and friends. She said she was cleaning the clutter from the cabinets, but she'd been cleaning the clutter since August. Aside from the bonnets she'd hung up in the hallway closet downstairs, there were few items left of my sisters. Day by day, she systematically removed any evidence that she had had five daughters. Even the house plants that my sisters had named had been gifted to a few older Amish who were in the hospital. When I asked her why she was giving away Gertrude, a hanging spider plant that outlived droughts and neglect in Katie and Ella's room, my mother contended that Gertrude needed a new home.

I remember stopping her in the hallway with Gertrude dangling from her forearm.

"Are you going to give me away, too?"

With that, Gertrude slid off my mother's arm and fell to the floor. She did not crash, but landed upright.

"Eli, why would you say such a thing?"

"You're getting rid of everything that reminds you of my sisters, aren't you?"

My mother crouched down and pulled me to her. I buried my head into her lavender sleeve that smelled of the same and my mother cradled the back of my head with her long slender fingers and held me until she stopped crying.

"I'm not ever going to give you away, Eli."

"Please don't stop making cookies," I pleaded.

My mother pushed herself away from me and wiped the tear that slid down her nose. She smiled, and I swear inside her dimple was a space large enough to pour batter.

"I'll keep baking for you. I promise."

I wiped my nose with the back of my sleeve.

"Do we have to have Christmas?" I asked.

My mother chewed her bottom lip, shifting her eyes from my face to the small square window cut into the hall wall. The first snow of December had started to fall.

"Yes, Eli. We will celebrate Christmas."

"Do we have to have it here?"

"Where else would you have it?"

"Bunker Hill," I said.

And so I counted the days until Christmas, not because I was excited to celebrate it, but because Mamm had given me permission to go to the cemetery, alone.

Although it is not a custom for the Amish to visit cemeteries, I had gone every week since the funeral. I would take a copy of the *Ausbund* and sing to my sisters, leaving half-eaten Whoopie pies as offerings. I never told anybody where I was going, but I think my mother knew. On the days I set off for Bunker Hill, she'd make extra Whoopie Pies and mark the pages of the *Ausbund* for the songs she had liked to sing most to my sisters, but wanted me to sing in her place. It was on these same mornings I'd catch her humming Marvin Gaye's "Let's Get it On." My mother never asked if she could come with me on those hikes to the cemetery, but I know she appreciated my effort at keeping my sisters' company. If anything, it gave her, and me, a feeling that they were somehow still with us.

When I arrived on Christmas, I realized somebody had already been there to visit my sisters. Boot marks in the snow led to my sisters' unadorned grave markers, on the lower left side of the cemetery where Amish children were buried. The Amish use flat stones for children, and upright stones for adults, which helped me to remember which ones were my sisters, although other children had been buried there, too. Just as I was about to kneel, I found, sticking out of the snow, a half-smoked cigarette and a plastic guitar pick that looked like a mini orange triangle reflector, like a warning that had fallen off the back of a buggy. Though I should have felt good that somebody else was keeping my sisters company, I felt sick. I remember dropping to my knees and pounding my fists into the snow, cursing the visitor for taking this last comfort away from me that year.

After six months of mourning, I needed something else to do, especially at night when the empty bedrooms in our house felt larger, the echoes more tinny and haunting. Though I knew that Ruth had always wanted the job, I asked Datt if I could be his apprentice. I knew full well that many of my nights would be tied up at the auction and that I would be expected to continue with my chores in a timely manner and do my school work without complaint. This I did not mind, and I had hoped my mother would hire somebody else to take my place at the candy stand on those occasions, leaving me free to join my father. He was happy to have my help, especially after Levi Esh had quit and become a cabinet maker. Levi told my father that he didn't like crowds, and my father believed him, sympathetic to his own quandary—being a private man in a public profession. I couldn't have been more relieved to follow him, shadowing his appraisals and studying his methods, which did not rely on the use of my hands.

Auctioneering, my father explained time after time, depended on a man's head. My father came from a long line of prominent auctioneers and he said all it took was a mind that could account for details beyond the fiscal. He always snapped when he said fiscal, then waved his arms over his head, emphasizing the importance of projecting an image of enthusiasm, which was his hallmark posture even when he was less than confident and in most cases, lost and sad after the accident. He had a clear, strong, booming voice too, one that people remembered and respected (the care of which consisted of the three cups of licorice tea he sipped prior to every calling). My first lesson was to pay attention to the amount of tea leaves and water he put into his thermos.

I got the proportions right the first time I tried, which didn't really matter when I accidentally left the thermos at home the night of the State Farm Show in Harrisburg. It would take me longer than most to advance in this business, but eventually I'd learn every aspect.

Eventually, my roles would include office manager, public relations manager, accountant, traffic coordinator and janitor. I could push a mop. I could poke numbers into a calculator, battery operated, of course. I could still make a good strong pot of licorice tea. None of these things depended on my hands being "normal" and my father took full advantage of proving to me that nothing was wrong with them. However, I'd often catch the nervous twitch in his eyes when it was my turn to hold a particular piece of merchandise, not because he feared I would drop it, but because the audience would turn its attention to my hands. The distraction would inevitably screw up the sale when folks who had never seen a boy with webbed hands would make some subtle gesture that my father would mistake as a bid. The disputes went like this, in English, above the hiss and screech of his bullhorn:

"I'm not paying thirty-six dollars for a rusted hoe."

"But you just made a bid, sir."

"I did not."

"You pointed."

"I flinched," the caller would blurt, breathless, then point again, "when I saw the hands on that boy!"

My father would take a deep breath and look over at me, chin quivering beneath the bush of his beard, fishing for the right lie, the softer lie that would prove this man was wrong. When nothing came, he'd chant again, resuming the auction. Between my father's often indecipherable yarn of words, I'd learn that most people had a fascination with the strange and grotesque, and I was never quite sure if his audience and business had not grown out of a curiosity people had with my hands.

It certainly stopped the nightly volley of money. I had never seen my mother so inflamed as the night she learned of these incidents of public humiliation, long after they had occurred. My father had told me not to mention them; he needed my help and I'd just have to learn to ignore, and forgive, the bidders who mocked me. But when my mother pressed me to understand why I had worn a hole in my pants, I reminded her that I still didn't have pockets to hide me. The night she learned of this we had been stuck in the house during a snowstorm. Mamm marched me downstairs to the kitchen and sat me in the chair across from my father, who sat forlorn in his roller chair. She cleared her throat and announced that she was taking all the money to the bank and opening an account in my name. Mamm said I could withdraw however much I needed when I started rumspringa. But it's not like I would ever buy a car. When I asked her what I would need that much money for at sixteen, she said, "The operation."

"For my hands?"

She nodded.

"I know of good doctors in Florida."

"What can they do?"

"Give you the separation you need."

And the way she said need made me flinch as if she'd stuffed inside the word an opportunity or a threat. I did not know which and did not have the courage to ask her.

My father, vexed, rocked back and forth on his roller chair, cigar smoke suspended in the light of the gas lamp over the table. My mother stood and marched to the sink, grabbing a sponge to scrub the counters for no particular reason other than to think. She spoke with her back to us, eyes fixed on the hazel tree in the garden, snow quilting the branches that had once provided the solace she needed then.

"You'll know what to do when you're 16," she said.

But I didn't. I only knew what I didn't want.

After the debacle at my father's auction, I decided to keep to myself, preferring the safety and comfort of dogs. I bred black labs with Rotweillers from the two pups I'd received as a condolence from an English neighbor, a widow herself, concerned about my loneliness. I was a good, kind breeder and kept the kennels clean, often netting $300 per month or more depending on the season.

Over the years, I met many Englishers, mostly divorcees, widowers and widows who needed companionship more than love, heartbroken young lovers, and love-struck children who craved the comfort of a cold nose and wagging tail. They would sit on a cage and tell me why they needed a dog, how some even believed that the purest people came back to this world in the form of a dog. And why not, they'd ask. What a better way to live your life, safe, fed and loved, don't you think? I would nod and remind them of their first shots, rarely extending myself beyond polite conversation. Never a handshake. I figured the less people knew about me, the less they'd ask and the less I'd have to tell.

I walked with my head down a lot and paid attention to the cracks in the road. The shame burned in my cheeks every time someone looked me in the eye and praised me for being "such a good boy" simply because I was quiet. Only God knew that my silence was a defense against all the consequences I had yet to face. I buried the secret deeper every year, refusing to give people a chance to love me so that I wouldn't have to disappoint them with the truth. Somewhere, somehow, I believed, a thief catcher would find me, too.

THREE

ON THE MORNING OF my eleventh birthday, I vowed to get rid of the camera. It would have been easy to take it to one of the pawn shops that my father frequented, and maybe even sell it for something more useful like a pair of work boots or a bolt of wool for a winter *wamus*, or coat, and later, when I found out how much it was worth, trade it for a fly reel.

Birthdays are celebrated among the Amish and we do receive small gifts, maybe a wooden toy when we are young or special cakes, candy, cookies or homemade ice cream. Usually the kids at school would sing happy birthday, but after the accident, I declined the song. It was too painful to hear because it reminded me of all the birthdays we had already missed since my sisters had died, and I didn't feel it was right to have anyone sing to me without singing to my sisters first. I avoided the quiet observation of my birthday and always hoped the day would quickly pass. I did not want a game, a ball, confections or consolations. There was nothing in the world, and I mean that literally, that anyone could give me that would make me happy on my birthday.

I would have to give that to myself.

I wanted to see my sisters.

The problem was not in parting with the camera, but with the images inside it. I would have been happy to give back the camera, and when I got older, I often thought about running an ad in the paper, making it look like I had only just found it at one of my father's auctions. But, like my birthday, every time I thought to ask a friend to write the ad (I couldn't type and the chance of deciphering my handwriting was as likely as identifying a horse by its horseshit), I knew they would ask questions about what I was doing with the camera in the first place. What I wanted was the courage to develop the film because the longer I waited, the more vulnerable to light those images would be. It terrified me that a thin piece of plastic and chemicals could be so sensitive, which is why, until my mother had set up the bank account and a safe deposit box in my name, I had stored the camera in the darkest space I knew in our house—between the kitchen ceiling and the floor beneath my bed.

I pried it open that September 6, took a deep breath and said to nobody in particular, but most likely to God, *I will see my sisters today.* I had a plan. I knew where to get film developed. I knew the rates of the drugstore developers and saved coupons when I saw they were having sales, just as Mamm did for cleaning supplies and toilet paper. What I didn't like about this option was that I'd have to deposit the roll into a big yellow envelope. I didn't trust that I'd ever see it again because most of the drugstore developers took a week. I didn't have that long. I worried they'd mix up my order and somebody else would see my sisters first. I imagined if they did, they'd be horrified and call the police, which would only make my shame and my family's story public again.

Over the years, small photo kiosks had popped up around the county in parking lots near banks and grocery stores. I had memorized every location and drawn a crude map in my notebook, noting traffic patterns, especially those near Amish farms. The point was to avoid being seen at any film developer by anyone I knew. This was not as easy as it would seem since the Amish can show up just about anywhere. There was a hitching post outside the K-Mart on Route 30, and who should walk out of the Red Lobster beside it with his entire family? Bishop Beiler. I remember trying to duck behind a huge white Cadillac in the parking lot, but Emma saw me and ran over, waving.

"Happy birthday, Eli!"

I stood up behind the trunk.

"Hey there, Emma."

She looked around, spotted our horse and buggy, then cocked her head, realizing that I'd driven myself to the shopping center. I was only eleven. I still had one more year until I could drive the buggy. "What are you doing here alone?"

I motioned toward the K-Mart. "Wanted to check out a new reel."

Emma's eyes narrowed. Her father called out to her.

"We're going shopping, too. Come with us."

"Sure," I said, seeing more Amish buggies pull up to the hitching posts. We don't live on reservations, but it would have been easier for me if we had—and if our two worlds had more physical boundaries than the lines drawn by our customs and beliefs.

The timing never seemed right for me to get the film developed. The second time I tried, I had woken up sick, with swollen glands and the beginning of strep throat. The third time, the floor boards in my bedroom had swollen in a rare October heat spell and I couldn't pry them up to get the camera. The fourth attempt failed when Emma and Mamm surprised me with two pairs of pants with pockets they'd sewn for my twelfth birthday. One was wool, for winter. The other was made of cotton. I didn't pay attention to which was which and put on the wool pants. I couldn't put them on fast enough. I was so overwhelmed by the gift that I scooted to Leroy Fisher's barber shop to show him. It was a hot day in September, right after Labor Day weekend, and the roads, for once, were free of tourists. Still, with the heat, it took me almost an hour to get to the barbershop. The Amish don't wear shorts and any pants would have been hot, but the wool just about melted me. I must have looked like I'd broken a fever when I knocked on the barbershop door. Leroy was with a customer and set down his scissors, rushing over to meet me. "What happened?" he asked, alarmed. Ever since Ruthanne had gone blind from diabetes, Leroy seemed a little on edge, always ready to put out a fire. But nothing was wrong with me. For the first time in a long time, it felt like things were looking up.

"Nobody can see them now," I said and grinned.

"See what?"

I dropped my chin, looked down at my pockets. "My hands."

Leroy scratched his neck.

"Guess that solves everything," he said.

"For a while," I said, feeling relieved, thinking about my father's auctions.

"Sure those pockets are big enough?"

"They are," I said. "Until I grow more."

He stared at me with a crooked smile, then pulled the door closed and whispered.

"Then I guess you can hide the camera in them, too?"

I stared at Leroy in shock. I had hoped he would be as elated as me about the gift I'd received, but Leroy obviously didn't see a reason to celebrate me hiding anything. I don't remember the scoot home to our farm, only the weight of the melancholy that had set in again, no thanks to Leroy. Though he knew I had taken the camera, I had never told him what I had done with it, which made me more anxious than ever to get rid of it.

I vowed never to visit Leroy at his barbershop after that, and stopped taking the loaves of bread Mamm baked for him and Ruthanne, now that she couldn't bake like she once did. Even on the rare occasions that he came to our house for dinner alone, I made a point to eat at Uncle Isaac's. Eventually, he stopped coming to visit us. Though I missed his company, and his jokes, I couldn't risk exposing myself. Leroy always looked like he knew something about me that I didn't, and that terrified me because I was certain I wouldn't like it.

No attempt to get the film developed was as memorable as the bungled attempt the next year, on my thirteenth birthday. Under normal circumstances, I would have walked to school, but my father asked if I wanted to ride with him in the buggy since he was going to my uncle's harness shop, where I had worked as a child oiling saddles. The men there loved to talk and I knew my father would stay longer than planned, which would give me time to drop off the camera at the English gift shop next door that developed film. The perfect plan. The one perfect chance. I hid the camera in my lunch box, but no sooner had we left our farm did Datt get pulled over by the cops, not because the officer wanted to arrest us; he wanted to hand back the orange triangle reflector he'd seen fall off the back of our buggy.

The officer spooked me and the horse when he poked his head into the buggy, recognizing my father. It seemed everyone knew us because of the auction or accident. From the way he spoke to Datt, I think he knew us from both.

"I'm surprised you don't have a hundred more."

My father took the plastic reflector and nodded, forcing a smile through the tangle of his silver beard.

"Thank you," he said in a quiet voice. "We'll be sure to tack it on tight next time."

"You be sure there is a next time, Mr. Yoder. People depend on you," the officer said looking straight at me. "Don't want to lose him, too. What you got in there, Eli?"

I swallowed. The horse whinnied. I clutched the handle of the small red and white Igloo cooler that we commonly used as lunch boxes, praying there would be no need for him to ask what was inside, or if I cared to share it. I was not prepared to surrender my sisters' souls to a man who wore a uniform. Dirk Willems might have had more courage, but at thirteen years old, I might have had more sense.

"Whoopie Pies," I said, averting my eyes from the man.

"For lunch?"

"It's Eli's birthday," my father said, his voice edgy, annoyed we had been detained, not because the harness shop would be busy or that I would be late for school, but because all the cars that passed us had slowed down to see what was wrong. They inched along the road, peering into the buggy. When one of the passengers stuck their arm out the window with a camera, my father began to twist the tip of his beard into a point with his thumb and index finger. If my father knew what was in my lunch box, I believe he might have ripped his beard right off.

The officer sniffed the air, as if his nose itself was powerful enough to detect what lay inside my lunch box. "Homemade?"

"Almost always," my father said and I could hear the gravel in his voice from everything he hadn't said.

"I love Whoopie Pies," the policeman said and clapped, then dug into his pants pocket and pulled out a cracked black leather billfold.

"Could I buy one from you?"

"Buy one?"

"Or two. I was just about due for a coffee break."

I shifted my eyes to my father who had stopped twisting his beard. His fingers, however, remained clinging to the tip. He was as stunned as me and the look in his eyes said, Does he see an auction block in here?

"They're not for sale," I said and gripped the handle tighter now, wrapping what I could of my hands through it. "My mom made just enough for everyone at school."

Knowing this was a lie, my father arched an eyebrow and I knew the lesson he wanted me to learn would not be in the distant future, but right there in the buggy.

"Your mother always makes extra, for the teacher, too. I think it would be kind of you to offer a pie to the officer since he's been kind enough to see to our safety."

I swallowed again. Nodded. And sunk deeper into the bench seat.

"I don't want to impose. Only if there's enough."

"There's plenty," my father said. "Just enough."

The officer smiled and lifted his eyes to the blue sky, the air sweet with the smell of fresh cut hay. In the distance, behind us, a team of field horses pulled a hay loader for our Amish neighbors and I cursed myself for having declined their invitation to join the work frolic. Every time the officer spoke, his words whirled and buzzed like a chain saw blade in motion.

"You're saving me a lot of time," he said. "I hope I don't make you late."

"You're saving us from accidents," my father said, and his smile flattened when he looked over at me, looking glum and forlorn and doing nothing to serve the officer.

"Eli? Go on. Give him a Whoopie Pie."

Never in my life did my hands shake as much as they did then. I could hardly work them out from under the handle without knocking the lunch box off my lap. I managed to hold it there and poke the small white button on the side of the lid, with my thumb, holding the handle with my other hand and sliding it to the left or right, in this case, to the left, to give the contents inside a little roof from the wandering eyes of my father and the officer.

"You need a hand with that?"

"No," I said, and managed to open it myself.

"You sure there's enough Whoopie Pies?"

I locked eyes with my father. "Think so. Should be."

I covered up the box with my left arm and cradled the rest with my right as if it were a puppy. I pretended to count the Whoopie Pies, bundled in clear plastic wrap, but arranged them instead to hide any parts of the camera. The lens poked through the center and I slid my arm over the middle then leaned over the whole cooler as I reached out and passed two small Whoopie Pies to the policeman.

"Here you go," I said.

"Happy birthday, Eli," he said, offering one dollar.

I nodded and forced a smile, feeling my heart pound, unaware that my bangs were flattened and sticking to my forehead. I kept my eyes on him, watching him strut back to his squad car, happy as can be, already peeling the plastic wrap and sinking his teeth into the dark chocolate cakes and the fluffy cream filling. When he got into his car and drove away, it occurred to me that his job, in addition to catching speeding cars, was to catch thieves. I could not bear the thought of running into him again and asked my father to drop me off at school immediately. I would wait three more years until I tried again.

FOUR

ON THE MORNING OF my sixteenth birthday, Uncle Isaac, a willowy gap-toothed and garrulous man, who lived on the thirty-acre wheat farm next to us, arranged for a hot air balloon ride, a privilege his own children had enjoyed when they had started *rumspringa*. It was as much of a gift as it was an announcement that I was of the age to gain a broader perspective on the Amish community and my relationship to it. The perfect gift, right?

According to my mother's youngest brother, there was no better way to usher in this rite of passage than with a ride in the sky that promised a new view of the people and the land I loved as much he did. The hot air balloon ride, Uncle Isaac contended, was a way "to lift people higher to God and hope they'd be better off and nicer as a result."

There were two problems. First, I was afraid of heights. I had avoided so many barn raisings in my youth that I'd developed the reputation as the only Amish boy who voluntarily worked as a dishwasher. I stayed in the kitchen where the women inevitably put my hands to use and where I suffered the run of rumors and idle talk.

I didn't like heights, not because I was afraid of falling; I was afraid of getting too close to God, and feeling compelled to confess my secret and return my sisters' souls. I wasn't ready for that, not then at least. When I rejected the gift, Uncle Isaac looked hurt.

"Eli, this is a chance of a lifetime! Only my own sons and the twins have been that high in the sky before."

I stared at him, arms crossed over my chest in his barn where I'd been asked to assist the delivery of a calf who shared my birthday. I squeezed out a bloody rag and Isaac picked the hay out of her small pink nose.

"What's the problem? Aren't you excited?"

"I know all about it. I feel like I've already been."

Ella and Katie had been the first girls to ride in Isaac's balloons when they were twelve, only because they begged Uncle Isaac. He didn't have any daughters and gave in. Katie and Ella flaunted their victory for a month, every night at dinner, by telling the rest of us in detail how small everything looked and how insignificant people were when you looked down on the earth. I was only four then but their descriptions made an impression on me and I imagined there must be a much bigger world than the one on our farm. But the more Isaac pushed me to see it, the less curious I was. I needed to figure things out for myself and I didn't like the way Isaac sometimes acted like he was my father. He was my uncle and I wanted him to be my friend, but every now and then I'd see the look in his eyes that suggested his concern for the direction my life was taking, as if he could see which road I would take before I even knew it existed. After the accident, he would sit with my mother in her garden and talk for hours about me, taking the place of my father whose voice was too hoarse after the auctions for discussing anything other than food.

"I'd rather stay on the ground," I said.

"How can you say that? You have to see it to believe it, Eli."

Maybe Isaac was right. The Amish were forbidden to ride in airplanes so a hot air balloon ride would be the closest experience. I would have to see it to believe how marvelous it was, to understand the value of a view, because until that day, I had only gone as high as Bunker Hill where my sisters were buried.

"Maybe," I said.

"Maybe? It'll change your life."

I said nothing and helped Isaac clean the stall around the poor heifer who lay panting and exhausted, relieved to see the bloody hay dumped into a wheelbarrow. She groaned and I paused to rub her neck. Her eyes went limp and her neck softened under my large hands, kneading out knots in the muscle. It had been a difficult birth and she had lost a lot of blood. I swatted the fly around her eyes.

"Is she going to die?" Isaac asked.

I lifted her eyelids and looked into that dark black pool, seeing my own reflection. "No," I said. "Not today."

I followed Isaac out of the barn where he dumped the wheelbarrow of bloody hay on top of the compost pile. I paused at the water pump to clean my hands. It was still dark out, the crickets loud before dawn with the air calm and the moon still hooked in the sky. Isaac turned to me with expectant eyes.

"Give it some thought, Eli."

I nodded, wishing to tell him I already had. I'd waited seven years to follow through with my plan and I didn't need a hot air balloon to change things.

When I got back from Uncle Isaac's, my mother beckoned me to the clothesline. She looked excited but it wasn't because her clothes had been hung just right. The line sagged with wet black pants and aprons, shirts and dresses that hung in order of color, light to dark, steam rising in puffs of pink clouds, the bright morning light silhouetting her face as she meticulously hung another shirt. My mother was as fastidious about the clothes we wore as she was about how they appeared on the line when they were hung to dry. This is not unique to Amish women. Although most would decline the association of pride with their wash, it was hard to find an Amish washline less than easy on the eye to anyone passing through Lancaster County. My mother's wash line was perhaps, besides her cooking, the only form of creative expression she had left since she'd abandoned her garden and quilts after the accident. As much as I had offered to help hang the wash over the years, no offer could lure my mother away from the control she had over the bold statements she could make with her laundry.

We were fine.

We had moved on.

We had forgiven.

But we hadn't moved on, not really. We'd moved away from anything that looked like our past, altering it by simply doing nothing to change it. I paused in the walkway, between the washline and the house, seeing in the flagstone squares the weeds my mother no longer bothered to remove, and the paint chips blown off our house in the wind. Even the panes in the windows had remained cracked. My parents had not bothered to fix them or repaint the trim that had peeled on them and the doors, making our farm the anomaly among the manicured gardens and whitewashed fences of our neighbors. Even tour buses and rental cars had eventually stopped coming past our place. The finest features of our farm, like my sisters' faces, had been smudged and blurred by time and memory. My parents had stopped making repairs since the accident, as if repairing anything was useless to them now, including the oak doors of my sisters' bedrooms that had swollen shut. The hinges had rusted and the knobs refused to turn. Even my mother's garden lay fallow and the hazel tree bare where our grief had grown old and wasted. My mother's washline was the only sign of hope; and it was the most appropriate place for her to give the gift she'd been waiting sixteen years to give to me. She turned, seeing my shadow in the sheet she had hung.

"I thought you'd be up in the balloon by now."

"Nah," I said. "You know me. I don't like heights."

"You said no?"

I nodded and stared at her, wanting desperately to explain, but she didn't give me a chance. Her mind had leapt a field ahead of me.

"Maybe it's just as well. I have a more useful gift," she said, her voice cheery, cheeks rosy, lips parted and curved into a smile broader than I'd seen in recent years. She moved to the far end of the clothesline and stepped behind a large white sheet, unpinning the coat hanging on the other side. At first, I thought it was my father's black sack work coat, but when she stepped out from behind the sheet, I realized she was holding a long overcoat with a split tail—a *Mutze*.

"We've been waiting forever to give this to you."

Her smile only grew larger when she walked over to me and pressed it against my back and shoulders.

"You're about a half-inch broader than granddatt, but once I let out the seams, this should fit just fine," she said stepping in front of me with arms outstretched, happy to pass on the coat her father had worn for fifty years.

I stared at the coat but did not take it, trying to make sense of my mother's gesture. I was not sure if I should thank her. That the *Mutze* was given to all Amish boys when they turned sixteen meant it could be a gift, but we were not permitted to wear it until after our baptisms. I couldn't understand the point in calling something a "present" when I'd have to wait to use it.

I would have decided it was not a gift had my father not just stepped out of the house and crossed the yard to meet us with a brown box, his pace hurried, as if he'd been timing his entrance and had been dismayed by its delay. He rocked on the balls of his feet when he handed the box to me. He seemed pleased to see my mother in good spirits, too, and it was the first time in a long time I saw their eyes connect for something other than a moment of shared grief. I stepped back, hoping not to snuff out the small expectant spark of joy I felt between them, because that would have made a far better gift.

My father handed me the box.

"Open it."

"Here?"

My father nodded. His palsied right hand shook the large brown box, the label of which identified that it once held ten pounds of black licorice wheels.

When I pulled back the flaps and looked inside, it was no camera at all, but a funny black felt hat with narrow flat sides, versus wide and round like most Amish men wore. I lifted my eyes, confused, wondering if maybe my parents were playing a joke on me because everyone knew narrow hats were the sign of a rebel. The more conservative the Amish, the wider the brim and the higher the crown. Even I hadn't dared trim my hat. Our dress code is as much a part of our protest against materialism as it is a symbol of solidarity among each other and our separation from the world. Over the years, I needed the protection of the three inch brim from the curious eyes of the English, and I had come to rely on the small shadow it cast on my face. There were many plans I had for my sixteenth birthday, but trading my hat for one with a smaller brim was not one.

My father pulled back the flaps and took out the oddly shaped black hat, exchanging it with the one on my head. He adjusted the brim, so that the corners came to a point in the middle of my head. Mamm folded her hands in prayer.

"A spitting image of Aaron!" she cried.

"It's close, huh?" my father said, pleased.

I sighed. Their comparisons to my grandfather did not bode well for my birthday, or the hope that any of this had been meant as a gift—more as a promise of who I would become that day. Not granddatt, specifically, but somebody just like him—a respected Amish man. The funny shaped hat and the limp heavy coat belonged to granddatt who, after being jailed for protesting mandatory high school education for his children, walked into and then out of the Lancaster County prison wearing them in 1956. The unique shaped hat had been the focus of every photographer that day, and oddly, our community, who took it as a symbol for all the ways we could acquire an education without having to be high-minded about it.

Upon granddatt's release, and later, we learned, at the daring of a bailiff, he cut the hat to look like a mortar board. When he burst through the prison doors, he said to the first reporter, "See? There are many ways to graduate."

My grandfather's peaceful protest coupled with the company of about fifty other Amish fathers preserved a tradition that has gone unchallenged ever since. What hadn't changed, however, was the style of our hats and the bishops took exception only to granddatt's until he died.

My parents did not intend for me to wear the hat on this auspicious birthday, only to embrace what it meant.

"Okay. Okay. Take it off," my mother said again, just as quickly shifting tones, eyes wandering the periphery of our property, searching for uninvited guests like a cousin. "No need to wear it for too long now."

She brushed off the top, picking off lint.

"Until Sunday."

"What about Sunday?"

"You'll be wearing both."

I shifted my eyes to the steam rising from the heavy wet wool of the *Mutze* and wondered if this was a test. I stared at her, curious. She could barely contain her smile or the excitement brimming inside her. Was she okay?

"Your first song group."

"Oh," I said, suddenly disappointed. "That."

"Aren't you excited to meet the girls there?"

"Girls? Yeah. Maybe. But I don't think I'm ready," I said, forcing my voice to crack. "See? Nobody wants to hear me sing."

"Emma Beiler does. She asked me to ask you."

I lifted my eyes to meet hers.

"I told her you'd be there," my mother said, lips spread in a mile-long smile. "It's her birthday. Remember?"

I nodded, feeling the dread. I would've been glad to celebrate Emma's eighteenth birthday, but Sunday night was the only night I was sure not to see any Amish adult at a public place like a photo lab, where I had planned to spend the night in the parking lot, sleeping in our buggy if I had to, while the technician brought my sisters back to life.

I sat on the edge of my bed, staring at the *Mutze* hanging from the hooks behind the door, feeling forlorn and anxious. What terrified me was that by encouraging me to accept Emma's invitation, my parents had given their consent to participate in the thousand-year-old ritual of "tarrying" or *Bett Schlupa*, otherwise known as bundling, the long awaited privilege of bed courtship (contested by some Amish and denied by others to even exist) that coincided with *rumspringa*. It surprised me that our bishop thought of bundling as "the smartest thing the devil created since the snake in the garden."

If I was old enough to make a decision about joining the church, my parents figured I was old enough to make a decision about the woman I was going to marry. My parents trusted that we'd only talk and touch lightly, then fall asleep. To keep us from acting on the excitement of our hormones, they encouraged us to use the bags, bolsters or bed board which I knew had been removed from many beds. By my pillow, they had left a yellow flashlight and a small transistor radio with extra batteries for both. I'd seen the flashlight and used it many times in my life, but I had never seen the radio in our house and wondered if my father had acquired it in an auction. I turned it on only to discover that someone had tuned it to a country station, and the sulky, squeaky, lovesick voices did nothing to quell or stifle my own. I groaned and turned it off.

Most every guy I knew would have been elated. Emma, the bishop's only daughter, was the talk of many guys who had set their sights on the girl with doe-shaped eyes the color of moss, and whose smell, they rumored, had been distilled from honey-suckle. I never noticed. I had known Emma most of my life and I would have said she smelled like sweat and cotton, but I liked the smell of honey-suckle. I even liked her father. He was personable and reasonable and didn't make me feel bad if I'd mixed up a Bible verse or didn't fully understand it, but the last thing I wanted to do was to bundle myself with his daughter, right under his own nose in his own house, even if he expected this and had done so as a youth with his own wife, perhaps, or who knows how many others before he was married. It was just the way it was—no gender differential. Bundling was as traditional as saying "bless you" when somebody sneezed. Although few Amish spoke of it, every adult had observed it. A preacher who spoke out against bundling was silenced for five years. Bundle didn't mean sex. It meant snuggle, cuddle, touch.

It's easy to understand why I was nervous. We had never even held hands.

We met in the barn behind the bishop's house and drank root beer and orange drink until our stomachs ached. I sat with a few guys my age and older, all single and in *rumspringa*, while the girls, wearing new dresses, mostly dark blue and green and very plain, sat facing us from a bench made of hay bales. We had played a game of volleyball earlier, tying the net between two unhitched buggies in the grass. Emma and I had been on opposite teams, and although she was fairly tall and quick, she hadn't moved fast enough to miss the ball I'd spiked. She sat on a hay bale with a swollen lip and a bag of ice that dripped on her new dress.

I had wanted to get up that moment to help, but before I could stand every guy in the barn leapt to their feet to bring her a fresh bag of ice. And that broke up the party. All the other girls who had been patiently waiting, having picked out the boy they liked earlier that evening, hoping he'd respond somehow, got up and stormed out of the barn then hiked up their dresses and hitched up their buggies in silence. They had every reason to be upset. They'd been outnumbered five to one. Although this seemed like a good thing when they arrived at the beginning of the evening, they suffered the worst kind of rejection, realizing the ratio was thirty-three to one. One being Emma. Emma with the fat lip and melting ice and swarm of male attendants.

This was no fault of Emma's. She got up to meet the girls at the door, pleading with them to stay and sing some more, but they made excuses to get home, eyes spitting glances at the boys who shamelessly waited with bags of ice, hoping to heal Emma and win her heart. If I'd been a girl, I would have left, too. But I was a boy. And Emma had invited me to stay even before they had left. She had no plans for the boys with bags of ice, especially the ones who wore English clothes and called themselves Leacocks, one of many buddy bunches, or gangs, that formed during *rumspringa*. Looking around the barn, I'd say there was at least one guy from every gang we knew including the Pinecones, Drifters, Shotguns, Snowballs and Canaries. She was obviously not impressed with them. At one point, she'd stepped away from the volleyball game to get a glass of lemonade and with the same fresh tartness said to the pursuing Leacock, who had arrived just then in his black Oldsmobile, "If you came to impress me, deflate those tires and walk next time." Emma hated cars as much as me, but what she hated more was the cockiness the Leacocks were known to flaunt because they drove them.

Weary of their advances, she excused herself for the evening, feigning a yawn, and walked across the lawn to her house. She closed the door behind her but did not say goodnight. The night was not over for her yet.

In fact, it had only just begun. Waiting in her bedroom, perhaps draped across her bed and bearing the shadow of an oil lamp that burned on her night stand, was the fated *nacht ruck* she'd probably made herself. The *nacht ruck* that every one of those guys who had come to her party would have fetched a few tons of ice to see.

Everyone wondered who the lucky one among us would be. It was known that unmarried couples rarely kept company in the daylight, when others might catch them together. Usually boyfriend-girlfriend relationships were private affairs, although a few quilting bees and work frolics offered a chance to speculate on these secrets.

We followed Emma outside, moving toward our hats that hung outside the barn on the fencepost, leaning against it, trying to act cool and calm in the moonlight. Reading the posture of every guy there, excluding myself, you'd think they all had been invited to bundle. Nobody was too quick to hitch their horses to their buggies and nobody was too bold to linger either. We grunted our own good-byes and took off down the same road until it split. I was tempted to keep going, to tell Emma I had a stomach ache, and I would have if I hadn't spiked the ball into her lip. I owed her an apology. I was not feeling good about my performance on the volleyball court, embarrassed by the control I had lost with my hands, and I hoped that Emma would reconsider her invitation to bundle.

I had been to the bishop's house many times and I knew my way around, but not in the dark. It was an old stone farmhouse with two sets of stairs and two front doors, one was better for going and one better for coming. I decided to use the back door by the kitchen and climbed the narrow flight of stairs. I looked down the long, dark hallway, smelling kerosene. I heard a match being struck inside Emma's room, whose door had been left slightly ajar. I held my breath and froze, hoping Bishop Beiler and his sons had drifted into a deep sleep because I knew they were not meant to see what I did.

Stretched across the wall in the hallway was Emma's shadow and I stepped inside it and pressed myself against the details—prayer cap lifting, fingers working their way through twisted braids and a bun, loosening a mass of thick dark hair that fell around her bare shoulders. I had never seen the shoulders of any girl, not even my sisters, and just the sight of their shadow had left me breathless.

Emma had blossomed over the years from a shy, gap-toothed skinny girl into a slender young woman whose skin held the luster of the moon. Overnight, it seemed, she had become a woman, and I had no vase big enough to contain this kind of blossom.

Emma lifted off her blouse and unpinned her skirt, letting each fall to the floor. Just as carefully she unlatched the bra I did not know she was wearing and draped it over the back of a chair. Then she stood and turned, her small round breasts in silhouette, hair tumbling down her back, following the curve in her waist.

I gasped and covered my mouth with my sleeve. My heart raced. I couldn't tell where I was, or why I was there, only the certainty of overwhelming ambiguity. As much as I felt horrible for knocking her lip with the volleyball, I felt shamefully excited by the invitation of Emma's shadow where it was safe to reach out and touch her with my hands.

I knelt in that darkened hallway on one knee and traced her body starting with her feet. I dragged my hands past her thin ankles, the mound of her calves, past her knees and solid thighs, then higher over her hips, into the valley of her waist, up over her stomach and breasts, the small hills of her shoulders and the slope of her neck, then slowly, and gently, my hands found her hair. Just as I leaned in to smell her shadow, she poked her hand out the door and with one long slender finger, beckoned me to enter her bedroom.

"You don't have to sit on the floor," she said.

I could not move. I could not breathe. I swallowed, feeling the stiffness in my body. *Eich bisht so dobbich*, I thought, desperate to be saved from my awkwardness. I got up and stepped toward her but paused at the threshold. I had trouble catching my breath the longer I stared at Emma in her *nacht ruck*. I'd never seen anything like it, a long sleeveless mass of light pink chiffon that hugged her hips and breasts. When I hadn't said one word, Emma wrapped her arms around her waist and stared at me confounded.

"Don't you like it?"

"No," I blurted.

Emma's mouth dropped open. She looked crushed.

"You don't?"

"No," I said, wanting to tell her No. It's one of the most beautiful sights I've ever seen! but I couldn't get past the first no without her beauty arresting me again.

I tried again. "It's beautiful, Emma," I said, then despite the heat scorching my neck and cheeks whispered, "You're beautiful."

"Oh," Emma said and ran her hands through her hair. Blood flushed her cheeks. "Would you like a soda?"

"Uh-huh," I said, feeling stupid again for how unlike me I sounded. I hadn't opened my jacket and my hat was cock-eyed from what I could see in the reflection from the window above the sofa. Emma crossed to a small table and took the root beer, then walked back to me and pulled the tab with her own fingers, like she'd done for years at the market when she brought me lunch. It was easier for her to open it and I had never objected to her help, but suddenly, I resented it and wanted to open it myself. Sensing this, she stared at me before she let go of the can.

"It's alright," she said.

I nodded, even though it wasn't. Whatever boy I had been before, whatever boy she had known me to be, I did not want to be then, but the man I had hoped to be had not yet arrived and there was no telling when he would. I took off the *mutze* and hung it on the small wooden pegs on the wall, beside her prayer cap, then hung my hat beside her bonnet and pretended, for a moment, that we lived together so that the distance I felt between us would disappear.

Emma moved to the couch by the window and lowered the green paper shade.

"You want to sit down?"

We sat. She on the right side and me on the left, with a gap large enough to fit both of us again. I sipped the root beer quickly, nearly guzzling it all. Emma watched. I paused, burped and offered the can. She took it. I smiled and cast my eyes on the rug at our feet. I couldn't think of anything to say. Every time I looked at her in her pink dress my mind went blank and I wondered if this happened a lot. I'd never had a reason to ask the other guys in *rumspringa* what really happened when they'd seen a girl in her *nacht ruck*. I couldn't imagine anybody holding on to much of a thought, yet I was still frustrated to speak nonsense. "Maybe you could brush your hair."

Emma moved her head so fast I thought she'd snapped her neck.

"What's wrong with my hair?"

"I've never seen it like that till tonight."

Emma scratched her neck. I could see the muscles in her shoulders and back tense up. She was used to boys and didn't get nervous around them with seven brothers, but she sure looked nervous. I would've preferred the opposite—a sleepy, sedated Emma who had drifted off to her dreams before I'd had a chance to see her in that dress. I cursed the frost and the cold and everything that had led me to this moment, and although I would never curse my mother, I cursed the promise she had made Emma on my behalf.

Emma got up from the couch to get the brush from her dresser.

"How's your lip feel?" I asked.

"It's getting better."

"Still looks a little swollen."

Emma picked up the brush and turned to me.

"No thanks to you, slugger," she said and laughed. I laughed, too, and we shushed each other, hoping not to wake anybody in her family. It felt good to laugh and I think I breathed for the first time since I'd stepped into her room. She walked back to the couch with the brush and sat closer this time, facing me.

"Why don't you do it?"

She handed me the brush. I wiped my nose. The can of root beer had sweated and left drops of condensation, but I felt the beads above my lip, and knew I was sweating. We didn't talk for a while longer than the first silence.

Finally, Emma said, "I'll show you." She took the brush and ran it through her hair. She lifted the long, wavy brown tress that hung loosely over her right shoulder and shone in the lamp light. She pulled the brush gently through it, smoothing the hair shaft with her own natural oils. Her hair was healthy, thick and wavy, and although she had cut it shoulder length, she would never cut it again once she kneeled for baptism. It was a beautiful burden to bear, I thought. She picked up the tresses dangling over her left shoulder and brushed them as if the glory within each strand was meant to shine.

I couldn't remember the last time I had seen a girl brush her hair like that, or the last time I had seen any girl's hair. The only time an Amish boy saw a woman's hair was after his mother or sisters had bathed. I had not seen a girl's hair loose like this in years and the sight of it excited me as much as it made me sad. It made me think of the braids my mother had cut from my sisters and the glory she had stolen as a result.

Emma paused and handed me the brush.

"It's your turn now."

I nodded feeling the root beer churning in my stomach. Emma turned her back, waiting for me to brush her hair and I tried, slowly, to please her. I picked up a clump of hair the same thickness that she brushed over her shoulder and did as she asked of me, careful to untangle the knots that had formed at the ends. I brushed with simple, long strokes, but was frustrated that the brush could feel more of it than I could. I wanted to run my fingers through it, but couldn't. When I finished I lay the brush on the couch.

"Let's play cards," I said, feeling my voice quiver. "I have Rook."

Emma's eyes got wide. She sighed.

"I don't want to play cards. I just want you to hold my hand."

I'm not sure how I looked but I could tell it wasn't good when Emma thrust her hand on top of my hand. I yanked it away and held it behind my back. Before Emma could move, I shot off the couch and crossed to the doorway, then took my hat and coat, feeling the tremor work its way through my entire body. It struck me, as I hurried down the dark hallway, that the cost of seeing beauty was facing what was ugly first.

I did not sleep that night. I hitched up the horse and rode home to walk the perimeter of our farm, the stalks high and dry, whipping in the wind. I followed the long white fence line over the toboggan hill, then ran down the slope to sit by the edge of the pond, dry and cracked from the heat of the summer. I pulled my knees to my chest and buried my face, feeling awkward even in the moonlight.

If I could have asked God for one favor that night, it would have been to stay fifteen forever. Only three days past my sixteenth birthday and my life in *rumspringa* had grown complex. I didn't need to go to bars and drive cars; I needed to change if I wanted any hope of fitting into the unchanging world that had already shaped me. This change did not involve new clothes or a new car or a new job or even a new religion. It involved new hands. Besides seeing my sisters again, there was nothing I wanted more.

FIVE

THE NEXT DAY I stood in line with a suitcase at Farmers First Bank feeling the long, hard gaze of the English who wondered what I was doing there. It's not our clothes that make people stare, it's the fact that we have money. The Amish forbid conspicuous consumption and we do not encourage excessive wealth, but we are frugal and we do save—some of us even invest in mutual funds. We don't hoard and we share what we have, but I can't tell you that I had any intention of sharing anything that day.

"Nice way to treat a girl, Yoder."

I turned, startled to see Emma Beiler's three oldest brothers. One carried a large black bank bag and the other filled out a deposit slip. They were part of a construction crew and on their way to work, hands already brown with wood stains. Usually, seeing other Amish people at the bank is a relief, but I felt no camaraderie with Emma's brothers. They were in their early twenties. All baptized. Ready to marry and be men.

I swallowed and nodded, fighting for air, for words, even one. "Hi," I managed to blurt, but my voice sounded scratchy and high-pitched and not at all like my own.

"You headed on a trip?" they asked, eyes pinned on the suitcase.

"Florida," I said, trying to sound less than scared. "Pinecraft actually."

"Quick get away?" the oldest brother asked.

"Quick enough," I said, adjusting my hat, pulling it lower to soak up the sweat on my forehead. It must have been a hundred degrees inside the bank.

"Good timing," the middle brother, Jacob, said. He moved toward me and laid his hand on my shoulder. "You ever pull a stunt like that again in our house and you'll think a gelding got lucky."

"What stunt?" I asked, stiffening, feeling Jacob's fingers wrap themselves around the ball of my shoulder. All the brothers towered over me.

"You may have turned sixteen, but you've got a lot to learn about becoming a man," he said. "You don't just leave a girl crying."

I stared at him, confused.

"Emma was crying?"

Joshua, the younger one, laughed.

"Sobbed so loud after you left she woke the whole house up."

I stepped back, feeling everyone, not just the Beilers, staring.

Jacob lowered his voice. "You know she really likes you."

"I like her, too," I said.

Joshua turned to Jacob, who looked at Aaron. Jacob, being the oldest, leaned in to whisper in my ear while Aaron grabbed my shoulder.

"Then don't ever leave her alone like that again. Got it?"

Aaron let go of my shoulder. He'd dug his fingers so deep into my flesh but I didn't feel anything. Just the burning in my face.

"Next in line. Hello? I can help you over here."

The voice arched over the din of chatter and the stutter of a broken ceiling fan. Jacob pushed me forward. I picked up the suitcase and moved toward the teller, my thick soles stumbling over the carpet. If it had been only money I'd come to withdraw, I wouldn't have minded that Emma's brothers were watching, but I'd have rather swallowed my fist than reveal the true source of my shame.

By the time I exited the bank, a black Dodge truck had pulled up beside my buggy. The drivers, Levi and Amos Esh, stood outside the Beiler's buggy. The Beilers didn't look at all interested in their request, and directed it at me.

"Eli can bring you home," they said with disgust, then waved and pulled out of the parking lot. "He belongs with you guys anyway."

Great, I thought. This was not good.

I nodded and forced a smile, then hid the camera behind my back, between the suitcase and my leg when the Esh brothers crossed the parking lot toward me. There were few indications that Levi and Amos were Amish. They wore bright t-shirts and baseball caps. I hadn't seen them in years. At 26 and 29 years old, they had to be the oldest guys in *rumspringa* ever. One look at their shingled hair, and I assumed they didn't have plans to kneel for baptism anytime soon. They were not the kind of guys most parents would want their sons and daughters to befriend. Rumor had it they'd thrown a few *rumspringa* parties in their barn, and once, made a music video with lewd portrayals of

Amish girls from Indiana looking like they'd posed for the cover of a dime-store romance novel.

"What's the problem?" I asked.

"The truck overheated. We need a lift."

"Oh," I said, seeing the black hood opened like the beak of a crow, smoke rising from the engine block.

"Thanks, Eli," Levi said and smiled. "You saved the day."

"I didn't save anything yet," I said, feeling the sun radiating off the macadam, soaking into my black pants. I needed shade. I needed to breathe. And more than the fear I felt from Emma's brothers, I feared the questions the Eshes might ask me along the way.

The road to the Esh brothers is a sinuous one, with dips and curves and twists crossed by the shadows of fence posts. There's no shoulder, which makes it a tough road for cars to pass on, which is what I wanted the white cargo van that had followed us out of the parking lot of the bank to do. I signaled to the driver, but the van continued to tailgate us, spooking the horse so much that it jerked the buggy off the road. We cleared a fallen tree, only to have the rear spoke get stuck in the stub of a trunk. Levi flew out the door with the camera. Amos, who had fallen asleep in the back, awoke with a howl, and the horse, who had been so spooked it broke the traces on the wagon and ran free into a meadow down the road, contented itself immediately chewing grass.

I looked in the side view mirror, wondering who was in such a hurry. White vans were common on back country roads and I thought perhaps it was a plumber, a milk truck, bread truck or even a florist. Three men stepped out of the van and approached the buggy slowly, speaking in whispers. When they were close enough in the mirror, I realized they were wearing nylon stockings over their faces. I had never seen this and I wondered if a new state law required bakers not only to wear hair nets, but face nets, too. I popped my head out the buggy to ask if they needed help but just as quickly whipped myself back inside when I saw a gun in the driver's hand. My heart pounded and I lowered my voice, speaking in Pennsylvania Dutch. "Sit on the money." Of course, Amos, who had a penchant for asking the wrong question at the wrong time, said in plain English, and loudly, "Why are you whispering?"

I shifted my eyes to the side view mirror, seeing the men standing behind our buggy now, the driver's hands behind his back, the gun no longer in sight but all the more menacing. Amos nudged me on the shoulder.

"Shove over. I got to pee."

Levi hadn't said a word. He had already seen the gun from his place on the ground and had lowered his head, in prayer or consternation, I'll never know. I had never seen Levi Esh's eyes. He wore sunglasses before sunglasses were fashionable and before his true fears were made clear.

Amos nudged me to get out, but it wasn't he who spoke.

"Don't move."

That's when we turned to my side where the driver stood, then looked over at Levi's side where the other two men stood hovering over him. A bee had flown into the buggy and Amos, who was deathly allergic to bees, screamed. The driver took out his gun and shoved it inside the buggy. He whacked the barrel against my cheek, then smacked my eye and aimed the gun at Amos. The men took turns speaking, each with a southern twang that reminded me at first of the bishop, but with more burn between the words, as if within each syllable was the cigarette they had just smoked.

"Scream again and you'll never hear yer voice."

"Now you boys listen and you won't git hurt."

"Y'all be the good Christians you are and move."

I closed my eyes feeling them swell, hearing the rush of wind through the buggy, the rustling of corn husks, and the caw of ravens that sat perched on the telephone wire suspended above us. My head throbbed and the pounding was so loud that I feared the men would tell me to make it stop. I would have covered the gash with my shirt sleeve but I was too afraid to move. Blood didn't bother me much. I'd seen plenty of it birthing puppies, but the dripping of my own blood on my hands made me dizzy and nauseous.

In any other instance, I would have considered this another day in Paradise. We had just passed the town hall where Amos had asked me to stop so that he could pee but Levi told me not to stop, to let Sweet-Tooth Amos learn a lesson about drinking too much root beer in the morning. But now, with the gun at my head and the suitcase in the back seat, this was nowhere near Paradise. We had read about muggings and homicides, but violent crimes rarely happened to the Amish, at least not in Lancaster County.

"I said git out!"

One of the men kicked the steel wheel so hard he stubbed his toe.

"When ya'll gonna use some goddamn tires? Ever hear of rubber?"

The driver looked over at the man who just spoke.

"Shut up. Just get the suitcase."

"Okay, boys. Time to step outside."

We did as we were told. *Fagelshtahra und eigevva.* This was a time of surprise and surrender. The horse looked over at me but didn't so much as whinny, content to chew wood while the three men with the nylon caps instructed us to face the field and remove our clothes, including shoes and socks, fold them as neat as our mothers had taught us, then place them behind us and get on our knees.

"You gonna kill us?" Amos asked.

"Not unless you give us a reason to," the driver said.

I unbuttoned my shirt and wiped my forehead with the sleeve, stained now, and stiff with salt. I did not want to take off my pants. They were still wet, but the man with the gun waved it around in the air and nudged my back.

"Off with them."

I looked over at Levi, bare-chested and bare foot, when he unbuttoned his pants. "Just given them what they want, Eli."

"Ya'll don't use no zippers?"

Amos looked over at the men. "We don't recommend them."

"Why's that?"

Amos looked over at me and winked.

"God made us big," he said, speaking for himself.

"What?"

"We've been known to get stuck in zippers."

Levi laughed and I closed my eyes, cursing both of them for trying to make light of all of this.

"Take a look at this."

One of the men fished the camera from Amos's pants.

"A Leica M3!"

"Looks like an antique."

"It is. And it's worth a fortune these days."

I swallowed, feeling suddenly woozy again.

"Built in '62 by the Germans. They don't make cameras like this no more. Best mechanical thirty-five ever made."

"What's that?" the driver asked, staring at me, trying to read my lips. Forgive the sinner and not the sin, I said over and over, hoping that if God knew I'd already forgiven these men, he'd show some mercy and spare the camera.

"You can have the horse," I said.

"What?"

"The horse for the camera. Look! She's got snap."

I walked over to the horse in my underwear and tried to grab the reins but she kicked and nipped all nasty. She wasn't done chewing that fence post and took off across the field, pounding the dry September earth, dust rising beneath her hoofs until she was gone for good. The men stood watching me, mouths agape, and as incredulous as the Eshes.

"Ya'll not supposed to use cameras, right?"

I nodded, feeling the road split and pull me into the darkest center of the world.

"See, then? It's a win-win. You get your life. We get the camera. You boys kneel on that there shoulder and face the field and count to one hundred, first in English, then in that funny tongue ya'll slipped between your sentences. Then you're free to get home however you choose. We're sure sorry for the inconvenience, but ya'll helped out some Christians in need and we're sure the Lord'll repay you."

The driver waved his gun around as if it were a bullhorn, directing his partners to collect our clothes. When they picked up my pants, they stopped, feeling the damp cotton, then they smelled it and looked over at us. "Who pissed their pants?"

Levi and Amos turned to me. I turned red.

"Did you piss your pants?" Levi asked, astonished.

"You pissed your pants?" Amos asked, too. "Goddamn. Guess I would, too, if I'd been stealing souls. What are you doing with a camera anyway?"

I squeezed my eyes shut, feeling the tears sting. I was scared. They were scared. But I was the one whose fear, it seemed, had flooded him. The driver cleared his throat, and for a moment, I was grateful for his empathy.

"Good thing he did," he said.

"Steal a soul?" Amos asked, mocking me.

"Pissed his pants. Done us a favor. Police dogs love a strong scent to follow."

He pulled the money from the buggy then swaggered back to the van as if he'd stopped to buy a cantaloupe. The two men followed him and climbed into the van.

"Go on. Start counting. We want to hear you."

We knelt on the side of the road, stark naked, under a blue sky with a hot breeze that rattled the corn husks in the fields. The gravel dug into our shins but we didn't dare stop counting to complain. It takes a long time to count out loud to one hundred in any language. We were scared and stuttered; and it's likely we counted to three hundred until we assumed it was safe to get up and go home.

Aside from the buggy, we had nothing to hide behind other than what those men had left us, our black brimmed hats and their shadows. We walked side by side, with our heads down, in silence, with Levi on my left and Amos on my right and me dripping blood between us. I was caught again in their argument over the best route to take. They ignored my pleas to walk away from town, and insisted instead that we turn back to the bank where they could use the pay phone to call one of the English drivers.

"Who are you going to call?"

"Leroy Fischer."

"What? Why? You can't do that!"

"Why not?"

"He doesn't drive anymore," I gasped. "He lost his license." The thought of seeing Leroy like this was unbearable so I lied, and did a good job of it.

Amos laughed and pointed to Levi.

"So did he."

I turned to Levi.

"You don't have a license?"

"Never did," Amos said. "Old Levi's full of secrets."

That's when Levi reached over and grabbed Amos's hat right off his private parts and tossed it like a Frisbee. We had to wait until they finished wrestling each other on the side of the road, oblivious to the semi-trailer that whizzed by us, stirring up dust and scattering empty soda cans. We stopped traffic only when we crossed Route 340.

Judging from the hooting and hollering and horns honking, we were the best show in town next to the Ringling Brothers Circus. It happened so fast that none of us could have ever predicted the cost of our exposure.

Tour buses skidded to a stop with open doors and passengers surrounded us within seconds, snapping pictures at dizzying speeds which only provoked Levi and Amos to keep one hand on their hats, for obvious reasons, and the other hand in the air extending a stiff middle finger.

I, too, was outraged and shoved my hand in the air only to realize the futile attempt I made to mimic them. My hands wouldn't separate, and this, beyond our nakedness, only encouraged the tourists to take more pictures of us standing with our hats over our balls and our shadows nowhere long enough to hide us at noon.

"Eli?"

I turned, tuning in to that voice distilled by honeysuckle and felt every-thing, inside and out, shrink. Emma pulled up beside us in her buggy, forcing the tourists to step out of the way when her horse dropped a significant road apple, the smell of which worked wonders to send the New Yorkers back into their buses where they managed to pry open the windows and snap more photos that would make us the talk of their friends for years.

"Eli, get in. You boys, too. Come now."

I stood stiff, feeling my entire body turn red. At first, I pretended that I didn't hear her and continued to walk through the crowd, not sure where to go, only that I didn't want Emma Beiler to see me in the buff any more than I had seen her shadow. I wanted to hide and I was searching that crowd for anything that could cover me, willing to untie the windbreaker from the waist of a tourist. I opted for the kiosk instead and walked to the steps of a small bookstore and took out a local map of tourist attractions, shook it open and wrapped it around my backside like a skirt, Dutch Wonderland spread across one cheek and a Shoofly Pie advertisement across the other. It was the best I could do, given the circumstances, but I was only making a spectacle of myself.

"Eli, you're bleeding!"

Emma followed me in the buggy. Levi and Amos, who had already climbed inside, stuck their hands out the door and swooped up my hat just as I was securing the map.

"Hey, gimme that!"

"Get in, Eli."

"No. I can walk home."

"Why? Don't be silly, Eli. You need to see a doctor."

I strained to lift my right eye, the good eye, to meet hers. A tear escaped her and she bit her lip then her eyes got all wide like she'd seen the funniest thing in her life, or the saddest. But she didn't laugh at me, not yet.

"The cops will be by any minute. Get in!"

I just stood there, deaf and dumb and dripping blood. She was right. I needed to see a doctor. But the only doctor I intended to see did not treat eyes.

"You need some water at least."

It was too hot to think straight so I said nothing.

Emma took a deep breath and sighed.

"Suit yourself," she said and snapped the reins.

"Suit yourself!" Amos repeated, howling at the double meaning.

Of all the people, God had sent Emma Beiler to help me, but being rescued by the bishop's daughter was not something I could accept.

SIX

THE SMELL OF HUMAN piss, not horse, woke me first and made me realize I wasn't home. A bright light shone above me and all I could hear were the murmurings of a nurse hunched over me. She hummed something low and soothing as she threaded a needle through my cheek. I lay on my side, lumped on a cot, eyes jumping between the blood drops on the floor and the parade of polished shoes trying to avoid them. Two German Shepherds sniffed my hand that dangled over the edge of the rails, though I was not in a hospital.

I moved only to the sound of a straw bending to meet my lips. I sucked. I swallowed, relieved by the cool liquid. The nurse repacked the dressing in my nose. "That should hold for another hour," she said. "Until he can sit and hold it. Any word?"

"Not yet. License plates were from Tennessee. Stolen vehicle."

The nurse got up and changed places with a tall man who swung his keys forward and dropped them into the remains of my hat, the brim mutilated. It was as much detail as I could see. Everything had taken on a variegated coarseness as if the world had been outlined and smudged with charcoal. The lines were thick and sudden and I read them as I did the storm clouds that gathered over our farm.

"Lucky day, huh?"

I struggled to hold the man's gaze. I looked away instead at the dogs. One of them swaggered with hip dysplasia and sauntered to a glass dish filled with water by the door. She ignored the group of reporters who had gathered, cameras aimed at me and the cop. All I could hear was the buzz of voices. Everyone was talking so quickly. Some with accents I hadn't heard. One like Leroy's jagged voice. Another with a twang. They brandished questions with a ferocity I had seen in dogs, but not people, and all I remember were the long white teeth that gleamed when they smiled at me before the flashes went off on their cameras.

"Get them out of here. This isn't a goddamn circus," the cop snapped, although it was, in a way. A guard slammed the door and the room grew quiet.

"Sorry about that," he said and leaned closer with a file I had not seen tucked under his arm. He smelled of leather and aftershave and he flicked the snap of his holster when he spoke. "I'm Captain Fowler. Jonathan Fowler. You can call me Johnny, okay?"

I nodded and it hurt to move my head.

"You're in the Paradise Township Police Station. We'll take you to the hospital if you want to go but we didn't want to force you. We respect the Amish."

"Got nothin' against hospitals," I said, straining. "I was born in one."

"That right?"

I nodded again, then tilted the good cheek up, the left one, to reach for the straw he offered. I tasted apple juice this time. It was room temperature but the can was cool against my chin and soothed the fire burning inside me. I realized I had been dressed in jeans and a T-shirt. They were not my own clothes. They smelled of cigarettes.

"We'll need your name to document all of this," he said and lifted the can of apple juice off my face. "We tried to look for identification. No luck with a driver's license. Can you tell me your name?"

"Eli," I gargled, swallowing the last sip, straining to read the words on the t-shirt. KISS. A man with a white face, long white tongue, frizzy black hair and huge stars painted around his eyes stared up at me from the shirt.

"Okay, Eli. Eli… Stoltzfus?"

I closed my eyes, tried to shake my head but all I could manage was a slight shift in my jaw. He understood.

"Beiler? Myer? Zimmerman? Schroeder? Yoder? Lapp?"

I parted my lips, opened my good eye at Yoder.

"Alright then. I knew it wouldn't take long," he said, pleased with himself, obviously aware there were only so many surnames among the Amish. "Eli Yoder. We're going to record all of your answers. It's important that you answer to the best of your ability. Do you understand? We need you to remember everything you can about today. You ready?"

I felt my stomach spinning.

"Take your time. It's important that you study each picture carefully."

Johnny pulled a chair over to the cot and opened the file. He took out a few sketches of men, mostly young men, boys not much older than me with short hair. He held up the sketches slowly, one by one.

"Do you recognize any of them?"

I shook my head. Even if there was a defining feature like a scar or a birthmark, I would have been lying if I said any of the faces looked familiar. I hadn't taken a good look at those boys. I didn't have a reason to pay attention to their faces smashed beneath nylon stockings.

"Would you recognize their voices? An accent? Slang? Did thay tauk laak this?" Johnny asked, sounding like the boys from the Carolinas who had supplied my sisters with smoke bombs. "Yes," I said, although Johnny's imitation was far from accurate. It was close enough to get him excited.

"What did they say, Eli?"

"It's… worth… a… fortune."

"What? What's worth a fortune?"

"My camera."

"What?"

"They said… my camera's worth a fortune."

Johnny lay the sketches down on the folder in his lap. What did I care if he acted surprised? All the English had cameras. Cameras were as common as cars and just as lethal, but the cop didn't know this or seem to care.

"How much money did they steal?"

I grumbled, "96,000."

The officer looked up, stunned.

"What's a boy like you doing with that much money?"

"It was given to us after my sisters died."

Officer Fowler paused. "Us?"

"My family. My mom put it into an account in my name. Said I could take it out on my sixteenth birthday."

"She did, huh? For what? New car? You people always pay with cash, huh?"

I stared at him and wiped the sweat on my brow.

"To move to Florida. I want… to start a dog business there with my cousins."

The officer stared at me, trying to detect the lie. He just shrugged.

"Good luck with that. So how much was the camera worth?"

"More," I said, knowing it was priceless.

"More? Hmmm."

I felt dizzy thinking about it.

"Can I go home now?"

"Sure you can. But we just got started. We let you sleep for a few hours but we need you to answer a few more questions about your assailants now."

The way he said assailants made me feel like we had been old friends.

"I won't testify. It's not our way."

"We realize this, but we need some more information."

"I've forgiven them," I said.

Johnny paused.

"Just like that?"

"Yes."

It's not like I needed a whole lot of time to decide. As long as they weren't the driver who killed my sisters, anyone was easier to forgive.

"Jesus Christ," he said. "Jesus Christ."

That's when Johnny felt it appropriate to share more about my assailants, three convicts who had escaped from a prison in West Virginia and robbed four convenience stores, two Wawas, one Seven-Eleven and a Turkey Hill, earlier that day after crossing into southern Pennsylvania. They'd left two clerks dead, one in critical condition, one stable, and one paralyzed, lodging a single bullet into his lower vertebrae.

"We'll need your help to stop them, Eli."

"I can't do anything."

"You'll have to try. Everyone thinks they're Amish."

I rolled over and pushed myself up from the cot, feeling the ache in my face.

"Why? You said they're from West Virginia."

"Yes, but they're wearing your clothes."

And with that, I collapsed back into the cot and fell asleep, dreaming of a life of crime among Amish imposters. I don't know how long I lay there but I remember waking to the smell of a ham sandwich that Captain Fowler got from the vending machine. He peeled back the cellophane and dabbed mustard under the thin white crust.

"You deserve your money back, Eli."

I shook my head. "I just want to go home."

Johnny bit into the sandwich. He studied me when he spoke, chewing with his mouth open and full.

"Been a long time since you've been in the papers."

"I don't make it a habit."

"Allegedly," he said and opened a file stuffed with yellowing newspaper clippings about the accident. He pulled out a photograph of my mother and me, kneeling at the edge of the road, the buggy, toppled and twisted behind us.

"No one's ever found the sonovabitch."

"Who?"

"The driver who hit you."

"No," I said.

"Not yet," he said and scratched his mustache, then he looked down at his file again. "I have no idea why nobody's touched this case for so long, but with your cooperation, I'd open it myself."

I stiffened in the cot.

"Cooperation?"

"Yes. Maybe he'll finally step forth."

"Why would he do that?"

"Because he probably feels guilty and wants to be punished. When we have some suspects, we'll ask you to look at their faces. You won't have to testify in court."

I stared at him and the room seemed to get loud with the telephones ringing and the typewriters clacking. I didn't like the idea of the police poking into my sisters' deaths. It was too late for that. The last thing I wanted was my parents to relive the accident again; however, if I cooperated with the police, my family might finally meet the driver. I leaned over the edge of the cot and vomited.

"Bathroom's on your left."

I sat up and swung my feet over the cot, touching down on the cool concrete, avoiding my puddle. I felt dizzy when I stood and braced myself against the wall, trying to find my balance. I walked slowly, catching the eye of the guard who glanced up from the newspaper. He puckered his lips and winced when I passed. "Ooo-eee. Cripe's Maggie. They got you good. I wouldn't look in the mirror yet if I was you."

"I won't," I said. "I don't like mirrors much."

I reached up and cupped my hands around my face. The guard spied the webbing between my fingers and quickly slid his eyes back into the paper. "Amish," he grumbled as if my hands, not my hat, had confirmed his suspicions. "Shit. When you people gonna import? Head to Atlantic City for a weekend. Take the train. Take a bus. Just do us all a favor and hit the jackpot with the gene pool."

I shuffled across the floor into the bathroom and locked the door. I turned on the water, cupped my hands and drank from the spigot without looking in the mirror once.

When I got home that afternoon, I found my father sitting in his roller chair with the *New Era*, the evening newspaper, spread out on the table. He glanced through his bifocals, eyes wide and bewildered by the sight of me in the jeans and Kiss t-shirt. His greatest nightmare, me looking English.

My father who rarely used the Lord's name in vain, said, "Christ Jesus," which sounded like Kraft Cheeses. He pressed his fingers against his lips and tapped them slowly, as if the rhythm could help to steady his own erratic heartbeat. I turned to see if my mother was within earshot, but there was nobody else in the kitchen.

"You've got some explaining to do."

I told him everything but left out the part about the gun and the driver. I told him the stitches would come out on their own and that I needed ice and aspirin and that I'd be okay. I told him I'd lost the money from the bank but I didn't tell him about the camera. I had hoped he would figure the 'personal property' reported by the newspaper meant my clothes. He didn't seem too concerned about my wounds. What worried him caused him to dig his elbows into the table and cover his mouth with a fist.

"What were you doing with the Esh brothers?"

"Giving them a ride. Their truck overheated."

"They could have walked."

"It's a long way to their farm, Datt."

"It's only three miles!" he blurted and shook the picture that showed them giving the world the middle finger. Ever since Levi had quit driving for my father years ago, he took him for having idle hands, which implied he was employed in the devil's workshop. It didn't matter that Levi's cabinet business was thriving among the English.

"See? They're anything but *Gelassenheit*!" he said, reminding me of the Amish code of conduct in the world, more specifically, the Frowned Upon behaviors, as if I'd forgotten how offensive a cocky spirit could be, let alone a boisterous laugh, quick retort, aggressive handshake, curt greeting, boldness, rebellion or worse, individuality. In less than a year, I'd be guilty of all eight.

"They needed help, Datt."

My father sighed and mumbled, his words cold.

"They've always needed help. But what about you?"

I stared at him. He threw his eyes on the photo.

"What are you going to do?"

I shrugged. There wasn't much to do. I didn't know if my father meant now or in general. It was one of those questions that seemed as wide as the moon, depending on where you stood when you looked at it.

"I'd like to get changed," I said, seeing him scowl at the Kiss T-shirt. My father, prone to sudden irritability, scratched the melted candle wax off the table.

"I mean about work."

"The auction?"

"Yes, Eli. Everyone will have seen you like this."

I hung my head, feeling the blood flush my cheeks.

"It's just a photo, Datt."

"Just a photo? It's your soul, Eli. Your soul!"

My father pressed his lips together, but it wasn't the same kind of tension I'd seen earlier on Emma's face. My father was not a man who laughed easily, and seeing his only son stark naked in the local newspaper (and God only knows where else) disgraced him. There was no humor in what he saw, only humiliation.

"Take the week off," he said.

"One week?"

"No. You're right. Take off the month."

I stared at my father, whose brown eyes were wide now, gleaming in the late day sunlight coming through the windows. My father had never once taken a day off, not even with walking pneumonia, despite the orders of two doctors after staying in the city hospital. When my mother asked him what in the world he thought he was doing getting up to milk the cows, he said, "I've got walking pneumonia, woman. If I had sleeping pneumonia, I'd be in bed!" My father, like most Amish men, worked to live and lived to work. Vacation was not something we even considered, except for the opening day of trout season when my father was the first to cast his line into Beaver Creek. That Redbeet Reuben Yoder would offer me a week off was an exception to his own rule. That he would encourage me to take off a month was dangerously un-*Gelassenheit*.

"A month! Why? What will I do?"

"Recover," he said and motioned to my face, my wounds more convenient to identify than the invisible ones in himself.

My mother never mentioned the photo. She worked around the humiliation as if it were a weed she didn't bother to pull because it would only grow back. She set to work, sewing me a new set of pants, with pockets, and a shirt identical to the one stolen off my back. Bright blue, too, to match my eyes.

After I had bathed and changed my clothes, I found her alone in the room she called "the nest," an alcove in our farmhouse warmed by southern exposure, where she and my sisters had spent hours quilting during the winter. The only thing left of my sisters was the last quilt they'd made, which remained on the frame, faded now. She kept the door closed, opening it only on the anniversary of the accident, as if the quilt itself could conjure up the faces of my sisters, smiling, wide-eyed, eager to create. I found her many times waking up with a craned neck from falling asleep on top of the unfinished quilt. She had no intention of moving it, as if it would erase her fondest memories.

She had been coughing from the dust in the room and I brought her a cup of chamomile tea. She had not seen me wearing the English clothes yet. I wore my night shirt and a pair of white cotton long johns and stood in the doorway, surprised to see she had pushed the frame aside to make room for her treadle machine, foot pumping the pedal, hands guiding blue fabric under the needle with precision.

As much as my mother took exception to some Amish customs, she was adamant about the quality of her family's clothing and insisted on making her own. Mamm dyed the cloth with natural colors she'd made from the trees on our farm. Even though by 1983 most Amish women had adopted the practice of buying fabric, my mother spent hours preparing her own textiles. Behind her were bins of untouched dyes that she'd made from sugar maple, hickory, black and white walnut, alder, hemlock, butternut tree, blue ash, sassafras and madder for reds, and dried up pokeberries, which my sisters collected, even though the purplish red they yielded was weak. I mention all of this because it reveals, to a degree, the pride with which Mamm took in presenting us to the world, even though it defied the spirit of *Gelassenheit*.

By making me new clothes, in the room she opened once a year, I think my mother needed to reassure us that no picture could steal the essence of what made us good. *Hochmut* or not. She lifted her foot off the pedal and paused, fixing her eyes on me through tiny wire-rimmed glasses.

"Where's your ice?"

"I already put it on."

"I called the doctor."

"I don't need a doctor."

"You need more ice for the swelling. It hurts?"

I nodded. She swallowed, eyes narrowed, as if the pain had just transferred itself to her. She looked down at the shirt when she spoke next, safer to see it than my face.

"You know," she began. "I've forgiven those men."

My mother had never lied to me, but something in her pale blue eyes told me she was having difficulty letting go of the rage shooting through her body again, as if every cell had been reawakened. Seeing the glaze over her eyes shattered for the first time, she looked human to me. I looked at her not as my mother, but as a woman who had been wronged too many times. Justice, she was teaching me, was an act more powerful in the absence of sound or spectacle. In her case she sewed, piecing together whatever scraps she had left of her faith and dignity, of my own.

"How much did you take out of the bank?"

I swallowed, feeling the sting of the confession that sat like a nettle in my throat. "A lot," I whispered, not wanting to tell her I took 9-6-67, which was not a locker number but the amount of my birthday, $96,196.70.

"I noticed you took the suitcase, too."

She looked up. I nodded, leaning against the door.

"And where did you plan to go with the suitcase?"

"Florida."

"Florida?"

"Only my cousins know me there."

"I see," she said and tore off a piece of black thread from the bobbin with her teeth. "Why does that matter?"

"Most people I'll meet won't know the difference," I said.

"In what?"

"My hands. After the surgery."

My mother set down the tea cup and shifted her gaze from me, fixing it instead on the blue fabric. Her eyes narrowed to tiny slits and I was not sure if she squeezed them shut to keep the tear from sliding out, even though it did despite her and splattered the fabric. Her fingers trembled, guiding the cloth under the hinged presser foot of the sewing machine, her nose grazing the tension block. I had not intended to make her upset. It wasn't the right time to remind her, but the operation had been her idea. She had opened the bank account in my name for this very purpose. But now, seeing her sunken face in the moonlight, I wasn't convinced her idea had been right. Or God's will.

SEVEN

I WOULD GO TO Florida. And I would get the operation without anyone's permission but my own. I had to get a few things straight before I left and that included apologizing to Emma Beiler. It wasn't the swelling in my eye or the itching of the stitches that kept me from seeing her sooner. I fretted over choosing the right words and the right time to tell Emma that I was leaving. The more I thought about what I'd say and the more upset I realized she would be, the less often I left our farm to meet her and talk. I gave myself a long project instead, and set to work scraping off the paint on the side of our house.

I wrongly chose the south side first, thinking that I'd be warmer working there, now that the frost lingered in the mornings. In every window facing south was the reflection of the walnut tree, which I hadn't realized that we'd all been facing when we gathered to eat and when we tried to sleep at night. It was no wonder that over the years my father's indigestion plagued him and my mother remained restless and sleep-deprived. I often wondered why we hadn't cut the tree down, but I now believe the real reason was to remind the driver of what he had taken from us, should he ever pass our farm again.

I thought about all of this, scraping away the paint on our house. By the third day I realized I had much more to tell Emma Beiler than that I was leaving. I was worried that the cop would open the investigation into my sisters' death, which meant I'd not only meet the driver, but I'd have to forgive him, too. I wasn't ready for that, and I wasn't ready to tell Emma that I couldn't do it.

Holding that cold metal scraper above my bedroom window, with the tree and my reflection in the glass, I realized that the driver had changed my life again. He had transformed me over the years, and slowly, subtly, I had become a coward, just like him.

There's a true story my grandfather told my sisters and me whenever we got into trouble for eating too much candy. We didn't know how to stop which is why I never really liked candy, even though I craved it from time to time. Granddatt advised us to listen to our stomachs more than our eyes, believing candy was the first lesson in discipline. The second was learning how to ask the right questions, which required the humility to admit we didn't know everything. He'd say, "Don't end up like Moses King," who, according to oral tradition, took his newly purchased tractor into the fields and began to harrow. He never asked the Englisher who sold him the tractor how to stop it, so Moses King drove it in circles until it ran out of gas.

People laughed whenever they heard the story, except for Granddatt who believed there was no pity for a person's stupidity. It was his way of teaching us how to trust our gut, and if I had had any inkling of what my gut was trying to tell me when I set out to talk to Emma Beiler, I would have stayed on our farm and scraped the paint off our barn, and then off our fence and every other building. I needed to stay busy. I didn't have the courage to hear what my gut was trying to tell me back then, which is why, I believe, Bishop Beiler took it upon himself to make it clear.

His words were no less sharp than the metal teeth on old Moses' tractor, but Bishop Beiler had not intended to break clods of dirt. We sat in the dark on the porch outside his house, rapt by the rush of the wind through the willow trees, elbows on knees, hands pressed together, chins on fingertips, each of us wrought by the wonder of the other, when all I had come to do was to apologize to his daughter, who, as my luck would have it, was helping her cousin deliver a baby.

Bishop Beiler couldn't have been more pleased by my timing. Apparently he had a few things to say to me, namely that he couldn't believe that I had already succumbed to the evil forces of the Outside World within my first month of *rumspringa*. His beard carried the scent of pipe smoke and every now and then he'd burp between words, then swipe the air to restore the decorum and fix himself another apple butter sandwich on slabs of raisin bread. He offered me one but I declined, too nervous to digest any more.

He reiterated what it meant to be Amish and of the importance of radical obedience to the teachings of Christ. He highlighted the ethic of love that rejects violence in all spheres of human life both verbal and physical. He spoke of the poison worms of worldliness and pride and the concept of the church as a voluntary body of believers accountable to each other but separate from the world. He reminded me that if I chose baptism, it would be my duty to submit to the church and to God.

"You understand? It's all about surrender."

I nodded. None of this was new to me.

What was new was the story of Joshua's Army.

"You haven't heard of it?"

"Nope," I said.

"Neither have the Esh brothers," he said and huffed.

Then we went on to remind me of the confession of hidden plunder made by Joshua's army before their battle against the people of Ai.

"You see it was their confession, not their weapons, that led this army to victory."

He waved his arms in the air when he spoke.

"Remember. Hidden sins of pride and disobedience, if not confessed, can lead to the Church's defeat."

He turned to me when he said confessed, then shifted his eyes to the fields and the darkness gathered around us. He stuck the knife back into the jar of apple butter and said nothing, waiting for me, I think, to surrender.

His silence pinned me in a place I didn't want to be, the proximity to a holy man and the power he had to make my ugliness bigger, which only made Bishop Beiler more dangerous than his words. He said he wasn't angry or mad about me leaving his daughter in tears; he was more concerned about the direction I was taking with my life. He said the Amish needed good souls like mine. I wanted to tell him he was mistaken.

"You're our future, Eli. Every time one of you choose to kneel for baptism, it's a victory for the Amish. Allowing you all to go through *rumspringa* is a riskworth taking even though we know we could lose in it."

I wanted to assure him that he wouldn't lose me. My plans for *rumspringa* only involved a few months in Florida, not years of sowing wild oats in Lancaster. I wished I had already pledged my allegiance to a respected gang like the Canaries. I wished I could have made plans to pick up Emma every Saturday for song group for the rest of *rumspringa* (when she chose to talk to me again) for three, maybe four, more years until I decided it was time to marry her, and only after I completed the required summer courses and had memorized the Eighteen Articles of Faith.

"Eli, is there anything else you want to tell me?"

"Other than sorry?"

Bishop Beiler lifted his eyes to meet mine in the moonlight, as if this was the moment that would define who I would become, under his guidance, within his district. This was my chance to clear myself, to earn the glory I had stolen from my sisters, that the driver had stolen from me. This was my chance to move on and become a man.

I closed my eyes and listened to my stomach, hoping that the voice everyone said was lodged there would speak. Some called it the Holy Spirit but I'd be lying if I said I heard a peep. I tried to hear what my gut was saying, tried to discern the direction it wanted me to take, but all I could hear was the wind in the willow trees and the hoot of an owl who swooped over us when Bishop Beiler burped.

It's not that I didn't hear anything. I heard the voice that hated the driver, the voice that promised never to forgive him, the same voice that had urged me once to steal a camera and to use it to take my sisters' souls. I wanted to bury these secrets more than I wanted to become Amish. And this was not right, I knew. And this was not holy. And this did not make me a child of God.

I figured the longer I stuck around the Amish, the more I put all of us at risk. It wasn't my hands that would separate me this time from the people I loved the most, but the web of lies I had spun to protect them from me.

◇

I was surprised to find my parents waiting when I returned that night. It was late. The dull glow of the gas lamp shone from the kitchen. I could see my mother wiping down the counters, pausing every few strokes to dab her eyes. My father, wrapped in a dark black cape, sat on his roller chair, the silver in his hair catching the lamp above the table and the mangled black hat that lay in the center.

I had that sinking feeling in my knees as if the ground had turned to mud. My mother opened the screened door, staring through me as if she were waiting for me to come inside to scrub the soil from my feet.

"How did it go?" she asked.

"Good, I guess."

"You'll stay then?"

I shook my head. "No."

I lowered my gaze seeing in her gray eyes the sadness and the disappointment. I wanted to tell her not to waste her tears. She dabbed her cheeks, flush now, and played with the tassel of her prayer cap. "Your father wants to see you," she said, then stepped inside the kitchen when the timer went off above the oven. I followed her and she pulled out a tray of pluckets, clusters of sweet rolls that filled the air with cinnamon and yeast. "Now don't eat them all before you get to Florida. Save some for your cousins."

Mamm made pluckets only on special occasions, usually on the last day of a visitor's stay. As children, we had taken great delight in devouring them. Usually the smell comforted me and had the power to make me homesick, even from my own bedroom where the odor drifted through the floorboards. Pluckets were the smell of celebration and sorrow. Of arrivals and departures. The last time my mother had made them was the day we buried my sisters. Standing there by the hot oven, smelling the sweet rolls again, made me sick and sorry.

I started into the kitchen but my father held up his hand, pressing the air, keeping me at the threshold. It was already three in the morning. He walked toward me with a suitcase, massaging the left side of his lower back where he had obviously pulled a muscle carrying it. He set it at my feet and handed me a long white envelope.

"You have a window seat."

I opened it and pulled out a one-way ticket to Tallahassee from the Lancaster train station. I'd never been on a train before and neither had my father.

He never saw the value of a vehicle that moved that fast. Until now.

"Your mother packed everything you'll need."

"I've put suntan lotion in a plastic bag," she said. "You must use it every day. The sun is much hotter in Florida. You don't want to get a burn."

I fixed my eyes on my father. He nodded.

"It's true," he said, as if he had reason to believe I questioned her or his reasons for buying the train ticket.

My mother opened the cabinet above the sink and took out a black lunch pail, normally reserved for my father's long-distance appraisals. She filled it with pluckets and a paper napkin folded into a triangle. Then she closed the lid on the lunch pail and snapped the latch into place, but she didn't flinch this time. She passed the lunch pail to me and her hand lingered on the handle. She and Datt stood there, waiting for me to move. I expected them to ask more questions or beat me with more reasons to stay. I'd have preferred a scene to silence.

All they said was goodbye. Once from Mamm. Once from Datt. Goodbye.

"I'll be back soon," I blurted because I couldn't bear the thought of saying it, too. I pried my mother's hand off the handle with the same brute force she used to cut off my sisters' braids. I tucked the lunch pail under my arm and lifted the suitcase, stepping out of the way to avoid my mother's tears.

The last thing I remember is the hand of my father on my shoulder when I turned toward the door. He squeezed me and I could feel the rattle of his palsy struggling against all the love he'd denied himself and me since the accident. He looked at me, his brown eyes black in the dim light, asking me why. That's when I heard Hanna's voice repeating what she had told me in the pond so long ago.

Sometimes you have to leave and you don't know why.

But I knew. I didn't deserve to be Amish. I stepped outside and my father closed the door. My mother stared out the window, face fixed and waxy, like a doll. Her blank eyes and crooked smile made me nervous. She stared through me, beyond me, as if that same smile revealed the hope she had for who I'd be when I returned from *rumspringa*.

PART THREE

◆

ONE

I WALKED DOWN THE ROAD in the dark and, for the first time in my life, watched the sun rise, not on our farm but at the intersection of the only two worlds I knew, Main Street and Decatur in downtown Strasburg, where Leroy Fischer's barbershop sat at the corner. It was a world of mirrors I had hoped to avoid. After the Beachy Amish had requested mohawks earlier that year, and Leroy had granted their request, the Old Order Amish forbid us from soliciting his services, saying that if we did, we had chosen to indulge in the "pleasures of sin for a season." But I needed a haircut. If I were to enjoy any kind of anonymity in Florida, I'd need to get rid of my bowl cut. I didn't want to be the brunt of bored English teens, who could point out the deception of gangs in *rumspringa* wearing jeans and T-shirts at local malls. I had no problem losing hair if it meant I could restore my honor. But I never said how much hair I was willing to lose. And Leroy never asked.

I stood on the sidewalk across the street from the barbershop, hesitant, watching Leroy watch me. He had put down his scissors on that clear, crisp blue morning and stepped outside, arms crossed over his white smock, lips pursed with a cigar, staring, waiting for me to make a move. It had been two years since I'd seen him. He had lost his hair and his sideburns had turned white and looked like two strips of bacon with nothing but the fat, which he hadn't been eating much from the looks of him. He was wiry and shorter than I remembered, stooped under the spiraling barber pole.

"Jesus. Joseph. And Mary."

"No," I said. "It's Eli."

I straightened, feeling suddenly exposed again. The men inside the shop pressed their ears against the glass, straining to hear our conversation. But we didn't say much.

The last time I had seen him was at the Gordonville Auction, two weeks after my fourteenth birthday. He had bid on a used Polaroid camera inside the fire hall, thinking it would make a great gift, but when he gave it to me, I turned and walked away. I thought it was a joke. I couldn't thank him for something that I thought he was using against me.

Leroy wiped his eyes with his sleeve and straightened. He stared at me like he didn't know who I was, so I held up my hands. "It's Eli," I said, seeing myself in the window, a good head taller than the man who had towered over me.

We stared at each other, long and hard, the kind of stare that holds life-times.

"Eli Yoder," I said, frustrated he had not recognized me yet. I thought I'd refresh his memory with my other name, the one I rarely said out loud, but silently every day.

"B i g U g l y," I said, hardly believing he'd forgotten.

"Oh, Big Ugly," he said and nodded his head.

"Yes. Big Ugly. I'm sixteen now."

"Pshaa. I'm sixty-three."

"You got old."

Leroy smiled and parted his lips to flash the gold cap on his front tooth.

"You got beat up, Ugly."

"Looks worse than it feels."

Leroy moved close to my face, examining the wounds with his dark eyes. He pried at the scabs with his fingers the way he'd done with his young boxers.

"What are you gonna do about you?"

"I need a haircut," I said.

"Your father know you're here?"

I took out the train ticket and showed it to him.

"He bought it for me."

"You gone leave us for Florida?"

I stared at the sidewalk, at the wad of pink bubble gum wedged between the crack and the small heart drawn with blue chalk. I didn't like the feeling of Leroy's eyes on me then. They felt heavy and made me ache.

"I'm sixteen," I said, trying to draw some sort of boundary around myself. "I'll be okay." I was no longer the gap-toothed boy he'd known at the market.

Leroy tapped the tip of his lip with his finger and studied me more. He drew in a wheezing, gurgling breath then coughed out a phlegm ball which landed on the bubble gum. Everything got quiet. Someone turned down the TV. Leroy's half-hound Caesar stood in front of us, black nose pressed against the glass.

"I don't have any openings today."

"I can't come back tomorrow," I said. Even if I could take another train, tomorrow felt like a long time from now with twists and turns and other trees on the road that had not yet been hit by Trouble. I did not trust any of the English to help me now. Only Leroy. He took out the cigar, narrowed his large brown eyes to reconsider.

"I'm all booked up today."

I handed him the lunch pail. "Take this."

He leaned in to look. "Pluckets, huh? That's quite a sacrifice for a hair cut."

"And this," I said and pulled out a pack of antique Rook cards, which my father had packed in the suitcase.

Leroy smiled, amused by my outrageous and desperate offer. The Amish don't tip; tipping was something I'd learned from Leroy in the market. I knew a tip made a man happy and a happy man was a good thing when you decided to put your life into his hands. I handed him the Rook set.

"It's a good set. Antique," he said. "You think it's worth a haircut?"

"Dunno. Depends how good it is."

"Then follow me," he said.

I marched behind him and into the shop where he shooed every one of the men with shaving foam on their faces and their hair half cut. For the first time in twenty-seven years, Leroy Fischer flipped the CLOSED sign on 826 Main Street at half past seven on a Saturday morning. Then he handed me a straight-edge razor, the kind of blade, I imagined and hoped, could separate webbed hands.

"Come on in, Big Ugly. Make yourself at home."

Leroy shook out a black cape and a few tendrils of curly red hair slid down it and landed on a white tile. He waved me to the seat in front of him and pulled a comb from the jar of blue Barbasol, then oiled a pair of scissors.

"Kid comes in here thinks he can wash the red out of his hair. Told him you can't wash out what's meant to be. Thinks I'm an old stooge. He's too young to understand."

"Maybe," I said, too fixated on the details of the shop to follow him—the stacks of auto magazines and others with bare breasted women on the cover, an assortment of bowling pins, a Coke clock, one card table with a game half played, an ashtray where Leroy's cigar sat smoldering. And where I expected mirrors, I found photographs instead. Not just one or two. Hundreds of photographs of peoples' faces. Big photos, small photos, color and black and white. Polaroids, too. I didn't know which was worse. Staring at yourself or a stranger staring back. They didn't look sad and they didn't look silly. Those faces looked helpless hanging there, tacked to the walls, eyes aglow and mouths gaping. I'd never seen so many photos in my life, not even at the tourist stands. For some reason, postcards didn't have the same impact as a photograph. But there was an immediacy and intimacy about those faces on the walls that made me uncomfortable, like they had all conspired to play some huge joke. Aside from the ticking of the ceiling fan, I'd swear the walls could laugh.

"Do you hear that?" I asked.

"What? Come sit, Ugly. We got work to do."

He flicked the comb and splashed the only mirror that wasn't covered with photographs. I followed the splash to the lower right corner of the mirror, then turned my head to get a better look at what was there. In the back of the shop, perched on top of what appeared to be a small stage, was an old barber chair sitting by itself with a wide red curtain draped on the wall behind it. I had never seen a throne in real life and I had never known anyone to own a throne, much less sit on one, but everything about this massive barber chair reminded me of the pictures we'd seen as kids in the English books that showed Jesus with lambs and children in his lap.

"What is it?" I asked and pointed to the empty chair.

Leroy cleared his throat.

"What? That? Just a stage," he said.

"What's a stage doing in a barbershop?

"Same thing as a boy just starting *rumspringa*."

"What's that?"

"You both just waiting around to be occupied."

I turned and caught Leroy biting his lip. He seemed nervous and excited, like he wanted to tell me more.

"People get their haircut up there?" I asked.

"Not in that chair."

"Then what's the point?"

"The point?" Leroy asked and scratched his chin. "The point is to confess."

I felt my body stiffen.

"Confess what?"

"Everything they wish they could've done differently in their lives. Man's gotta live a while to sit up there."

"You don't have to be old to make mistakes," I said and shifted my eyes to the floor. "I already made plenty."

"Well, go on, boy. Go climb up in that chair and tell old Leroy all about it before you shove off to Florida."

"I'd rather just get my haircut," I said, feeling the nudge of Caesar's cold nose against the back of my palm.

"He wants you to sit down. Come on."

I approached the chair slowly, looking over my shoulder, terrified of the bigger chair at the back of the shop and the way its shadow seemed to find mine on the floor. Leroy held out his hand and took the razor back.

"Here," he said. "I'll need that now."

Before I could ask him why, he pushed me into the chair, draped me with a black cape, snapped it around my neck, stuck a comb in my hair and started to cut. Caesar sat at my knees looking up at me, panting, smiling, it seemed, at the spectacle I'd just become.

"What's he laughing about?" I said.

"Him? Oh, nothing much."

Leroy whistled while he worked. He didn't talk except to tell me to lift my chin and not to slouch. I wasn't sure why that mattered until he told me not to move. That's when I glimpsed in his hand an electric shaver, something I'd seen plenty of times at the auction, but which no Amish man had ever placed a bid on because they saw no need for shaving off their beards or anything else.

Leroy set the shaver on the counter and continued to cut. Large clumps of my bowl cut fell to the floor and collected in the dip of the cape covering my lap.

"Whoa," I said. "It's a little short."

"Hardly, Ugly. This is short."

That's when Leroy lay down the scissors and picked up the electric shaver. He flicked it on and the tiny motor whirled inside it. Caesar barked. Leroy clapped and the rest I would rather forget.

Leroy chopped my hair as short as he could and buzzed off the rest, leaving the top of my head all fuzzy like the belly of a puppy. When he was finished, he took the razor, slapped shaving cream over my head and scraped off whatever stubble remained. Then he swatted the hairs on the back of my neck with a soft brush and pointed to the mirror. "Have a look at the new you."

My heart raced and I could hear the heavy breathing of everyone in the shop who had barged through the doors when they heard Leroy clap. Caesar licked my hands clamped to the rails of the barber seat. The room seemed hotter and suddenly crowded. More men had gathered on the sidewalk outside, apparently lured by the rumor of my initiation. They pretended to stop in for hair wax and tonic and cigars, but I suspected they wanted to watch my hair fall, cheering like they were watching a football game.

"Don't you want to look?"

I opened my eyes and looked at the floor first. Clumps of the page boy littered the ground, all dark and shiny and streaked with copper. Six-inch strands as wide as the tiles, brown on white. Brown on black. Hair everywhere. Bits and pieces of me on the floor. And then there was the rest of me in the chair, too scared to see what remained.

"See? It's not that bad."

Leroy splashed aftershave on his hands and patted the top of my head. I reached up after him and ran my fingers over the smooth skin. He was right. It was not that bad. It was worse. I was completely bald. Aside from my clothes, there was no evidence now that I'd come from the Amish.

I felt my mouth drop open but no words came out. Just a stifled, short breath.For all the legends surrounding Leroy's barbershop, none involved going bald voluntarily. Sure, I'd seen short cuts. Buzz cuts. Cuts that made the boys in *rumspringa* look like they'd joined the military, which we forbid. Such a cut certainly curtailed their desire to flirt much longer in the Outside world where Army recruiters swarmed them and promised a life of honor. But we had known another kind of honor, the spirit of *Gelassenheit* and solidarity, and part of that honor required us to look like each other so that our age-old choice to remain separated from the Outside World would remain distinct and dogged.

I tasted something sour, the kind of bitter taste I had come to believe meant a man's soul had gone bad. I snapped my mouth shut then opened it again.

"You shaved it all off."

Leroy laughed.

"It'll grow back in a few months."

I groaned and ran my hands over my slippery head.

"Months. Months?! How many months?"

"Five. Or six."

I sank into the chair. My heart slid into my stomach.

Leroy ran the brush over my neck again. It tickled but I didn't laugh. He pointed to the mirror. "What are you waiting for? Take a look!"

I refused. Six months, I thought. Then groaned.

"You look good, Ugly," he said, but I heard, *you look good ugly.* Nobody looks good ugly.

"No, I don't."

"Sure do. You wear it well."

I turned to one of the men behind me. A man in a pin-striped business suit who stood eating a hoagie, picking flecks of oregano out of his teeth with a toothpick. Others gathered behind him along with a local photographer who snapped my photo and pulled blood into my cheeks.

"Hey, hey. What are you doing? He's still Amish," Leroy crooned, jabbing his pointer finger at a middle-aged man with a receding hairline who stood by the door with a long-lens camera. Even when Leroy had worked in the market, nobody dared take our photo while he was cutting our hair. After Marcus Paoni had taken my photo, Leroy had posted a sign on the back of his chair that read inside a humongous hand-drawn camera:

DON'T EVEN THINK ABOUT IT. $100 PER PHOTO.
DOUBLE FOR BARBER. CASH. NO CHECKS.
MONEY ORDERS ACCEPTABLE. NOBODY WILL
BE TURNED AWAY FOR LACK OF FUNDS. AMEN.

The sign made folks giggle nervously when they passed him sharpening a razor on the portable strop. But the man with the camera wasn't giggling then. In fact, nobody spoke except Leroy. "Patton, that you? I told you I'd crack your knees if you ever took a shot at these kids. The sign might be missing, but you owe me a hundred bucks. Actually, give it to Ugly. He could use a few extra dollars these days."

The men turned to Jack Maxell, all five-feet-five of him and his flabby jowls. He looked like a Pit Bull with a mustache. He was the coach of a high school track team, but he'd never run a mile. People called him Patton because he watched movies every Friday night about a military man with the same name. Mr. Maxell had adopted his motto, which became the insignia on all the track kids' uniforms: **There is no substitute for victory**. Apparently Patton didn't dare say that to the cops who'd pull him over on his fifth count of drunk driving. Leroy would tell me he'd taken a job with the newspaper to earn money to pay off his fines.

"That's a cheap shot," one of the men said, to which the businessman hurled his hoagie across the room, knocking the toupee off Patton's head. It landed on the camera.

"Dirt bag! Put that goddamn gun away and get the hell outta here, you bastard."

That's when the men started to unleash a torrent of expletives that rattled my head and my heart. The room started to spin but I was sitting still, trying to figure out how many hairs I had lost and worse, the respect I would lose among the Amish.

Leroy climbed on top of a chair and waved a cape, trying to get everyone's attention, keeping at bay what could have easily turned into a brawl.

"Gentleman. Gentlemen! Let us not stoop to his level. Patton, hand over the money or we'll kill you."

The room got quiet again, but nobody took their eyes off the photographer who had walked up to me, digging in his wallet, pulling out soft crinkled bills. "Here's sixty-three dollars," he said. "I owe you twenty-seven."

"You owe him more than that."

Leroy stepped off the chair and walked over to us.

Patton lay the money on my lap and extended his hand. He had good hands, strong hands with long, slender fingers, and small wrists which didn't match the rest of his body. He cradled the camera lens the way I'd seen the English do at the market with loaves of fresh-baked cinnamon bread.

"I'm sorry," he pleaded. "I just thought—"

Leroy cleared his throat. "What? What were you thinking?"

"He seemed… relieved."

"Relieved?" Leroy asked, incredulous.

I clutched the sides of the barber chair.

"Yeah. You know. To be one of us."

TWO

I WANTED TO LAUGH but I screamed instead. I had felt like a thief most of my life, but now I finally looked like a convicted one thanks to Leroy. When I caught a glimpse of myself in the reflection in the back door of the shop, I wasn't sure who was staring back at me. He didn't look familiar. He didn't just scare me; his baldness spooked me, and I couldn't imagine how much he'd bewilder the Amish.

It was one thing to wear English clothes around the Amish. They expected this from the guys in *rumspringa*, but there was no way I could show up to my cousins in Florida (or anywhere else) without hair for fear my relatives would think I'd joined the Catholics. A very long time ago, the pope had cut his hair short and shaved his beard to spite the Anabaptists during the Reformation. Song #102 in the *Ausbund* recounts our criticism of him. I could think of no greater offense. Joining the Catholics would be a far more bitter betrayal than simply inhabiting the Outside World. There was no way to convince anyone that all of this was an accident. Or God's will.

My big bald head looked like a lawn ball.

I suspected my story would topple Moses King's story. Everyone who knew me would pass this on to their children and grandchildren to warn them about my stupidity. I stood there, squinting from the glare, thinking that maybe God had not just made me ugly, he made me stupid, too, not to know any better than to avoid Leroy.

I don't know how long I stayed in the shop after everyone had left, but I remember the smell of pot roast roused me from my shock. Leroy banged on the back door for me to join him and Ruthanne for dinner. I took a deep breath and stepped outside, crossing the courtyard to the old carriage house behind the shop where they lived, even though I wasn't hungry.

"Where's our refugee?," Ruthanne asked, caning her way to greet me at the door. She was a small round white woman with arms and thighs as thick as hams, but carried herself like a thoroughbred. Anybody who knew anything about the reflexes of her tongue would have said the woman had snap. At sixty-nine, she was legally blind and attributed it to seeing too much TV in the dark. She left candy wrapper trails wherever she went and her pockets were full of sweets. She pulled out a roll of Life-Savers.

"You like Butter Rum?" she asked and peeled the silver foil with the tip of her thumb nail as if it were a pairing knife, and a little green thread, like mint dental floss, fell out like a snake on the floor. She didn't pick it up. Leroy looked at me and shrugged.

"Don't get him hooked, Ruthie."

"What's a matter with a little something sweet? It's not like the Amish don't eat sugar. Take as much as you want, hon," she said waiting for me to take one off the roll. "Just make yourself at home."

"Okay," I said, but I didn't eat it and slipped the Life-Saver into my pocket.

"You can leave your hat in here," she said and opened the closet door in the hallway. A dozen hats, mostly black felt, sat piled up as if they'd been flung over a fencepost during Sunday services. Below them, on wooden hangers, was a row of black broadfall pants, black suspenders and solid hook-and-eye shirts in alternate shades of purple and blue. The whole display resembled a bruise. I'd never seen so many clothes in one closet and I ran my hands along the shirts, surprised to find sweat stains in the armpits as if they'd only been discarded yesterday. For all I knew, they might have been. For nearly thirty years, the barbershop and the carriage house behind it had been the way-station for wayward souls like me passing between two worlds. It was the first stop to freedom for those of us naïve enough to believe we could find it in the Outside.

"I didn't bring my hat," I said.

Ruthanne straightened.

"You're in that much of a hurry to be English?"

I cocked my head, watching this plump pale woman with frying pan ear-rings sniff the air, pleased by the sweetness and smoke of the pot roast and mashed potatoes that Leroy graciously scooped onto my plate. The veins in his forearms bulged from the weight of the spoon.

"Not really," I said. "Leroy kinda sped it up."

Ruthanne reached out to find my head and froze when her fingers touched my skin. She gasped.

"Leroy!"

Leroy looked over at me and glared. He slapped a finger over his mouth, then slid it across his throat.

"He asked for a hair cut, Ruthie."

"That's right. You show me the hair on this boy!"

Leroy shrunk at the table. The steam from the mashed potatoes rose to his face and fogged his glasses.

"What's he going to do now, Leroy? He can't go back like this! His poor head's as bare as a baby's bottom."

Leroy shredded his paper napkin at the table.

"Suppose he could work here," he said.

"Maybe he doesn't want to work here."

"Sure he does. Who wouldn't want to work here?"

"Why you always answering for everyone?"

I watched them like a volley ball game, back and forth, Leroy getting smaller and Ruthanne getting bigger.

In all the years I had known Leroy, I had never seen him in public with his wife. Ruthanne had nursed Leroy back to life in Korea and he proposed to her on a gurney with a washer that had fallen off his tank and fit her pinky. If I hadn't just met her, I would have believed it was the color of their skin that kept them apart in public places, but it was Ruthanne's power that I marveled at most. She was a blind woman who claimed she could see shadows and I believed her.

"You better have a plan this time, Leroy."

"I do. Trust me, Ruthie," Leroy pleaded, whispering as if I weren't already listening, "I have a plan."

"That's what you said about the Esh brothers. And look what good came of it. They started a band."

Leroy sat back in his chair. It creaked, scaring the black cat curled under his feet.

"Now you listen to me, Leroy, and you listen good. We'll help this boy as much as we can, but we won't hinder him. I hope you have a way to make up for his loss."

"Ruthie, for God's sake. It's Redbeet Reuben's Eli."

Ruthanne recoiled and her voice shrank as if knowing my name made a difference. "Big Ugly?"

"Bigger," I said. "And uglier without hair."

I pulled her hand away from my head, her fingers cold, stiff. Trembling.

Leroy stood from the table.

"Come sit everyone, before dinner gets cold."

He offered me the seat facing the window. Caesar lay under the table looking up at all of us, catching my eye, as if he, too, was in on this cruel conspiracy to welcome or reject me, I wasn't sure which.

◇

We didn't pray. And we didn't say grace. We just sat there and ate in silence. Although it felt awkward not to say something to the Lord for the food set before us, it felt more awkward to speak to strangers I hadn't seen in two years. I didn't want them asking any questions that I couldn't answer yet. If I had my mouth full, I'd be saved from talking at all. The food was good and Leroy offered me another slice of pot roast after I burped, a custom among the Amish meant as a compliment for the cook. Ruthanne lifted her face and smiled, even though I could see her fingers shaking. She picked at her food.

"Do your mom a favor and don't get too used to it."

"It's okay," I said, being completely honest. "You're a good cook, Ruthanne. But Rachel's better."

Leroy laughed. Ruthanne cleared her throat.

"Is that right? How's she doing?"

"She don't use too much salt."

"I mean what's she been up to?"

"Oh. She's sewing again."

Ruthanne's eyebrows arched across a high forehead. My mother's quilts had fetched a decent price and, although my father could not sell them in his auctions because of a conflict of interest, she sold her quilts to art dealers in New York city. We could afford the best buggies at the time, all paid for through the sale of a single quilt that my mother and sisters had made. Five-thousand dollars was the average, but the last quilt they had made had sold for seven thousand five hundred dollars. It didn't matter that Ruthanne could not see them now. She understood their value, and the value of Mamm's return to the quilting frame.

"I can't believe it's been what? How long has it—"

"Seven years," I said when Leroy's mouth started to move.

"You still selling puppies?"

I shook my head and felt the blood flood my cheeks.

"Sold the business last week."

"Moving on?" Ruthanne asked.

"Growing up," Leroy answered for me.

"Yeah," I said, feeling afraid for the first time.

Leroy caught my eye and we shared a knowing look. He knew I was lying, trying to be polite. I was far from grown up or even close to fine. Everything was a mess but there was no good reason to share this with folks I hadn't seen in a long time. At least Ruthanne hadn't seen my recent photo in the paper, but now that she'd run her fingers over my bald head, I didn't know which was worse.

"You grown taller than your dad," she said.

I nodded, then said, "A bit."

"How's old Reuben doing?"

"He limps now," I said. "But he gets around."

Ruthanne pinched her lips together and shifted uncomfortably. She tapped her fork on the table. She seemed distracted for the rest of the meal and said no more aside from asking Leroy to pass her the salt.

When we finished, I was surprised to see Ruthanne get up and wander over to the record player to listen to a lady named Ella sing of building a stairway to the stars. She sat in an old chair facing the window where the sun slipped into the lower third of the frame, as if she could see it. Leroy motioned for me to get up and help with the dishes, which no man I had ever known had done for his wife.

"What's a matter?" he said, snapping on a pair of yellow rubber gloves.

"Nothing."

"Don't look at me like that."

"Like what?"

"Like I just lost my balls."

"You didn't lose much," I said and got up to join him.

Ruthanne chuckled from her perch by the window but I don't know why she laughed. I was serious. I didn't mind doing dishes because it almost always got me out of those perilous days where the men I knew scaled heights to build barns. We worked together in silence listening to Ruthanne sing, which made me think of Emma.

What made me miss her even more was seeing Ruthanne and Leroy dance in the middle of the kitchen floor, hands clasped, faces pressed into each other's necks while the dishes dried. I stood by the sink, shifting awkwardly. The Amish are taught to reserve displays of affection for the space between the sheets. And we rarely discuss touch. Aside from my mother's care, she rarely touched us, and we never saw her touch my father. Or him her. There were no clues that my sisters and I had been conceived out of love.

Watching Leroy and Ruthanne glide across the kitchen floor, entangled old quilts stitched from the same cloth, made me marvel at the patchwork of people's hearts that seemed to assemble when people danced. I had felt the power of this expression watching Hanna in the dance studio so long ago; and

I always wondered if any of the Amish I knew had done the same, together or apart, or if they had, why nobody ever talked about it. Perhaps they believed that beauty was the flip-side of shame.

To flaunt it was to be shameful, but to hide beauty, I would learn, was the most regrettable kind of shame.

At first it had felt wrong watching Leroy and Ruthanne. I told myself to look away, to look out the window at the crescent moon and the blue-black sky of dusk, but something kept my eyes on them, as if the secret to my survival remained somewhere in their embrace.

Caesar watched them, too, but soon dropped his head between his paws and dozed off, as if this ritual were the very thing he needed to sleep well. I envied him. I was tired, too. I closed the closet door and slid the latch into place then made my way outside, through the courtyard, passing the trampoline and a garden sculpture of a small bronze dog I remember Leroy used as a mascot at the market. For years he had told me that the dog grew wings and could fly at night, which I had believed with little convincing.

I stooped down to pat its smooth metallic head, then lifted my hand and felt my own, wondering if I had become a mascot in the Outside World. I needed a reason to believe in flying dogs here and all other possibilities.

THREE

I TRIED TO SLEEP on the cot that Leroy had set up in his office above the barbershop. The room was small and cold and the windows rattled and shook the tiny potted violets on the sill every time a car passed. I lay there, listening to the ticking of a wall clock, feeling restless and worried. I felt the first of many twitches of homesickness, a longing we call *Zeitlang*, or in my case, the dull ache that comes from being wedged between two worlds. I could not stop myself from touching my head and ran my hands over the baldness. No amount of blankets or bedding could provide the comfort I needed then, because below me, in the shop, was a chair where men were expected to confess their secrets. This new knowledge hardly encouraged sleep.

I knew enough about confessions in one world to fear them just the same in the other. If the Amish act against the church after we choose baptism— divorce, file a lawsuit, join the army, connect to public power lines, install wall-to-wall carpeting, use rubber tires, drive a truck or a tractor, to name a few offenses—we face public shaming. Communion is not enough to ensure our obedience to the Ordnung, but confession, either by free will or requested, seems to keep us straight. The point is to remind us of our sacred vow of submission. From what I'd heard about the Catholics, climbing inside a little wooden closet to tell a priest what you'd done wrong was far less humiliating than standing before your entire congregation.

I wondered if perhaps the old barber chair was Leroy's way of connecting to God, even though I couldn't imagine what a man like him could have done wrong in his life. Whenever I had asked him about the scar on his face, the one he got in Korea that looked like someone had sewn a purple zipper across his jaw, he said a shark bit him. Then he'd laugh and shrug, "Gotta watch out for them Great Whites."

Maybe it was Leroy's poking fun at us, in public, at his makeshift stand in the market that he regretted, and why he dedicated so much space in his shop to that big old barber chair on the stage for confessions. I walked down the spiral stairwell to see it and paused at the door, hearing a murmur. It grew louder, then tapered off into a syncopated hissing before starting up again.

I opened the door a crack expecting to see Caesar, but the dog was not in his bed beneath the cash register. He guarded the barber chair instead, perched on the stage littered with crumpled paper balls. Leroy sat in the chair with a pen in his hand, a notebook on one knee and a plate of peanut butter sandwiches on the other. He managed to light a cigar and smoke while he wrote, puffing as the words came through his pen. I'd never seen anyone write so much. I didn't know there were that many things a man could say. It amazed me to see the fluidity of the pen across paper, like a dance.

Leroy flipped the page every minute. He never once lifted his pen off the page, as if any sudden movement would arrest the flow. I have to admit, watching someone write is not interesting. I was more curious about the phenomena I was witnessing that night—the more Leroy wrote, the more he disappeared. First hands, then legs, arms, torso, neck and face. All I saw was the pen moving across the notebook pages.

I stood there in awe. The only man I knew who could disappear with as much ease as he could walk on water was Jesus himself, but it didn't look like Leroy was trying to perform any miracles that night, or impress God.

Staring at Leroy made me realize that the bishop had been right. God has no face. It was the only explanation for what I was seeing. A part of Leroy became God when he wrote and I wanted to know what that felt like. If writing this fast with this many words was a way to escape, I wanted to hide there until my hair grew back. Somewhere, somehow, far from my father's Kingdom of Simplicity and beyond any faith I had put in Florida, I was determined to disappear. Just like my sisters. But it would not be dark and sad like death. It would be full of light, this place, where I could be happy.

◇

After Leroy finally fell asleep in the chair, I climbed the stairs and crawled back into the cot, only to wake to the familiar scraping of steel wheels in the road and the clop of hooves. It was a glorious Sunday morning in October, the sky a breakable blue, the air crisp, the light offensively bright. For a moment, I thought I was home, but seeing the fields of our farms framed in the windows of Leroy's office did nothing to inspire me to rise and start my new life in Strasburg. I did not want to think about Emma and what I was missing with the Amish. I wanted to be busy and I told Ruthanne to put me to work. She handed me a plate of soggy waffles that I'd seen come from a box she'd pulled from the freezer, then she pointed her finger in the direction of the barbershop.

"See the boss about that."

I found Leroy wearing his white smock. It was Sunday, but the Lord's Day wasn't only for the Catholics and Amish. I knew the Atheists took time off, and Agnostics, too, but not knowing which faith Leroy followed, it didn't surprise me that he exempted himself from rest of any kind. He zipped about the barbershop, whipping up shaving cream, blowing up red balloons. I thought maybe he was preparing for a birthday party, or surgery with the number of cold steel razors that gleamed from the tray at his chair. The old chair on stage had been draped with a white sheet, as if whatever use it had had for him at night was now a distraction. Although he had cleared the floor of crumpled paper balls, he left my hair in clumps there, and I stepped over them, trying not to feel angry about how much he had taken from me.

Leroy didn't seem to notice. Or care. He was too busy sharpening a razor on his coveted strop, a Pearlduck, which I'd seen him wear around on his belt buckle for years at the market. The sound always disturbed me and I felt my hair rise on the back of my neck when I heard it again, *tffffft tffffft*. He glanced my way and smiled.

"Good morning, Ugly. How'd you sleep?"

"Alright," I said. "Never been much of a sleeper."

tffffft tffffft.

He paused, motioning for me to eat my waffles.

tfffft tfffft.

"Me neither. Never been a good sleeper. I'm one of the worst sleepers in this town. When I woke up this morning, Ruthanne asked me, 'Did you sleep good?' I said, 'No, I made a few mistakes.'"

Leroy stared at me. I thought he was waiting for me to finish eating. I struggled to chew the waffles. The center was still frozen, even though the edges had been burnt.

"That it?" he asked. "That's all you got?"

"What?" I asked, my mouth full. I was not used to standing up and eating, but I figured this is what the English did and I better make it a habit. I offered the other half to Leroy, even though he didn't want a waffle, but the acknowledgement of his joke.

tfffft tfffft tfft tfft tf tf tf

"Guess it's hard to sleep right in a chair," I said.

"Mmmmm. Uh-huh," Leroy grunted, eyes narrowed, slits as sharp as the blades on his tray. I set the plate down on the chair beside us, feeling awkward under his gaze.

"They're sharp," I said, shifting my eyes to the razors.

Leroy picked one up from the tray.

"German-made. From the great Solingen manufactures. Your father probably knows all about them," he said, then rattled off names like Graef & Schmidt and Twin Works. He said one of the razors was from the Civil War and was used to shave the faces of Confederate defectors.

"You ever use a razor blade?"

"With my hands?" I asked and laughed.

"No. With your teeth. What's so funny?"

"I can't use a razor, Leroy."

He grunted again then took his reading glasses from the pocket of his smock and crouched to study my hands. He traced the webbing with his own fingers, careful not to touch me, as if there was an invisible wall between us. It had been a long time since anyone had gotten this close to my hands and I stiffened.

"Why not?" he asked.

"You know why."

Ever since the day Leroy had tried to come between Marcus and me in the market, he had never mentioned my hands again, but I thought I'd have the first words, to remind him of what he'd forgotten.

"They haven't changed," I said, and my words were as cold and sharp as the steel blades he coveted.

Leroy looked up at me and nodded.

"They're bigger," he said and uncurled my right fist. When I started to tremble, he let go just as quickly. He stood, then waltzed over to the rack on the wall and tossed me a white smock.

"Only the pros wear these."

"Pros?"

"You're hired."

I dropped the smock on the chair. I had never been hired by anyone outside my immediate family to do anything. As far as I knew, I was unemployable.

"To do what?"

Leroy cocked his head and smiled.

"To put a man's life in your hands. Go on, try it on."

I narrowed my eyes, suspicious. I was the last person to trust with another man's life. I could hardly trust myself with my own. I'll admit I was slightly disappointed, too, because, for a moment, when Leroy was tracing the webbing in my hands, I thought he might be thinking about slicing through it to spare me the humiliation of having to go to Florida six months after my cousins expected me there. But this was not his plan. I felt my heart sink and reached for the smock, but Leroy handed me the straight edge razor.

"I mean try this on. Hold it stiff. Like this."

Leroy picked one up from the tray and showed me.

I slid the bone handle of the razor into the only space between my fingers where the webbing stopped, a fraction below the first knuckle, between the middle and ring finger of my left hand, surprised how easily it sat there. Leroy was impressed, too. "You're meant for this."

He picked up a mug of shaving cream. "You know the Egyptians kneeled on the edge of the road while the street barber shaved their heads?" he asked, whipping up foam.

He set the mug of shaving cream on the chair and took out a black marker from his coat pocket and drew a face on the balloon. Eyes. Ears. Mouth. Throat. He carved the face into fourteen sections and numbered each one. Six sections along the throat, including three beneath the chin, five along the chin, sweeping across the face in an earlobe to earlobe arc. He left a square patch beneath the bottom lip, two above the upper lip, adding arrows in every section to help me direct the razor up or down.

"This is your map," he said. "As long as you follow the lines, you won't get lost."

I nodded reluctantly, unable to find the value of a map drawn in magic marker on a balloon. If this was the way I was supposed to navigate my new life among the English, I was bound to get lost, just like the tourists.

I studied the diagram. It was a jumble of arrows and numbers with the words freehand and backhand repeated all over with various combinations of up and down. It looked confusing. I turned to Leroy who slathered another balloon with shaving cream, using long arm strokes as if the balloon itself were a canvas that promised great art.

"Follow the map," he said, pointing. "Stroke one. Right cheek. Beneath the earlobe."

One freehand down, two backhand down. Upper lip. Three freehand down. Moving below the chin. Four freehand down. And the throat. Five freehand up. Right side. Repeat. Six backhand down, seven, freehand down. Right side upper lip. Eight backhand down. Below the chin. Nine backhand down. And throat. Ten freehand up.

Leroy stroked and spoke. He said the word barber comes from the Latin word *barba*, which means beard, and that a long time ago, barbers were considered the most important men of their tribes. They healed and cured and blessed. He said barbers arranged marriages and baptisms, too, and that during exorcisms, barbers encouraged evil spirits to come out of a person's body by permitting their hair to hang loosely over their shoulders.

"Hold up," I said. "My hair was hangin' loosely over my shoulders yesterday. Why did you shave it all off?"

Leroy jabbed the razor in the air. "After an exorcism dance, barbers would cut the long hair of the possessed then comb the short hair tightly against the head so that the bad spirits stayed out and the good spirits stayed in."

"But now I have no hair. How's that protection?"

"It's not. It's honor."

He said that shaving dated back to Alexander the Great, who ordered the soldiers of Macedonia to shave before going into battle to prevent the enemy from pulling his men to the ground and slaughtering them like the Persians had done. Many men followed the trend, creating jobs for barbers.

"See? There's even economics in shaving."

I wasn't thinking about economics. I was concerned about the duties of my new job and how I'd ever get past the red balloon with a razor.

"Watch carefully," he said, moving the razor across the middle of the chin for stroke number ten. Stroke eleven. Freehand across. Base of the throat below the Adam's Apple. Then above to the jugular, which he called the BB, The Big

Bleeder. Twelve freehand down. Thirteen freehand up. "This here's your power point. Don't let it scare you. Barbers have always been equipped for blood."

According to Leroy, priests and monks were the doctors of the Dark Ages. They employed barbers as assistants, and this partnership worked for 1,700 years. Barbers had the sharpest tools and knew about human anatomy. Bloodletting had become a typical service to clean out toxins, and they advertised it by placing troughs of fresh blood in their shop windows. (Apparently, George Washington died as a result of this well-intentioned service.) The red stripe on the barber pole denoted the blood taken, and the white stripe, the bandage given in return. Leroy paused to look at me.

"If you haven't struck an artery by now, you can proceed with the final stroke, below the bottom lip."

"The Soul Patch?" I asked, reading the map at fourteen freehand. "Up or down. There's no arrow."

Leroy smiled. "Whatever you want. You're home free at that point. The man is alive. You ready to try?"

FOUR

I WANTED DESPERATELY TO retain the value Leroy had assigned to my hands that day. Not because I wanted a job in the Outside World; I wanted a reason to belong. Leroy warned me that learning to shave with a straight-edge razor would exhaust me, that there would be days when I'd curse him and his bag of balloons but the real work was keeping Emma Beiler off my mind. I put every effort into forgetting her by popping my way through a bag of 300 red balloons. Caesar had grown so used to the sound that he'd no longer bark, but he'd whine whenever they popped, feeling my frustration.

When Leroy and I got tired of blowing up balloons, we used Ruthanne's Styrofoam dummy heads, which Leroy would inspect for scrape marks. Finding many, he'd say try again, promising me I was almost there. Once I shaved him without nicks, I'd be ready for his clients. He didn't want me practicing on the balloons in front of them either. "Don't spook them before they can trust you," he said.

In the meanwhile, I swept the floors, answered the phone, took appointments and took out the trash. At night, I worked on my shaving skills, conveniently interrupting the thoughts of Emma that drifted through my head.

Rather than dwell on my stupidity for rejecting her, I focused on the foam dummy. I found it to be a strange comfort, too. It was faceless, for starters, and holding it, wrapping my hands around another white bald head, made me feel less alone. Leroy would often find me in the morning, asleep with my arm draped around it, tucked warmly beneath the covers. I became Leroy's apprentice the day the head felt smoother than when we'd pulled it from the box.

One Tuesday in November, Leroy introduced me as his partner to a room full of men, who'd been curious for months about the new "man" they'd be trusting with their lives. Ruthanne ordered donuts for the occasion, and the powdered sugar had dusted their suits and coats, all of them dressed for the rite of passage when Leroy abdicated his art to a boy with webbed hands. None of the men seemed convinced or excited about my appointment, only baffled when Leroy made the transition, handing me the Civil War razor, asking his patrons, "Who's a brave man?"

They stood still, donuts suspended above coffee cups, arrested in mid-chew. It seemed they all scratched their necks or noses at once. Nobody spoke.

"Don't tell me you're afraid of a little blood," Leroy said, eyes locked on the taxidermist, who had only two days prior sat in the shop for hours, recounting the details of how he'd shot and stuffed a fourteen-point buck. Even the Amish hunted and I was impressed with the aim of a small man whose eyes constantly twitched. His name was William Nepher, but he preferred to be called Willy even though Leroy called him Tooth because he lost his big one on the sidewalk outside the shop one night drunk. Apparently Tooth had always had a lisp, but now he whistled through the gap when he talked, drooling and slobbering his protest against Leroy's volunteering him for death.

Leroy stuffed a fresh donut in his mouth and pushed him in the chair. The other men, already late for work, decided that seeing me shave Tooth's beard was something not to miss, and so they scrambled to the telephone, forming a line to call their secretaries and bosses to tell them they'd "witnessed an accident" and would be late.

Leroy draped a silver cape over Tooth's shoulders and turned to the growing crowd, which had now extended out the door and down the block, drawing more and more passersby to the window. Even school children paused to identify the source of wonder and terror. Leroy rolled his eyes and told me not to worry, to focus on the diagram, which he had asked me to mount on the mirror above my work station, along with a wishbone he'd hung for good luck. Not that I needed it, he said. It was simply a marketing tactic to put his clients at ease.

I would not say Tooth was at ease. He shivered under the cape while Leroy sharpened the razor on the Pearlduck strop, testing it against his thumbnail. He decided it was sharp enough to cut through the tangle of beard, which looked no different from my father's or that of any other Amish man who had worn one since the day he got married. It was thick and tough, like stale bread crust, and I wasn't convinced that two hot towels would be enough to soften it. Sensing my unease, Leroy handed me two more towels, then pointed to his neck, reminding me to put a third there to soften the insides of a nervous man. I lay the others on his face, and despite being buried beneath hot wet towels, Tooth managed to speak.

"How many other men have you shaved?"

I pointed to Leroy, "Besides him?"

Tooth gasped and Leroy patted his shoulder.

"Deep breath, Tooth. You'll be done soon. Eli's fast."

But I wasn't. Not then. I had grown so used to the Styrofoam dummies, that the warm flesh of the man made my hands slow down and shake. It was not the blood I resisted as much as the notion that I'd betrayed Tooth in some way by shaving him. I didn't know his faith and paused in the middle, at stroke seven, to ask him if he had ever been an Anabaptist.

"The hell kind of question is that? You preparing me to meet my maker?"

I told him, no, he'd have to wear better clothes for that. Tooth snarled under the towels, but Leroy howled, and the men watching hooted and hollered and cheered me on. It got quiet as I got closer to the Big Bleeder, then everyone chanted the stroke numbers, following Leroy who clapped to pace me. Swift and sure, he mouthed whenever I looked up, hesitant to touch Tooth's throat with the razor.

"We don't have to do this," I said.

Tooth said, "Shit or get off the pot."

I looked up at Leroy who shrugged. I could feel all the eyes of the men on me, waiting, eager for me to finish. For a moment, I felt as if I were in the middle of a volleyball game. It had been a long time since I'd voluntarily put myself in any situation where people were focused on me. I imagined Tooth's neck as the net and the razor as the ball. I looked down once to visualize the man's neck, then closed my eyes. The men gasped as I felt my way along Tooth's throat, clearing the man's Big Bleeder with three swift strokes. That's when the men let out a collective sigh and erupted in applause.

Leroy slapped aftershave on Tooth's face and told him to take a look, but the taxidermist remained in the chair, staring up at the ceiling with a smile wider than the moon. He kept feeling his face with his hand, rubbing it over each cheek, cooing and gurgling like a baby. He stared up at me out of his twinkling blue eyes and threw his arms around me. I tried to wrestle myself free, but he hugged me harder, saying he hadn't had a shave that close since the day he'd been married and that I'd just made his wife the happiest woman on the planet. He kissed me on the forehead and hugged me again, leaving me dumbstruck and stiff. Everyone said Tooth looked twenty years younger and acted like it, too.

After he paid, I swear he skipped down the sidewalk, but I can't be sure because as soon as he walked out the door, the line pushed itself inside and everyone demanded a shave. Leroy took names, assigned times, and promised ten-minute appointments. He offered donuts and coffee while they waited and called Ruthanne to bring more of each. Not a single Englisher complained about the wait, and for the next three hours, they stood quietly, determined to experience my services, which in that first morning were rumored to have tripled Leroy's business.

My hand cramped up after the third hour and Leroy ushered me into the storage room to show me how to massage it and shoved it into a tub of Ben-Gay. "You're doing great," he encouraged.

"This is beginner's luck."

"You're no beginner, Ugly. You're a natural."

He wrapped my wrists with medical tape and sent me back on the floor to shave two lawyers, a doctor, three professors who looked like Amish men in cardigan sweaters and bow ties, an Irish plumber with a red beard, an Italian electrician with no beard but black stubble, young men who hardly had more hair on their faces than I did, old men with bad eyes and more hair than they could see. They all seemed pleased with my work. They wanted to know who I was, where I'd come from, how Leroy found me and how long I'd last, because everyone knew Leroy Fischer's employees had the shelf-life of a pear. They bruised easily, too, wounded by his razor-like tongue and brutal hours.

"Ugly comes from good stock," Leroy said, promising them I'd be setting a world record that day, which only encouraged them to linger and share the historic moment. When I had finished that night and sat weary, soaking my hands in a bowl of warm water and Epsom salts, it occurred to me that none of the English had asked a single question about my hands. Leroy didn't seem fazed.

"Who cares?"

I stared at him, trying to remember a time when my hands were of no concern to strangers.

"Ugly, look. Those men don't even see your hands."

"That's impossible. What do they see then?"

"They see a pro."

FIVE

I WANTED TO BELIEVE Leroy. I wanted to believe that as long as I worked in the barbershop, nobody could see what made me different. The more I worked on the men, the more they liked me. I was quick. I 'turned' a dozen chairs a day, twice that on Saturdays. Sometimes the English would find excuses to hang out at the shop just to watch me work. I found it curious they had so much time on their hands. I imagined the exasperated look on granddatt's face had he seen them standing around doing nothing, offering idle hands to the devil's workshop. But the men were happy doing nothing, and even if my job didn't serve the Amish, I was happy doing nothing, too. The more I engaged with the Outside World, the less I thought about how to re-enter the Amish, though the past was always there to remind me of who I was. For the first time in my life, I did not feel compelled to hide from the English, but sought their company.

They opened their homes to me and introduced me to their favorite television shows, taught me the basics of football and included me in their Monday Night pools. They brought me baseball cards, taught me how to read the Wall Street Journal, gave me tips on the stock market, how much and when to invest. They brought me magazines of girls and cars, even though I had no use for either. I couldn't understand their generosity. I didn't give them gifts. Leroy said that wasn't the point.

"Sometimes a man doesn't need to know much about another to decide he likes him. They sense your intentions, Ugly."

True, I wasn't after their money or their gifts. I wanted to do good by the Englishers, because as far as I knew, they were good people and it felt good to be liked and needed by them.

I could fix their roofs and leaky faucets, help them churn over better soil by building compost piles in their yards. I hadn't realized how much I'd learned growing up on our farm, but my education from the land often seemed more practical than the higher education of the English I was meeting. They often seemed incapable of the kinds of duties we'd assumed as children, basic cleaning inside the home and repairing washers and dryers (ours ran on air compressors and gas), and later, lawn mowers and clocks and anything that had a spring- loading device. I helped the English with unskilled jobs, too, like hauling junk out of their basements and garages. I even taught a few of their wives how to can fruit and vegetables, which I'd learned from spending time with the Amish women while the men raised barns.

They wanted to repay me and offered driving lessons, but I declined, accepting lessons in golf instead. When the course froze, they ushered me into their private gyms. The first time I went to 'the fitness center,' a YMCA in the city, I stood stiff and open-mouthed, staring through the large windows to the room where men and women shared sweaty mats and bicycles that didn't move. Even more astonishing were the number of legs and shoulders and arms I could see. Besides the night I'd tried bundling with Emma Beiler, I'd never seen so much bare skin in my life. I must have alarmed the trainer, a red-haired woman named Marion the Barbarian who looked like a cross between Uncle Enos and our Clydesdales. She stepped out of the sweaty room and snapped her gum when she spoke. "Stop gawking, kid. I'm too old for you."

The girls at the front desk turned and giggled, then elbowed each other and said, "We're not." I was hungry and they offered me a granola bar and I ate standing up. When I finished, I handed back the wrapper and they batted their eyes and said, "You're cute, Ugly."

I didn't return to the 'fitness center' after that and told the insurance agent who had taken me that I would find enough to do at the shop. He seemed concerned about my "getting enough exercise" there. I couldn't understand the obsession the English had with physical fitness, when all I'd ever seen them do was eat too much at the market. I guess I'd never noticed living on our farm, but I had no idea how much time the English spent jogging. A group of men from the shop invited me to join them, but when I outran them by six miles the first time, they didn't invite me back. Even Ruthanne was "Sweating to the Oldies" through some tape she'd borrowed from the public library. A man named Richard Simmons would teach her the steps and it was my role to correct her form. Once a week, she'd call me to sit on the living room couch and watch her—a blind woman doing aerobics with a fat man. As soon as she was through, she'd reward herself and me with pints of ice cream, which she sent me to get from the Strasburg Creamery next door, without Leroy ever knowing.

What was just as strange about these invitations is that they happened every Tuesday night. Leroy had given me my own appointment book to mark the date, time, and place I had agreed to meet his clients, declaring Tuesday my official day off. I objected. The Amish aren't used to free time like the English. Free time makes us anxious. Makes us think that something's wrong—like we've neglected a farm animal or rushed our chores, making waste with our haste. The first thing I did every morning before breakfast was to check the appointment book to see if there were any gaps in the schedule, and if so, I'd devise ways to fill them by doing chores for Ruthanne. She said in the thirty years they'd been living in the carriage house, 1983 was the cleanest. She said Mamm had done a good job of raising me.

I told Leroy it wouldn't be fair to schedule me to a four-day week when he worked six. We were supposed to be partners and I wanted to do my share; two shaves for every one of his haircuts to keep our earnings the same, which meant I really couldn't afford to take Tuesdays off. When I suggested we stagger the invitations throughout the week rather than stuff them all into one day, the men turned to Leroy for answers. He ignored them, but later, at dinner, he'd remind me of what exactly I had agreed to do the following Tuesday, with whom and for how long. He was especially concerned about when I'd return.

"If you plan to be out past two, just give us a call. Let it ring a few times so we're sure to wake up though."

"Okay," I said, trying hard to think of a reason I'd have for wanting to stay out past two o' clock. The last time I'd been up that late was to help Uncle Isaac and his heifer deliver her calf on my birthday.

I wondered if Leroy expected me to go to parties like the other Amish kids who passed through his shop. When I asked him, he said, "I don't care if you party or not. Go to a movie. Or the mall. You just need some time off."

At first, I thought he was being protective. He emphasized that if he didn't give me enough free time, he'd be liable for violating child-labor laws. I stared, head cocked and said, "Leroy. I come from an Amish family. Child labor *is* the law." He'd grunt and tell me things here were different and that English teenagers were supposed to stay out past midnight at least once a week.

I had never heard of this custom and reminded him there was no curfew during *rumspringa*. He'd huff, "Then why not make the most of your night?" as if Tuesday was the only night I'd be permitted to explore the Outside World.

Potluck dinners at Evangelical churches and bingo halls filled with peg-leggers from the V.A. and Kiwanis Club were not my idea of adventure. Ruthanne had insisted they would be by asking me to take her on my scooter, and stay to make sure she marked her cards right. When I told her I didn't gamble, she rubbed the stubble on my head. "You asked Leroy to cut your hair. That's about the greatest gamble you've ever taken."

Maybe she was right, but even if I had indulged in 'sin for a season' like so many Amish kids, I would not have chosen to gamble. I decided only to engage in activities I imagined the bishop might have done while he was going through *rumspringa*.

◇

I went to the movies. A lot. I had never been to a movie theater and when the men in the shop found out, they fell silent and covered their gaping mouths.

"Ugly, you're a heretic to pop culture. What'd they do to you on the farm?"

I shrugged.

I expected the professors to educate me on the wonders of the silver screen, but it was the taxidermist, Tooth, who knew the most. He'd rise from his chair with great deference when he spoke about men named Truffaut, Fellini, Bergman, Wilder, men whose names he'd spell out with bars of soap on the mirrors. He liked to argue over the merits of a new young filmmaker named George Lucas and needed me to settle his dispute. He took me downtown to the Brunswick Theater to see George Lucas' film about a space farmer. It kept me awake for a week thinking about all the things I'd seen like spaceships, robots with odd accents, and tall hairy creatures who spoke by grunting.

I kept looking around the theater. When Tooth asked me what I was looking for, I told him and he laughed. "You have to go to Hollywood to meet George Lucas."

I asked, "Where's that?"

After that, other men from the shop fought to take me to the movies and "give me culture." They were Leroy's oldest clients, The Double OO's, he called them: Outrageous Octogenarians, a bunch of widowers, whose children had long since left Strasburg. They took me to see silent films and films about true things, but I liked the stories best. They asked me if I liked to dance. I said I wasn't much of a dancer, but I liked to watch dancing and they said, "done." I wasn't sure what they were so worked up about in "Flashdance". It seemed the story was about a dancer who changed her leg warmers in every shot, which depressed me, not because she was being extravagant (they said everything in Hollywood was excessive and to find a way to accept it), but because the old warehouse where she danced reminded me of Hanna and my sisters.

I sat in the lobby until the movie ended.

After that, I decided to ask a bit more about the movies they suggested. I wanted to see nothing that had a girl as the lead, or girls who danced. They chose "Octypussy" but Leroy said it would be too much stimulation for me, that "Return of the Jedi" had already threatened my alertness and that they would be the ones who suffered from my lack of sleep should a razor ever slip. They insisted on comedies after that. They gave me the choice between "Trading Places" and "Risky Business."

One Tuesday night in late December, when I asked which theater was showing these movies, because location often determined my choice, Leroy looked up from the paper and said, "Only one. Dutch Wonderland." This was not good. Anyone who knew anything about the culture of *rumspringa* knew that Amish kids parked their pick-up trucks at night in the parking lot of the amusement park and theater, where they blended better with tour buses and cars than the buggies and wagons on their farms. A crowded tourist-trap parking lot on a Tuesday night during the darkest and coldest days of the year meant one of two things: a storm had stranded motorists along Route 30, or Amish kids planned to meet.

A full moon filled the sky that night, the kind of night when most Amish don't worry about traveling in the dark no matter what they're driving. I stood outside the door, shivering and hesitant. Tooth, my chaperon for the night, flipped up the rabbit collar on his coat. "What's wrong, Ugly?"

"Nothing," I said, worried for the first time that I didn't look English enough. I was wearing a pair of used brown corduroys with thick ribbing, a T-shirt, and a flannel button down, but the sleeves were too short and the pants too long. It was one thing to wear these things in the shop, where Leroy's clients didn't care what I wore. But standing there in the parking lot, looking into the lobby of the theater at Amish faces I had known for years, made me feel like an imposter.

I didn't realize that Tooth had opened the door. Warm air rushed out to meet us.

"Go on in," he urged. "Get warm."

From an outsider's perspective, nothing seemed unusual. The theater staff ripped tickets and handed back stubs and throngs of pimple-faced teenagers milled about the concession stand, hauling off buckets of popcorn, candy, and sodas the size of small wells. But if you looked closely, you'd notice that none of the teenagers ever stood alone, not like the English, who were in the minority that night. Among the majority, there was no specific crowd either, only small clusters separated by gender, just one of several clues that these were Amish kids in *rumspringa*. The English wore faded jeans and T-shirts;

the Amish kids who looked like they'd been dressed together in very stiff, dark blue jeans. It was their shoes that gave them away—work boots, heels stuck with chicken feathers, and the odor they carried on their coats, a kind of sweet sweat that comes from the work done before dawn. If I'd closed my eyes, I could have been in our barn.

I walked behind Tooth with my head down, grateful for his height and the dozens of donuts he consumed in the barbershop each week. When he turned to ask if I'd like some popcorn, I whispered, "Not now." And he said, "Now's the only time to get it." Tooth refused to see a movie if he got there late, and he bragged that he could hold his pee until the final credit. He boasted to the men in the shop how he'd once watched a double feature after consuming a 64-ounce Dr. Pepper.

I decided now was the time to relieve myself and told Tooth I'd meet him outside the theater door, but no sooner had I walked out of the men's room did I stop, arrested by the sight of a young woman leaving the women's room at the same time. She was wearing stiff blue jeans and a pink sweater that clung to her hips and breasts. Her long dark hair hung loosely over her shoulders and was pinned behind her ears by two pink sparkly barrettes that had replaced her bobby pins and prayer cap.

"Eli?"

"Emma?"

"I thought you were in Florida."

"I thought you'd be baptized."

That's all we said. I don't know whose face burned more. Emma turned and ran past the door for "Risky Business," then ducked under the Exit sign and disappeared outside. I ran after her and searched the parking lot, hoping to find her in one of the trucks, but I found nothing, only one couple who had skipped the movies and decided to keep each other warm by making-out. They didn't notice I'd opened the door. They hadn't even bothered to change out of their Amish clothes, or what remained of them. Black suspenders dangled over the seat. I closed the door over the leather fasteners and stood exasperated. I had no idea where Emma had gone and, against my will, I turned back to the theater to watch a movie about trading places. I didn't need Hollywood to tell me what I already knew about trying to be somebody else.

SIX

GREISLICH WAS THE WORD that came to mind. Horrible. My mother used to say it after the accident, and it rang in my head for days after Dutch Wonderland. Though I didn't mention anything to Leroy, he sensed my sudden gloom and thought it'd be appropriate to cheer me up with a gift.

"Your girlfriend stopped by this morning," he said and handed me a small package wrapped in brown paper.

I was working on the postman and set the razor on the edge of the sink and turned to Leroy. He flashed his gold tooth and I could feel all the eyes of the men on me, too. They'd even turned the radio down and shut off the TV.

"Ugly's got a girlfriend?"

They seemed baffled and sat up in their chairs, and those who had been waiting, drinking coffee or doing the morning crossword puzzle, folded their newspapers. Even Caesar, who'd been sleeping in the puddle of sunlight by the door, got up and wagged his tail, sniffing the string dangling from the package, pulling it with his teeth.

"Leave me alone, dog. I can open it myself."

"Sure you can."

One of the men got up and crossed to the door, poked his head outside and called to anyone within earshot.

"Big Ugly's got a girlfriend. She left him a gift, and he's opening it right now."

Leroy walked over and shut the door.

"For Christ's sake. He's not a circus performer," he said and the man shrank back and sat in his seat. "But he is a magician. How come you didn't tell us you had a girl?"

I narrowed my eyes, feeling the first swell of anger.

"Because. That's one of the Five Forbidden Topics."

Leroy nodded, and I pointed up to a faded poster that listed, in order of offense, the things Leroy forbade anyone to talk about in his barbershop. Politics. Religion. A man's reputation. A man's salary. And his romantic relationships.

"Are you in love?"

"No," I said. "I don't even know who sent this."

"Sure you do. Pretty young thing. Tall for a girl. Slender. Big green eyes and a smile that could melt steel?"

I pursed my lips, folded my arms across my chest.

"I don't know anybody like that."

Leroy paused, arched his eyebrow.

"Seems to me she'd be pretty dang hard to forget."

My hands started to shake and I tapped the sink with the razor. The postman sat up, alarmed.

"She break your heart, Ugly?"

"No," I said and swallowed, wishing I had the courage to tell them I'd broken hers. "Did you tell her I was staying here?"

Leroy snapped the cape in his hand.

"She didn't ask. She figured that out on her own."

"Why don't you open her gift?" the postman asked.

"I will later."

"We want to see," the other men said, urging me on with their chanting, banging the bottoms of their coffee cups on books and magazines. *Ugly. Ugly. Ugly.*

I squeezed the package, feeling something squishy, and peeled back the paper to find a hand-knit black wool cap. Hoots and hollers from the men.

"Somebody's keeping an eye on you, Ugly. Try it on!"

I stiffened, but managed to pull the hat over my head. They clapped and cheered. I cringed, feeling stupid. I didn't like how the English seemed so keen on spectacle. They sought it and where there wasn't any, they created it, even at the cost of a man's humility.

"Looks good," the postman said. "Fits you well."

"You should see the girl," Leroy bellowed.

"She cute?" one of the men asked.

I didn't like them bringing Emma into the shop. It felt wrong to hear them talk about her with the same kind of excitement I'd hear when they talked about the swimsuit girls in the magazines.

"She's the bishop's daughter."

"Woweeee. You aiming high, Ugly. Getting in with a holy man's daughter! That's something to tell the folks."

"I'm not getting in anywhere," I said, feeling hot and crowded and very small.

"Now you're talking some truth. You know you can't just up and marry an Amish girl if you're not Amish yourself," the postman announced.

"Marrying?" I asked. "Who said anything about marrying? I just learned how to hold a razor straight."

The men laughed but Leroy walked over to me and lowered his voice.

"She said you're missed."

I stared into the sink and the grey scum of stubble floating above milky water, relieved that I could no longer see my reflection. "I know," I said, my mind far from the shop, adrift in Paradise and Providence.

I was upset that Emma knew where I was living now, and I wondered how many others she might have told. I wished she had left a letter with the hat, even a short note. I needed to know what she thought of all this, and perhaps learn how she thought I might proceed. I went to bed early that night. Leroy knocked on the door.

"I'm sleeping," I said, smelling peanut butter.

"Don't sound like you're sleeping."

He opened the door with a plate of sandwiches and crossed to the window to water a new row of violets he'd potted that morning. Since I'd arrived, he'd filled two small shelves he'd built from 2x4s and crowded them with violets of every variety.

"You know if you keep a violet in good shape it'll flower almost continuously?"

I shook my head and pulled the sheet higher over my face, groaning.

"Nope. Didn't know that."

I was sick of those tiny plants with their thick, green hairy leaves. Leroy was in the process of collecting and alphabetizing every variety. He had started from Z and worked backward through B. I thought he was joking when he told me the names of his favorites, each a certain shade of white, violet, or pink with a distinct petal size and shape: Baby Bell, Baker's Hot Lips, Bambino, Barbie's Dream, and the Barbara's, Barbara Ann, Barbara Jean, Barbara Sisk - then Bean Jester, Becky, Bayou Baby, and Bell Ringing Fool.

"Bell Ringing Fool?" I asked.

"Speaks to you, does it?" he asked, then pulled the violet off the shelf and handed it to me with a sandwich. "Misery loves company."

"I'm not miserable," I said and set the violet on the small table beside my cot, where a Bible had been opened to Revelations. Leroy, of course, took notice.

"Hmmmm. Learn anything new?"

"To love my enemies."

"How's that going?"

I stared at Leroy, feeling my jaw stiffen. It drove me crazy to see him amused by my reactions. He smiled.

"So?"

I closed the Bible. "Why do you love violets so much?"

"What's there not to love?"

"You love flowers more than Mamm."

"Your mama's not alone in her affair, Ugly. There's loads of us violet lovers. Whole societies. We love violets for their character. They're durable, especially for the unskilled thumb like mine. Violets love even a black thumb almost unconditionally. They're a very forgiving plant. Even when I forget to water them, they still flower."

I stared at him perplexed, this dark man with the white hair and plaid pajamas, shuffling around wooden floors in moccasins he'd bought from a Cherokee shaman, which Leroy pronounced shay-man, and I mistook for the Deitsh word *shenka*, which means to give a gift or pardon.

Leroy sat down beside me on the bed and opened an Auto Trader magazine on his lap. He reached over me and took a pen from the desk.

"You know what your problem is?"

"I don't love violets."

Both of Leroy's eyebrows jumped up and he smiled.

"Maybe. Seems Doe-Eyes has the quality of a violet."

"I don't want to talk about her. And her name is Emma. Emma Mae Beiler. Not Doe-Eyes. And I don't love her. Yet."

"Okay. Fair enough. Let's talk about your name, Ugly."

I lifted my eyes to meet his, regretful I'd not locked the door of the office and pretended to be sleeping. He scribbled in the Auto Trader and pointed to the letters he'd scrambled across the windshield of a truck, caught beneath the wiper blade like an insect, each letter as vulnerable as a wing. It read L I E.

"You know there's a lie in Eli?"

"I can't imagine," I murmured, wishing Leroy would turn off the light and leave me alone. Instead, he tore off the crust on the bread and chewed and swallowed it without blinking or looking away. Only the flitter of Leroy's photographs, lifted by the cool breeze coming in through the window, broke our silence. Leroy got up and left me alone when he finished his sandwich. He did not mention the lie again.

The only direction I moved that night was down the stairs and up on the stage to sit in Leroy's old barber chair. I clicked on the spotlight. I'd brought a notebook and a pencil from his desk, hoping to disappear, like him, by writing a letter to Emma. I had never successfully written anything longer than my name, address, a date, the phone number of a veterinarian, the numbers for the auction. Holding the pencil in the half-inch gap between the webbing and my fingers was no easy task. As soon as the thoughts came, the pencil seemed to slip, jerked about by the unsteady stream of such thinking. I couldn't keep up with the thoughts and had no way of keeping track of them, let alone making them legible. No matter how hard I tried, the bulbous letters looked like they'd been written by a child.

Sitting there alone in Leroy's barber chair made me realize how much I hadn't said in my life and how much I needed to say it. I wondered if this was the lie that Leroy had seen in me. Even more frustrating was the realization that as long as I couldn't write, I would never disappear. Feeling the blood surge in my hands, I hurled the notebook across the stage floor and snapped the pencil in half. Then I heard a clap and turned, seeing Leroy at the door with his own notebook, a pen behind each ear and a plate of 'cigars,' thin bologna slices rolled up in white cheese—Leroy's signature.

"Got a confession?" he asked, trying hard to keep from smiling, but he snorted his laughter instead. I scratched my ear. I didn't like him snickering.

"Nothing that I'd want to share with you."

"You sure? Who would I tell?"

"The whole world. You got a mouth bigger than Jonah."

"I don't know the *whole* world. Only half. What can't you tell half the world?"

I looked down at the bits of broken pencil, the lead and the wood in my lap, as if they were parts of my soul that had to split open to let my heart write. I whispered the words as they struck me. "I don't know how to forgive."

Leroy walked over and handed me a bologna cigar as if discussing this would make us both hungry. He studied me in the funnel of light from the spotlight and said two words that sounded vaguely familiar. "Just laugh."

SEVEN

OVER THE NEXT FEW weeks, I struggled to see the connection between laughter and forgiveness. Sensing this conflict, Leroy turned to me in the barbershop one day when a group of high school girls, mostly cheerleaders, pressed their lips against the window, trying to get my attention. They made me nervous. I didn't want them licking the glass like that after I'd spent so much time cleaning it. I marched to the window and squirted it with a bottle of Windex, hoping that when I wiped the glass, the girls would disappear, too. But no matter how much I tried to avoid them, they showed up, trying to get me to talk. They said my accent was sexy. Finally, I hung a sign on the door that read: Patrons Only. No Loitering Please.

I was tired of feeling like a zoo animal inside the barbershop. At least none of the clients ever bothered to comment on my hands. After all, they were trusting me with their lives, no matter how much they wanted to joke about the webbing. The high school girls were different. The truth is, I liked the attention that the girls were giving me, but I didn't like how they reminded me of Emma.

"What you'd do to that poor girl, huh?"

"What girl?"

Leroy stood by his chair, oiling scissors. "The only one that matters to you."

"You wouldn't understand."

"Try me."

"It's too complicated."

"Can't be more complicated than the arrangement between you and me."

I sighed and tossed a wadded-up paper towel in the trash can.

"Trust me. It makes this look easy."

Leroy grunted and laid down the scissors. "This secret of yours. Did you hurt another person?"

I stared at him. "Not really. Not exactly. No."

"Did you kill somebody?"

"No, Leroy! Of course, not. Why would you say something like that? I didn't kill anything."

"Sometimes you sure act like you did. Like you regret the very air you're breathin,' boy. But let me tell you, if you didn't kill nobody, you're in pretty good shape."

I stared at him, but Leroy cast his gaze into the mirror and spoke to my reflection as if there was some kind of salvation in his message. "The only confession you need to make is to yourself, Ugly. You take yourself way too seriously. Life is not a test. The test is whether or not you can allow yourself to enjoy it. The minute you can laugh at yourself, you can forgive yourself. Easy."

I wanted to believe every word he said was true, but I had never been taught to focus on enjoyment. I did not come from a people who relied on humor for their survival, like Leroy did. Part of me envied the ease with which he embraced it, calling laughter the True Messiah. From what I understood, life was a test, and one that I'd been failing each year. For the Amish, life is a serious matter, but more serious than life was death, which made us even more serious as we prepared for it. It's hard to laugh when you know every thought, word, and deed could be used against you someday. I believed that by taking the photos years ago, I had already doomed myself, and there was nothing funny about that.

The Amish intend to serve others as a way to serve God, but I had not, until then, ever distinguished our purpose, what we did, from how we did it. It struck me that there was an element of joy to almost everything we did, alone or together, washing the dishes or digging a drainage ditch. I couldn't recall a single work frolic that had not turned into an enjoyable event: the buzz of the laughter that filled our homes after a quilting bee, the sense of abundance when the pantry was filled with canned fruits and vegetables—small joys that sustained us during long winters and suspended our complaints through the labor of working the earth. Even then, the harvest was one of the most exciting times of the year, bringing us together again and fostering the community we held sacred.

If Leroy was right, then I had been wrong my whole life about my purpose. Maybe God's test was to see if I could enjoy my life, find the humor in the things that made me frown. I wondered if Jesus ever laughed. For Leroy's sake, I wanted to believe he did. I recalled the night I'd opened the box of comic books and found the note, the cryptic message that read *courage is the hero that helps a boy laugh*. When I'd asked him the next day if that's why he gave me Captain Courageous, he'd said, "Just one reason. There's more," even though there was never anything funny about those cartoons.

That evening, I followed Leroy up the spiral staircase to the office where I'd slept for twelve weeks. He lead me to the floor-to-ceiling bookshelf that I'd been staring at with no interest. He stood in front of it, beaming, hands on hips, roving the shelves with the kind of reverence I'd seen reserved for sturdy work horses and harvested tobacco. Besides the Bible, the only books that commanded as much respect among the Amish were our hymnal, the *Ausbund*, and our recorded history, what we called the bloody theater, or *Martyr's Mirror*, neither funny, which Leroy guaranteed his books to be. Laughter, he said, was the greatest offering a man could make to the world, which is why he called the bookshelf his altar. "Bet you never took a look," he said.

I shook my head. "They're just books."

"Just books? You been here all this time and you weren't even curious to take a peek? What about the records?"

I shrugged, feeling the heat in my cheeks.

Leroy pulled out a small chair that flipped on hinges into a step ladder. He took two steps up and turned to me.

"This here's my life savings. Gonna make me rich."

I scratched my head, confused. Caesar had followed us in and hopped on my cot and burrowed his nose under the sheet, looking forlorn and forgotten beside Leroy's altar. Leroy pulled out books and records, introducing me to the men and women whose faces graced the covers, people he considered living saints like Richard Pryor, Bill Cosby, Carol Burnet, George Burns, George Carlin, Robin Williams.

I realized then that all the photographs on the walls of the office and the shop featured these same folks, their smiling eyes invoking the laughter they hoped to hear from their audiences. He said he'd listened and memorized the routines of Lenny Bruce, Carl Reiner, Mel Brooks and Brother Dave Gardner on used records he'd collected from local garage sales, claiming one man's junk was another man's fortune.

He climbed the ladder to the highest rung.

"Here. Supplemental reading to your Bible studies."

He passed me a pile of books, dog-eared and highlighted biographies of men whose names sounded harsh and English like W.C. Fields, the Marx Brothers, Charlie Chaplain and Sid Caesar, whose story I would come to read as a manual for understanding the heart and soul of Leroy. Lastly, and with both hands, he placed on top of the pile a book called *The Fate of Humor* by James M. Cox. Then he stepped down.

"Ever hear of Mark Twain?"

I shook my head. Aside from the occasional copy of *The Call of the Wild* in the Amish-owned and operated Gordonville Bookstore, we didn't read much high-minded literature. We read the Bible. We read the *Ausbund*. We read the land.

"You never read *Huckleberry Finn*?"

Leroy sucked in a deep breath. He held his hand over his heart, pledging his allegiance to a man he considered one of the greatest humorists of all time. That Mark Twain happened to be American was pure luck, he said, believing it was the Russians who occupied the pinnacle of humor because they created mordant wit. I had never heard such ideas, which the Amish would have construed as high-mindedness and a threat to my attention on God. As far as Leroy was concerned, humor was a god and it was his job to keep me focused on it.

I set the pile of books on the cot, reserving what Leroy had hoped would become my new bible, *The Fate of Humor*. The cover was the color of cocoa and the book had been preserved in a plastic jacket. The pages possessed the golden yellow of a fried corn fritter and smelled of pipe smoke. I flipped through it reading the subtitles: Romance, Idyll, Yankee Slang, the Ironic Stranger.

"What's an ironic stranger?"

Leroy pointed at me and said, "That's you, Big Ugly."

It felt good to hear Leroy laugh like that, bent over, grabbing at his sides as if his laughter kept him from falling off the edge of the world. He stood and wiped his eyes with the cuff of his barber smock, then held my gaze, not with a threat but with a promise to help me. "Go find Doe-Eyes and cheer yourself up."

"I'm not ready," I said and set the book down.

"Your hair's almost grown back."

"Not enough."

"Enough for you to go home."

"You want me to leave?"

"You want to leave?"

"Where would I go? What about the business?"

"Ugly, you are my business. What concerns me is that you're always thinkin' about this and that, and I know it ain't good, but you're too young to worry so much."

I nodded. He was right. I did worry.

"I have a lot to be worried about," I said.

Leroy sighed and reached out to my shoulder.

"Whatever it is you done, remember it can't be that bad, especially if you can find something funny about it. Make a man laugh, and he'll love you. Make a man laugh, and he'll forget what he hates about you. Make yourself laugh, and you'll forget what you hate about you."

Standing there, staring into Leroy's big dark eyes made me realize that humor was the sharpest tool in his survival box. He'd already taught me to use a razor. I'd seen his power at the market, how he unleashed the sparkle in our eyes and the gleam in our teeth when we smiled. I've never asked any Amish, but I think we'd all agree that we found safety in Leroy because of this. His sense of humor had sliced through the lie we kept telling ourselves, that there was only one way to be.

EIGHT

I WOKE UP AT dawn to read from Leroy's altar and I fell asleep late to finish what I'd started. I spent the nights listening to Leroy's record collection, learning the acts of Lenny Bruce and Mel Brooks while Leroy mouthed the lines. He borrowed old Groucho Marx and Bill Cosby records from the library and played them in the shop, claiming to be one of Cosby's inspirations. Apparently he and "Cos" grew up in the same building in Philadelphia in the Richard Allen Homes, the city's first housing experiments for the poor, "efficiently designed" to contain as many people as possible in one room. Leroy said he'd climbed the building at 919A Parish Place and changed the sign, painting an "e" over the first "a".

Although Leroy liked Cosby, he loved a man named Richard Pryor, simply because he endured heckling better than most other comics, and this encouraged him. When Leroy received the laser disc of Pryor hosting Saturday Night Live in 1975, we'd sit on the couch burning our tongues on bubbling pot pies or scraping burnt brownies from the trays of our TV dinners, a novelty I'd grown to love. He'd been talking about the laser disc for weeks, and when it came he'd stopped everything to watch it, even if it compromised his poker schedule with the men from the shop. I think he offended the Irish and Italian Catholics when he said Richard Pryor's routine was a real religious experience, comparing it to a visitation from the Pope or Christ Jesus himself. He shared a bit about Richard Pryor's famous moment at a place called the Troubadour in 1976, a year we both had hoped to forget.

"Rich was in the middle of a routine about black folks and religion. Rich says, 'Black people didn't have a God, we just worshipped nature… Then the white man said, "Why not worship me?" Then Rich turns to his mostly white audience and says all straight-faced, 'Now when I say white man, I don't mean everybody.' He pauses and laughs before he continues, 'But you know who you are!' That's when the hecklers started up. Hooting and hollering like they did. One heckler shouts, 'You better be glad I have a sense of humor.' And Rich? Oh, man, he just pause up on the stage and look real thoughtful and says real quick, 'Yeah, I'm sure glad you have a sense of humor, because I know what you white people do to us.' Then he got all kinds of claps from the good folks, 'cause he sure did handle that well. Don't know if I could do it."

I told Leroy I once thought that God was a black man until the bishop told me that God had no face. Leroy said he agreed, then hooked me on Saturday Night Live that winter and another black comedian named Eddie Murphy. We passed many cold nights on Leroy's old couch with Ruthanne, who evaluated the quality of Eddie Murphy's delivery since she couldn't see what he was doing.

"Eddie's good, but Richard had a bigger gift," she said, lamenting the fact that he'd set himself on fire a few years ago, admonishing, "When you get discovered, dear, don't you dare set yourself on fire and leave me here to deal with the press. Always carry two matches. One for each of us, okay?"

According to Leroy, "The truth will be funny, no matter how awful it is, even it if scares the shit outta folks, or makes them cry like a baby." If this were true, that meant my whole life had been funny, though I couldn't see the humor in any of it. Leroy said I hadn't developed a "playful mind" yet, even though his mind didn't seem playful at all the way he focused so viciously on the books he was reading. Looking back, he was never without a book. I adopted his habit and read while I worked, pausing one day with the *Fate of Humor* in my hand while I swept.

"How do you know if you're funny?"

Leroy looked up from the cash register.

"You don't. You need an audience for that."

And so I waited for Emma every day Christmas week, hoping she could come by again and give me a chance to explain my leaving the Amish. I wanted to make her laugh and show her I'd applied myself among the English, that I was perhaps better off among them. But Christmas came and went and there was no more promise of Emma visiting than Richard Pryor answering one of Leroy's fan letters. Leroy sulked. I sulked. Grumpy and sullen, we worked in silence venting our disappointments with blades and scissors.

As much as I wanted to tell Emma the truth, to lift the burden of the real reasons for my departure—my hands, the photos, my unwillingness to forgive the driver, I couldn't bear the thought of disappointing her with who I'd become. No matter how hard I tried, I found no humor in any of it. Despite what Leroy believed, I was a thief, not a comic.

My mother had told me the night I received Leroy's comic books that laughter was the sound God made when he forgave us for making mistakes. I tried to hear that sound in the awful truth that plagued me but was met by silence. I practiced telling the big chair what I'd done when I was a boy but only got as far as the camera. I had never been able to tell anything, not even a rock, that I had not forgiven the driver. Looking back, I'm not sure how much permission I had given myself to hate him for everything he had taken. No matter what other people believed about where my sisters had gone, they were not with us.

New Year's Eve, 1984, I watched the ball drop from Times Square from Leroy's TV along with his friends who'd come over for their annual PDDLC: Potluck Dinner and Dirty Limerick Contest. The only PDDLC rule Leroy established was that nobody's limerick could start with anyone from Nantucket. I didn't know what Nantucket was and I'd never heard of a limerick. I sat on the couch and listened to a retired math professor.

There was a smart dog named Horatio,
who devised a mathematical ratio:
The sum total space
From his crotch to his face
Was equal to solo fellatio.

Everyone laughed, but I was trying to translate from English to Deitsh, having never heard of fellatio either. I forced a smile, and one of the men came over and slapped me on the shoulder and said, "Ugly, it's your turn."

I shifted on the couch, feeling the expectant eyes of the men, even Ruthanne, who sensed my fear. "Go on, Ugly," she said gently. "Everything's fair game."

I set the cupcake that I'd been eating back on the plate on the coffee table and wiped my mouth. I had always been good at rhyming, especially learning all those lyrics to rock songs with my sisters. After hearing at least two dozen limericks that night, some dirtier than others, I knew what the meter was and had worked out my own limerick even though I wasn't sure if the translation into English was correct. But everyone was waiting.

Have you heard of the Diesel Fitters
who never had time for the shitter?
They worked not for free

To make hose for ladies
And for this they were often quite bitter.

Nobody said anything at first. Ruthanne offered me another cupcake, unable to see I hadn't finished the first; then Leroy clapped and encouraged me to tell them more.

"What's a diesel fitter?" he asked.

I told them what I'd heard about Levi and Amos Esh, who were let off their jobs at a tobacco warehouse one fall but found work in a lingerie factory, making ladies' "panty hoses," as they called them. "But they lost that job, too, and went to a job bank in the city to find another job, and the woman working there asked them what they did, and they said they were Diesel Fitters. She looked at them all cocked-eyed and said she never heard of such a job. Amos pointed to Levi and said, 'I checked the quality of the panty hose, and Levi checked the length and said 'Diesel Fitter.' They went into construction after that."

The men and Ruthanne howled, asking for more. I told them I wasn't trying to tell a joke. It was a true story. Everyone knew the Esh brothers weren't the sharpest blades in the saw mill. But the more I thought about how ridiculous their story was, how stupid it made them look and how it lifted us all in comparison, the more I laughed, too. Our laughter filled Leroy's living room like the hot air in a balloon, and it dawned on me—whenever people laughed together, they created community.

I trusted this could only be a good thing, and the men trusted I was ready to join it. They turned to Leroy and announced, "Ugly's ready to see you Behind the Chair."

I stared at them, thinking this was their joke.

"I see Leroy behind the chair every day," I said.

"No. *Behind The Chair with Caesar: Confessions of a Barber*," they said and laughed, tipsy, "You haven't seen him on Tuesday night."

Leroy seemed nervous that first Tuesday of the year. It was the first Tuesday since I'd arrived that he had not asked me about my evening plans. He hadn't even pestered me about Emma. Bigger threats distracted him. Looking back, I'm sure Leroy would have preferred to take himself to the movies, but the men had pressured him into confessing to me this time, not them. This was half their fun, to see my reaction to the real Leroy, but nothing could have prepared me for who I'd meet January 3, 1984.

It was no wonder that Leroy needed Tums. Until then, I had always cor-
related his anxiety around the first of the month with his rent and utilities
payments, not the fear of rejection that reared its head whenever he had to
perform *Behind the Chair with Caesar: Confessions of a Barber,* a stand-up
comedy routine that he'd created after years hearing his customers confess
something they wanted only Leroy to hear. "I get more truth from the chair
than most shrinks get their whole lives," he said, even though I didn't know
what a "shrink" was then. I guess he figured all that patient listening to strangers would pay off in the end. He dreamed the routine would get him to New
York and Hollywood, and eventually around the world.

"Got another belly ache?" I asked him while we set up lawn chairs, cram-
ming as many on the floor as we could.

"Nope."

"You've eaten half the Tums today."

Leroy's cursing punctuated our work. Apparently the Jehovah's Witnesses
had refused to renew their rental contract with him for folding chairs on account of his absenteeism at their meetings after he promised to attend. When
they showed up at the shop that morning, he said, "To quote our dearly de-
parted Ms. Dorothy Parker, I've been too fucking busy and vice versa. Try
bearing witness to that!"

I stared at him, wide-eyed. He just said, "Sorry."

He was anxious about the usual crowd of rowdy college students and young
patrons he invited (he started the show late, at 10 p.m., to deter old folks from
coming, claiming anyone that close to death was too bitter to laugh). To add to
his anxiety, he was uncertain that the material he had written was appropriate
for me, or had any power over the folks who would fill the shop, expecting to
laugh.

Most of them were white and young, except for the Hispanic boys he knew
who helped him on occasion to paint the shop. A horde of college boys had
arrived drunk from parties, smelling of beer and cigarettes. I stood at the door
taking coats and collecting money that Leroy donated to a shelter in North
Philadelphia. Beside me, sitting on a bar stool, was Ruthanne who had stayed
home from bingo to offer Leroy moral support.

I would learn that Leroy's Confessions had drawn folks from all over the
county without advertising. He relied on word of mouth and figured that if
any of his material had a chance, he'd know by the turnout. That forty-five
men had packed a barbershop on a week-night past ten o'clock said as much

about what they desperately needed in their lives as it did about the faith they had in Leroy to deliver it.

He climbed into the old barber chair and got real quiet, folded his hands across his lap and adjusted the microphone, then wiped his glasses that had fogged up with the heat of the spotlight and all those men.

"You boys ready for a good story?"

YES!

"You made your resolutions?"

YES!

"Good. Now it's my turn to sweat."

Laughter.

"This confession's new. You probably wonderin' which one of you I'm gonna pick on next, right? Which secret Jeeter gonna unload up here at the start of the year? Well, sit back and relax. This confession's not from any one of you. It's my own. So you can relax and stop guessin' who it is tonight. Ole Leroy got a stocking stuffer for the boys. And you should know this delivery won't be grammatically correct. Or even politically so. Hope you don't mind."

Cheers, then giggles from those nervous about another man making himself too vulnerable in public. Leroy kept looking over the boys' heads, searching the darkness for my gaze, and finding it, took a deep breath and began.

"I'm a bastard."

He didn't need to go any further. Everyone had already bent over laughing to release the awful pain of it. I'd been around the English enough to know that nobody called themselves bastards. They called everyone else that.

"Now you laugh, but I'm telling you the truth. I never knew my daddy. My mama was a waitress worked at a diner and she got her own eggs done over easy one day by a man who drove a forklift in a lumber yard. That be my daddy. My mama, she didn't want me to end up driving no fork lift. She wanted a good education for me. She teach me to read when I was a boy, ran for miles to catch the Book Mobile when it missed our neighborhood. The driver, she be all scared and didn't dare drive into The Jungle, what we called our hood in North Philly.

I got real good at readin' and mama had incentive. She keep the pies and cakes that her customers didn't eat and save 'em for me, cut the portions off that didn't touch their lips and say, Leroy, you read that book, you get some cake. So I did. After a while, I didn't need no cake. I just wanted more books. So my mama she started to take me on the bus to the public library where we'd spend the half day she had off each week, and we'd sit in the childen's section and read books. She knew I like A Snowy Day, *and I asked her to read it every time we went to the library, and she say, 'Leroy, all these books here and you make me sound like a broken record?' I'd say, again, please mama. I love that book. Somethin' about the rhythms.*

But one day she force me to explore the shelves some more and I find me another book, Frog and Toad, *and it had this big shiny silver sticker on it. Win some sort of award. So mama and me take it up to the check-out counter and the lady look at me and mama and she say, 'I'm sorry. This book's on hold.' Mama look at me then back at the lady all cross and say, 'Who put it on hold? Ain't never come here and find a book on hold. Take me four months for my son to find him another book he love and you tell him it's on hold? We can't read Snowy Day again. No way. He want Frog and Toad.'*

The librarian, she all old with beady eyes, looked out of glasses hooked up to a chain on her neck and say, 'I'm sorry. But this book has been reserved by a very important elementary school teacher. At a private school.'

Mama squeeze my hand. I could feel the heat in her skin. She get mad quick. And I put my hands over my ears thinkin' maybe her fuse gonna blow. 'Well why don't she get books from her own liberry. This is a public liberry!' And the librarian, she swallow and look up from her glasses, and her eyes go all wide and she point behind me and mama.

'Maybe you can ask her yourself, ma'am.'

Mama look down at me but I already turned to see whose comin' behind us. A tall, slender woman with a fair skin and big green eyes as bright as the grass, with long dark hair that curled around her shoulders. Mama was pretty. Don't get me wrong. But this lady, she like an angel. She had a boy with her. He be my age, with skin as white as hers and freckles that made the Milky Way look empty. His hair all red, too, curly, and his eyes like emeralds. He looked like a doll and I wanted to poke him to see if he was real. The Angel, she introduce us right there like we had planned a meeting.

'Frog and Toad is Liam's favorite book, too. But he's read it quite a few times and I'm sure he'd love to know somebody else loves it as much as him.'

Red Liam, he look over at me and smiled and said, 'It's the best book ever.' And I say, 'Do you like Snowy Day?' And he says, 'Too cold. I like rain better.' And my mama and the Angel? They laugh and the librarian wipes her eyes and hands me Frog and Toad. *Mama and me, The Angel and Liam walk home together and Mama brag about how much I like to read, how I read her Bible verses, pronounce the words better than our preacher, in her mind. The Angel, she listen and tell us her name is Maggie O'Brian. We walk past our school and Maggie stops all concerned and tells mama that she'd like me to come to her* school, as her guest, and I go, thinkin' it be for one day, but she turn out enroll me in Liam's second grade class! And even though Mama not big on Catholics and confession and the Holy Mother Mary, she decide it was a good choice. That maybe the nuns knew a thing or two about educatin' her boy. She agreed to take another shift to pay Maggie O'Brian back for my uniform, even though Maggie O'Brian insisted it was a gift. And even though Maggie O'Brian had arranged financial aid for me, mama insisted on payin' that back too. When Maggie O'Brian asked her how she plan on doing that workin' at a diner, mama got a big smile on her face and said 'Forklift,' meaning my daddy and the money he owed her for child support but had spent on booze and gambling. As much as mama wanted me to get an education, she wanted to educate The Forklift on the consequences of his irresponsibility. Sending me to Catholic school was the best revenge she could ever take against a man who didn't see the value in education but believed people learned best from a fist.

I liked Maggie O'Brian's school. She was a reading specialist and one day, this day, December 6th, she come in to read us Where the Red Fern Grows and we all sitting on the carpet, riveted by the story of those dogs when we hear bickerin' outside. Maggie put down the book and walk over to the window and she pause and look real concerned and she freeze right there when the bickering turn into a blood curdling scream. I recognized the voice yelling 'You son of a bitch. You pay me for my son's education!' Uh-oh. Mama. Fuse gonna blow, I thought. Maggie tells me to sit back down when I get up from the carpet, but as soon as I turned to the window, I sees Santa Claus! And Mama curled around his back, yanking off his white beard and scratchin' his face until it bleed. Santa shout, 'Get off me bitch!' and fling her to the ground and take out a gun and aim it a her head. I had no idea it was my daddy. I wouldn't have recognized him in the Santa Suit that he'd stolen from the Salvation Army to collect money. Not for gifts either. That's all I remember about him. And the sound of his gun. One shot and mama slumped to the ground. Died right on the hopscotch grid we'd drawn in pink chalk that morning. Imagine a dead woman and Santa on a sidewalk. The cops come and wonder who been naughty or nice when Santa say he shot her in self-defense.

Years later when I took my first real job at a grocery store, they asked me to write down who to contact in case of an emergency, and I wrote Santa. And they read it over and give me a call back and said this is not a joke, young man. And I said it wasn't either when he killed my mama.

He gets out of jail Friday. Been a long time since I seen the Forklift and I doubt he still fits in his Santa Suit. We been writing every week for the last forty-five years. Forklift always asks for one thing when he gets out of the clink. He *wants to go to Friendly's for a grilled cheese.*

I write, "Dear Daddy, I can take you any place you want. Why Friendly's?'
And he writes, 'cause they'll let me use the bathroom there with the other folks.'"

Nobody moved but Leroy. He took a sip of water and stared at us, looking bigger now in that chair and more expectant. He did not crack a smile but looked as though he might crack. I had never seen him so weary and vulnerable, as if whatever energy he had put into his confession had cost him more than the hours of sleep he had lost preparing for it, or preparing for me to listen.

I had no idea that Leroy's mother had been killed by his father. It sounded better in my mind to use 'Forklift' in place of father, but it did not soften the jagged edges of the picture I now saw when I looked at him, on stage. I knew that Leroy had come from a rough part of Philadelphia, that he had lived in a ghetto as a child. I knew that his family did not have a bathtub for the first six years of his life. Who knows how many other things I had taken for granted that Leroy never had: the safety of a school yard, the peace of a farm, the emptiness of open roads, and the community they connected. Leroy had never known the promise of my paradise. His childhood was beyond anything I could ever imagine. I had never known anyone who had deliberately killed another person and I wondered if the 'Forklift' was sorry for what he'd done. That Leroy should share this about his past made me fear him, because it was not humor that made him powerful. It was the courage he had found to forgive the Forklift.

For this reason only, I was the first to clap. I applauded his courage and the awful truth he had revealed to us, which was big and ugly and beautiful because of that. Slowly, with the other men rising from their lawn chairs, we cheered for Leroy Fischer and the pain we never knew he carried in his heart. We cheered for the pain in our own, inspired to find a way, like Leroy had done, to find and bind the broken pieces.

Ruthanne reached out and tapped my shoulder and asked me to guide her through the maze of lawn chairs to the stage where she stepped up and wrapped her arms around Leroy and made the room ripple with whistles. I stood behind them like I'd done the first night I had arrived, but this time I understood the secret of their embrace. The difference between Leroy and me was as plain as my people. It was not the color of our skin that separated us, or our age, or education or life experience. It wasn't even that Leroy was a bastard and I wasn't. Or that I was a thief and Leroy wasn't. The startling difference was that I had loved poorly, and Leroy had loved well.

NINE

THE NEXT TWO DAYS were a flurry of frantic activity and frayed nerves. It was hard for me to understand Leroy's giddiness and the genuine interest he had in meeting his father. He spoke of all the things he looked forward to sharing with him: golf lessons, baseball games, long overdue talks on the porch.

It was as if Leroy awaited the arrival of an old friend. The Forklift had already become a cherished guest and he had not even arrived. I couldn't understand this and it bothered me, not because their relationship threatened our own, but because it kept me thinking about how I would have prepared for the driver if I knew I was going to meet him. This made me angry, but mostly sad, because I had never considered welcoming him. I could never imagine loving him as much as Leroy loved his father.

Leroy hauled a bed frame into the shop the day before the Forklift was due to arrive. He said he'd struck gold at a garage sale down the street. At first I thought he was swapping the cot for a bed for me, and I was touched. Halfway through the assembly, Leroy mentioned the need to move my cot aside for a nightstand.

"Why do we need a nightstand?" I said, perfectly content to use an old Coke crake for my books.

"The Forklift loves to read. I thought I'd surprise him with something he'd remember from the good old days."

"What's that?" I asked, wondering if the Forklift's reading consisted of those girly magazines.

"Comic books. Thought I'd let him leaf through my collection of Captain Courageous. You still have them?"

I nodded. "You want them back?"

"Just for a while. Until the Forklift reads them all. Maggie gave them to me."

"The Angel gave you Captain Courageous?"

Leroy looked up from the bed. "Day before Christmas. At my mama's funeral. They were supposed to be Liam's and she tried to explain to him why she gave me his gift. She said it was important to find a way to laugh again. 'Courage is the hero that helps a boy laugh,' she told me. That's why I gave them to you. I was hoping my daddy would... You ever get much out of them?"

I nodded. "Yes," I said, feeling the sting of giving away my buddy books.

"Good. I hope they make him feel at home."

"Home? I thought he was visiting?"

I picked at the screwdriver in my hand, feeling the prick of the words. Leroy took out a dirty hanky from his back pocket and wiped his sideburns.

"I thought you understood, Ugly. The Forklift is coming to live with us."

"Live?" I asked and gulped.

"You'll be roommates."

I looked up at him, feeling a sickening combination of anger, grief, despair, and betrayal. It was like a tornado, flash flood, hurricane and earthquake had gone off at once, and I was scrambling to find the ground but couldn't. I remember the ticking of the wall clock and the chill of that January gathered around my heart. It was as if my journey to the Outside had come to this and ended here, too. I refused to share a room, or my life, with The Forklift. I got up and took my coat.

"Where you going? It's almost midnight."

"Out," I said, taking the leash. "I need to walk."

"Good idea. Me, too."

"I don't want your company," I said. "Or your dad's."

Leroy paused and met my cold stare, incredulous, his body suddenly limp, as if I had just shot *him*.

I wanted to get as far from the Outside as I could without going home. There were only two directions to go from Strasburg. An eighth of a mile north and I could walk over a miniature red covered bridge of the "Amish Village," a hideous attempt by the English to duplicate our real life and sell it at a premium to tourists. Leroy called it a Potemkin Village. Bogus was the word he'd say whenever we'd drive past it, heading west, into downtown Lancaster, taking Ruthanne to doctors for more shots and lectures about the sugar in her blood. Heading east would take me to familiar places like Intercourse, but I didn't want to risk running into any of the buddy gangs who stored their trucks in the parking lots of Kitchen Kettle, hoping their parents would think they belonged to the tourists who shopped there for jams and jelly. The only direction fit for me was south.

I stopped where the sidewalk ended, letting Caesar off the leash. The street narrowed into a two-lane country road then shot straight past Bunker Hill, where a wrought-iron fence surrounded my sisters' graves.

I opened the gate for Caesar, making fresh tracks in the snow to my sisters' unadorned grave markers. I had not come to offer them company that night. I had come seeking their own. There was nobody in the world that had the power to comfort me or soften the blow of Leroy's news. I wanted to punch him and hug him at the same time, which aggravated me even more because this rage was not good and in no way helpful. It was real, and sharp, like a cramp in my side and would be my torture. Feeling nothing at all might have served me better. The Forklift's arrival had unnerved me the way a whip breaks a wild horse. Forgiveness would require me to accept everything that was and is, which, unlike Leroy, I loathed and wanted desperately to change. This is why I didn't want to look in the mirror. I'd see Leroy staring back at me, waiting for what I had not yet given the driver, or myself.

It was officially the Epiphany, Friday, January 6, a day when my family visits with friends in observance of the visit the Three Wise Men made to the baby Jesus. It was meant to be a day of peace. But if peace came at the price I was paying, I figured I'd be one poor man for the rest of my life. This made me laugh so hard that my head ached. It was an uncontrollable laughter with uncontrollable tears that froze on my cheeks and chin. I slumped into the snow, feeling the wet cold soak through the knees of my jeans, my shoulders bobbing like loaded springs. I pounded my fists against the snow, laughing so loud for so long that, later, I would learn I'd woken up everyone in the valley, including my parents. Hearing laughter rumble from the cemetery on Bunker Hill made them trust the power of their prayers that had asked God to bring me home.

I finally understood what Leroy meant about laughter being a criticism flung at the absurd. I sat against the grave markers and looked up at the black sky, wondering if God and Leroy had conspired to teach me what it meant to be forgiven. My heart felt like it was collapsing and I pulled my snow-soaked knees to my chest. Through my tears I saw a vision of a young boy sitting across from me in the snow. I could not see his face. He was wearing a dark hooded cloak and he shivered. I got on my knees and stood, moving slowly toward the vision, then crouching before him, wrapped my arms around his tiny shoulders and held him until my own body shook with the cold and he disappeared. I don't know how much longer I stayed in the snow that night but I had fallen into the deepest sleep of my life.

I woke up to the sound of my sisters' voices.

What I heard through the wind blowing off Bunker Hill was their request to be free. *Let us go*, they whispered over and over, as if they were pushing me to move on, too. Until then, I had never considered letting my sisters go because holding on to them was all I ever knew about our survival. Losing this part of myself didn't terrify me as much as not knowing what would occupy the hole it would leave. This made me shudder. I needed time to practice taking myself less seriously. I needed time to laugh again. I needed time to live among the living, not the dead.

I did not expect to find the barbershop locked when I returned from the cemetery. And Leroy didn't expect to see me again. He had packed my suitcase with my clothes, half Amish, half English, and set it outside the stoop by the back door with a brown bag of peanut butter sandwiches. Beside it was a small violet, a Bell Ringing Fool, wrapped with a piece of white silk to keep it from freezing; and wedged between the leaves was a note that read:

KNOCK WHEN YOU'VE LEARNED TO FORGIVE.

PART FOUR

◆

ONE

NOBODY TOLD ME THAT going home would be the hardest part about *rumspringa*. If I'd had any doubts about fitting in with the Amish before I left, I doubted myself even more now because I had no idea if I'd ever find the camera and could do what my sisters wanted. I was confident only in my mission. Something about freeing my sisters made me feel like Captain Courageous, but I was not trying to be heroic. There are no heroes among the Amish, just martyrs and men serving God. But I have to admit it did feel good knowing I had a chance to serve someone else, and for once in my life, make things right.

I carried the suitcase to the edge of Decatur and thumbed a ride with a dairy truck driver who delivered me to the Strasburg Railroad, where I would stay in one of many cabooses that had been converted into motel rooms. The owner was a client of Leroy's and I had shaved him several times. I asked him if I could pay for a room with a shave once a week. He felt sorry for me, assuming Forklift had kicked me out. I didn't correct him. Sympathy had its benefits now. He gave me the key to a bright red caboose from the turn of the century, refurbished with a potbelly stove and a small TV. Then he reached into the flap of his flannel coat and handed me a pack of Trues and a can of Budweiser.

I thanked him and promised I'd be gone by the end of the month. I figured it wouldn't take long to find the camera. After all, my father was an auctioneer, and I had been to enough pawn shops to know to look there first. But before I got started, I sat on the edge of the bunk bed and lit my first cigarette and drank my first beer, until I got dizzy and burped and fell asleep like an English man.

◇

Once I had read in Leroy's dictionary that pawn was also a verb that meant to pledge your honor or life on something, which is exactly what I intended to do with the camera. I took the bus into the city and walked two blocks through gray slush to the pawn shop on East King Street. The owner recognized me and waved. He stood in the door of his storage room with his back to me, facing customers I could hear but couldn't see.

"How's your father been?"

"Good," I said, hearing oddly familiar laughter from the other room.

"Haven't seen him much lately."

"He doesn't like to drive in snow," I said and ducked behind a row of antique lamps, then turned at the end of the aisle to the shelf of cameras, seeing mostly Minoltas and older Kodaks, but nothing that came close to the Leica I had lost. I had never seen a single lens reflex camera and picked one up, unprepared for the distortion I'd see through the lens. Stepping out of the storage room and standing at the counter was Emma Beiler; beside her were Amos and Levi Esh, who I hardly recognized, except for that laugh. My own hair was shorter than his now. Long gold locks hung over his eyes and framed his cheek and chin like a curtain. If he had worn anything other than jeans and a Rolling Stones hooded sweatshirt, I wouldn't have recognized him at all.

It was Amos who bore the greater disguise. His were the markings of a respectable, responsible, baptized Amish male: black wool coat, black vest, black pants, crisp white shirt, and black felt hat. But even a wide brim could not hide the wily look in his eyes, the innocence he had lost and the trouble he'd caused in the decade he ran around with his brother in *rumspringa*.

It was a good thing that I had to look down to see them through the camera because I certainly didn't want to look up and say hello. Looking down to see the things in front of you is a strange way to view the world. It made me feel as if I'd invaded their privacy, because none of them knew I was watching. It also made me feel like God, even though I had no power to change what I saw.

They were assembling pieces of a drum set on the floor in front of the cashier's counter. What was most startling was the artwork depicted on it. Wrapped around the base of the biggest drum was the silhouette of an Amish girl, leaning out of a buggy. She struck a provocative pose. Her bonnet was falling off and her back was arched, white neck elongated, arms outstretched to retrieve it.

"Come on now and we'll *ferdail* the stuff; that's a way to get *shut* of it,"

Amos said, directing the assembly of the drum set. It all looked so organized, like they were setting up a fruit stand at the market.

I had never witnessed any leadership in Amos, even though he had always seemed to have the upper hand, despite his brother's height and good looks. But what I was slowly beginning to learn that year was that nothing is as it appears. Any honest Amish person will tell you that much about us.

Amos wanted more for the drum set than the owner was willing to give him. He persisted, stressing the originality of the artwork. The pawn shop owner disagreed, telling Amos that he was lucky to get even half for the set. Take it or leave it, he said.

I didn't listen to the debate once I saw the way Emma was looking at Amos. She stared at him, not with the consternation most folks had when they looked at Amos, but with a softness and compassion that disturbed me. The gaze in her eye suggested not only interest but admiration, as if she'd been the recipient of a precious gift—his simple presence and the "sacrifice" he was making on her behalf by giving up his drum set. He grazed her arm and she did not move, but met his gaze and smiled.

I stood there, biting my lip, trying to understand the series of events that had led Emma Beiler into the Esh brothers' lives. It was unlike most Amish girls to hang out with boys who weren't already friends of their own family, especially of her brothers, which always made it more acceptable in the eyes of the community. The Esh brothers were the last boys in the county Emma's brothers would ever approve of accompanying her. It's not like they had a good business or even a future. They were in a band.

But as soon as the cash register opened, and the owner put a few small stacks of money into Amos's hand, their band was broken up. It was as if the floor had split and some invisible line separated them even more. Amos held the counter, his back toward Levi. Emma looked relieved and wiped her hands on her apron as if having touched those drums was the dirtiest thing she'd ever done in her life, and hopefully the last thing before she was baptized.

Then she turned to Amos and hugged him.

Amos smiled and snorted like some wounded animal who'd been rescued from a barn fire. I should have been happy for his good fortune. I should have felt good about seeing him dressed up and representing us so well, but I felt sick. Jealousy, my sisters had taught me, was the trick the devil used to turn your attention away from what God had already given you. If this were true, I was no doubt focused on the wrong thing that day.

I grabbed hold of the shelf to keep from dropping to my knees, praying they wouldn't see me. But as luck would have it, the opposite happened. Not only did I fall to the floor, I brought the entire rack of cameras down with me, shattering every lens. I lay on my back, surrounded by cameras, some on top, some beneath me, the crook of my arm bent around a long lens.

"Eli? Is that you?"

I opened my eyes to see Emma, Amos, and Levi staring down at me. I felt a knee against my back, propping me up. My head throbbed, and I rubbed the back of it finding a small lump. The pawn shop owner sifted through his battered inventory and cried, "You'll pay! You'll pay for this!"

"I'm sorry," I said. "It was an accident."

"His hands get him in trouble," Levi said, swooping in under my arms to lift me off the floor in front of Emma. She stared at me with those mossy green eyes. "Let us help," she said and reached out to pluck the glass stuck in the pads of my palms and fingers. I stiffened. Standing this close and smelling her after all those months made me tremble from the inside out. As much as I wanted to stop shaking, there was nothing I could do to stop the current inside me. I wondered if this feeling was electricity and the real reason the Amish forbade it.

Nobody said anything for a long time until Emma spoke, keeping a straight face. "You're back from Florida already?"

I nodded, feeling the eyes of the Esh brothers crawl over my head and the hair I hadn't intended to lose.

"They give crew cuts in Florida?"

"Sometimes. If you ask," I said, avoiding Emma's gaze.

"Good for the weather, huh? It's hot there."

I nodded.

Levi, who seemed unfazed by most things in life, stared dumbfounded.

"That's uglier than my worst haircut," he said, which set everyone laughing, and we laughed so hard I didn't feel the million little pieces of glass stuck in my hands. The pawn shop owner didn't see the humor, but because he knew my father and needed his business, he left me alone and stormed back to the counter. I asked him for a broom and swept up the pieces, and Emma crouched down to pick up the glass in a copper dust pan. Levi and Amos straightened out the shelf and helped line up the cameras but the owner told them to stop; there was no point without lenses.

"What do you want with a camera, anyway?" the owner asked. I swallowed, feeling the eyes of everyone, but Emma's most—barbed exclamation points that made me consider what I'd say. Amos spoke for me.

"Didn't you know?" he asked.

Emma shook her head.

"Eli's in the business of stealing souls," he said joking.

I felt the leaden weight of his stare. Then Levi shared a look with me, and as gently as he could, pushed Amos out the door.

"Let's go warm up the truck."

Emma paused at the door, her curiosity getting the best of her. She looked at me and fixed her prayer cap.

"Eli," she said.

"Yes?"

"We'll wait for you," she said then pushed open the door and crossed the parking lot to climb into the black Dodge truck that spat smoke into the bright white winter.

The pawn shop owner glared at me, still angry, and sighed, "What kind of camera did you want, Eli?"

"Leica M3."

"Surprised your dad hasn't run across one."

"Not yet," I said, my eyes still on Emma.

The pawn shop owner lowered his gaze.

"Did he tell you what they're worth?"

"No," I said, wishing that Emma didn't have to sit squeezed between the Esh brothers in the front seat.

"This might come as a shock, but those cameras are worth a thousand bucks. Thank god you didn't break one."

I stared incredulous, shifting my gaze from the parking lot to the owner. "A thousand bucks?"

"Collectors' items. Head to the Philadelphia Camera Show in March," he said, handing me a card with the address of the Radisson Hotel on Old Lincoln Highway in Trevrose. "Two bucks gets you in. If the Japs don't buy them all up, you'll have a chance of getting your hands on a few." Then he looked down at my hands and said, "Maybe."

I had not intended to get into Levi Esh's truck after I left the pawn shop, but he honked from the driver's side and called out the window.

"We'll give you a ride home."

I groaned. That's the problem, I thought.

"What's the problem?"

Levi drove up to me and waited, the engine sputtering, him pressing on the gas, trying to keep that rusted carcass alive. I stared at the metal name plate 'Dodge' and wondered if this was a direction from God. But because I had never been great with directions and wasn't truly listening that day, I received no help in getting out of Levi's way. Emma called out from the truck.

"Come on, Eli. You'll freeze to death."

It was strange to see Emma's face distorted by the frost on the windshield. I stood before the snow-crusted hood, the chrome shiny and wide with dirty brown ice fangs stuck in the grill. I had ridden once in the black Dodge as a kid, but it still looked like a monster, and I knew better than to get into it.

"I'll take the bus," I said.

Levi lit up a cigarette and cleared his throat.

"It's not safe."

"Driving with you is?"

"What's that supposed to mean?" he asked, hurt.

"What it means," snapped Amos. "He'll go slow."

"He'll go slow," Emma pleaded. "He promised me, too."

It wasn't going slow or going fast that terrified me as much as our destination. Levi had offered to take me home, but I did not know where home was for me.

TWO

WE SAT FOUR ACROSS on the front bench of the truck and didn't say a word. The snow was thick and the streetlamps of the city glowed behind us like scattered halos in the dying light of late afternoon. We had slid through a stop sign and one intersection where the red light was blinking. Levi leaned on the horn as we skidded across a patch of black ice.

"Aren't you supposed to stop?" I asked, feeling my heart pound. Emma was scared, too, and had dug her hands into her thighs, gathering the black apron into her fists.

"Usually, yes. But the blinking makes it optional," Levi said.

I caught Emma raising an eyebrow. We didn't know if Levi was telling the truth about running the light. He was the more experienced driver even though we'd all been driving buggies since we were twelve. The difference between the English and Amish drivers is that the Amish are always defensive drivers. Cars were the bullies whom buggies obeyed. That is, of course, when you could see them coming.

"It's not optional, Levi. Red means stop," Amos hissed.

"I thought it was yellow."

"Yellow is the middle. Red's on top. Green's on the bottom. No wonder you still don't got a license," Amos said, as if he'd gone over this a thousand times.

"What?" I asked.

"Levi's got a blind spot. He never passed his test."

Levi sighed, eyes safe behind his sunglasses.

"That had nothing to do with it. I can't parallel park."

"Hates to merge," Amos said as if to explain his brother's entire relationship to the world itself.

The snow was falling faster now and the visibility was no more than a foot. Levi liked to smoke when he drove. He said it calmed his nerves, but he was anything but calm that afternoon. He gripped the steering wheel and stomped on the gas, sending us into a fishtail where we narrowly missed hitting a telephone pole. He seemed pleased to see his brother flinch, but it was Emma he heard, seeing her trembling hands fold into a prayer position on her lap.

"Just get us home safe," she said. "Please?"

We turned down Lincoln Highway East, passing a hardware store and industrial plants puffing smoke into the winter sky. Traffic had slowed to a crawl and we pulled over for an ambulance to pass, seeing several other cars that had slid off the road into a shallow embankment.

"Maybe we should wait," I said.

"For what? To get stuck here overnight?"

"The snowplows will be here."

"No matter. If we wait too long, the gas'll be all," Levi said, meaning out of gas in Pennsylvania Dutch slang.

Amos leaned over to read the gauge.

"It's full," he said.

"The needle's always on that side," Levi said. "It's been broke awhile now."

"How much you got?" I asked, feeling the cold wind coming in through the crack in the passenger's side window, the glass patched with duct tape.

"Enough for now," Levi said.

"He always says enough when he means we're all."

"Are we all?" I asked.

"A few more miles."

"Emma's clear on the other side of Strasburg. And there's hills to climb."

"Lucky for you," Levi said. "It's all downhill from there." He sounded optimistic but Amos sneered, catching the smirk on his brother's lips.

"You think this is funny?"

"No, brother. I do not."

"You know how important it is for us to be at the bishop's house tonight."

"Don't hold your breath. Bishop Beiler hasn't painted his fence blue yet."

Amos sucked in his cheeks and his eyes got as wide and wild as any bull I'd ever seen. Painting a fence blue meant, according to a contested Amish folk tradition, that one of the daughters in the house was of marrying age, giving potential suitors an invitation to come knocking. It was all starting to make sense, but it was the kind of sense that made my head throb.

"Go ahead, Amos. Tell her. We've got plenty of time."

"Tell me what?" Emma asked.

"I'm joining the church," Amos declared.

"You are?"

Amos nodded. Emma smiled.

"My father will be very pleased to hear this."

"But that's not all he plans to join," Levi announced. "He wants to marry you, Emma. Isn't that the greatest news you and your father could ever hear?"

Emma snapped her mouth shut with the force and speed of a camera shutter. Levi howled. Amos shrank. I cleared my throat, trying to find the sound of my voice, but my heart was beating too loudly. It felt like a fist was pushing through the inside of my chest.

"You can't marry her," I said.

"Why not?" he asked.

"Because… Because she's not baptized yet," I managed to say, even though I wanted to say because I'm going to marry her, someday, when I learn more about love.

That's when Levi pulled the truck back on the road, feeling the tension between us, the vinyl seats squeaking beneath our shifting weight. It did not look like Emma had breathed since Levi had mentioned the blue fence, and her panic, I presumed, had less to do with driving in the storm than with everything that I had left unspoken.

Levi hadn't lied about the gas gauge. The tank was empty by the time we turned past the brewer's outlet. We managed to coast for an eighth of a mile before the truck slid over a frozen bridge and ended up in a snow drift. The hood of the truck was buried and the wheels were submerged under the icy waters of a creek running below the old mill.

Levi's side was butted against the flagstone wall of the bridge and we had to crawl through the window of the passenger's side. I got out first and sank into the snow, the bones in my heels and ankles feeling the cold first. I didn't have time to consider stepping out of it when Emma began to dive through the window, hands outstretched for me to pull her through. I stood there, as frozen as the snow freezing me, the cold wind grazing my nose and cheeks.

"Give her a hand, Eli," Amos shouted from the truck.

"Eli?" Emma waved to me. "Come on!"

I looked at the angle she was coming through the window, considering the alternatives to giving her either one of my hands. My hands still ached from the accident in the pawn shop and I wasn't sure every shard of glass had been removed. I decided I would grab her under her armpits, like a small calf, and yank her from the window, but I ended up pulling her too quickly and she fell on top of me, pushing both of us into the snow drift. We landed with a silent, soft thud, her body on top of mine, faces pressing, the warmth of her cheeks like a million sunsets I had not yet lived long enough to see. I swallowed and the lump of my Adam's apple pushed against her smooth neck once, and lightly, but long enough for both of us to feel. Then I swallowed again so that we didn't forget it.

Although the world was spinning, I was lying as still as I'd ever been in my entire life. Maybe it was the snow itself, but I had not experienced a more quiet moment, not even when I prayed. I felt that electric current again, and I wanted to ask Emma if she felt it, too, but I listened to her heart instead. Hearing this breathing beauty made me smile and feel warmer than I had on any sunny day.

I believe if we had stayed pressed against each other any longer, Emma and I would have melted the snow drift. Amos pulled Emma off me and pelted me on the head with a snowball, knowing the red on my face had nothing to do with the inclement weather. He grumbled, "Maybe that'll cool you off."

Levi tossed another snowball and said, "Nice work."

Emma, whose neck and cheeks had blossomed like a red tulip in spring, gathered the prayer cap that had fallen in the snow and tied it beneath her chin, making sure to tie the tassels into a cross. She smoothed out the black apron and flicked off the matted snow like soap flakes. Her fingers shook and her jaw rattled, but she managed to crouch, and before any of us knew what she had formed in her hands, hurled three perfect snowballs at each of us.

"Ouch, Emma!"

"Whoa!"

"Is that all you got?"

We all looked at Levi, incredulous. Emma hooked her fists on her hips and with a fury I have yet to see her emulate, made more snowballs in thirty seconds than I'd ever seen her make of dough. She was a baker, after all, and although the snowballs were small, she knew how to pack the snow just right.

She fired off each of them, offering a few to Amos and me, and together we bombarded Levi Esh with everything he deserved for getting us into this mess.

When we finished, Levi remained kneeling, and we didn't know if we'd hurt him or not. All of this was about to explode into a bloody nose or laughter. It could have gone either way. I started to laugh. Emma and Amos sank into the snow, and soon we laughed so hard our jaws stiffened and we couldn't speak.

"Letsgetyouinside," I said, my words slurred by the cold, not knowing how we'd get into the old mill.

I looked up at the windows, covered with plywood that looked tired and weathered. A red sign hung cockeyed from the wooden stairs by the front door that read, NO TURN AROUND. We all read the sign, but none of us took to heart its true meaning. It was cold. We had run out of gas. We were not walking for miles in a snow storm. We would freeze before we got Emma home. No Turn Around. And so we didn't.

We wrapped ourselves in old black theater curtains and tried to get comfortable in the middle of the dance floor, but there's nothing too comfortable about sleeping on hard wood when you're not even tired. The windows had been cracked from what looked like the beak of a bird and the wind blew in and grazed our necks. By six-thirty it was dark and moonless. I was hungry and tired, but wide awake with the electricity of Emma still revving inside me. It would have been easier to sleep through the storm than to stay awake and think about what had happened between us.

Amos hadn't stopped talking since we arrived, and Emma had wandered off to find her own space in the mill. She was angry at all of us, mostly at me, I suspected by the way she moved around me and avoided my eyes. She seemed irritated, too, and had grown weary of the game Amos had devised to prove his commitment to the Amish and to her. It was not a fun game, like corner ball or volleyball. It was a test of Amos's memory, and of our patience. He had pulled from his coat pocket a copy of the Mennonite *Confession of Faith* and handed me the putty-colored booklet.

I held it up to the light coming in through the window, the soft pink hue of the streetlamp showing the tobacco juice stain on the cover. At first, I thought he wanted to remind me of the basic confessions, but he wanted to perform them instead. The light in his eyes suggested he'd waited a long time for the show.

"Go ahead. Quiz me."

"Give it a rest, Amos," Levi said lighting a cigarette.

Amos tried again. "Pick a number, Emma."

"You guys play by yourselves. I'm tired."

Emma, who had gone off into the corner, sat wrapped in a theater curtain, staring out the window at the falling snow, and did not turn to us.

"Eli, pick a number," Amos said, even though I didn't want to play, either.

"Six," I said reluctantly.

"Okay. Look it up. See for yourself."

What I held was a combination of the Schleitheim Confession—the first confession of faith created by our predecessors, the Mennonites, adopted by a Swiss Brethren Conference on February 24, 1527, and the Dortrecht Confession, written and adopted more than a century later, at a Peace Convention on April 21, 1632. It was a declaration of what we collectively called the Chief Articles of Our General Christian Faith, the foundation of our unwritten rules, the Ordnung (pronounced Ott-ning). A good Amish man or woman memorized them for life and recited them during his or her adult baptism. It was common to memorize the Articles of Faith eight weeks before baptism, not eight months.

Amos cleared his throat, wiggled his fingers as if he were about to perform a piece on a piano. "Article Six," he began and shifted his eyes to Levi when he spoke. "Repentance and Amendment of Life."

"That's it?" I asked, impressed that it was only one line. Maybe memorizing the eighteen articles of faith wouldn't be that hard after all.

"That's the title," he said. "We believe and confess that the imagination of a man's heart is evil from his youth, and consequently inclined to all unrighteousness, sin, and wickedness; that, therefore, the first doctrine of the precious New Testament of the Son of God, is Repentance and amendment of life."

"I think we've heard enough," Levi said, and stamped out the butt of his cigarette with his shoe.

Emma stifled a yawn. "You've done a good job. My father will be happy."

"Let me finish then."

"*Shvetzah*," Levi barked, calling him a talker.

Amos handed the booklet to me. "Read it yourself."

I looked at the top of page 41. The words poked my heart and made me despair, because what they were telling me was not to find the camera. More precisely, to put off the old man with his deeds and put on the new man.

I looked up and handed back the booklet.

"It's getting too dark to read the rest."

Amos tucked it back into his pocket and said nothing. I had read enough to feel the weight of those words. I didn't need to memorize anything for the message to sink in.

We feigned sleeping on the cold, hard floor of the mill, our thoughts burdened by the Sixth Article of Faith. I got the sense that each of us wanted to change something about our lives, perhaps a wish gone wrong, or a deed that had turned dark. I wanted to ask Levi if my oldest sister had gotten to the Sixth Article and had given up, knowing she was not changing anything about her life, at least the one that existed on the very floor holding us, the one on which she had once floated in pink satin shoes.

I poked Levi in the shoulder. He groaned as if I'd woken him from a long and restful sleep. I whispered.

"What did Hanna want to change?"

He rolled over and sat up on his elbow, eyeing me in the dark with a sadness I had never detected in him, or rather had mistaken as anger.

"The only thing she couldn't."

I stared at him. "What was that?"

"What she loved," he said, dejected. He rolled away from me, pulling the heavy black theater curtain over his shoulders. He sat with his back toward us, facing the mirrors on the walls and the demons staring back at him.

"She was happy here," he said.

I didn't know if he meant there in the dance studio, or on earth with the rest of us, because I was old enough to know the difference. I was old enough, too, to understand what Hanna had tried to tell me by the pond, *sometimes you have to go and you don't know why.* I think she knew all along.

I poked Levi's shoulder again.

"What, Eli? At least pretend to sleep."

"I can't," I said. "My mind's mixed up."

"About what?"

"Did you love her?" I asked.

Levi turned to me and laughed.

"I asked her to marry me."

I waited for a moment, catching my breath. "What did she say?"

It was Amos who answered.

"Your sister was a smart girl. She said no."

Levi did not challenge him, too tired and cold that night to fight his only brother over a bitter truth.

We lay silent for hours, huddled together like long black cocoons, shifting and rolling our way to more restful positions, as if somewhere on the knotty pine floorboards we'd find comfort where none was ever intended.

When the snow stopped falling, Levi and Amos went outside to dig the truck out of the drift, even though it looked like it would take a team of horses to pull it out of the creek. I joined Emma at the window to watch them. They were arguing about something again, slinging insults at the other with snowballs.

Emma pulled the curtain tighter around her shoulders and hips, her form, a young black plum beneath the window sill, waiting to ripen.

"You know, I used to be afraid of the snow," she said, refusing my gaze when I asked why.

"I used to think the snow would never melt, and I'd never get to see my mother's garden, or our fields. When it snowed this much, I thought maybe God was overworked and I worried that he might forget to thaw it."

"You don't have to be scared," I said. "We'll get you home."

"Maybe," she said, but she didn't sound convinced. "Everything's frozen."

She was right. In a way, the world as she knew it had frozen in that storm. Her liberty had been threatened by the plans of a man eight years older, who, while pleasing her father by selling his drums, had done nothing to comfort her. Gauging the deep furrow in her brows, I'm sure she worried more about this than about any bit of snow.

"The snow always melts," I said, trying to reassure her, and myself.

She shifted her gaze to me and nodded, chin propped on the back of her wrist, pulling me into the dark green pools of her eyes, a wet and slippery warning in the cold light of morning.

"How come you never said goodbye?"

I felt the blood fill my neck and cheeks. She turned toward the window, again giving me only her profile—her nose almost blocking the sight of the tear sliding down her cheek. After a long silence, she whispered, choking back a sob, "I waited at the train station. I was going to come with you to Florida. I wanted to leave, too."

I pressed my hands against my stomach because that's where I felt her words first. "What? Why?"

Emma said nothing, stared out the window, beyond the lace spun of frost, watching the Esh brothers digging themselves out of the hole they'd created with the truck. Amos was careful to clear the rear window, especially the huge sticker that had been prominently displayed there for years: *Jesus Loves You, Everyone Else Thinks Yer An Asshole.* He cleared only enough snow to read: *Yer An Ass.*

Emma pointed to the sticker then redirected her finger to me.

THREE

THERE WERE NO SIGNS outside the old mill that warned me against moving forward. I couldn't go back to who I was before Emma's touch, and I dreaded leaving the old mill. I wasn't going back to Leroy's and I wasn't going back to our farm.

Follow the right. No matter who you are, what you are, what your lot or where you live, you cannot afford to do that which is wrong. My mother often quoted this Mennonite directive, and since I had known her to take exception to Amish custom every so often, I believed that I could move left and still arrive at the same place.

Rather than decide where I was going in the long run, I decided where I was going that morning. I didn't want Emma's father worrying about her. I volunteered to go get gasoline for the truck while Levi and Amos continued their battle inside the old mill. Emma offered to come with me. Amos was not happy about her announcement.

"Stay here. It's too cold," he protested.

Emma turned to me. "What if you get stuck in the snow?"

I held up my hands. "I've got these. They're almost as good as a shovel."

Emma smiled. "Good. Maybe you won't leave me this time."

◇

We walked two slow miles, southeast and uphill, post-holing our way through snow toward the BP service station on the corner of Route 30 and 896. It was bright and the light burned our eyes bouncing off the snow, but it felt good to get out of the old mill and its streaming confessions. I breathed in the snow-sweet air of Lancaster County and marveled at the difference two miles could make.

Emma and I didn't talk much, and neither of us complained about the snow in our shoes. Our feet were soaked and freezing, yet we'd managed to find a small degree of contentment in this misadventure. Emma hummed a hymn, plodding through drifts as high as her thighs. I felt happy and, for some reason, oddly at ease, too. Until then, I had preferred the company of dogs, but dogs didn't sing; and although dogs didn't mind the cold, Emma didn't seem to mind it either. She panicked only when she realized that she had lost her prayer cap.

"We'll find it when we go back," I suggested, but Emma's eyes filled with the fears imposed on so many Amish girls I knew, my sisters included, who were told what would happen if they ventured out without their heads covered. Folklore suggested evil spirits would penetrate the unprotected. I pictured Emma at Dutch Wonderland, bareheaded, wearing barrettes in her hair.

"It didn't seem to bother you last time," I said.

Emma shielded her eyes from the rising sun, and my accusatory look.

"I never lost it," she snapped. "I knew where it was."

"You were on a date at Dutch Wonderland."

Emma huffed. "I wouldn't call it a date."

"You wore a pink sweater."

"I liked dressing like the English. Don't you?"

She swallowed hard and I wanted to reach out and press my mouth against her neck to soften the stone lodged there.

"Emma," I said, my voice sounding tinny. "Why did you want to leave?"

"Why not?" she asked, offended. "I'm only eighteen."

"Yes, but most girls—"

"I'm not most girls, Eli. It's different for me."

"Because you're the bishop's daughter?"

"Yes. Why can't I have as much time to decide when to join the church as the rest of you?"

A crow flew over us, cawing and flapping its wings. "What's there to decide?" I asked and felt stupid the minute the question flew out of my mouth. I looked up at the crow and glared. I'd never really thought about this Amish standard. I figured it worked out well to have the girls kneel first. We can't marry unless we've joined the church, and it always made sense that the girls were the example we followed. Standing there in the open field with Emma, I wondered what had held her back.

"You have your reasons. And I have mine," she said. "Come and help me find my prayer cap."

"Now? We can come back when the snow melts. It's here. Keep the faith."

Our eyes locked. Emma's lips turned up into a crooked smile.

"Funny you should say that."

"Why's that?"

"I thought you forgot about the faith."

"Almost," I said, and offered the hat she'd made me. "Until I got this."

Emma took it and pulled it down around her ears, and for a moment looked English again with her brown hair hanging loose around her shoulders and blowing in the wind. Her hair was thick and shinier than I'd remembered it in the movie theater, and longer. I wanted to touch it.

"It looks good like that," I said.

"Don't get used to it," she said. "I could kneel for baptism any day."

We stepped off the road for a snow plow to pass, scattering salt crystals that looked blue in the light, signaling the stranded motorists at the gas station to start up their cars. They had been gathered around the pumps, drinking hot cocoa from Styrofoam cups, looking shocked and forlorn, obviously shaken by events that had nothing to do with the storm.

A band of yellow police tape marked the parking lot. Several policemen moved in and out of squad cars, speaking on walkie-talkies. The convenience store door opened and a man in a trench coat, wearing white rubber gloves, carried out a small clear plastic bag that held something long, bloody, and shiny. Emma gasped when the detective passed us, carrying a finger.

"What happened?" she asked, but she already knew the answer, even though the only dead body she had ever seen was that of a relative dressed at a funeral. She reached for my arm and held it, feeling the eyes of everyone on us. We were used to being watched, but not in places where there were locals. January was hardly tourist season in Lancaster County.

"Why are they staring, Eli?" she whispered.

"Maybe they're surprised to see us at a gas station."

She was scared and cold and reached for my hand, but thought twice and wrapped her arms around her shivering body. The ends of her hair had frozen and looked like an old brittle paintbrush. Someone tossed her a wool blanket from the back of his station wagon and another, wearing a hunting cap, gave me his scarf and handed each of us a cup of hot chocolate. I recognized him immediately. Tooth. He looked concerned. "Ugly, you sure you want to be here? I'm surprised the cops haven't called you in for questioning."

I turned to Emma, who was already taken by our familiarity.

"Questioned for what?" I asked.

Tooth glanced back over his shoulder to the store.

"Those three ghouls came in here dressed like the Amish again. They gunned down the cashier last night."

"What?"

"That's right. She was the top in her class. High school girl. Your age," he said to Emma. "Asked her to get milk, then shot her in the head. All for less than five hundred dollars in the cash register. It's got your bishops in a tizzy."

Tooth motioned to the policemen walking out of the store. They paused, seeing me. Emma tugged on my arm. "Let's go," she whispered.

"I can give you a lift," Tooth offered.

"We're walking," I said.

"You sure? I was hoping to catch up on the show I missed at Leroy's. I hear it was one of the best. The fellas say you've got a gift for ticklin' a man's funny bone, too. Diesel Fitter?" he said and chuckled.

I scratched my ear. Everything was starting to feel itchy beneath the wet wool and jeans. "I guess," I said, desperate to change the subject. "Would you happen to have a gas can we could borrow?"

"Sure thing," Tooth said, and walked to the back of his car and popped the trunk. "You and Leroy could take your show on the road. A barber chair is big enough for two."

"I don't plan to take much of anything on the road."

He rooted around the back, pushing aside a bag of golf clubs then pulled out a rusted gas canister. "I use it for the snow blower, but you can take it."

"I'll make sure you get it back."

"Keep it. But if you're ever on Saturday Night Live, you be sure to get me tickets. You owe me a few."

I took the gas canister from him and he held out his hand.

"Deal?" he said.

"What's Saturday Night Live?" Emma asked.

"A television show," I said, and felt ashamed that I even knew this.

"You been watching television at Leroy's?"

I shrugged, raising my eyebrows to meet the steam rising from the cup in her hands. "Sometimes."

"You like it?"

"Dunno. It's alright," I said, trying to read her face. I couldn't tell if she was curious or cross with me.

"Alright?" Tooth said, stricken. "Pales in comparison to the entertainment inside the shop. Ugly, you should take your girlfriend. That'd be something."

"Girlfriend?" Emma repeated. The fear in her eyes turning venomous. "You're a performer now, are you?"

Tooth choked out a laugh, then snorted. "Not yet. We're hoping. Ugly's got a chance to make it in show business. New York. Los Angeles. Maybe Las Vegas!"

"His name is Eli," Emma said, indignant. "Not Ugly!"

"It's just a nickname," I said.

Emma dropped the cup of cocoa and a brown stream trickled into the snow at her feet. "Is that what the English call an insult?"

"Term of endearment, honey," Tooth said.

Emma hissed, and then in her very lilty Pennsylvania Dutch accent said, "Is that right? How about asshole?"

Everyone within earshot, including the police, paused, trying hard to hold back their laughter.

Emma stomped on the cup. "Shame on you for letting people call you Ugly and answering to it like it's true."

The other folks in the parking lot had shuffled across the snow-pack and climbed into their cars, trying as hard as they could to get the engines started. I turned back to Emma and whispered.

"You don't have to take everything so seriously."

"Hating yourself is a serious matter!"

"I don't think you understand me."

"No, Eli. You're wrong," Emma said and her words were cold and heavy. "I don't think you understand yourself."

Emma didn't give me a chance to explain. She stormed across the parking lot, past the police, and, rather than turn back to the old mill, she set out in the opposite direction, across a field, prodding her way through frozen corn stalks.

◇

I limped back to the old mill with the gas, following our tracks in the snow for the longest two miles of my life. The last two people I wanted to see were the Esh brothers and explain why Emma had left.

"Where's Emma?" Amos asked. I wiped my nose with the back of my sleeve, crafting a lie. I tried to sound as casual as I could. I was taller than Amos now.

"She got a ride with one of the English."

Amos looked up at me, digging his foot into a slush puddle, crushing ice beneath his heel. He seemed impatient and assertive and not the Amish man he wanted to be.

"Home?"

"I don't know. Maybe. Was that where she was going?"

"Where else would she go, Eli? Not all of us leave home during *rumspringa*. Her father's probably been up all night waiting. We've got plans for supper."

I looked over at Levi who had crawled out from under the bumper of the truck. Somehow these two had managed to lift the truck from the creek, and both were soaked and muddy. Levi took the gas canister and filled the tank.

"You need to leave that girl alone," he said, paused at the back of the truck, seeing the distance between his brother and me. He smiled and nodded, as if he saw something we didn't. He raised a finger to his mouth and plucked his lips. "She's in shock," he said.

"Really?" I asked, feeling more an authority on Emma Beiler's state of mind than anyone else. "She's angry."

"Of course. She feels betrayed by you lunkheads."

Amos cocked his head.

"We've done nothing for her to mistrust us."

"Uh, let's review, Amos. You sold your drums under the premise that you are joining the church, not her family."

"I figured it would be a nice surprise."

"Based on her reaction, you honestly think she was enjoying herself?"

Amos nodded and folded his arms across his chest.

I shook my head. "She'd rather watch paint dry."

"Listen to Eli. He knows about girls. He grew up with sisters. Asking a girl to marry her in front of her entire family without asking her first is not ideal."

"It's the thought that counts, right?" Amos asked.

Levi pulled out his cigarettes and offered me one. I took it willingly, leaning into the flame of his lighter. Amos stared at me dumbfounded.

"You're smoking now, too?"

I coughed. Levi spoke for me.

"What's the matter, Amos? You too holy to smoke now?" he asked and waved the cigarettes in front of him. It was one vice that Amos could barely resist, and he turned red from the taunting. "Guy can't live on sunflower seeds forever."

"Don't even need 'em. I've already quit smoking."

"And drumming," Levi said and elbowed me.

"I've quit drinking beer, too."

Levi howled.

"Oh, that's a good one. Emma will catch on to you sooner or later. She'll see all of this is for her, not the church. Only way to a girl's heart is to be yourself."

"Hanna made no promise to stick around for you," Amos barked.

Levi puffed on his cigarette, seemingly unaffected, then blew on his hands to warm them up. "And do you see Emma waiting for you?"

Amos kicked the wheel of the truck, then bore his small dark eyes into me. "You let her get into a car with a stranger?"

"I didn't let her do anything."

Levi laughed and pulled on his cigarette.

"Emma's more hard-headed than her father, with twice the bite. She's got snap, but Amos thinks he can break her."

"I never thought Emma needed breaking," I said.

"She doesn't. I keep trying to tell Amos that girl will find her own wind to ride, and the harder he holds onto her wings, the sooner he's gonna pull 'em right off."

"At least I'm trying," Amos huffed. "That's more than you've ever done for love, by giving up on it."

Levi screwed the gas cap shut. I felt like I was in the middle of a corner ball game. Every word the Esh brother's hurled at each other seemed to hit me in the groin. I knew they argued a lot, but I'd never seen the contempt they had for one another until now. It made me sad, and I wanted them to stop fighting before I had to choose sides.

"You don't know what Emma needs," Amos said.

"She needs her violet. Do you have it?" I asked.

Amos pulled it out of his coat pocket and handed it to me.

"She needs more than a flower. I can tell you that."

I took the violet, seeing only the thick hairy leaves.

"Emma doesn't need to be controlled by you," Levi said, and wiped his eyes with his sleeve, wet and covered with dirt from the pond. He looked tired, worn from this age-old argument that I couldn't fully understand. "You think love is power, and this is why you'll lose her… if you ever have her in the first place."

A raven cawed, as if applauding. Amos cleared his throat and walked closer to me. "He's just sore 'cause he couldn't keep hold of Hanna. No wonder he ran out of gas here," he said, waving his hand at the old mill. "Place is haunted."

I stepped back. I didn't like how close Amos was or what he was saying.

"Levi's scared 'cause his time is running out," he said, and his words were clear and loud enough for Levi to hear every one. I stared at Levi, seeing for the first time a terror in his face, though I could not understand his brother's power to threaten him. Levi held out his hand, palms up, as if to receive the whack of an invisible paddle. He drew in a deep breath, but his voice shook. "Go ahead, Amos. Why don't you tell him."

"Oh, no. That's your job, brother."

"Tell me what?" I asked.

Amos shifted his weight and toed another ice puddle, crushing it beneath his heel. He looked over at Levi and spoke slowly, with authority. "Why I should trust what Levi says about women when he's still in love with a dead one?"

Levi let out a long, slow gasp, then lowered his head and walked to the truck. He climbed in and started it, then leaned across the seat to knock on the window, gesturing for us to climb in. I sat in the middle, feeling awkward, cramped by the ghost between us. We pulled away from the mill, crunching snow beneath the tires, and said nothing, our minds restless in the silence.

FOUR

LEVI WAS SWEATING. I thought he was trying to be a good driver and compensate for the hazardous turns of yesterday, but his mind was far from the road beneath us, focused instead on the road ahead, a white, sinuous lane. At one point, he pulled over, got out of the truck, and vomited in the snow. When I asked him what was wrong, Amos answered for him and said, "Mourning sickness," which I interpreted as "morning sickness." I stared at him incredulous, and suggested he eat some snow and he did. With his back to us, he took off his sunglasses, dragged a forearm across his eyes, then quickly put them on and turned back to the truck.

One thing I noticed was that Levi never looked in the rear-view mirror when he drove. In fact, there wasn't one attached to the windshield, just a long line radiating like a spider vein from a stone that had cracked the glass. He could only see what was in front of him, and that seemed appropriate. If he was really still in love with my sister, maybe this is how he kept going.

If Levi had married Hanna, he would have been my brother-in-law, and this relationship was something that even death would not have been able to take from us. Sitting there, staring through the windshield across the snow covered fields that connected our community, it occurred to me that Levi might have been as alone with his grief as I had been, and perhaps, just as angry at the driver. Aside from the rumors that had run rampant, I knew very little about the Eshes, but this sudden tie to Levi gave me a reason to figure some things out.

I wondered how he felt about the driver, if he had found a way to forgive him. And if he had, I wanted to know how. But this was not something I could ask him as if I needed a loaf of bread or a ride. I needed him to consider me a friend, and this, I knew, would take some time, which is about all I had then.

I did a lot of figuring that afternoon, riding between the Esh brothers on the bench seat of The Monster. I had to think quickly when Levi asked me where I'd like to go. I figured if Levi still loved my sister, he'd be interested in helping her.

"Can I stay with you?"

Levi turned so quickly I thought he had let go of the wheel. "Today?"

"Yes. And tonight. Tomorrow. A few more days, maybe."

"Don't you want to go home?" Amos asked, equally struck by my inquiry. It's not that they were surprised I had asked for lodging. This was common among the Amish. What perplexed them is that I was asking to stay with them.

"Don't you want to see your parents?"

I shook my head, feeling the shame heat my cheeks.

"Not like this."

"Like what?"

"Dressed like Levi. Like I'm English."

"Isn't that why you went to Florida?" Amos asked.

"No."

Levi turned to me, brow arched above the rim of his sunglasses, as if to confirm a lingering suspicion. "What exactly did you do in Florida?"

"Nothing," I said.

I held up my arm, letting the sleeve of my coat expose the pale flesh of my wrist. Aside from my haircut and jeans, there was no other evidence to convince the Eshes of my journey. I had nothing to lose by telling them the truth. "It's not exactly sunny at Leroy Fischer's."

"Christ," Levi said, then ran his hand over my head. "We should have warned you to stay away from that place."

"All I wanted was a haircut."

Amos and Levi laughed and, for a moment, shared the kind of peace I would have wished between brothers, even though there was usually no safety between their words.

"Sorry *rumspringa* didn't work out like you planned," Amos said.

Levi sympathized. "But you can't stay with us."

"Why not?" Amos asked him. "It's not like you're getting baptized anytime soon. We could use the company."

"Where would he stay with Mom still sick?"

"In the barn."

Levi slapped the steering wheel and turned to me. I felt his eyes fixed on me behind the black lenses. "No."

"You're going to leave a brother out in the cold?"

"He has parents. He has a home. We are not family."

Amos turned to me. "Why can't you go home, Eli?"

"Because," I said. "I'm not ready."

"Ready?" he asked, sensing my awkwardness. "You mean to get baptized?"

I nodded. It was half true.

Levi sighed. "Trust me. You don't have to be ready to kneel to go home. You don't want to end up like us."

"Like you," Amos said. "I'm the one getting baptized in the fall. You should really consider it, Eli. It's harder the longer you wait."

I pressed myself into the seat, feeling young. The last thing I expected from the Eshes was a lecture about *rumspringa*. I felt like a lost calf then wandering an electric fence line, zapping itself with the current.

"If you help me, I promise I'll leave you alone."

It was Levi who answered.

"Help you? We'll hurt your reputation more than you can imagine."

"Not any more than I have. I stole my sisters' souls."

◇

It felt good to say it. I had kept quiet for nearly two-thousand five hundred fifty-five days, or eighty-four months, but now the silence had ended in one breath. Five words in my confession. One for each of my sisters. My words hit the windshield and ricocheted back and bore through us all like bullets.

I stole my sisters' souls.

Levi did not pull over to vomit this time. He pulled over to listen in the empty parking lot of a one-room Amish school house, my breath fogging the truck windows. Amos sat beside me, quiet and shaking. He took out the booklet of the *Confession of Faith* and opened to the Dortrecht Confession, Article II, a thumb grazing The Fall of Man—prepared, it seemed, to offer me grace.

They hung on every word, every detail of my confession, dumbstruck and awed by my honesty. I experienced the same sense of power that Leroy must have felt from his barber chair. I didn't care if only two people heard me. I needed only one.

When I was finished, Levi sat slumped over the steering wheel. The *Confession of Faith* had dropped from Amos' hand and landed on an empty can of Coke. I couldn't read their faces. They were as blank as the sky, as ashen, too. Amos held his right hand over his face and looked at me through spread fingers, like a rake he needed to remove the debris that had suddenly blown over him.

"Is that all?" Amos asked, but he didn't sound interested in hearing any more. "Yes," I said. I did not tell them about my mother cutting my sisters' braids, because I knew somewhere in the book of Articles, Amos would point out that my sin was no worse than my mother's. I didn't tell them that I could not forgive the driver. This was enough revelation for one day. At the rate I was moving, I could end up kneeling for baptism in the spring, and baptism was not something I had even begun to consider.

I crossed my arms over my chest, feeling cold and exposed now. I knew what I had done was probably worse than anything the Esh brothers ever had done, but I didn't expect them to be speechless. I needed their help.

"I want to find the camera. I want to destroy the film and let them go."

"Let them go?"

"Yes. You know. Give them back to God."

Levi pushed himself off the steering wheel, his hair matted against his forehead. He looked feverish. "You really believe in graven images?"

I turned to him, then Amos.

"What's not to believe?"

Levi's jaw tightened and I felt the seat bounce when Amos shifted. He rolled open the window to get some air. Despite the weather, it was hot and stuffy in the truck. There was a long moment of silence. A state trooper had passed the school house a few times, and had finally pulled into the parking lot, lights flashing, but no siren. He got out of the squad car and walked toward the truck, the freshly fallen snow squeaking beneath his boots.

Levi glanced in the side-view mirror, seeing the officer split in the cracked glass. "Shit," he said.

Amos turned around and popped open the glove box, suddenly frantic, searching through cigarette boxes and pouches of chewing tobacco. There was an ice scraper and a flashlight. Three Musketeer wrappers and a tooth brush. I wasn't sure what they were searching for, but I knew they didn't find it when Amos slammed the glove box closed. He turned to Levi. "I knew this would happen sooner or later."

"What?" I asked, confused. I wanted their help in finding the camera, but rescuing lost souls was the last thing they wanted to do when they were struggling to save their own. Whatever line had been drawn between them at the pawn shop seemed to grow longer when the police arrived. They sat quietly in the truck, Levi pressed against the seat, drumming the steering wheel with a thumb and a cigarette. It was an erratic rhythm and I wondered if it matched his heart beat. The officer knocked on the window. Levi rolled it down and the cop shined a light on us even in the daylight.

"Good afternoon, boys."

"Everything alright?" Levi asked.

The officer shrugged and poked his head into the truck. He wore a thin silver mustache that looked like overused steel wool. "Sure, if you consider trespassing and forcible entry legal," he said. "Or driving without a license and failing to register this truck since 1976. Then yes, it's alright."

I didn't think we had done anything wrong at the old mill. Broken a door lock, yes, but our damage could be undone. We hadn't stolen anything. We even folded up the theater curtains when we left. I had seen enough episodes of "CHiPs" at Leroy's to understand what an accomplice was. Regardless of the truck, we were all guilty of trespassing and forcible entry, even Emma.

"Please don't take us to jail," I said. "We're Amish."

The officer chuckled.

"You think the Amish are exempt from jail?"

"We didn't mean any harm."

"But you did harm, son, didn't you?"

The officer didn't give me a chance to answer. By the time he opened the car door, another police car had fishtailed into the parking lot of the one-room school house. The window was down and a bloodhound was barking in the back seat. When the car stopped, the dog leapt out of the car and ran toward the truck, snarling, lips curled back, baring her teeth. That's when the cop shouted, "We have our guy."

FIVE

I HAD NO PLACE to hide my hands at the police station, and I felt more humiliated in the half hour I spent there than in the sixteen years I'd been alive. Parading in front of a room full of real criminals violated any kernel of faith I had left in the Outside World, where my sisters' killer had remained unknown for nearly a decade.

Levi and Amos tried to convince the police they had made a mistake, that I was not one of the three young men who dressed like the Amish and killed convenience store clerks. But the cop from the parking lot wedged me into a line of a dozen dirty, dark-eyed men. Apparently, the bloodhound had smelled my urine *and* blood, and matched it to the men who had robbed us and stolen our clothes the year before.

I smelled alcohol and cigarettes on these men who did not seem young to me at all, but weathered, chiseled, pock-marked and scarred. They did not seem scared. One yawned loudly. Another said, "Shut up, Carmack." Even with their hands bound by cold steel claws, a few of the men managed to crack their knuckles and their necks. I couldn't crack anything, certainly not even the riddle of how we'd ended up in this tight white room buzzing with fluorescent lights.

We walked in a short ellipse, like horses, cramped by the confines of the stage. Whoever was watching through the one-way window wanted me to step forth, and I did, when the voice of the policeman called to me through the small speakers on the wall. He asked me to turn left, then right. I did. The voice told me to turn to the side, so that they could see my profile. I heard more garbled voices through the speakers, and then a booming "Eli Yoder, come down off that stage." It didn't sound like the officer who had taken us into the station. I recognized the face when he barged into the room, nearly doubled over, cackling like a Grade-A hen.

"You boys wouldn't know your elbows from your assholes if you didn't have a map. Let the kid go," he said to his staff of six at the Paradise Township Police Department. They moved toward the young Hispanic man with a shaved head standing beside me until the officer at the door yelled, "The tall one. With webbed hands!"

The officer removed the handcuffs and struck me on the back with a soft blow intended to comfort me. "Go on. Get out of here."

It was the first time in my life I was happy that my hands had identified me unmistakably as Eli Yoder—and not the escaped convicts of a West Virginia state prison who had been impersonating me and the Esh brothers since September. Killing in our pants and shirts and suspenders, God rest their souls. Officer Fowler ushered the Eshes and me into his office and told us to sit down, that we were not off the hook, that we had a price to pay for trespassing and breaking into the Hottenstein's mill.

Levi cleared his throat, his face pallid and green. He hadn't spoken since we were shoved into the police car. "How much do we owe?"

"For trespassing or breaking and entering?"

"Both."

Officer Fowler leaned back in his chair. He tapped his pen on the desk, then flicked the clown-like head of a Pez dispenser and offered each of us one pink tart candy. He sucked and spoke and smacked his lips.

"Was the mill locked when you arrived?"

Levi nodded. "Yes, but—"

"You broke the lock and entered."

"Yes. The storm," he said. "We had no place to go."

"But you weren't licensed to be there."

Levi shook his head. We followed. My head felt heavy and cloudy. My stomach growled, and Officer Fowler handed me the Pez dispenser. It was an odd gesture, but I took it anyway and forced a smile.

"You realize that's second-degree criminal trespass."

I felt my stomach drop. Hearing the phrase second-degree anything was not good, especially since most Amish associated it with burns. We knew about fires. We knew about trespassing, too, but nobody I knew had ever been charged for spending time on a neighbor's hillside, or hunting ducks in their pond.

"It'll cost you $1,000 each and six months in jail."

I dug my heels into the floor, bracing myself against the back of the chair in front of me. I took a deep breath, acutely aware of the danger of going to jail for this stupid and silly mistake. I had heard tales of men in modern prisons that didn't sound much different from my ancestors' songs about surviving their tormentors for 400 years. It didn't matter if it were 1584, 1684, 1784, 1884 or 1984. The cruelty of men against Anabaptists had been as big a theme in our lives as finding a way to love our tormentors. But this was different. The Esh brothers and I could not say we had been martyrs, willing to risk our lives for our faith. We were second-degree criminals. We could not bring honor to the Amish by serving jail time, only shame.

I wanted to believe that $1,000 and half a year in prison was a small price to pay for the true crime I had committed. That crime was something I believed I'd be paying for the rest of my life. I had learned about garnished wages from the men in the barbershop, and I wondered if perhaps this was God's way of collecting from me what I owed. Just being with the Esh brothers felt like a full sentence, but no matter how much trouble we had gotten into that day, we had no business going to jail for trying to survive a blizzard. This thought got me so worked up that I spoke out loud, hearing Emma's voice.

"You know, you're an asshole if you send us to jail."

Levi and Amos turned to me aghast. I thought Officer Fowler was about to fall off his chair. He gripped the edge of his desk and pursed his lips, trying hard not to laugh, but also impressed by whatever it was that had suddenly emboldened me. "Thank God," he said. "Because I'm not."

"You're not? Why?" I asked.

"I have a better idea."

He got up and opened the door and told us to wait for him in the squad car. He was taking us to Twirly Top, he said, and he hoped we had a big appetite.

I groaned, nauseous, slumped in the front seat. I had avoided Twirly Top over the years by taking alternative routes home, even if it made the trip longer. The thought of eating there made my stomach twist again and, this time, the knot worked its way into my throat.

"What's wrong, Eli?" Officer Fowler said. "You don't like ice cream?"

I was grateful Amos spoke up.

"It's not that. It's Sunday. We're supposed to meet the bishop for dinner. He'll be worried about us."

"He has a reason to be worried," Officer Fowler said, and he turned up the radio. We stared out the windows while he sang, looking up at the troubled sky. Unlike us, Officer Fowler had been in a cheery mood ever since we had left the police station. He seemed glad to have us alone, a captive audience to his offer.

"You boys familiar with moles?"

I turned to him, feeling my lips curl in a half-snarl, like my dogs did whenever I'd asked them something dumb.

"We go to school until the eighth grade."

Officer Fowler nodded.

"I know that."

"Then you also must know that we can read and write."

"We know what a mole is," Amos added. "Know how to trap and kill 'em."

Levi laughed. Officer Fowler knuckled the steering wheel and flicked a bandage stuck around his middle finger.

"These moles are protected. Nobody can hurt them."

This made me sit up. "What's so good about saving a mole?"

Officer Fowler pointed at me and scowled. "They help catch bad men."

"I thought the police used dogs for that."

Levi and Amos were silent, as lost as I was.

Officer Fowler cleared his throat. He honked at a passing UPS driver and waved at the big brown box on wheels that had pulled out of the Twirly Top parking lot, spitting snow and gravel under its tires. The snow had piled up outside the door and two of the waitresses were shoveling the walkway. I wanted to get out and help them. I wanted to be anywhere but in a car.

"Being a mole is a civic duty," Officer Fowler said.

I turned to Amos and Levi, who shrugged, as we pulled into the parking lot.

"Civic duty?"

Officer Fowler nodded and grabbed a pack of Camels from the dash.

"It's a real honor to see justice served."

"Justice?" I asked, full of the words that didn't mean much to the Amish. We didn't serve on juries or serve as witnesses in trials. For the most part, we avoided courtrooms. We didn't need them. Forgiveness was our civic duty.

"Don't you want to see those men go to jail?"

"If that's what it takes to help them," I said.

"You're the exception. All of you are the exception. Everyone else'd like to see them hung, if they could."

I imagined this, seeing in my mind the three men with nylon stockings pulled tightly over their faces, flattening their noses and the rolls on their cheeks, bodies limp and hanging, like a piece of loin that's been tied in string and dangles off a butcher block. I felt ill again, picturing it.

Officer Fowler spoke quickly now, in a low voice.

"Consider it an adventure," he said, as he stomped on the brake. The squad car slid across a patch of ice into a snowdrift as high as the bumper. He yanked the keys out of the ignition, and the engine thudded to a stop. "Don't you want to help catch those bad men?"

"So we're the moles?" I asked, finally catching on. Officer Fowler nodded. "Might make martyrs out of you all," he said and his voice fluttered as if a little bird had flown out of his throat just then. "What do you say?"

◇

We sat in a booth by the window, near the jukebox that Officer Fowler continued to stuff with quarters to make sure nobody could hear us, even though we were the only customers in the diner. We were hot and sweaty and upset that Officer Fowler seemed so delighted to have such control over us.

"Why don't one of you go undercover?" I suggested, remembering the cop shows I'd seen on Leroy and Ruthanne's sofa. The poor guys who had to hide always seemed to get the bad end of the stick. Besides, I was already hiding.

Officer Fowler tapped his teaspoon against a coffee cup and smiled.

"It's an inside job," he said.

I had always thought that Amos was a lunkhead, but now that I had been united with the Esh brothers, I was willing to defend Amos against a man who was beginning to appear the biggest lunkhead of the English.

"You want us to go undercover as ourselves?" I asked.

"That's right. During the parties," he added.

"Parties?"

"*Rumspringa* parties. It's the most obvious place those men might go."

"Why?" I asked. "They'll stick out like a sore thumb."

"Exactly, which is why they're taking notes, studying how to be Amish while your friends stumble around drunk."

"They could kill us!" I blurted.

"That's why you'll have one of these," he said, and tapped the holster of his gun. I dropped my french fry. Amos set down his root beer. Levi swallowed a hunk of hamburger. I lowered my voice, matching that of Officer Fowler.

"You want us to carry a gun around the Amish?"

Officer Fowler nodded. I studied his eyes, as my father had taught me, to detect his bluff. There was nothing but a glint of earnest amusement.

"Don't tell me you've never broken the rules to get what you wanted. Not even the Amish are that good."

That was all he needed to say.

I nodded. Amos and Levi nodded, too. More than you'll ever know, I thought. More than I'll ever tell the police.

Office Fowler paid for our meals then drove us back to the one-room school house. On the way, when Levi asked if he could drive the truck unregistered, Officer Fowler looked at him in the review-mirror. "It's registered now."

"How's that?" Levi asked. "Don't I need to pay?"

"You'll pay, trust me," he said. He waited while we climbed into the Monster, and when Levi was able to start it in the cold, he said. "See? It really is your lucky day, boys."

Then he reminded us of our deadline. We had one week to make a decision. Until then, the charges for criminal trespass would not be dropped. Six months in jail or six months seeing that justice was served. Our choice, he said.

It was late by the time we reached the Esh's dairy farm in Leacock, where a white silo stood out against a dark winter sky streaked with silver and purple, as if it had absorbed our bruising. Aside from the one afternoon Levi had taken me to his barn when I was a boy, I had not spent time on his property or ever been inside his house. It was built from field stone in the traditional Pennsylvania German tradition, with an off-set door and only three rooms: one where the Esh brothers had been born, another where their father had died, and where their mother lay dying from colon cancer.

The Monster more than anything seemed to belong in this odd portrait of dilapidation and unrest. The house, now cracked and tilting, sat on the slope of a gentle hill crowded with elm trees, root-collars ringed white with fungicides and looking strangely like disembodied halos in the darkness. A gas lamp flickered from the lower right window in the house but was soon extinguished by the shade that Mrs. Esh pulled down when she saw the head-lights against her walls. Like my mother, she believed it was bad luck to have unnatural light enter her home, which was yet another source of contention between her sons.

"Why do you do always have to wake her up like that?"

Levi pulled up to the barn door and turned to Amos.

"Since when has she ever slept?"

"Your mamm doesn't sleep?" I asked.

"Ever since Levi bought this truck," Amos snapped.

I looked over at him, calculating. Seven years seemed like a long and painful time to stay awake. I could hardly keep my eyes open by then, and it had only been nine hours since Emma and I had left to get gas. I yawned.

"Doesn't she have any dreams?"

"Yes. One," Amos said.

"What's that?"

"She wants us both to join the Amish, but as long as Levi keeps driving this truck, she knows he won't."

Levi shut off the lights and reached for the pack of cigarettes wedged between the dashboard and windshield.

"Shall we?"

"Join the Amish?" I asked.

"Go undercover," he said, cupping the lighter around his hands. "You ready?"

Amos got out of the truck.

"What's it gonna be?" Levi asked, turning to me. "You know we won't sleep if we wait a week to decide this thing."

"We should sleep on it," I suggested, offering the advice Leroy had doled out to his clients who suffered from indecision.

"You actually think you could sleep now?"

I nodded. Everything felt like it was buzzing inside me, but it wasn't the kind of hum that came from singing hymns or reciting scripture. I had not slept in three days, unless you consider the hours we all tossed and turned in the old mill restful. Answering anything other than the spelling of my name seemed cause for great suffering.

I got out of the truck and Levi pulled it into the barn, its walls covered with hundreds of guitars of every shape and size—electric, bass, and acoustic, most of which Levi had made himself. This was no ordinary barn but one huge workshop, with half-finished cabinets laying in rows on the floor like overdone coffins. More overpowering than the tang of hay was the acrid bite of wood stain and varnishes of every potency available. Scraps of sandpaper littered the floor, along with a trail of cigar stubs and beer caps. A leather recliner had been pushed against a support beam. In front of the chair was a large television perched on an overturned apple crate, a VCR balanced precariously on top, its extension cord running the length of the barn to a generator outside. If

I had had any doubts about the rumors that Levi and Amos had watched videos of Van Halen, here was the evidence. Beneath the wall where the guitars hung were posters of rock stars. Levi's face had been superimposed on Sammy Hagar's, which made me laugh because they didn't look much different.

Amos lit an oil lamp and grabbed a blanket from the truck, obviously too shaken to face his mother and share the news, which Levi had begged him not to do. Levi crossed the barn and returned with three beers in green bottles and plunked them down on the hay bales where we waited, brooding over what to do. Levi popped the cap on one of them with his teeth.

"Here," he said and handed the beer to me. "Don't try this on your own. Hurts like hell if you get it wrong."

He flashed the cracked molar in his mouth and smiled. "Bet your hands are strong enough to open one."

I took the beer and looked up at him, weary.

"You think so? Won't it hurt?"

Levi smiled.

"Hurt? A bottle cap? Naw. Not as much as love."

"Levi. Let him alone," Amos said.

"Why? That's the last thing I want to do. Since you're leaving, now's the perfect time to have another brother. You said so yourself. We have the space."

Amos pulled his knees to his chest. I wanted to feel sorry for him, but I wanted to impress Levi more. He handed me the other bottle of beer and I took it in the palm of my webbed hands and cupped it, twisting the cap open, breaking enough skin to bleed. I laughed nervously and said, "Guess this makes us blood brothers now?"

"What do you mean now?" Amos asked.

Levi took the beer from me and drank it all, then fell back against the hay bales and looked up at the stars through the holes in the roof, as if each star were the hope he needed to keep his fragile world from collapsing. None of us spoke for a while, burdened by the decision we had to make. We listened to a screech owl hoot and our eyes followed a rat that scurried along the eaves of the barn. The pawn shop seemed like a million years ago, yet Emma's touch lingered. I wondered what she was thinking and how I would ever win her back if I cooperated with the police. But we were a people who had been known to strike a deal in order to survive. And so I offered up a prayer. *Dear God, I will go undercover if it means I can return my sisters' souls to you.* Just as I said "Amen" in my mind, Amos stood up. "There's nothing to decide," he said. "I'd rather go to jail."

◇

What Amos Esh was driven to decide that night was not if he would go to jail, but if doing so was worth losing his only brother. The sibling rivalry that had smoldered for years had flared up into a war. When Levi offered to drive Amos to the station to turn himself in, Amos told him he'd never ride in The Monster again. "It's over, brother," he said. Then he walked up the hill toward their house and, after telling his mother what had happened, framing it as a true martyr's mission but omitting the part about Levi becoming a mole, induced her first night of sleep in years.

When I asked Levi if he was upset about Amos leaving him, he looked at me and said, "I don't have a brother." That motivated me to replace the one that he'd lost. I was eager to do whatever work he needed on the cabinets (I could sand) or on the guitars (I could stain), but he put me to work scraping paint off the barn so that I could work from the ground. Levi used the ladders and climbed around the roof, scaring his mother who'd rattle the windows from the house, watching us, concerned about "the Englisher" with her son.

I don't blame her for being afraid of who I was and what I was doing on her property. I suggested I speak with her, but Levi had said it would only make her more anxious. It was her mind that worried him more than the cancer. She had been calling him Gideon lately, mixing him up with her late husband. Sometimes when we were working she'd holler 'Gid!' and Levi would take off to see what she needed, which was usually just a pillow that had fallen on the floor. Even though nothing was ever a real emergency, I'd never seen Levi move so quickly. He cooked for us both but delivered my food to the barn, where I was sleeping on a bed of hay, under an old wool blanket that smelled of beer and cigarettes and stank of schemes.

SIX

OFFICER FOWLER COULDN'T HAVE been more perplexed yet pleased by our decision, which we announced on a blue bird Friday afternoon even though Levi and I had already decided by Monday morning.

"You changed your minds?" he asked.

We stood in his office again, but this time, he told us to sit and make ourselves at home. He offered a box of Dunkin Donuts, mostly powdered holes, and encouraged us to eat as many as we wanted. Then he listened to our offer. We told him we would go undercover as long as we didn't have to carry guns.

He stared at us, stymied.

"How do you plan on protecting yourselves?"

"Prayer," we said at the same time, then looked at each other surprised. I didn't know that Levi still prayed.

"That's not enough. These men are very dangerous. They're escaped convicts, and armed, for God's sake!"

"So are we," Levi said, then shifted his gaze to me, nonplussed.

We hadn't discussed this concession. We hadn't said much of anything since Amos had turned himself in.

"Prayer, huh? Stronger than a bullet?"

Levi and I nodded.

Officer Fowler studied us, scheming, calculating the reward for our cooperation. He turned and unlocked a black filing cabinet and pulled out a coil of plastic-coated wires and pocket-sized battery packs, one for each of us. He showed us how to keep the wires under our clothes, and how to hide them should they poke out for whatever reason. He told us that even on the hottest day to make sure we wore long-sleeved shirts and coats. Then he unlocked another small box and pulled out two black guns that gleamed in the morning light streaming through the window behind his desk.

I looked at the guns and then up at Officer Fowler.

"We told you we're not using guns."

"I know. These aren't real guns. They're tasers."

I turned to Levi. He reached out and picked up a gun, running his finger along the gleaming black barrel. "Sure looks like a real gun."

Officer Fowler took the gun from Levi and shoved it against his heart. He fired and Levi doubled over, then slumped to the ground, clutching his chest.

"Hey. Hey!" I said and turned to help him when Officer Fowler turned the gun on me and grazed my right butt cheek. I felt my knees buckle and fell to the floor, too. Levi and I peeled back our clothes. He lifted his left pant leg and I looked into the darkness inside my pants, expecting to find blood. There was nothing but a burn mark.

"Why'd you do that?" I growled.

Officer Fowler burst into laughter.

"Stun gun, boys. Can't kill a man, but it can make him stop in his tracks."

Levi groaned and muttered "Shit."

Officer Fowler said, "That's right. That's exactly what those men are, and we're going to catch them and put an end to their senseless killings."

I turned to Levi, searching his eyes. They were as big and bugged as mine. I didn't know who was more senseless, the Amish Imposters or the man in charge of finding them. Officer Fowler ripped a tissue out of the box on his desk, dabbed his eyes, then walked over with extended hands and hoisted us off the floor.

"Scared you both, didn't I?"

I nodded. Levi clenched his jaw.

"Remember who's the boss," Officer Fowler said.

I wanted to say the bishop, but bit my tongue. Officer Fowler handed us each a stun gun. "Don't lose them."

I held mine like a dead rat.

"What's the matter? It can't kill anybody. It'll just help keep those men stuck for a while until we come in."

I shook my head and swallowed, anticipating not only the shame I would feel and bring upon my entire community if anyone ever saw me with a gun, but the disintegration of any hope I had of earning back Emma's trust. It was one thing to serve justice. It was another to violate the Amish belief in nonviolence. Stun gun or not, it inflicted pain on people. Officer Fowler said the easy part was that we only had to use it once. The hard part was knowing when.

I was now not only a thief but a new recruit of the devil. Wearing stun guns and stupid grins, Levi and I hunted *rumspringa* parties that winter, trying to detect the Amish Imposters. We didn't feel safe with stun guns inside our jackets and wires slipping out of our clothes, but we had no luck in finding *rumspringa* parties anyway, a feat more difficult than squeezing the teat of a cow with a pinky toe. Although the Amish advertise in *Die Botschaft* for farm equipment and services, there are no announcements for *rumspringa* parties. That's the whole point. They're kept under wraps. Not even the parents of the kids hosting them know they're happening in the far corners of their fields.

We didn't lie to Officer Fowler when he asked us "what in the Sam Hill" we'd been doing with our time when the Amish Imposters struck again. He told us every second that we wasted risked the lives of innocent citizens. He had expected us to have a few leads by then, but we had only ticket stubs. There was simply no action in February, when most of the kids stayed indoors anyway. We went to the movies with the money Officer Fowler had given us to pay for gas. We'd just wait at a gas station and ask somebody for their receipts, then, fill the envelope Officer Fowler had given us to keep track of our expenses. Levi paid for popcorn and drinks with his own money, and said it was the least he could do.

"You wouldn't be in this mess if it weren't for me," he said.

I couldn't argue, but still felt guilty about using police money to fund our trips when they thought we were part of the force, "serving justice." But going to the movies helped to pass the time. We knew the party scene would pick up when the snow started to melt, not because the Amish don't go out in their buggies in inclement weather, but because with the ground thawing and not much field work, they found themselves with more time on their hands. That's when we knew we'd find volleyball courts drawn in the remains of dirty snow.

The games meant more than winning or losing. They meant talking, and talking is all we wanted the players to do. The way Levi figured it, the more they talked, the more information we'd have on the Amish Imposters. One day, he tossed me a ball and said, "Start serving." Besides shaving men's beards, it was the one thing I was good at, and my absence from the court over the preceding months hadn't weakened my spike. Levi knew people would still fight for me to be on their team, and this, he said, would guarantee we'd find out when and where the parties were.

We hadn't discussed engaging in sports to see justice served, but it was the best plan we could come up with. We chatted up so many Amish youth about who was visiting their farms, working with them, even living with them, that a few of our friends thought we'd become real estate developers.

"Why would we do that?" Levi asked, offended.

"To carve up all this land and make a killing."

"That's exactly what we're trying to prevent," I said.

But even a hundred games of volleyball delivered no information about three men who dressed like us but killed like English. At times, our inquiries were met with great animosity for mistaking anyone's relative for a killer from West Virginia. No Amish we spoke to wanted to believe that a man could kill in cold blood like that, even though we pointed out, through the newspaper articles, that three men had done so, several times. Most startling was the future many of the Amish saw for these men who had wandered down a very crooked road.

"Maybe they'll straighten themselves out among us," they said in defense of the three men. We would have argued, but after three weeks of inquiries, the convenience store robberies stopped. The convicts had likely moved on to

Ohio, where they'd have even more Amish to hide behind in Holmes County.

"They won't catch them there," Officer Fowler said, brandishing his Pez dispenser. "They don't have the infrastructure or the task forces like us."

When I asked how six officers made up a task force, he snapped, "Six? We got eight. It's about time you boys understood you're part of the team." To be sure that we fulfilled our agreement to serve justice, Officer Fowler assigned us all kinds of paperwork and filing, which had nothing to do with catching our assailants. We were not moles in the station. We felt more like mice, scurrying here and there, filling coffee cups and making photocopies for officers too busy, or too lazy, to do it themselves. It bothered us to be used like this until Levi flashed the greatest idea since a group of bishops decided the Amish could use air compressors for milking cows.

Levi proposed we use the station's photocopier to make fliers about the camera and then post them on every windshield in every public parking lot in the county. It would take a while, but at least we wouldn't have to use our stun guns, or wear wires. Getting access to the photocopier was easy when Officer Fowler wasn't around. We were not questioned by his deputies or the bailiff, who no longer looked up from his paper when we passed his desk. Everyone assumed we were tracking down our assailants. When we'd enter the station, they'd ask us if we had any leads. Not yet, we said.

We took full advantage of the photocopier and made hundreds of flyers. Levi had helped me draw a picture of the camera and suggested we include a $10,000 reward. When I questioned this, he snapped, "Your sisters' souls are priceless."

"What if there's no film in the camera when we find it?" I asked.

"If that's what you believe, that's what you'll create."

He warned me not to give in to my fear and said I needed faith now. Like in God's will, which surprised me, because I'd never expected Levi Esh to believe in God's will. "Do you believe in that?" I asked.

Levi shook his head. "I believe in accidents more."

SEVEN

I REMEMBER LEANING AGAINST the photocopier one night in late February, watching it spit out image after image of the camera. We'd hadn't had many leads on it yet, and we'd called every pawn shop in the county. The camera show in Philadelphia looked more and more promising, but I didn't have the nerve to ask Levi to take me now that neither of us had the money or the time, which certainly didn't help to elevate my mood. I'd been melancholy, which wasn't entirely unusual, partly because I missed Leroy and the men in the barbershop and the safety of Ruthanne's kitchen. I missed shaving the men and didn't find much satisfaction scraping paint off the barn. The wood didn't talk, didn't say, "Hey, there, Ugly. What you got goin' on today?" The barn didn't care how I was feeling, didn't praise me for my work or criticize me, either, which was better than no talking at all. I missed the chatter of the barbershop. I even missed the sagging cot and wet-nosed Caesar nudging me awake each morning.

What disturbed me most of all was that I had been dreaming about Marcus Paoni lately. He kept showing me the camera, but he refused to give it to me. I would have liked to blame him for everything (didn't he start all this?), but my bad mood had nothing to do with him.

February was the hardest time of the year because it reminded me of Mamm on the 14th, the twin's birthday on the 3rd, and Sarah's birthday on the 27th. I couldn't wait for March. Maybe it was the weather. There had been nothing but gray skies since Amos had left. I knew he had written a few times, but Levi refused to share his news. He'd take the letters behind the barn with cigarettes and a bottle of booze; beer no longer interested him and he left the rest of the Rolling Rock for me. I don't know how many times he'd read the letters, but he'd review them long enough to fall asleep. Usually, in the morning, there'd be nothing left of the letter but a small heap of ashes, and an empty bottle stuffed with the butts of his Marlboros. I'd cover him with a blanket, then stand over him, feeling like I'd been called into his life to protect him. It was in those moments, in the dull gray dawns with frost on the ground, that I wondered if this was God's will.

All I knew was that the more time I spent with Levi Esh, the more I wanted to know this man who loved my sister as if she were still alive. I never mentioned her name for fear that he would stop talking to me altogether. We didn't talk much as it was, especially after he'd started to drink, and it worried me. As much as he said the booze made him feel better, I knew it made him worse.

Most mornings, he couldn't tolerate any loud sounds, so we'd wait around the barn reading magazines until his hangover wore off and we could work again. That was usually after noon, when he finished feeding his mother and cleaning up the kitchen, which he insisted on doing himself even though I told him I was good with dishes and could wash them outside where she wouldn't see me. I wanted to help him focus on work. Not only had he been slow renovating the barn, he'd been falling behind with his customers, too.

One of the clients, a white-haired Englisher from Vermont, drove by the farm a few times, threatening to take Levi to small-claims court if he didn't finish the kitchen in his 1781 farmhouse-turned-bed-and-breakfast. He wanted it done before the Gordonville Auction, which was in two weeks. Levi told him it was hunting season even though Levi didn't hunt. When I asked him why he was ignoring his clients, he told me they could wait. "I'll tell you what my priority is. Finding your camera," he said.

I couldn't help but think about the accident when an image spat out of the copier, and I wondered if that was his priority, too.

"Do you think it was God's will?"

Levi shook his head. "They were too young and too beautiful to die like that. It was a stupid, stupid accident."

"That makes it easier," I said, feeling a chill despite the warmth of the machine against the back of my legs.

"Easier for what?"

"To stay angry."

Levi turned to me. The photocopier had stopped spitting out flyers, and he gathered them and squared the edges, banging the stack against the machine. I felt the sting in my heart and threw my gaze at the coffee stain on the floor. A phone rang in the office on the other side of the wall. No one answered.

"I thought we didn't believe in accidents," I said.

"There's a lot of things we're supposed to believe, Eli. And that's what makes me different. No matter how hard I try, I can't seem to believe what I should."

"I never knew you were trying so hard."

"You're funny."

"I'm serious. Is that why you're not baptized, yet?"

"Shit, no," he said, and handed me the stack of flyers.

"Let's go. We have work to do," he said, moving past me toward the door. "I've called four more pawn shops and we've got a lot of driving to do in the morning. Your little treasure hunt has us going from Ephrata to Brownstown to Harrisburg. I want to be awake when we drive into the capital."

I didn't move.

"The camera can wait. I want to know why."

"Why what? Jesus, Eli. Let it go."

"What can't you believe?"

"In forgiving the driver. Okay? Can you stop asking me questions now?"

I swallowed. "I haven't forgiven him either."

"Promise me you never will," he said and for the first time in my life, Levi Esh faced me and lifted the black lenses off his face, revealing a socket where the left eye should have been; it was empty and red, marbled with capillaries. His right eye looked like the hard mints we sold at the candy stand, the kind of clear blue I'd seen glowing from the salt on the road. It was beautiful, almost jewel-like and I couldn't imagine what it would be like to have only one. I couldn't mask the horror on my face. I imagined it was the same look most people gave me when they first noticed my hands. I was sorry, but I couldn't change my face for Levi, at least not then.

"Hang your mouth open any longer and the flies will land on your tongue."

I closed my mouth. "I'm sorry. I didn't know."

"Amos poked me with a stick when he was two."

"Is that why you're always arguing?

"No. It was an accident. I lifted him up to pick an apple and he grabbed a branch instead. He was just excited. He didn't mean no harm. We don't argue about that. It's the driver that draws blood."

I stared at him. "You argue about the driver?"

"It's nice not to have Amos around anymore, telling me I need to forgive him. What he did was an unthinkable crime, and he should pay for it with his life."

I nodded and closed the door, annoyed that a few officers seemed to be huddled nearby, listening.

"That's why I'm here," I whispered. "In *rumspringa*. I have never been able to forgive the driver. I need to see him."

"Why?"

"I want to know what he looks like," I said, feeling awkward sharing this, even though I couldn't stop. "I need to see his face. He's always been this dark cloud, not a real person. I always thought if I could see him, it'd be easier to forgive what he'd done to us."

I was surprised by Levi's response. So quick. So dismissive. He flicked his wrist when he spoke.

"What if he doesn't want to be forgiven?"

I stared at him, exasperated.

"Then it will be that much harder for us to move on! I know my mother wanted to forgive him. She says she has, but I know she wanted to know who he was. If he had troubles of his own, you know? She always told us that every person you meet is fighting their own battle. But we never saw his."

"Maybe you're not supposed to. Look, I don't care what the bishop says. Promise me that you won't give in. You hear me? Never. No matter what anybody tells you. He doesn't deserve our sympathy or forgiveness. Let the driver fight this battle on his own."

I nodded my head slowly, feeling the prick of his words in my heart. Though I had not been able to forgive the driver, I never thought that forgiveness was something to earn rather than something to give away. Levi spoke like most of the English, and his words reminded me of the letters I had read, but this time, I did not find comfort.

"Okay," I whispered. "Okay."

Levi swallowed and scratched the back of his golden hair which had almost grown to his chin. Ironically, he had never looked so Amish, or grown up. He would be thirty in September, and he looked so oddly out of place in the police station with its electric lights and wall sockets, standing beside a hulking piece of metal made to duplicate things.

"You promise me?"

"Yes," I whispered, feeling sandpaper in my throat.

"Give me your hand. We'll shake on it."

"What? Why? I don't... shake hands like that."

"I know. Trust me. This will be better."

Levi lifted the lid on the photocopier and lay his hand on the glass.

"Just do it. Put it beside mine."

The glass felt warm beneath my hand. Levi hit the button and the arm below the glass swept left and right. A bright green light flashed and out popped a piece of paper with black-and-white handprints. Nothing was different about mine. The scanner didn't pick up the webbing. Just a hand, like everyone else's.

"That's your promise," Levi said and handed a copy to me.

That's when things started to go very, very wrong. Whatever deal I'd struck with Levi did nothing to comfort me. As Leroy would say, I was caught in the eddy of a shit river with no oar. No matter how much I wanted to believe that I was loving Levi well by promising never to forgive the driver, I was feeling worse and worse. If this was love, and moving toward God, I was in deep trouble.

Every now and then, when we were working on the barn, Levi would catch me frozen in thought, paintbrush poised in the air like the front paw of an Irish Setter. This particular time I was stricken by the fear of not reaching heaven. The odds were stacked against me. "What if I don't get in?"

Levi looked down on me from the roof. It was an unseasonably warm day in early March. The smell of grass and dirt in the air. The twitter of birds in the breeze. We worked with our shirts off, skin soaking up the first warm sun of the year. Levi had been playing his Who tape again on a battery-operated cassette player, singing along to "The Real Me." "Can you see the real me, preacher? Preacher? Can you see the real me?"

He turned it down.

"What's that?"

"I don't think we'll make it into heaven."

Levi pushed himself off the roof and landed on the ground.

"What? Why?"

"If we don't forgive the driver."

Levi scratched the stubble on his chin.

"You really want to go to heaven?"

"Don't you?"

Levi actually paused to think about this. There are many reasons that ninety percent of Amish youth return to the community after *rumspringa*, but none are more prevalent than the fear of dying alone and not going to heaven. As long as Levi refused to forgive the driver, he was not in God's good graces. Didn't he know he was making things hard on himself? I wanted to remind him that he had done nothing wrong but this. He was no thief. He was no soul catcher.

"Heaven's not a place for a guy like me."

"Why not? Don't you want to see your dad again?"

"I don't believe that I will. I hardly remember what he looked like. We were so little when he died."

"You don't remember anything?"

"Not his face. None of the details, at least. Not anymore. You know the real shitter? I forgot what his eyes look like. I don't know when it happened. I just know one day they weren't there anymore in my mind. Like a chalk drawing someone had blown off the board without asking."

"What if you had a photo?"

"That might have been nice."

"The English are lucky. They keep all those albums."

"Maybe," Levi said. "Maybe not. I suppose if we could see the dead, we'd miss them even more, which is probably why God never wanted us to have our photographs taken."

Levi grabbed a glass of iced lemonade that had sweated on the ground in the sun. I tried to resume the painting, but I couldn't concentrate.

"What about Hanna?"

"What about Hanna?" he asked, snatching the rag from the loop in my jeans to wipe the sweat from his face.

"Wouldn't you want to see her?"

"In a photograph? No way, Eli. She hated cameras."

"In heaven," I said.

"How? I don't believe she'd remember me, either."

"Why not?"

"I don't believe she'd want to," he said.

"You don't believe a lot, do you?"

"Only two things," he said. "Your promise and—"

"I'm telling you, I don't know if I can keep it."

"Then you're not trying hard enough, Eli."

I nodded, feeling ashamed for even thinking of breaking a promise to Levi after all he'd done to help me. He handed me the dirty rag.

"You're going to go to heaven, Eli."

"It's not guaranteed. And you hardly know me."

"I know your heart. And so does God."

I wanted to believe him but my face fell flat. I stared at him in the shadow of the roof, helpless and frightened, like a small rabbit that had come out of its hole too soon, only to stare into the barrel of a rifle.

"Trust me, Eli," he said, then whispered, his own superstitions hard-wired into his brain. "There's more than one way to get to heaven."

Levi Esh was teaching me a great lesson about trust. He was letting me figure things out for myself and that made him, in my mind, an exemplary brother and good friend. Maybe the best friend I ever had. The problem was that he was half right and half wrong, and I didn't know which half to trust.

"I'm worried," I said. "I've never broken a promise."

"Me neither," Levi said. "We're going to find your camera once and for all."

"How? There aren't enough pawn shops in this state."

"Maybe not. But I have a plan."

I was unsure if I wanted to know it, but he told me anyway and grinned.

"If it don't get you to heaven, you'll at least have a friend in hell."

EIGHT

LEVI'S PLAN WAS PRECIPITATED by two words I had spoken in my sleep through clenched teeth. Marcus Paoni. Enough for Levi to wonder who he was. And ask. I did not lie. I told him I'd stolen his camera, and why.

"Big Ugly?" Levi asked, trying hard not to laugh.

"Big Ugly," I said. "I'm serious."

"You sure he wasn't talking about your pecker?"

I stared at him. "No. That would be Big Beauty."

Levi smiled, but didn't laugh.

As much as I tried to tell Levi that my dreams were getting better, they were getting worse. I'd seen Marcus Paoni almost every night since we'd started to distribute the flyers, which suggested that I owned the camera. Levi asked me the obvious one night after we'd distributed another batch. He drove us to Your Place, a small bar and pool room on Route 340 in Intercourse, between Leacock and Paradise, the place where Amish guys in *rumspringa* hung out on weeknights. We ordered a pepperoni pizza and beer, but Levi didn't drink that night. He told me that no matter what, he'd never drink and drive. He poured me another beer. My teeth always felt a bit numb when I drank beer, but I didn't tell Levi. I drank another. When my shoulders drooped and my eyes glazed over, the earliest indication of my intoxication, Levi launched his inquisition, which sobered me momentarily.

"Have you ever considered telling Marcus the truth?"

"Why would I do that?"

"If he still has the warranty on the camera, chances are he still has the serial number, which will identify yours from the hundreds out there. Once we find that out, we can notify every dealer from here to Juneau with a phone call."

I hadn't said a word about the show in Philadelphia and thought now might be a good time, since Levi had mentioned a place as far as Alaska. I imagined the adventure we'd have driving The Monster across the country, bound by our mission to find and free my sisters' souls. But the thought of sitting in a truck for hours on end, day after day, made me cringe. There had to be another way to find the camera, and I truly hoped that Levi's plan was it.

"It was his grandfather's camera," I said.

"Then you'll have to tell his grandfather, too."

"His grandfather died," I said, recalling the flyers Marcus had posted around the market in the summer of 1976.

"See that? It's getting easier already."

"How will we ever find Marcus now?"

Levi smiled. "Voting records."

"You know where he lives?"

I stared at Levi, my eyes clouded with questions. I choked back the tears. "You've done everything to help me. Why do you care so much?"

Levi smiled and reached out to put his arm around me.

"I want you to find your peace."

Levi had found the address of Marcus Paoni. He lived on the western side of the county, in a subdivision of Hempfield Township. Apparently, Levi had clients in the neighborhood and built the cabinets in their kitchens. He knew that Marcus was a mailman, and he knew when Marcus was home. He said Marcus was harmless, somebody he believed, between us, who sat on the pot to pee. But that was no concern to me. I had bigger puddles to jump. One moment I'd be ready to talk to him, one moment I'd be worried sick. My indecision tortured us both. Levi said I reminded him of every guy he'd ever known who, on the Saturday before baptism, knew it was his chance to turn back. He said if I didn't stop pacing, he'd tie me to a post in the barn and tell Marcus Paoni himself.

"You can't tell him!"

"You want the camera or not?"

I paused. We'd been outside all morning repairing a fence post by the creek that had buckled under the last snow. Levi paused every thirty minutes for an aspirin and a cup of coffee from his thermos. I'm sure my worrying was another hammer in his head. He reeked of alcohol and his shirt was stained with salt from his excessive sweat. His hair lay like strings of wet gold across his forehead, and in the lenses of his sunglasses were the cars passing us from the road.

"This is my battle," I said. "Let me fight it."

"That's the problem, Eli. You don't want to win this battle. You're too busy fighting the wrong one."

"What's that?"

"Your sisters."

I stared at him, vexed, parched from our work.

"I am not fighting my sisters."

"Oh, yeah? Then why won't you let them go? I've given you every chance to meet Marcus. He's the only person who can give you that serial number, if you even stand a chance of finding the camera again. But I don't think you really want to find it."

Levi was wrong. I wanted to find the camera. I was even willing to surrender it to its rightful owner. What tortured me was knowing who would get to keep the film.

"What if he asks me why I want it?"

"You tell him the truth."

"That I'm a soul catcher?"

"Yes. If that's what you believe. You know what Hanna used to say whenever we argued about her spending so much time in the dance studio? She said we don't regret the things we do, only the things we haven't done."

I stared at him, watching the postal truck rise and fall on the ridge above us. He had accused me of not being a fighter. I felt the heat of the anger flaring inside me and I wore it on my face.

"And you think this will bring me peace?"

Levi pounded in the last stake.

"Yes," he said then turned to his shadow. "And Emma."

A crow swooped down over us, attracted to the gleam of the metal thermos. It was quiet and still, the earth soaked with snow melt, the creek solid, swollen with its silence, creaking in the winter sun and threatening, any moment, to shatter our secrets.

I hadn't slept much thinking about it. I lay in the barn on a pile of hay, watching the stars through the holes in the roof and said a prayer for my sisters' souls, hoping they were safe wherever they were. I did not trust grace to bring us together. Not that meeting Marcus Paoni was a blessing from God. It was the closest I'd ever come to starring in the devil's playground. In the morning, I read the sky and looked for any signs that our plan was not worth pursuing. I saw only cloudless blue. We showered and shaved for the occasion. Levi insisted we wear Amish clothes when we met Marcus, but I couldn't understand why it mattered.

"You think we'll look more... forgivable if we're Amish?"

Levi brushed the lint off my purple collar.

"Forgiveness isn't what you need right now. You need the serial number of that camera. First things first. We're talking survival now. Not fulfillment."

Levi directed me to our reflections in the side of The Monster. We had dressed in the barn. I wore Levi's clothes: a bright blue long-sleeved shirt, black pants, and black suspenders. Levi wore the same, but with a purple shirt. We looked like two big bruises. Levi turned to me.

"You ready to meet your maker, Big Ugly?"

I nodded and stood taller, feigning courage.

I hung my head out the window of The Monster for most of the ride, searching that cloudless sky, wondering if Levi's plan was a mistake. Should anything strange suddenly appear, I made it clear to Levi that he was to turn around immediately and deliver me to the barn. If it all went wrong, I wasn't sure that I was equipped with enough kindness to be a friend to anyone in hell.

We stood on the front porch of Marcus Paoni's house in the dappled light of a birch tree. There was an overturned baby pool in the front lawn, a brown and brittle patch of land that looked forgotten. I was not ready to ring the bell yet. Levi turned to me and smoothed out my hair, which had grown just long enough to be blown by the wind.

"How do you feel?"

"Miserable."

"Understandable. It's not meant to be a party, Eli."

I stared at the brass knob on the door.

"Levi," I said and turned to him, my heart pounding, "no matter what happens, you'll still be my friend, right?"

"Eli, of course. Don't ever question that."

"Even if I make a fool of myself in there?"

"You're trying to make things right. Only a fool wouldn't try as hard."

I caught our reflection in the door knob, hearing voices inside the house. A small child, a dog, another voice that sounded like a man's.

I quickly pulled out of my pocket the photocopied handprints we'd made weeks before, unfolded the crinkled paper and solemnly lay my hand on my print. "Friends?"

"Even in hell," Levi said and put his hand on his own.

"You're too good a man to go to hell," I said.

Levi punched my shoulder. "Just tell the truth. And break a leg," he said. This time, I nodded and knew what he meant. I could only hope the legacy I'd leave in this thorny path was worth something good.

I rang the bell and a small round girl with red hair in pigtails opened the door. She stood staring up at us with a Barbie in hand, eyes wide and wild, taking us in. She looked back over her shoulder, down the short hallway and into the kitchen, where a young man, around Amos' age, sat reading the newspaper.

"Marcus, the Mormons are here."

I turned to Levi who shrugged, trying hard not to laugh. I wanted to punch his shoulder and make him stop.

Marcus looked up and folded the paper.

"We're not Mormons," I said. "We're not here to convert you. We're Amish."

Marcus stood up and walked toward us. He was dressed in his postal uniform, wearing shorts, thick socks, and boots that could make a fine dent in plaster, or bone. I froze, watching him approach, remembering the red-cheeked, red-bellied bully of my youth. His sister stayed in the hallway until he shooed her out with a gentle tap on her backside. "Tell mom you're ready for school." But the little girl had run to the window and pointed to the truck. "You're the Amish robbers. You're driving!"

I looked at Levi, helpless. Marcus looked at me.

"What do you want with us?"

I cleared my throat, feeling every tendon and nerve in my body shake. Even my tongue trembled when I spoke and my words were rushed and crowded, like grain in a silo. I had never been in more of a hurry to tell the truth.

"When we were young, you left your camera at my candy stand and I stole it. And I'm sorry," I said and scratched my neck. Everything was starting to feel very hot. "You posted signs and I tore them down, and I've never tried to find you all this time. Then the camera was stolen from me last year. I need it back now, and I need help finding it. My life depends on it. Actually, my sisters' lives depend on it. Their souls are inside it."

I turned to Levi when I finished. "Was that okay?"

Levi said nothing, focused entirely on Marcus, who looked shell-shocked.

"Who are you?"

"I'm Eli," I said. "Big… Big… Big Ugly, remember?"

I showed him my hands.

Marcus nodded and his lip quivered when he spoke.

"How could I forget?" he said in a high-pitched voice that was not at all what I imagined from a guy his size. He could have tackled me, but he hugged me.

"It's all my fault, Eli."

I squirmed inside his embrace.

"But I should have returned it," I said, feeling awkward and stiff and not at all comfortable with Marcus so close to me.

"I tried to find you," he said. "After my baseball game that night at Twirly Top. I saw you through the window with your dad. I wanted to apologize, but you ran outside."

"Why didn't you?"

"I was too embarrassed to say anything in front of your sisters," he said, looking back over his shoulder, as if to make sure his own wasn't eavesdropping. His voice quivered. "The tall one looked like she might kill me."

Then Marcus sobbed into my shoulder. Levi stepped aside.

"You're not ugly!" he wailed. "How could I say that! You're a beautiful boy! I never want to see that camera again."

"You don't?" I asked, startled.

Marcus met my gaze in the hallway. "I just want you to forgive me."

NINE

IF GOD HAD TOLD me that Marcus Paoni would be asking for my forgiveness one day, I would have believed it was the devil talking in my ear. I don't remember the ride home. I was in shock, not because Marcus had forgiven me, but because in patching together the ever-fading pieces of August 14, 1976, I realized we might have avoided the accident if I had faced Marcus then.

"I messed up," I said to no one in particular, although Levi was the only one within earshot.

"What's wrong? You did fine."

I shook my head. The world had taken on that nebulousness again, and everything, especially the cars whizzing beside us on the freeway, looked smeared.

"The driver might not have hit us if we'd stayed, but I was too scared I'd get caught for stealing Marcus's camera. I wanted to go home."

Levi reached for the cigarettes on the dashboard.

"You can't beat yourself up like that."

"But I knew better."

"You were just a kid, Eli. You were scared."

I shook my head, buried my face in my hands, smelling the smoke of Levi's cigarettes on my fingers.

"Look at the bright side. He forgave you."

I nodded and took one of the cigarettes to smoke because I had nothing more to say. Marcus' forgiving me did nothing to help my sisters. I still needed the camera, and Marcus was of no help. His grandfather had received it as a gift. He had called his parents, but from what they knew, there was no warranty. The only way to identify the camera, they suggested, was to develop the film left inside it.

This was hardly news. I was so despondent over the whole ordeal that I slept for three days, roused only by the smell of Levi's chicken corn soup. He nudged me awake in the barn where I lay on piles of hay, wrapped in wool, warm and drowsy with depression, lulled into a deep sleep by the tinkling of rain on the roof. The days had grown warmer and longer but nothing about spring seemed hopeful. I wanted to sleep forever and I told Levi to go away. He ignored me and nudged my back with his knee, then wedged the bowl of soup into the divot he'd scooped out of hay.

"Wake up, Big Beauty. You've got to eat."

"Save it for your mom. She's the one who's dying."

"Broken spirit'll kill you first," he said.

"Then let me die."

"I'll let you die trying, but not like this."

"But my life is over," I groaned.

"You can be sad, not pathetic. Get up. We're going to a *rumspringa* party."

It was one of those acrid March nights that smelled of woodsmoke and ash, the apocryphal musk of beginnings and endings. We didn't wear our wires, and we left the stun guns in Levi's barn. Every time we passed a phone shanty, it occurred to me that we should stop and call Officer Fowler to tell him where we were going, but as soon as I'd open my mouth, I'd shut it just as fast. I didn't even ask Levi how he'd found out about the party. He was in no mood to talk on the drive and listened instead to songs on the radio. The mailman had delivered another letter from Amos that day and it had thrown him into a spin. We both had a lot on our minds, our worries punctuated by the crush of fallen cherry blossoms that lay damp and decayed on the road to Gap.

"Are you going to drink beer tonight?"

"Yes. A lot. They let Amos out of jail."

It was more than Levi had said all day and I trusted the conviction in his voice, even though neither of us had any idea how unprepared we were for their reunion. From the look on Levi's face, I believed he was more terrified than happy for his brother's freedom. I could not understand why the cops had let Amos go after only one month in jail. When I asked, Levi just turned and said, "Good behavior."

"Probably spewing off the Confession of Faith," I said and reached for the handle above the window when we hit a bump. "Besides, he's not that free. He still has a fine."

Levi turned to me. "He already paid it."

"How's that?"

"The bishop."

"Emma's father bailed him out?"

"Amos wrote to him every day. Must have made some kind of impression, because the bishop sent cash."

We said nothing more for the rest of the ride, my mind tethered to the thought that Bishop Beiler had found a way to forgive Amos, and that Amos had had the courage to ask. Sitting there in The Monster, I wondered how many chances I had had, and wasted, when it had come to confronting the bishop about what I'd done when I was a boy. If it had been as simple as writing letters to him every day, then I was equally angry at God for making it so hard for me to write. I wondered if in the silence between the ink and paper my secrets would have been safer, my confession more sincere.

I crossed my arms and pressed them hard against my chest, feeling my heart beat through my coat. Levi picked at his nails. We were as glum as two fellas can get, and though we had no plans on making friends that night, we didn't intend to lose any.

We followed the flames of a bonfire that flickered in the distance, then turned down a narrow lane flanked by plum trees in bloom, stars studding a tobacco warehouse that stood stark, stripped of paint. In the gravel parking lot were several black trucks like The Monster and several dozen buggies, horses gnawing on the fence posts where they'd been tied up. Groups of Amish guys milled outside, throwing horseshoes into a ring; others gathered around the bonfire, and more spilled in and out of the warehouse, standing and sitting in the windows, looking down on the spectacle of Amish guys playing corner ball. I watched one of the guys, a short skinny kid, leap up and roll onto the hay after being grazed in the balls. He covered his crotch and winced.

"They play hard here," I said, looking out the truck window.

"They're just acting."

"But I think it really hurts. Look at him."

"True. Makes it a better performance for him," he said and pointed to the edge of the circle of spectators, where a photographer crouched with a camera, aiming his lens at the players. His flash illuminated the bodies of two players in the middle, one jumping, the other tucked and rolling to the edge of the court, where the photographer tossed him a wad of bills. I don't know if I was more surprised to see this form of compensation or that the boys who accepted the bills were Beachy Amish, with shaved heads that looked like mine had.

"The Leacocks are here," I said.

Levi laughed.

"So is everyone else. It's a party, not a song group."

"They don't sing songs at this party?"

"Only after they've finished the keg. Come on."

I got out of the truck and followed Levi but walked past the Leacocks with my head down. They were a rowdy gang comprised of the more liberal Amish, the Beachy, a splinter group that had separated from the Old Order in 1910, when the telephone started creeping into the homes of Pennsylvania farmers. In addition to holding private Bible readings and meeting in churches, the Beachy used electricity and telephones, drove cars and wore plain yet modern clothes. Everyone had their own take on why the Old Order prohibited the use of electricity and telephones in the home, but some would argue it had less to do with keeping us disconnected from the Outside World than with saving face with the Beachy Amish, a battle that had been ongoing for seventy years. We all knew the Beachy took pleasure in challenging the Old Order, however subtle the jibe. I was still surprised to see the Leacocks dressed in traditional garb that night. They wore black pants, black vests, and white button-down shirts. They appeared as if they were about to kneel for a baptism, even though it would not be their own.

"You want a beer?" one of them asked me when I passed him at an empty corn crib, where he stood peeing.

"Yeah, sure," I said, looking for Levi, who had disappeared inside the ring of corner ball players, taking his place in the queue, ready to defend his championship title.

"Keg's inside. Make yerself at home."

I paused, hearing the guy's accent. At first, I thought it was the beer that had slurred his speech.

"What's that?"

"Go on. Git yer beer, boy."

I stared at him and we locked eyes for a moment before he filled his own cup and walked away, leaving me alone. I walked to the door looking into the truant world of the warehouse beyond the kegs and broken chicken crates, declining its invitation to explore. Everything in the warehouse, including the hundred-some young people gathered there, had suddenly taken on a grainy texture. Nothing was as clear or defined in *rumspringa*, and that made me uneasy. I knew enough about boundaries to need them now.

Just then, I noticed, hanging from a rusty hook on the door, an upside-down horseshoe. It wasn't just any horseshoe either. It was dipped in silver paint and hand-painted with flowers. It had chipped in places over the years, but not so much that the artwork couldn't be identified as my sister's. It bothered me to see it hanging the wrong way. I reached up and turned it right-side up, but it slid clockwise until it hung like a frown again. I don't remember how many times I tried to right it, but I jammed the loose screw into the rotted wood with my thumb until the screw fell out, and the whole thing dropped on my foot. "Jesus, Joseph and Mary," I cried, sounding like Leroy.

One of the Beachy passing me laughed. "That's good. You almost sound like us," he said and bent down to pick up the horseshoe. I turned and stared at him. He lifted his hat and scratched the stubble on his head. "Itches, doesn't it?" I asked, curious to hear him speak again, wondering what he meant by "us."

"More than a leech on yer crotch."

I cocked my head. We didn't have leeches in our local waters, not in our ponds, rivers, or crotches.

"Where do you fish?" I asked him.

"I don't," he said, handing me the horseshoe. "Make sure ye hang it straight this time. Don't let it cruck-ed."

I took it and forced a smile. Of all the signs I had wanted the day we'd gone to meet Marcus Paoni, I only needed this one to know something was wrong.

First the upside-down horseshoe, and now the odd accent this guy possessed. I didn't know of a single Amish man who couldn't say where he fished. I should have gone out and told Levi about this, but I was more compelled by the photographer. I leaned against the frame of the warehouse door, watching him in the firelight, studying his features, adding them up in my mind, sickened by the sum. Patton. Unmistakably. He shoved his lens into their faces, doling out wads of bills to each boy who permitted access to the shadow side of our culture. I did not move but waited, watching him until he turned, feeling my gaze.

"I hope you have a hundred dollars for each of them!" I yelled.

Some of the guys ran off to their buggies with the money, securing them in the back inside lock boxes. Patton got up and marched toward me.

"I'm doing nothing wrong, Ugly. They invited me," Patton said, then smiled, eyeing me through the lens.

I stepped out of his way, but he followed me back into the warehouse. I jumped when I heard the first snap.

"Please don't take my photo," I said, grinding the words between my teeth, searching desperately for Levi.

"It's okay, Ugly. I got enough to pay you now."

Then he took another photo. I paused, hearing the sound of paper being thrown, then felt the lump at my feet. I saw the wad of bills on the floor but I didn't pick them up, hoping the heel of a brother would grind them into the boards. "Take your money," I said.

"What's the matter? It's not enough?"

"It's plenty," I said and moved out of his way, trying to navigate through the crowd to the keg. At no point in my life did I want a beer more than I did then. I filled up a red plastic cup while one of the Beachy watched me sweat.

"Who invited him?" I growled.

"He followed us from Gordonville."

I shook my head seeing his front shirt pocket stuffed with bills.

"He shouldn't be here," I said.

"Maybe you shouldn't," he whispered, staring at the beer in my hand.

I drank quickly, without letting the head settle, and the foam clung to my chin. Patton snapped another photo. "It suits you," he said. "The guys at the shop are gonna love these. Big Ugly grew a beard!"

The Beachy kid stifled a laugh.

"Go home, bishop," he said, but I didn't know if he was talking to me or to another Amish kid, a Canary, who happened to pass him then, holding out a copy of the *Ausbund*, which the Beachy guy flicked away with his hand.

The Amish kid froze and watched the book of hymns fall on the floor, between my toe and the Beachy's heel, but the Beachy kid didn't bend to pick it up. He lifted his beer and drank. He was drunk, but not even a drunk, blind Amish youth would let the *Ausbund* touch the ground like that.

"What's yer problem, bishop?" he asked, and this time turned his eyes on me, all dark and hollow and dead.

I shook my head, studying him. He was the third Beachy guy with the shaggy remains of a crew cut growing back. If it weren't for my own hair in shambles, he would've passed me unnoticed. Just another derelict in *rumspringa* sowing his wild oats until he joined the church.

"I know you," I said and looked at his clothes. He was Levi's height, tall, but not as lean, and the jeans he was wearing were unbuttoned at the top and a bit of his stomach bulged over the flap of denim. He burped and waggled his finger.

"Nope. Don't think we ever met."

"Good Christian?" I asked him, remembering the cadence and tone of his voice and the cool metal of the barrel of his gun pressed against my cheek bone. I shifted my eyes, wondering how I'd ever slip out of the warehouse fast enough to run to the phone shanty at the end of the road and call Officer Fowler. I didn't even know if the phone worked, but I knew I couldn't let him get away.

He leaned closer to me and studied my face, then my hands, and his lips turned up in a smile. He threw his arm around me and beckoned Patton to take our photo, but I slipped out from under him and excused myself, then moved through the warehouse and pushed open the back door. I felt my heart pounding. I searched the corner ball court for Levi, but he was too involved in a game to be bothered. I waved to him but he seemed to ignore me, even when I jumped up a few times and kept pointing back at the warehouse. We had found our guys, and it was up to me to do something about it. I didn't want to run and draw any more attention to myself. I ran down the road a half mile in the dark and called Officer Fowler from the telephone shanty.

"You're absolutely sure these are the guys?" he asked.

I nodded, holding the cold plastic receiver in my hands, feeling the metal chord hit the back of my head. My whole body was trembling. Officer Fowler asked me to slow down. "It's them," I heaved. "It has... to be... them."

Officer Fowler praised me and told me he'd send a few of his men over right away, but they'd be in black cars and would be driving without lights. I told him they wouldn't need lights and to follow the bonfire. He made me promise not to tell anyone else, not even Levi, and to act as calm as possible. Then we hung up, and I walked back up the hill in the dark, my steps heavy with dread.

I forced myself back into the warehouse, took a beer, then pushed my way through a group of gangs I knew, feeling safer in the clutches of the Canaries and Pinecones, even the Drifters, hoping to slip into a safe conversation which was anything but. They smothered me with their welcome.

Eli Yoder? Where you been? Why'd you sell your dog business? Why haven't you come to song group? Good to see you, brother. We've been waiting for you.

I couldn't handle it anymore and snapped, "Look at me? Can't you see? I'm not your brother," I said. "Not yet."

I stepped back, reading their faces, grim and stunned. I went outside to find Levi. I didn't want to be there when the cops came, but no sooner had I reached the door and picked up the horseshoe lying across the threshold that I felt the ground begin to shake. Levi was being chased up the hill from the corner ball court. He ran toward me, shirt torn, nose bloody, his face and his pursuer's back-lit by the bonfire.

"Get in the truck, Eli!"

"Why? Did you see them?"

Levi paused to catch his breath and pointed to The Monster.

"I'll explain later, but we have to go home. Now!"

The pursuer waved his arms.

"Not until you tell him the truth!"

I recognized the voice. My stomach folded seeing Amos, his fists curled at Levi. "You owe Eli that much!"

Suddenly the guys from the horseshoe pit and the corner ball court started running toward them. I had never heard such panic in Levi's voice.

Amos tackled Levi and the two rolled down the hill, flailing and fighting, wrestling like the brothers at war they had always been. I ran after them, picking up Levi's sunglasses that had been knocked into the grass.

"Not here," Levi pleaded.

"Yes. Right here. In front of everyone."

Amos pinned Levi to the ground and drove his knee into his back. He turned Levi's bloody face into the hay from the corner ball court, and with his other hand grabbed a fistful of his hair. "You will tell all of us!"

"No!" Levi screamed, his eye red and swollen now. There had to be at least two hundred guys standing there, lured to the bigger and better fight than the one they'd been watching in the corner ball court. It didn't surprise me to see Patton pushing his way into the center with his camera.

"Eli, come!" Amos said, beckoning me forward. I could only see hundreds of black broadfall pants. I did not want to look up. I wasn't sure what they had in mind for me at the warehouse, but my heart was pounding and my hair was already soaked.

Levi bucked, trying to jerk Amos off, but Amos managed to hold on, digging his nails into his brother's forearm.

"You will tell him, you coward. Tonight."

Then Amos punched him in the jaw.

I swallowed, feeling helpless standing there, wanting to reach out and pull Levi off the ground. Get up. You're stronger than your tears, I thought. You're wiser! Get up and fight. But Levi lay on the ground and cried.

And Patton took more photos. Snap. Snap. Snap.

Levi moaned, slumped on the ground. He could barely see me through his swollen eyes. "Eli, I'm sorry."

"Why? What is it?"

"It was me," he groaned, his voice hoarse.

"Who?" I asked, meeting Amos's eyes, wet and glazed.

"The driver," Levi whispered.

Patton fired another shot and I turned to him.

"Stop taking those goddamn photos!"

Levi took a deep breath, and with the last bit of energy he had that night, shrugged his brother off and sat up, searching for my eyes in the firelight. He hugged his knees to his chest, but his whole body shook, like he'd been lost in a storm all night. He somehow looked smaller there, frightened, certain only of the fact that everything I had thought was true between us would change. A tear slid down his cheek as he spoke.

"It was me, not the English, who killed your sisters."

I just stared, unable to speak.

"In the truck. I didn't see your buggy in the rain."

I slumped to the earth, kneeling, seeing only the flicker of the fire. Everything else was a blur. The truth made no sense to me then. Levi could have told me he was Christ Jesus himself and my face would not have changed. All I remember is that everything inside me shut down. I could make out only forms, not faces, but I finally understood the formality of it all: black hats, black pants, black vests like the wings of a hundred ravens, swooping in over me while I knelt. And Patton's camera. He hovered, crouched before me, taking my photo, taking my grief. Taking Levi's shame. Exploiting the feelings we kept private and exposing us to the Outside World. The longer we remained silent, the faster his finger flicked the shutter. Shot after shot. After shot.

After all the years I had held back, I exploded in front of the very people I had hoped would never bear witness to this side of me. It was like something or someone had split me open. The half I did not like, with all its shadows and secrets, fought to stay alive, as if it knew this was its last chance to live.

I could not hold back, even though Amos and Levi worked together to restrain me. I didn't know how strong I was. I had never known the forces locked deep inside me that moved me to such violence. It felt right in the wrong way and wrong in the right way, and nothing, not even God, could make me let go of Patton. And the Amish Imposters? They didn't move until the cops came. The cops would tell me later it was the perfect distraction, though no one condoned my actions.

I know the details of what happened only because the Eshes were there to witness it, along with two hundred other Amish guys. I would read about it later in the newspaper. According to all accounts, I struck Patton in the eye first and he dropped the camera. Then I struck his nose and jaw and kicked his stomach until he could no longer tell me to stop. Then I pulled the horseshoe from my pocket and struck his right hand until I heard the bone snap and was sure his wrist had broken. Then, when I knew he could not take any more photos of us that night, or ever, I smashed the lens of his camera and hurled the rest into the fire. Only then, on my knees, did I meet God.

PART FIVE

◆

ONE

FOR THREE DAYS I stayed kneeling on the cold concrete floor of the Lancaster County Prison while reporters from around the county and the state clamored outside my cell. It was not the first time an Amish person had gone to jail. It would not be the last. Every reporter wanted to compare me to my grandfather Lapp, who had served time in the 1950s for protesting the higher education of his children. That's the only reason I agreed to speak with them. I needed to tell them there was nothing to compare. My jailing had nothing to do with peaceful protesting. I told them I was not Amish now. And after the calamity at the warehouse, I believed I never would be Amish again.

"Would you consider yourself an exception?"

I cast my eyes to the floor to avoid their microphones and the screech of the tape in their mini-recorders.

"We all make mistakes, if that's what you mean. But we're not excused from the consequences of our actions."

They battered me with facts and figures. Four counts each of assault and battery. One count for resisting the law, which I don't remember doing, but there were bruises on my arms and legs from the batons of the officers who found me first. I didn't know how much of a fight I had put up that night, or why I had tried to resist. I don't know if I knew how seriously I had hurt Patton, or how much I would suffer if convicted on all four criminal counts. But I knew my life had ended.

"Can you please go now?" I asked the reporters.

"You do understand your life depends on the truth?"

I nodded, feeling sick. The truth had ended my life.

"Then you need to tell us everything you know."

I knew my jaw ached every time I tried to open my mouth to answer them. I knew my heart was broken, too, because it ached without my moving.

"Are you sorry, Eli?"

I was sorry that I had violated the essence of *Gelassenheit* in every way. I had been resistant. I had used force to confront another, rather than allow silence to speak for me. I looked down at my bare feet. I was sorry the guards had taken my shoes. My feet were sore and cold. But Patton?

I was not sorry for him. I was glad that he'd suffered beneath my hands. I was sorry only that the cops didn't give me a chance to talk to Levi Esh before they took me away. I wanted to know why he hadn't told me sooner; why he had helped me only to hurt me again.

"Did he go home?"

"He's at the hospital. Scheduled for surgery."

I stared at them, feeling my stomach drop.

"I hit Levi, too?"

"No. Just Patton. He's at Lancaster General now."

I let out a quiet sigh, relieved I had not hurt Levi, even though everyone else believed I had reason to. They were not so much interested in the play-by-play of events with Patton as they were about the hit-and-run with Levi.

"It was an accident," I said, wanting to be certain they got that part of the story right. "Levi said it was an accident. He didn't see our buggy in the rain."

"You're sure about that?"

I swallowed, watching their eyes. They seemed to know something but held back from speaking.

"Yes. That's what he said."

"Is that the whole truth, Eli?"

"I want to see him," I said, feeling panicked. "Will you tell the warden that I need to talk to him?"

"What will you say?"

"I need to ask him some questions."

"Sure. Not a problem. Just as long as you answer a few more questions before we talk to him."

Then my heart went limp. Did I hate him? Did I love him? Did I think I could ever forgive him? I did not tell them that we had been friends. That he was the brother I never had. I wanted to love him but I didn't know how or how long I'd have to wait to be his friend again. I wanted to know if he had told me the truth. If he had told me everything about the accident. Or who he had told.

"Eli? Here. Sit up."

I opened my eyes, realizing I had been squeezing back the tears. One of the reporters handed me a tissue. She reached through the cell bars and dropped it on the floor with a peppermint, but I did not pick either of them up.

"Eli, please answer me. Do you think Levi would have told you the truth if Amos hadn't forced him?"

"I don't know," I said, my voice cracking. I wanted to believe that Levi would have told me some day, but when? I wondered if he planned to tell my parents, or if telling me was enough. It didn't matter now. My parents, along with the entire state, and possibly the country, would read about it in the paper. Their daughters' killer had confessed. But not to them. I would not be there to console them, and realizing this, I buried my head into my hands and prayed for my parents' peace, and for my own.

"Did you know him well?"

I shook my head. I wasn't lying. I had thought I knew him. I picked up the tissue and blew my nose. "I met him only once when we were kids."

"Is it true that he was in love with your sister?"

I looked over at the reporter, stunned.

"Who told you that?"

"I'm sorry, Eli, but we can't reveal our sources."

It didn't matter. I already knew.

"Is there anything else you want to say?"

"Yes," I said, choking back the tears. "I'm sorry."

One of the reporters clicked on a tape recorder.

"Could you say that again?"

"I'm sorry," I repeated, and my words were hard.

"For breaking Mr. Maxell's hands?"

I blinked, trying to see them beyond the tears.

"For not destroying his camera sooner."

One of the tape recorders clicked off.

"Thank you, Mr. Yoder. That's all we need tonight."

I looked up, startled. Nobody had ever called me mister. It sounded wrong. It made me sound too grown up and I wondered if losing my innocence by shedding the blood of an enemy meant that I had become a man among the English. I caught the reporters' long faces fixed on me, their eyes as swollen and bloodshot as my own. They didn't know what to say and just stood there staring, like they wanted to say more, but it was late. We were all tired, but they needed to turn the thick lens of their attention on Levi next and, I imagined, fry us both like ants under a magnifying glass.

Some time after two in the morning, they left to speak with Levi, and sometime after that they left to file their stories. I worried that the warden wouldn't come, and he didn't; and I worried that Amos would say too much, and he did. At six o'clock, a guard slipped a copy of the morning paper into my cell. Levi had made headlines above the fold along with the capture of the Amish Imposters:

AMISH HOEDOWN TURNS GRIM:
HIT & RUN DRIVER CONFESSES

I made headlines below it:

HIDDEN RAGE AMONG AMISH YOUTH?
SURVIVOR LASHES OUT

I only had to read the headlines to shred the paper. There was no good that could come of this, no apology powerful enough to erase the attention I'd drawn to the Amish, to myself, and now to Levi. I tried to imagine what he was feeling, how he was doing, what he was doing, what I would do if it had been me, not him, who confessed. I wanted to be there for him, to cheer him up, to tell him it would be okay, that no matter how bad it was, he was still my friend. I wanted to tell him a joke. I wanted to bring him soup. I wanted to take him to a party where he could play corner ball all night and leave as a winner. For the first time in my life, I wanted to break a promise. No matter what became of me, I wanted to be sure that Levi knew I had forgiven him.

I don't remember falling asleep, but I must have drifted in and out of consciousness. I dreamed that I stood outside a forest wrapped in barbed wire, and Levi was waiting for me under the bough of a fir tree. In the grass, beside him, was his leg, bloody and unattached. Skeins of barbed wire had punctured the calf muscle. I wanted to help him but stood helpless, realizing that the barbed wire had bound itself around my wrists and pinned my hands in front of my chest, palms out. I could not move, and I was furious. I could only stand there and watch while he died. The feeling I had watching him was what I had felt watching the paramedics zip up my sisters in black bags. The moment I believed Levi was dead, I woke, feeling the warmth of the light on the palms of my hands. I smelled coffee and fast food.

"Eli, wake up."

I rolled over onto my side, feeling the light work its way through the bars, warming my neck and face. I opened my eyes to Officer Fowler, arm out-stretched through the bars, offering a bag of Twirly Top hamburgers.

"You mean to make it a habit of being locked up?"

"No," I groaned and pushed myself up from the floor.

Officer Fowler pulled up a chair and urged me to eat.

"Go ahead before it gets cold."

"Thanks," I said, sniffing the food.

"I heard the reporters came by last night."

I nodded, working my hands into the bag, cupping a wad of french fries between the webbing, stuffing my mouth. I didn't realize how hungry a person can get when he cries himself to sleep.

"Did you say anything else they didn't print?"

I stared at Officer Fowler and swallowed a lump of the hamburger and fries.

"Not much," I said. "Why?"

"Oh, I don't know. I was just a little worried."

"Worried? Is Levi going to jail?"

Officer Fowler shook his head.

"Statute of limitations was only two years in 1976."

I cocked my head. "Statue of what?"

"Liberty," he said and smiled. "*Statute* of limitations means how long you have to file a claim against Levi, but since the Amish avoid legal confrontations, that probably wouldn't have been an issue in this case. He can't go to jail now. The statute ran out five years ago."

I swallowed. "You sure he won't go to jail?"

"Not unless he does something as stupid again."

I stared at him and shook my head, speaking as if I were Levi.

"He won't. I promise."

"Life's unpredictable, Eli. You never do know."

"What were you worried about then?"

"You."

I paused, mid-chew, touched by his concern. Officer Fowler had never struck me as a genuinely kind man. He was always on a mission, and whatever kindness he'd shown me and Levi, it seemed, had only been to get what he wanted.

"I'm okay," I said. "They haven't hurt me here."

"Good. Good," he said, averting his eyes from my face to the floor, avoiding whatever it was he wanted to say. He flicked the lid on his Tic-Tacs. "I was worried you might have said something that should've been off the record."

I had reached in for another hamburger and paused. "You read the papers," I said and shrugged. "Didn't say much of anything interesting. Just wanted to be sure they got the record straight, that I'm not my granddatt."

"I think they crossed their t's. I was worried you might have talked about your work with me," he said and slurped his coffee as if he intended to dunk the lump of words into the hot black liquid.

I shook my head. "No. I didn't say a word about being a mole."

"Good. I didn't say a word about your trespassing violation, either. You did a good thing by calling us."

I stopped eating and folded down the white paper bag, hearing only the crumpling between us. I did not want to hear of my heroics. I did not want him to thank me.

"They said I have four counts of assault and battery."

"That's about right."

"How long will I be in jail?"

Officer Fowler leaned back in his chair.

"Depends on how sorry the judge feels for you."

I swallowed, feeling the food in my stomach like one huge greasy ball. "I don't want his pity. Tell him all I want is to see Levi. I need to talk to him."

TWO

ON THE MORNING OF the fourth day, a prison guard pried my hands from the bars, pulled me to my feet, and told me to walk. He did not handcuff me, even though I offered my hands, compliant, thinking he was taking me to see Levi.

"He's been waiting all night," the guard said.

I stared at him, puzzled. He handed me my hat and a garment bag full of clothes, then unlocked a door, pushing it open to a men's bathroom.

"Change in there."

The bag was heavier than I'd thought, and I lifted it higher to avoid a small pool of urine collected in the square of broken gray tiles. I hung it from a stall door, then unzipped it, seeing a pair of pressed and starched black broadfall pants, a clean white shirt, a black vest, and a pair of suspenders. At first, I thought it was a joke and turned back to see if the guard was watching, but the door was closed. He rapped on it.

"Make it quick, Eli. Don't hold everyone up."

I didn't know who "everyone" was and thought maybe the reporters had put the prison up to this to have another front-page story when I met Levi again. No sooner had I thought this than a breeze drifted in from the window and lifted a familiar scent off the clothes. I pulled the sleeve of the shirt to my nose and inhaled, smelling the yeast and cinnamon of pluckets, but I didn't know if this was the smell of an arrival or a departure. I was beginning to lose the ability to tell the difference.

The guard knocked again. I quickly changed and turned to see myself in the mirror above the sink. There were cuts on my cheek, and above my eyes and my jaw was green with bruises. I turned on the faucets and ran the water over my wrists, feeling the cold against my veins, waking me up. It wasn't the swollen eyes, bruised from lack of sleep, that caught my attention, or even the greasy haystack of hair. I stared at myself, realizing that the broadfall pants had been sewn with large pockets. At any other time in my life, I would have been eager to shove my hands into them, but I kept them out for Levi so that he could see the promise in them. I was ready to forgive him, and I was willing to shake on it.

I opened the door and the guard led me down a long corridor flooded with daylight to where a tall man in a dark brown suit was waiting for us.

"This is the warden," the guard said.

"Hello, Big Ugly. You really ought to get out more."

He walked over to me and straightened the collar on my shirt, then swatted a few hairs off the back of the vest.

I recognized him immediately.

"We miss you at the shop. It's not the same without you around. But I suppose you'll be in a better place now."

"Where am I going?"

"The only place I can send you at sixteen."

"Without shoes?"

"You won't need them."

I noticed a few more men had opened their doors and stepped out into the hallway. I didn't realize that my request to see Levi would be such a big deal to everyone. "Thank you for making this happen," I said.

"I've done nothing. It's all them," the warden said, directing the guard to open the front door. Beyond the huge glass doors of the Lancaster County Prison, hundreds of Amish had gathered outside. Standing halfway up the steps were my mother and father; and at the bottom were Amos, his sickly mother, and Levi, who stood with his hands on the back of her wheelchair. He wore new sunglasses, but I knew he was staring right at me. I swore I saw him grin, then too self-conscious to reveal any more, he let his lips flatten just as quickly. Behind him, hundreds more Amish, young and old, were spilling out of the two dozen or more buses that lined the city sidewalks. Children too young to understand where they were skipped over the cracks in the sidewalk and laughed. Officer Fowler directed foot traffic in the street, which had been blocked from motorists with police cruisers on both ends. Aside from the Gordonville Auction each year, I had never seen more Amish gathered in one place in my life. Not even at a barn raising, which is why, I'm sure, Officer Fowler didn't want to miss out. He waved to me, but I didn't wave back. I stood there taking it all in, trying to believe that all of these Amish people had come to see me.

My eyes swept over the crowd again and settled on my parents. My mother dabbed her eyes with the corner of her apron. My father held her hand. I had not seen them show any kind of affection since my sisters had been killed, and it was this subtle gesture that made me wonder if this was all part of the strange dream I had had the night before. I searched the crowd, hoping to find Levi, but it seemed he had stepped away. The bishop waved to me and worked his way through the crowd. He bounded up the stairs with a large metal bucket, water sloshing over the edges, then set it down at my feet with a towel he'd slung over his shoulder.

I turned, seeing the warden and the prison guards step out to watch us. It was an overcast, quiet day, with only the clinking of a flag against the pole. Pushing against the crowd were several other reporters, who had come to witness a centuries-old Anabaptist ritual that nobody had ever seen performed on the steps of a prison.

Which is why I didn't need shoes.

"Welcome home," the bishop said.

Rather than kneel, which I would have preferred for a man his age, the bishop stooped low enough to humble himself, then plunged his hands into the cold water and began to wash my feet. When he finished, he dried them off with the towel, then stood, slowly, his knees cracking. He clasped my trembling hands, then leaned forward to give me the Holy Kiss, a symbol of love and friendship. It was the most significant display of acceptance I had ever seen the Amish give anyone, and it filled me with hope.

I choked back the tears, feeling the connection I thought I had lost. Even though I didn't know every face or every name of every person who had come on my behalf, I knew the size of their hearts. I don't think there was a silo in heaven big enough to hold the love of the Amish that day. It flowed as freely as the wind rapping the flag pole, and it stitched us together in our silence.

While the bishop wiped his hands, I saw Levi on the sidewalk, standing alone on a slab of broken concrete. He turned, shielding himself from a reporter who had gotten too close. Officer Fowler walked between them and motioned for the reporter to step away, which he did, and the bishop, who stood watching, seemed satisfied. He beamed a smile at me and bent down to pick up the bucket, but I swooped in and took it from him, causing a stir among the crowd. The bishop and I shared a knowing look and he draped the towel over my shoulder. I lifted the bucket and walked down the steps toward Levi, then set the bucket down and knelt before him and began to untie his shoelaces.

"What are you doing?" he whispered. "Get up, Eli."

"I will. I'm breaking my promise to you," I said.

"What? Why?"

"Because it's time to make a new one."

I looked up and caught the tear rolling down his cheek. He flicked it away with the back of his hand as if it were an apology that had come too late. He took off his shoes and rolled down his socks and lay them on the cracked concrete; and then, in full view of everyone, I plunged my hands into the bucket of water and began to wash Levi's feet. Not just once, but seventy times, as many times as Dirk Willems called out the day he died, to make sure his assailants, and God, knew that he had forgiven them. I plunged my hands into the bucket and poured the water over his feet again and again, surprised at how easy it was to forgive Levi. I had hoped that the water would be strong enough to wash away the pain and shame and suffering he had endured, but I would later learn that it was not. While the bishop had forgiven me, and while I had forgiven Levi on behalf of the Amish community, it was no substitute for the forgiveness Levi and I had yet to give ourselves.

THREE

MY DECISION TO FORGIVE Levi had reset the way people saw me. It was as if I had suddenly become a man. People looked up to me, although sometimes in fear. They said I was the light and darkness of our community, "its longest shadow and its greatest strength." Young children whose parents had been friends with my sisters clamored around me at work frolics and church services, hanging on my legs, swinging from my arms. They wanted me to play with them. They wanted me to see them, to see their goodness, as if I had suddenly become the example. Even the bishop had taken me aside to thank me for my courage at the prison, and his deacons, not entirely joking, said they could imagine God calling on me to speak for the church one day. But I was no more ready to serve the church than I was ready to admit I was in love with Emma Beiler, or give up on my sisters, which made my homecoming all the more awkward.

The house smelled of pluckets and pies and my mother's stovetop bubbled with soups and late winter stews as though she were preparing for a wedding and a funeral, since my homecoming was a bit of both. If anything, I think she wanted to keep herself busy and give all of us a reason to tell the reporters to leave. Our road had become a thoroughfare for TV vans from every major affiliate in the mid-Atlantic region. Helicopters swarmed our farm all day and night. I don't know what it was they wanted from us, pulling up the past again like an old root. Wasn't it enough that they had talked to me? Why did they need a statement from my parents about how we felt? Relieved? Confused? Betrayed?

My mother, tired of hearing the ruckus, lifted up the window over the kitchen sink and yelled across the lawn, "I don't know what you people think is news. Seems to me you're too late. We forgave him nearly a decade ago."

But the reporters could not see what I saw in the kitchen, how the news had ruptured any semblance of a rhythm my parents had established since 1976. My father had never helped my mother cook, but there he was, taking orders, hoping to be guided by domestic details and distracted from the truth: the driver had been Amish.

It was all very strange. Surreal, as Leroy would have called it, to move about our house with the media staked outside, trying to act as though nothing had changed. The Amish are good at this, at keeping a tight upper lip, chin up, eyes focused on the future. There was church on Sunday. Laundry to wash. Quilts, hope, to stitch and sew.

What nobody said that night is that although they might have forgiven Levi for killing my sisters, they had yet to forgive him for waiting so long to tell anyone, or to understand why he had never stopped to render aid to us.

"Do you think he's a coward?" I asked my mother, setting the table while she beat eggs. She banged the whisk on the side of the bowl.

"He's *mitt-daylah*," she said, a sharer of a similar fate. "I think he's scared of being happy. Like you."

I stared at her and she turned away to beat her eggs into a frothy foam, which she poured into a bowl of flour to make more pluckets.

"I'm not afraid of being happy," I said.

"Well, you sure don't look happy to be home."

And I cannot say I felt at home when I joined my parents at the table for our first meal together, not that eating Mamm's cooking didn't comfort me. Nobody mentioned the impending trial. Unlike Levi's case, the statute of limitations had not run out on mine. Patton had two years to file a claim against me. From the rumors circulating, it was likely he might do just that. I would turn eighteen in less than two years and could be tried as an adult. Datt told me not to worry about it and to focus on Patton's full recovery instead. He said we would avoid legal confrontation and any further publicity. We prayed that we could settle out of court. He told me I would be paying for Patton's medical care, replacing the camera, and reimbursing him for all the assignments he was missing.

Then, over the rattle of the helicopter hovering our roof, my father spoke of brighter things: fish, fishing rods, tackle boxes and auctions. He passed me a cigar under the table and said, "Save it for Gordonville," as if he expected me to join him at the biggest auction of the year.

◇

I had given very little thought to what I would do now that I was home, other than find a way to pay back Patton. My parents made a list to help me, but it felt awkward to discuss the mundane things that needed to be done on the farm without mentioning all the things I hadn't done right, or had undone, since I had left. They didn't mention my hands, which surprised me most of all. The only thing they did discuss was my hair.

"It's short," my father commented.

"It was shorter," I said.

My mother added, "At least it's growing back."

They didn't ask about Florida, or Uncle Enos and cousin Lydia. When I asked why, my mother just pointed to the stack of yellowing issues of *Die Botschaft* that she had kept since September and now asked me to take out to the trash. I didn't toss them immediately, seeing the wind pull back the pages, revealing orange columns. My mother had always been a careful reader and she scrutinized the letters written, the form of news in *Die Botschaft*, with the same judicious eyes she used when she shopped or composed her *Fraktur* work. At the top of each letter was a heading that contained the writer's name and the Amish district he or she was writing about. While there were letters sent from all over the country, Mamm highlighted only those from Florida, searching for news of me. She caught me reading them by the garbage cans beside the barn.

"I should've stopped saving them in October, but I figured you might want to get caught up on the news."

I turned, startled. "October?"

"Emma followed you to Leroy's the day you left."

I dropped the stack into the cans and closed the lid, wishing to crawl inside it. Not only had Emma known my whereabouts the whole time, my parents did, too.

"She told you?"

"She needed your head size."

"For what?"

"She was worried you'd catch cold being bald."

My mother bit her lip, trying to hold back the laughter. "I hear you're very skilled with the razor."

"Did Emma tell you that, too?"

"No, but Ruthanne did. Wish we had stayed in touch all these years, but we sure made up for lost time. I visited every week to hear about you."

"When?"

"Tuesdays."

"Tuesdays?"

"Yes. On my way home from market."

"I know," I grumbled and kicked the garbage can, only to upset a nest of rats under it that had burrowed a hole.

"There's been a rat problem here," my mother said and tried to stifle another laugh. All of this was fun for her.

"Apparently," I huffed.

She added that to the list of things that I needed to do. I was curious that every project required not just days but weeks or months. My parents had built into my schedule a commitment that I would stay. In the meantime, they busied themselves with everything they could think of, because they were not prepared to discuss my violence against Patton. It hung between us as thick and heavy as cigar smoke, with no promise of lifting. The pluckets that my mother had been baking were not for me but for the package that she intended for me to deliver to him, along with two pies and a pot roast.

"You want me to go to the hospital?"

My mother, who had been baking most of that first night, ripped off two sheets of tinfoil and covered the pies. "It's not a question of what you want to do. It's what you will do because it's right. He'll need visitors. He had surgery Monday morning."

"Surgery?"

"Yes. The doctors put his wrist back together with a metal plate and two screws. God forbid you need to be reminded."

"No. I don't," I said. "It's just that—"

My mother read the apprehension on my face.

"What? I pray you have not forgotten what Jesus taught us? We must love our enemies, Eli. Not bleed them."

I forced the words out. "He's not really my enemy."

"He's bleeding," she said. "He's in pain."

"Not any more than us."

My father stepped into the room just then, as if he had been listening the whole time, or trying to with the helicopters still buzzing our house at night.

"How did you ever come to hate this man?" he asked.

"I don't hate him. I hate what he doesn't understand."

"Well, then. That makes three of us," my mother said, snatching her wool cape from the peg by the kitchen door. She let herself outside to the driveway, refusing to speak to any lurking reporters, bypassing them, crushing stones beneath her shoes. She found her way in the dark to the telephone shanty at the edge of our road and opened the squeaky spring door, then slipped inside to learn the status of her son's enemy.

◇

Critical condition is what they said. He would not be leaving the hospital soon. This news did not make sleeping easier. I sat in our barn and worried. I worried about the extent of injuries Patton had suffered, and I worried how long it would take to pay him back. I certainly wasn't earning any money completing the tasks my parents had asked of me.

I would need a job that made a lot of money fast, but I had no skills, aside from shaving men's beards, that would ever earn enough to pay off my debts. I worried about the packages that had been delivered to me, too. Our English neighbors had stopped by with a chocolate cake and a baseball glove that had been sewn to fit my webbed hand. I worried about the mail I was getting. Filling our box were welcome home cards and invitations from less rowdy buddy gangs to join them for fishing trips and golf outings.

I did not expect to find anything from Leroy, but there was a card that had been signed from all the men in the shop. It simply said: WHO HAS THE BIGGER BALLS? YOU DID WHAT WE ALWAYS WANTED TO. There had been nothing from Emma.

◇

It's not that I didn't deliver the care package. I took it to Strasburg instead. It was a brisk spring day in late March, unusually cold with the forecast of snow. The daffodils in the box outside Leroy's shop had frozen and did not appear to be thawing under the half-smoked cigars, tossed, I presumed, from the dark, cagey man who sat on a folding chair and stared at my black pants, black vest, crisp white shirt, *Mutze* coat and black hat. I must have spooked him, because he gasped, then grasped the armrest when he saw me.

"The hell are you? A pilgrim?"

"Ugly," I said. "You must be Forklift."

"Big Ugly?" he asked and extended his right hand.

I offered him the basket of pluckets instead. He leaned forward in his dark green Philadelphia Eagles sweat suit. Sideburns as grey as ash crawled out of a knit cap. He looked scruffy and his beard had grown in patches. He looked like a very old Leroy. They had the same nose and hooded eyes. He reached into the basket, flicked open the cloth napkin to get a better look then flicked it back.

"I'd rather have a shave," he grumbled and scratched a patch of his beard. "I had better shaves in the clink."

"I'm not here to shave anyone," I said, hoping to keep Leroy's attention. I knew he had seen me through the window, standing there behind a chair with an electric clipper, finishing a cut on a client. It was early on a Thursday morning, yet busy, and the glass in the windows rattled from the bass thumping from the stereo playing Motown.

"You know how to get a hold of me," he shouted and turned up the volume. I could see the recent newspapers piled on the bench beneath the window. My story had made headlines from the major papers to the local rags.

I turned from Forklift and carried the basket to the door. I did not open it but stood outside and spoke to him through the glass. "I came to apologize," I said.

Leroy read my lips.

What? he mouthed back.

"I'm sorry," I said and lifted the basket, hoping that it might keep his attention, or ease his temper. He turned down the stereo and marched to the door. The men in the shop turned to each other, hands over mouths, trying to quell their laughter. Leroy opened the door a crack and whispered. "I don't want your damn apology, Ugly. I told you before how to get my attention."

"I'm still practicing," I said.

"Then come back when you're ready."

"That's the point. I need your help."

"I'm all outta help for you."

I bit my lip, feeling the eyes of the men on me. Rather than greet me with smiles, they threw their gaze into the papers they were reading, or fixed them on the TV. I felt rejected by them, but I didn't have time to worry about what they thought of me. Only Leroy. I reached beyond the pluckets to hand him the pies. "What's that?" he asked, nose twitching, already drugged by the smell of fresh Amish baked goods.

"An offering. Homemade."

"I can see that."

Leroy sniffed the pies. He lifted his eyes to meet mine and scowled. "Hm-mmmf. Shoofly and pecan?"

"My mom made them… just for you. And pluckets."

"Damn, pluckets? I'm supposed to watch my cholesterol."

"Maybe this is a time to break the rules."

He stared at me, considering, his white brows knitted tighter than his father's. He jabbed his finger in the air.

"This is no substitution, you understand?"

"For what?"

"Whatever it is you need from me can't be any more important than what I need from you. You follow?"

I nodded, feeling the rush of hope fill me.

Leroy glanced back at the wall clock.

"Come back at noon on my lunch break, and we'll talk."

I did. We sat in his office with Forklift and spoke.

Leroy pulled the blinds shut and locked the door.

"What about your trial?"

"It hasn't been set. I need to go to Philadelphia before it starts."

I shifted my eyes to Forklift. He only laughed.

"Why don't you take the train?"

"I need your help looking for the right camera."

"Which one is that?"

"The one with my sisters' souls."

"Jesus Christ," Leroy said, staring at me in shock. "That one?"

I nodded, and lowered my voice, confiding in both. I told them about Marcus Paoni, feeling strangely at ease telling The Forklift. He sat there on the edge of the cot that I had used and listened without judgment or comment.

"How do you know the camera will be in Philadelphia?"

"I don't," I told him. "But I have faith."

The old man had opened a jar of Skippy and licked the peanut butter straight from the knife, then stuck it back in the jar and stared at me. He had not put his teeth in yet and softly gummed the spread with dark lips that looked like long crinkled cinnamon sticks.

"Faith's all you need," he said and looked at Leroy. "Isn't that right? Saved me. Could save you, too."

I nodded. "Let's just start with my sisters."

◇

I saved the pot roast for Patton and took the bus into the city and dropped it off at the nurse's station on the fourth floor of the hospital. They did not ask for my name. My clothes were enough for them to know where I came from. I stood outside the door, watching him sleep while the TV blared cartoons of Rocky and Bullwinkle. The nurses pointed at me. "Aren't you the—you're him."

I nodded, smiling politely and stepped past them.

It was a relief to see Patton at rest, his moon face puffy with dreams, lips curled into a crescent. Clusters of shiny balloons clung to the ceiling, and plants, flowers, and cards lined the windows that overlooked the city cemetery. It surprised me that so many people cared about Patton. I guess I never considered that he had ever been a friend to anyone. I didn't realize that he was married, either, until I saw on the night stand a small picture of a woman and three young girls, who I assumed were his daughters.

Tucked under his left arm was a stuffed elephant with a red ribbon tied around its neck. Seeing him cradle it made me realize how young we look when we are hurt. He wore a plaster cast on his right arm, which lay across his chest, rising and falling slightly when he breathed. On the tray at the end of his bed was a set of markers. I was not adept at signing my name on anything, much less plaster, but I approached him slowly and took the black marker in my hand and wrote Big Ugly across his arm, hoping that when it was time for the doctor to remove it, they'd cut through the words and give Patton that added relief.

FOUR

I DID NOT GO straight home, even though the sky looked colorless and pressed. There was a dampness in the air and everything about it suggested more snow, spring snow, but I decided to take my chances and stop at Hoffman's Seed store to buy as many packets of violets as they had on the shelves. I asked the cashier, a pimply-faced Amish boy a few years younger than me, when they would be getting more. He pushed up the glasses that had slid down his nose and stared. "More? What do you need more for?"

"In case they're no good."

"Them seeds are good."

"How do you know?"

He stared at me through the thick glasses, rolling his big brown eyes like I was the dumbest cluck he'd ever seen.

"They're violets," he said.

"Yeah? I know that."

"Them seeds would take root in paper if they could."

I gathered up the packets while he opened up a small brown bag and slid them inside. "We'll see about that."

I hitched a ride to the Esh farm with an Amish man who owned a carriage shop. He seemed pleased to give me a lift and equally respectful of my space. He didn't ask me any questions, just where I needed to go. I stood outside the door in the dark, waiting for someone to answer, hoping that Levi was home. I was excited by the idea of building a greenhouse on our farm and wanted Levi to help me.

Building a greenhouse was not on my parents' To Do list. I figured this would be the best way for Levi and me to spend time together again, and for my parents to get to know him. Work would give us a sense of purpose and a new language that had nothing to do with the accident. We would speak only of the present and the future, of life, not death, in the greenhouse. And this gave me hope. If my idea worked, I wouldn't just be knocking on Leroy's door, I'd be busting through his heart.

I could see Amos through the window, hunched over the kitchen table, his face illuminated by an oil lamp. He was studying from the little book of big ideas, *The Confession of Faith*, then looked up, seeing my shadow cross him. I was surprised that he seemed genuinely glad to see me, although I would not say he looked happy. He looked sad. He opened the door and covered his mouth with his finger when I started to talk. He stepped outside and pulled the door shut, and we stood on the porch in the cold.

"Our mother is not well. Levi's getting the doctor."

"She's gotten worse?" I asked.

He whispered, "She said she saw our father."

"What?"

"She said he's come for her. Because it's time."

I swallowed hard, hearing the grave tone in his voice.

"She's dying?"

"She's been dying for a long time," Amos said. "But the news. Everything lately. It's been too much for her."

"I'm sorry," I said. "She didn't know?"

"Levi showed her the newspaper. He wanted to tell her the truth, before… you know… Before she…"

"She'll get better," I said, hopeful.

He shook his head and I could see him clenching his teeth. His throat tightened and he wiped his eye. I shifted uncomfortably, hearing the wooden boards creak beneath my weight. Amos searched my eyes in the darkness.

"She wanted you to know that you did a good thing."

I stared at him and he continued.

"At the prison. She wanted to thank you."

"Does she know I hurt a man?"

"She knows you forgave the one who hurt you."

I lowered my gaze and nodded, wanting to believe that he had done a good thing, too, by forcing Levi to confess.

"So did you," I said. "You wanted the truth known."

He shook his head and let out a long breath.

"It needed to come from Levi. Not me. You know, I've learned a great lesson from all of this."

"What's that?"

"We all move toward God at our own pace."

He was right. It was the most compelling thing I'd ever heard him say.

"Yeah. Some of us stumble," I said.

"And some of us trip," he said, and we laughed. It felt good to laugh with Amos, rather than laugh at him. It had started to snow and the flakes were thick and sticking to the ground. Amos stuck out his tongue and caught one.

"Do you want to wait inside? Warm yourself up? You'll freeze if you wait out here 'til he gets back."

I flipped up the collar on the *Mutze*. Freezing was something I'd risk rather than step into the house of the dying. I turned, straining my neck, trying to see beyond the window to the bed where Mrs. Esh lay.

Before I could answer, a horse galloped down the driveway, pulling a buggy, and Levi jumped out. He'd brought a local doctor, a tall man with a distinguished white beard and an eyeglass that dangled by a chain around his neck. He caned his way to the porch with a carved stick. Levi carried a lantern and a medical bag and paused, seeing me at the door. It was very awkward to stand there and not know what to say, or where to begin. I noticed in the lamplight that he had shaved his face and cut his hair like an Amish man. Gone were the jeans and the T-shirt and baseball hat. He was wearing Amish clothes, and he looked older in his leaden posture, more tired, and even sadder.

"Did you come to help?" he asked.

"No," I said, then saw the disappointment on his face, which confused me because in the two months that I had lived in the barn, Levi had not once allowed me to help him. "I mean yes. Of course. You need help?"

Levi cracked an ironic smile.

"You know that more than anyone in this world."

He climbed the steps and pushed open the door. Amos and I followed, but by the time we stepped into the house, the doctor, who had gone in before us, stood over Mrs. Esh and closed her eyes.

I helped Levi and Amos build her pine coffin with a hatch that opened on hinges so that people could see her face during the viewings, of which there would be three: one before the funeral, one during the funeral, and one at the gravesite. Although Mrs. Esh would not be wearing any makeup (no Amish woman ever does), she would be embalmed, which gave us a full day to make sure the varnish on her casket had dried.

Even though it was *hochmut* of me, I was proud of my work on the hatch, which Levi had shown me how to make. Aside from building kennels for the dogs, I had never built much of anything and it felt good to help the Eshes when they needed it most, especially after Levi had refused my labor for so long out of some debt of guilt he'd thought he was paying.

I made sure to screw the hinges tight and wondered if, maybe, I'd have a chance at being Levi's apprentice when all of this was done. I liked to work with wood and he had already taught me a great deal about carpentry while we repaired his barn, although I can't say he gave any thought to employing me then. He seemed relieved to have my help, yet rather reluctant to accept it, and I could see in his eyes the desperation, if not the filial obligation, he felt to resolve the awkwardness between us.

I was relieved to be in the barn working while they were with the body. They would wash her first, following a Lancaster County tradition, before the undertaker took her away for embalming. When she was returned, they would dress her in traditional white garments. I did not want to stick around to see them dress Mrs. Esh in her wedding dress. Even though my sisters had never been married, we had followed Amish custom and dressed them in white, too. I remember helping my mother while she attached the hair she had bought from the milliner to replace the braids she had cut. My father hadn't known what we were doing, too busy clearing the house of furniture to make room for benches for the first viewing and the funeral.

When I got home that night, I noticed the furniture in our living room had been pushed aside again, or taken out to our barn, and several benches had been lined up parallel with the walls. I stood by the door while my mother washed the floor; my father was outside, gathering a bundle of wood to feed the old stone fireplace. I did not need to ask them what they were doing. They had already assumed the role of family when the Eshes had none. Word travels fast as lightning among the Amish. It made me think that maybe Mrs. Esh had chosen to die then, so that we could all move on with our lives. It was thoughtful of her to share her fate with us, to help us acknowledge that; although we were preparing for only one funeral, there had been more than one death.

We should have known better than to haul a coffin up Bunker Hill after a snow storm, but we really didn't have a choice. We dressed warm for the trip. The roads were still covered with fresh snow, and while most folks traveled by buggy, a few arrived in a horse-drawn sleigh like us.

My father and I rode with Levi and Amos as pallbearers. We were surprised they had asked us and not other family members, though my father didn't hesitate to help. Like my mother, he was relieved to have something else to focus on. He tossed them an extra felt strap for the toboggan that would carry the coffin up the hill to the grave, which we had spent most of the morning digging. No sooner had we dug one more foot into the earth, then we'd have to shovel the snow that filled the hole. Before everyone arrived at our house for the funeral, Levi and Amos took turns sleeping in my room, then greeted friends and relatives they hadn't spoken to in years. It was a trying morning, to say the least. I don't think it had registered that their mother had died, that they no longer had parents in this world. They were exhausted and naps didn't help.

With the help of my father, we slid the casket off the wagon and onto the toboggan, then hauled it up Bunker Hill. I had never carried a coffin before, and I was surprised by how heavy it was. Mrs. Esh was not a small woman; she wasn't a large woman, either, but this phenomena everyone called dead weight could break a man's back. I'd been too young to carry my sisters, and I didn't realize the dead could weigh so much. We had screwed thick fish-eye hooks into the sides of Mrs. Esh's casket so that we could pull her up on the toboggan with ropes. Levi suggested it and we trusted him. After all, he was a carpenter. He understood the nature of wood.

I remember the quiet crunch of snow beneath our boots, and the creak of the iron gate when it was closed behind us by the English undertaker who was present, by law, to witness the burial. A small crowd had already gathered at the top of the hill by the grave site and was standing on the edges of a black plastic sheet that we'd put over the hole.

It was windy, and the drifts were as high as the fenceline. Someone had trampled a trail for us in the snow, to make the ascent smoother. Usually, we would be walking, carrying the casket on poles up the hill, but there was no way to guarantee that all of us would make the climb without slipping. Amos and my father walked beside the casket and kept it from sliding off the back by the ropes they had looped through the fish-eye hooks; Levi and I held either side of the thick hemp rope attached to the front of the toboggan. We walked backwards, taking careful but assured steps, digging the heels of our boots into the snow. We moved slowly, and the whole thing seemed to take forever. By the time we reached the hilltop, our hands were burned and blistered from the rope.

Just then, Levi let go to pull out the felt straps he'd stuffed between the top of the coffin. Amos and my father, whose hands were just as sore, let go of their ropes and started to unscrew the fish-eye hooks from the coffin, making sure Mrs. Esh would be buried without ornaments. I was the only one left holding the rope. Levi slid back the latch on the hatch for the final viewing but did not yet lift it for the crowd to see. He signaled to someone in the crowd to remove the black sheet of plastic off the grave, and just as he did, the wind blew the familiar scent of honeysuckle, which hit me with the force of an anvil. I know I wasn't the only one who smelled this. Levi sneezed. Amos lifted his head so fast to catch this fleeting scent that his hat fell into the snow. I looked up, searching the crowd, trying to follow this scent to its source, and there, between her brothers and behind her father, was Emma Beiler staring right at me. Even though we were at a burial, she pinched her lips together and bit back a grin, then lowered her chin and cast her eyes on the heels of her father. Amos had shifted just then, as did everyone else, and I, stricken by the site of Emma, let go of the rope and the toboggan slid down the hill, knocking four funeral goers out of the way before it slammed into the fencepost.

And believe me, it wasn't the runaway casket that startled us as much as the effect of the crash. Mrs. Esh's head unhinged the whole lid upon impact. Her eyes opened, her lacquered licorice-like hair fixed in place like a helmet, and the only hint of an expression on her face was in her gaping mouth. It was appropriate to see her for her final viewing at the cemetery, but nobody expected her to sit up and see *us*.

"Put her back in," somebody shouted, and somebody tried, but to no avail. We were all too shocked to move. I caught Emma's eye again and looked away, ashamed that this indignity Mrs. Esh was suffering had been my fault. The two crows that sat perched on the fence post fluttered and cawed, as if to urge one of us to do Mrs. Esh the favor of stuffing her back into the box. Still, no one moved but the English undertaker, who had sneezed. Aside from the crows, there was silence—until Levi and Amos started to move, although not toward their mother. They turned to each other and started to laugh, setting off the longest string of laughter I'd ever heard among the Old Order Amish.

It is Amish custom to follow the burial service with a fellowship meal, which we held at our house. Although normal conversation was expected to resume, none of us could get ten bites into our meal without somebody recalling the runaway casket. The girls who were helping in the kitchen could be heard giggling when they finally caught the story as it had been told and retold by the many witnesses that day. Even Bishop Beiler had to contain his laughter by coughing, punctuating the rise and fall of bellies and long white beards and the bent-over men wearing them. Nobody had been immune to the grace of God. My mother had stopped me in the hall when I got up to use the bathroom. She put her finger over her mouth and leaned against the wall, feeling it vibrate with everyone's laughter. It was the most people we had had inside our home since my sisters' funeral, and I could see from the light in her eyes how much she had missed the joy, not only of friends, but of strangers, too. She opened her eyes and reached out to hold my arm. "You remember what it is?"

"What?"

"This sound."

I smiled, remembering what she had told me years ago.

"It's the sound God makes when he forgives us for making mistakes," I said, in Deitsh. My mother dabbed her eyes with the cuff of her sleeve and stared at me, pleased. I wished Leroy had been there to hear us. He would have been pleased to know that laughter, more than anything, had ended our grief.

There were still questions about my trial, about the status of Patton's and Levi's futures, but it seemed that God had clearly wanted us to reset the bar to zero and start again; however, Amos did not want to reset anything he had worked so hard to establish with Emma, and he made sure she knew it. It is not common to see an Amish man cry, and although I wouldn't call the stifled sobs at the post-funeral meal an outburst of emotion, I would say he didn't do much to grieve in private. He seemed to enjoy the attention of the young Amish women who made sure to keep food on his plate and his glass full of water.

I was on my way back from the bathroom when I caught Amos and Emma talking in another room in hushed whispers. Amos wanted to see her at the next song group. I could not see Emma from where I paused in the hallway, but I could tell from her voice that she was hesitant. Amos pressed again. "If not for me, for my mother," he pleaded, and Emma accepted his invitation.

That's when my mind started to speed up. I had to act fast if I wanted Emma to give me another chance. After Levi and Amos went back to their farm and the other guests had left, I asked Emma to stay and help us finish cleaning the kitchen. Her father was outside with my father hitching up their buggy.

"It's all done," she said, looking at the stack of dishes by the sink.

"Yeah, but we need to put them back."

"We?" Emma cocked her head. She'd flung her wool cape over her shoulder but pulled it off and hung it back on the peg. "If you want me to stay, just ask."

I nodded, feeling the burn in my face. We hadn't said a word to each other during the meal. We'd exchanged glances. Once my mother had left us alone to talk, I didn't know what to say. Emma walked over to the door and called out to her father.

"Datt, go on home. I'll walk with Eli."

Then she closed the door. I had already pulled out a chair at the kitchen table and sat down. "What about dishes?" she asked.

"Let them dry first."

Emma caught my eye. "Why did you want me to stay?"

"Because... I have something to ask you."

Emma crossed the floor and pulled out a chair across from me and sat down with her back to the wall. A car passed on the road and illuminated the window. For a moment, it looked like Emma was wearing a crown. I shifted in my seat, trying to find the words, any words except the wrong ones, to say to her.

"I don't know what happened today," I said.

"I don't know anybody who does."

"I mean with me. And you. It just that sometimes..."

"What?"

"I feel like... like we collide," I said, and instead of the words feeling hard as rocks, they felt soft and mushy like pudding sliding down my throat.

"We do that well," Emma said, then swallowed and pressed her thumb into the hot wax that had dribbled from the candle burning on the table.

"I'm tired," I said.

"Of colliding with me?"

"Sounding like I'm eating corn on the cob every time I try to talk to you," I blurted, exasperated, and surprised I had actually uttered a complete sentence in front of her. Emma stood and went to the sink to fill a glass with water, then walked over and handed it to me. "I don't care how you sound," she said. "I just want to hear you say something you mean for once."

I stared at her, stricken.

"I do mean everything I say."

"To me," she said.

I took the glass and drank it all. I didn't realize I'd been holding my breath ever since I stepped into the kitchen. I hated how awkward it felt between us, and I hated that my body remembered her touch and longed for it. It didn't matter where I saw her or when, she always took my breath away; and that current I felt in the old mill revved up again and made me uneasy. She was wearing a new dress, bright purple with a black apron that made her green eyes sparkle. She seemed content to stand in our kitchen, and I wondered how many times she had sat at our table in my absence during *rumspringa*. She obviously knew her way around. She opened the cabinet where my mother kept the tea cups and pulled out two, opening drawers, mixing teas. It didn't bother me to see her so at home, it's just that she felt more at ease than I did.

"Do you ever think about that day in the market when we were kids? When the boy in the market took my photo?"

Emma stopped stirring. She lay the spoon on the counter and turned to me, nodding. "Never forgotten it."

I rubbed my nose, trying hard to keep my eyes on her and not get derailed from what I wanted to say.

"I stole his camera."

"Didn't he put up signs?"

I nodded. "I took those, too."

Emma took a pot of water from the stove and carried it and the tea cups to the table. She poured us each a cup and sat down beside me, wisps of steam rising between us, infused with rose hips and chamomile, teas my mother usually brewed when we were sick. Maybe Emma thought I was sick. She leaned closer to me, and I could feel her hot breath on my shoulder through my sleeve when she whispered.

"I never forgave him for calling you ugly," she said, then laughed and wiped her eyes. "He made me want to hurt him, and I've never felt that way about anyone before or since."

I nodded, taken by her confession.

"You want to know something else?" I asked.

"What?"

"I met him lately."

She pulled back and stared at me, incredulous.

I told her what I'd told Leroy and Forklift. When I finished, Emma and I sat in silence, sipping our tea. Her eyes were swollen, spilling with tears. I didn't know if she was more concerned about my welfare or my sisters'. "How will you ever find the camera without mixing yourself up with the English again?"

I looked at her, seeing the glow in her eyes from the candlelight.

"That's why I need your help Sunday."

"What about church? You can't miss communion."

"We'll have our own. I want to take you with me."

FIVE

AS THE SON OF an auctioneer, I know that when two parties want the same thing, common sense can go out the window. My father explained this theory once as the only way a person might get more than he thought he would. I had one day to pray for a miracle. I had to walk the crooked way one last time to walk the straight one forever, I hoped.

I needed God's cooperation. I wanted Emma Beiler's help and I wanted the expedient release of my sisters' souls, which I figured God would want even if he hadn't planned on my taking up much space in Emma Beiler's heart. I decided to pray out loud, just in case God hadn't heard me the first time. I figured if the admission to heaven ran anything like an auction, there was hope that God would want to settle the disputes of any disgruntled bidder whose bid had not been heard. I hiked back to the cemetery on Bunker Hill and shouted my request into the wind on that cold, crisp Saturday morning in March.

"Help me help you!"

Later, just in case the message had been lost in the wind, I spoke it again to the pond. I figured that I had learned to fish in those waters as a boy, and if I had any chance of guiding my message to heaven, it was there.

When I was certain God knew exactly what I needed, I did what I would never do under normal circumstances. I ate sugar-free chocolates. Not just a few pieces. The whole box. All twenty-four squares, one for each hour of the day that I had left to pray. I ate the chocolates completely, thoroughly, as if they were the last meal of my life. I sat on the edge of the pond and chewed and chewed until the sorbitol worked its way into the basement of my bowels. Sorbitol was the sugar substitute we had used in our chocolates for folks with diabetes. It's what Ruthanne should have eaten, but I knew why she hadn't. My grandfather had offered my sisters and me boxes of sugar-free candy, without telling us they were sugar-free, to teach us how harmful candy was. I'm sure we would have been sick either way, gorging ourselves, but something about sugar-free candy left an impression in the stomach.

I thought about Granddatt then and wanted to laugh, but I hurt too much. I remembered Leroy telling me about the first time he had eaten a Shoofly pie. Nobody had told him only to eat a small sliver, a few bites at most. He ate the whole pie in one sitting. When I asked him why he didn't stop, he said, "Hell. I don't know why, Ugly. It was like an affair I should have never started." Although I didn't really know what an affair was, I knew it was no good thing to involve myself in, and I knew that I would suffer as a result.

I ached so much on the way back to the house that I could take only one step before I had to wait a few minutes for the cramps to pass. Suffering like this was a sacrifice I was willing to make. The only legitimate way to be in two places at once was to be in a third: bed.

My mother attributed my sickness to pluckets, believing I'd eaten the leftovers from the funeral, when my father had. He thought my sickness was because of nerves. I told them it was the flu, and this reason sounded most believable since half the kids in the local schools had been coming home with a stomach virus that week. After all, I was learning how to be part of a group.

My plan, for the most part, worked. I would miss the spring communion, one of the two most important church services per year that encouraged any wayward soul to come forward, admit his wrong doing, and ask for the community's support in keeping him on the straight path. Any members whose behavior had been in question were given the chance to recommit themselves to the Ordnung. It's not that I didn't want to recommit myself to the community; I had already committed myself to recovering the camera, and the camera show was the same day. It was what Leroy had called a double-bind.

My mother, although disappointed that I'd be missing communion, seemed somewhat cheerful. She scrubbed the floors in my room and changed the sheets. She opened the windows and pushed my bed closer to them, encouraging me to get as much fresh air as possible. It had been a long time since I had been sick enough for my mother to take care of me like this and I think it soothed her.

My father seemed hopeful the virus would pass.

"Tell the bishop I send my best," I said, pulling the sheets tighter around me, terrified they would see that I was fully dressed.

I admit I felt a bit guilty luring Emma into my plan. I hadn't even told her the plan. I just told her to meet me at Leroy's barbershop, in her English clothes, at nine o' clock Sunday morning. When she hadn't shown up by half past, I figured she had changed her mind.

Leroy caught me pacing when he stepped outside to start the Austin Healey. He pushed back the sleeve of his coat and checked his watch.

"She's late."

"She's coming," I said.

"She's got more sense than to hang out with us, Ugly."

I glared at Leroy.

"Don't call me Ugly when she shows up."

Leroy looked over at me and zipped up his mouth. His father had hobbled outside with a cup of coffee. He was wearing a suit and a brown fedora. For a man who had spent most of his life in jail, he looked like he owned the world. He jabbed his cane in the air.

"The Amish get stood up?"

"I didn't get stood up."

"Your girl didn't show yet."

"She's not my girl. She's my friend."

Forklift looked over to Leroy and flashed a smile.

"Owwee! Boy's in LUUUUUVVVVV."

"I am not in love with Emma!"

And just as I said it, Emma scooted up to the sidewalk.

"You're not?" she asked, feigning disappointment.

Leroy answered for me, "Must be the other girl who looks just like you, and makes him just as crazy."

Emma parked the scooter in the bike stand and held back a grin with her fist. I caught a flash of the pink sweater beneath her coat.

"You look nice," I said. "For an Englisher."

"You look awful," she said. "What happened?"

"I made myself sick,"

"I can see that," she said and walked toward me.

"No point in going to church sick, you know?"

"Pity for you," she said. "I told the truth."

I stared at her. "What?"

"My father knows I'm going to Philadelphia with you. I had to tell him the whole story."

I covered my face with my hands, wincing.

"But that's the whole point!" I cried.

"Of what?"

"Dressing English. So nobody would recognize you."

"I thought it was because we were going to have fun."

"We might, but, oh, geeze... You told your father?"

"That's why it took me so long to get here. He wanted to know all the details. I'm sorry I kept you all waiting."

Forklift, who had pretended to sift through the frozen daffodils in Leroy's flower box, stifled a laugh. "Goodie," he said. "We got the bishop's blessing."

Emma turned to me and shook her head.

"I wouldn't call it a blessing."

"This is a blessing," Leroy shouted and gestured to us to climb into the Austin Healey. He tossed us two blankets. "What's a matter, buttercup?" he asked, reading the concern on Emma's face. "I may be old, but I drive fast."

Emma found no humor in Leroy.

"I thought we were taking the train."

Leroy and Forklift turned to me, the engine humming now, the radio turned down, Forklift whistling instead.

"Uh, well, we're not really going directly into Philadelphia. Not exactly. More like Trevrose."

Emma stared at me, head cocked, eyes fixed on the four-seater convertible. "All of us?"

"You'll see," I said. I glared at Leroy, whose eyes were wide and wild, shoulders bobbing from the silent strain of giggles he and his father suddenly contracted.

"You ever been in a convertible, buttercup?"

Emma shifted her eyes to me. I'm not sure if she was annoyed with Leroy's
nicknaming everyone he knew, or if she was quietly acquiescing to this tradition among barbers, knowing it was, perhaps, a quirk no more harmful than any of our own customs.

"You think it's a good idea to ride in a convertible on communion?"

I shrugged, suddenly regretting my decision to invite her. "Do you want us to wait while you ask your father?"

"Is that a dare?"

We stared at our reflection on the car doors. I had never heard Emma speak about cars. Something about the red Austin Healey, its sleek lines, the shiny chrome grill in the front, and the white leather seats made Emma appear more eager than anxious about riding in it. The Healey was a classic. According to Leroy, the British made only 5,095 BT7 four-seater Tri Carb (three carburators) series between 1961 and 1962. It was a racing car, and Emma walked around the machine, eyeing it as if she understood, or wanted to understand, its power.

"How fast can it go?"

"Faster than your buggy," Leroy said, although I could tell from the way he smiled, lips pushed into a pout, that he doubted he had the power to persuade an Amish girl to do anything.

But Emma climbed in and said, "Good. Then I expect you to get us to Trevrose and back promptly."

"I'll see what I can do, buttercup. Bundle up."

She looked up at me from the backseat. "Get in!"

I wish we could have kept driving in Leroy's car. I wanted to hold the look on Emma's face in my mind forever. I don't think I've ever seen her smile so much, maybe because she felt free to do so, dressed English. We hadn't sat that close since the old mill, and it was all I could do to keep from touching her hair, which hung loosely past her shoulders and grazed my hand every time she moved. I also felt her body against mine with every turn Leroy took, which he took fast to thrill us both. The Forklift seemed to be enjoying himself, riding with his hands up in the air as if he were riding downhill on a tractor. He whooped and hollered and every so often turned back to check on us.

"This is something, isn't it?"

"Sure is," Emma said.

"Feels good to get out and about, don't it?"

Emma nodded. I'm not sure how far Emma had ever been from Lancaster County. The landscape hadn't changed all that dramatically on our way into Trevrose; the land rolled on indefinitely.

"The sea is that way," I said, pointing east to the nose of the Austin Healey.

"I'd like to go to the sea," she said.

"You've never seen the ocean?" Forklift asked.

Emma shook her head and looked at me. "Have you?"

"Not yet," I said.

"It's a crime never to have seen the ocean," Leroy said. "Everybody needs to see the ocean once."

Emma shifted her eyes to mine and they were wide and wild as Leroy's. He caught our glances in the rear-view mirror and smiled slyly, scheming.

"Don't get any ideas," I said. "We're on a mission."

Leroy saluted.

"You're the boss," he said and winked, but he was looking right at Emma.

With every mile of farmland that lay behind us, Emma inched further away from me, a little less comfortable with our adventure, and a little less sure she was meant to share it with me. When we finally stopped, she stared at the large hotel. The sign was supposed to read Radisson, but the R was missing. The parking lot was full, and Englishers of every nationality spilled in and out of the building. Dirty snow pressed against the walls, crusted with cigarette butts and beer caps. Emma picked them up and tossed them into the trash.

"I wouldn't worry about that, buttercup. You could spend your life cleaning up the mess the English make."

Emma stared at him and wiped her hands on the sleeve of her coat. Forklift opened the hotel door and a blast of hot, stale air greeted us. He pointed inside with his cane.

"Game on," he said and led us into the lobby, where signs directed us past red carpeted hallways, puffy chairs and public telephones to the conference room.

Each of us was as perplexed as the other. Even Forklift took off his hat, an odd gesture of deference. I stood in the doorway, taking it all in, trying to determine how many sellers were there and how many buyers crowded their tables. I had never seen more cameras in my life, and I couldn't imagine how many souls had been sucked through the lenses.

I had gone to hundreds of auctions with my father, but nothing compared to the energy inside the conference room. We could barely hear each other over the frenzied din. The pawn shop owner had been right. There were crowds of Japanese buyers, and everywhere we looked, one of them was peeling back crisp bills from wads of money as thick as his fists. Many wore Band-Aids on their fingers and I wondered if this was a Japanese custom. Leroy shook his head.

"Paper cuts. I bet those bills were printed today."

One of the sellers walked past us with a tray of coffee and donuts and paused. At first, I thought we must have looked stunned because he offered some to us, but it was we who had stunned him. I had gotten so used to being with Leroy that I didn't even realize that we stood out like a shovel in the sand, two black men with an Amish boy, dressed for church, and a young woman who didn't look like she belonged to either. The seller turned to me. "I thought you folks didn't take photos."

"We don't," I said.

"We're not supposed to," Emma corrected me.

"Hard to resist a good shot, isn't it? I tell you what. You all better get in there now. There'll be nothing left after the Japanese take lunch."

"So what's the plan?" Leroy asked me.

"You two take the aisles on the right," I said. "And you take that one," I said to Emma, pointing to the left. "I'll take the middle two. And remember. Only look at the Leica M3s from 1963. With film."

We moved through the throngs of international buyers, hearing not only Japanese, but German and French, too. I wished I did not understand the Germans, but I did and felt defeated. They, too, had come to buy the Leica M3.

Best mechanical camera ever made. Worth roughly one thousand dollars, maybe more. Would I like one or two? Maybe a third for a friend? Buy two and get the third for half price. Pay cash, get a set of lenses, too. Don't wait. Buy now while supplies last.

I was weary of explaining why I needed to find a Leica with film in it. Every dealer gave me the same response. "Good luck, son. If there was film, it's bound to be developed by now. Why not buy another?"

They persisted, trying to sell me a "perfectly good Leica M3" for those with a few mechanical issues, "a well-loved" one for those in less than mint condition, and "like new," selling for $2,000, almost twice what the pawn-shop owner had quoted. I looked back at the clock. It had taken ninety minutes to move through one aisle. I had never handled so many cameras, and I can't say that seeing all those Leicas made me feel hopeful because not one of them had any film.

When I finished sifting through the last pile in the last aisle, I looked up to see Forklift and Leroy approach me with Emma. Gone was their sunny disposition of the morning. They looked weary and shaken, and not at all happy to be there, jostled by the international camera hunters. I had hoped to see a Leica in someone's hands, but they were carrying Cokes and huge hot dogs.

"Any luck?" I asked, even though I didn't have to.

"Lots of Leicas," Emma said.

"No film," Leroy added.

Forklift shrugged, eyeing me.

"Better pray there's a Lost 'n Found in heaven."

Instead of driving west toward Lancaster, Leroy drove east for sixty minutes into New Jersey, where the farmland gave way to tall marsh grasses, and the wind carried the salt of the sea. We passed through a wind-swept town of gray clapboard houses and condominiums made of metal and glass. We followed the road until it ended at a large sand dune, which Leroy told us to climb. Emma was the first to scramble to the top and she waved, eager for us to join her. Even Forklift managed to hoist himself up the dune, and together we stood side by side facing a vast stretch of water that lay before us like a pewter plate. I had never seen a body of water as big as the ocean.

"What's a matter, Ugly?"

"Nothing," I said, stunned. "Not a thing."

"Then go on!" Leroy said and took off his shoes.

Emma had no problem with the order. She kicked off her shoes and ran down the dune squealing, arms outstretched as if she were flying. I left my hat and shoes on the dune and ran after her, prodded by Forklift's cane. We met at the edge of the water. It was windy, and the spray misted our hair and put a wave in Emma's. She toed the foam and flicked it onto my feet, then splashed me with the wave that had just then rolled over us. She hadn't stopped smiling and ran ahead, teasing me. I ran after her until we were out of breath and stood there waiting for Leroy and Forklift to catch up. They ambled down the hard sand, pant legs rolled up for the surf. Leroy had reached out to hold his father's hand. I would have liked to have had a photo of this moment, and I told them this when they reached us.

"You sure keep on wanting what you don't have," Leroy said. Forklift took a deep breath, puffed out his chest, and watched the waves curling into the sand.

"Maybe it's not meant to be," Forklift said.

"What?"

"The camera. Maybe you ain't supposed to find it today, or ever. You ever think about that, Ugly?"

I shook my head. I had been quiet on the ride. The hot dog had miraculously stayed in my stomach, but I wouldn't say it settled it. The nerves were still there, but now they felt like thick ropes, and it was my thoughts that tugged them and made my stomach gong like a bell. I felt Emma's shoulder rub against mine. I looked over and she offered me an apologetic look, as if she held a part of my defeat as her own that day, and I loved her even more.

Forklift dragged his cane in the sand, making a cross.

"Now I don't know you any more than my son here likes to think he knows you, but I can tell you one thing from spending most of my life in jail. Not everything we think we need is what we need to learn. You all pouty now that you didn't find the camera, but you know what old Forklift thinks? Forklift thinks you looking at the wrong thing. Maybe you don't need the camera after all."

"But what about my sisters' souls?" I said, then wished I hadn't because Forklift laughed as soon as I did.

"Daddy," Leroy said, and I looked at him, cock-eyed because I had never heard him say this to anyone. Forklift poked his shoulder with the cane and continued.

"Hush up. Now let me finish, Leroy. I'm talkin' to Ugly here but you ought to listen up, too. Don't you see? You ain't supposed to free your sisters' souls. You supposed to free your own. Trust me. Your sisters' souls are smarter than that. They of spirit. Not here. In your head," he said and pointed to his temple.

"Soon as we nothin' but spirit, we make a bee-line to the gates up there. Soul's no fool. Not gonna wait around 'til some dumbass human like ourself set 'em free. They gone soon as they die."

I swallowed, watching a flock of seagulls fly over us.

"How do you know?"

"I don't," Forklift said. "But I can tell you my wife done leave the moment I popped her good in the head. Now she one of the brighter bulbs out there, but even if she some dim Nelly, I think she would have found a way to get to heaven even if I stitched up her soul in a burlap sac."

Emma turned to me, startled, and I stared at Forklift, wanting desperately to believe this man who had stolen from God, this man who had taken Leroy's mother when he was too young and powerless to stop him.

"Soul's gonna go where a soul needs to go. Dang! Ain't no way you stole your sisters' souls by taking their photo. What kind of crackpot thinking is that?"

It was getting dark and we turned back to the car, walking in silence, considering the truth in all of this. If The Forklift was right, I'd been spending my whole life trying to undo something I'd never done, and this was hard to handle, knowing it came from a man who had killed his own wife. Leroy sensed my unease and reached out to me, taking my elbow, pretending he was trying to steady himself on the dune.

"You gonna be okay with or without that camera, Ugly," he said, catching his breath after he had climbed back up. "It'll save you some trouble now, right?"

He sat down to put on his shoes, but I paused.

"Then why did you ever show me how to use it?"

Leroy looked up, meeting my eyes in the dying light.

"I thought it could teach you something."

"About what? Pain?" I asked, incredulous, wondering if this was a joke. Leroy shook his head and pointed at Emma.

"How to see beauty."

SIX

IT WAS AS IF a hex had been broken. Even though I didn't have a camera to use then, I could begin to see the beauty I had missed all those years. Emma was only one of the beauties in my world, but there was a whole palette to behold on our farm, even in its disrepair. It had never occurred to me until that day that my world could be beautiful, again, even without my sisters.

This was a staggering thought and it made me brace myself against the kitchen doorway for balance when I got home. My parents, who had been waiting for me, looked up from the table. My mother spoke first, eyes fixed on the window, watching Leroy's headlights illuminate a buggy, taillights fading in the darkness as he drove on.

"I thought you were done with all that business," she said.

"What business?"

"Running around with the English."

"I am," I said, and meant it. I didn't tell them I had been with Leroy.

"Then where on earth have you been?"

"Out," I said and made my way to the table in a daze.

"Out?" My mother stared at me, vexed. Out was not a word that registered among the Amish. We didn't just go "out" and wander aimlessly, especially on a Sunday. I wanted to tell Mamm that I finally had a new direction, but I couldn't empty everything in my mind on the table just then. I sat down instead and drank a glass of water as if I had just returned from a long drought.

At first, I'm not sure my parents believed the change in me, the eagerness to assume my role on our farm. I completed the entire To Do List in one month, then started my own, which included more ambitious tasks than repairing fenceposts and floorboards. For years, my mother's summer kitchen had been left half-smoldered by a grease fire that started when my sisters were making funnel cakes for a work frolic. We had never taken the time to repair it, and I asked Levi to help.

My mother was working in her garden when I told her. Her spade had just struck the rocks beneath the soil, and she looked up. It was a warm day in late April and she was perspired, cheeks ruddy from the sun.

"What did he say?"

"He will work for free," I said. "In fact, it was only under that condition."

My mother wiped her forehead with the back of her gardening glove.

"He'll repair the whole summer kitchen?"

"He's going to build you a new one. He's ready to start as soon as you say."

"Here? He's going to come here?"

I nodded and smiled. "You'll see him every day."

My mother could barely speak. Levi had refused all her offers to join us for dinner, thinking she and my father had already done enough to help him and Amos. For weeks after the funeral, she made dinner for them every day, and she continued to cook for them on Sunday. She had no intention of stopping either, even when they left her notes that said she was spoiling them and they'd be "ruined" by her good cooking. Whatever she cooked for us, she doubled and sent out with me in the buggy. Driving to Amos and Levi's gave me a chance to visit them, and try, as awkward as it was, to create a new relationship. We'd end up playing Rook. Actually, Levi and I would play while Amos studied the *Confession of Faith* and tried to hatch clever ways to win Emma's attention. He couldn't understand why she seemed so busy lately, uninterested in any kind of date.

Little did they know that on my way home each Sunday after making my delivery, I'd stop by Emma's house to say hello. Something had shifted after our adventure with Leroy, and we were less nervous around each other. The only thing that remained awkward was that whenever Emma reached out to hold my hand, I'd pull away. I wasn't ready to hold her like that, not yet, even though I did want to kiss her. From what I knew about kissing a girl, you had to hold her hand first.

We played a lot of cards. The Rook set was especially large and could hide the hand holding it. Still, our conversations flowed, and we had finally found a way to trust silence between us as a good thing. The more nights we spent together that spring, the more comfortable we grew, and the harder it was to be apart during the day. It was this need to see her more that prompted me to rebuild the summer kitchen. I wish I could say that my motivation was entirely for my mother's sake, but Emma and her mother needed to use the summer kitchen, too, since their own had been flooded that spring.

It wasn't only the summer kitchen I asked Levi to rebuild for my mother. I wanted him to build a greenhouse. By keeping ourselves busy with jobs like this, we avoided thinking about the statute of limitations that Patton had to file against me. We were digging the foundation in early May when Officer Fowler pulled up to the edge of our farm. He didn't dare drive down the driveway if he saw mamm in her garden, knowing she would chase after him with her hoe. After the reporters had taken liberties with our property, my mother had no qualms about keeping the police away. But this particular hot day in May, Johnny Fowler persisted.

He left his squad car in the small square of gravel we'd built for the roadside stand, where buckets of pears sat lonely in the shade of an umbrella. Our dog bounded at him, fearless and deaf to his demands to sit and heel. She snarled at him and Mamm said nothing to calm her down.

"I need to speak with your son, Mrs. Yoder."

"He's busy digging a hole."

"Yes, well, it's nice you people are consistent."

My mother said something to the dog in Deitsh, and the dog jumped up on Officer Fowler. He pulled out his Tic Tacs and rattled them at the dog, trying to distract her and move toward Levi and me. He looked frantic and out of breath. "You two get harder and harder to track down."

I leaned against my shovel.

"I haven't left since the week I got back."

Officer Fowler turned to Levi.

"I thought you'd be gone by now."

Levi turned his back, trying to ignore him, but I could tell that he wasn't wiping sweat from his eyes. I was livid at Office Fowler and felt my jaw tighten.

"Where would he go? He's home," I said. "It's his mom who left."

"Your mom?"

"She died," I said, wanting him to leave us alone. Even though it was hot, we had established a nice rhythm that morning and were making progress on the foundation. We'd gotten proficient at digging holes lately. We actually thought Officer Fowler might give us a break after everything that happened outside the prison, but he carried that look in his eye, the one that blazed with heroics.

"Oh, I'm sorry," Officer Fowler said. "I didn't know."

Levi begin to dig again, detecting his insincerity.

"Don't apologize. It's life. We've moved on," he said. "We would hope that the rest of you could move on, too. You gave your word."

Officer Fowler stared at him and paused, taken by his tone.

"Well then, I'd like to reconsider my words now that the Hottensteins have agreed to drop the trespassing charges if you both fix the lock and window." Levi nodded and resumed digging the hole.

"I think we can do that. Eli?"

"Okay," I said unable to believe what we were hearing. We were both sweating through our shirts and our backs were stained with salt. "What about Patton?"

Officer Fowler held up his hand.

"Just keep on doing your job, and I'll do mine," he said and turned and walked away. It would be the last time I would ever see Officer Fowler on our property. When he was far enough down the gravel driveway, I reached out and took Levi's shovel.

"Have you really moved on?" I asked.

Levi stared at me. "What are you trying to ask?"

I straightened, feeling the sweat down my back. I wanted to look Levi in the eyes, but he was wearing those sunglasses.

"I meant what I said. This is your home now, too."

"Yeah," Levi said, looking faded and weary in the sun. "Whatever you say."

I knew from the look on his face that he didn't believe me, and I was angry.

"Then you haven't moved on," I said. "You've lied!"

We both looked over at my mother, who had paused in her garden, over-hearing us. Levi kicked the edge of the trench we'd dug. "I haven't lied to you," he whispered.

"Maybe not to me. But you haven't forgiven yourself yet, have you?"

Levi took off his glasses, shielding his eyes from the sun.

"The night of the accident," Levi said, "I saw Hanna at the market. She was on a quick break and told me she didn't have time to talk, but that she was leaving for good."

He stared at me as the news registered.

"Where would she have gone?"

"New York. To dance. She was that good, Eli."

I felt the sun on my neck and scratched at it, realizing how far away New York was from us. Levi kicked the dirt and continued.

"I was so upset thinking about her on the way home. Then it began to rain. My mind was anywhere but the road. When I saw that tree," he said, pointing to the old walnut tree on the edge of our road, "I slammed on the brakes and turned, trying to avoid it, but didn't, then smashed your buggy against it. I didn't even see the buggy. I just heard the crunch of steel."

His voice quaked and I could hear him choke back the tears and stifle a sob with a swear word or two. He spit and stuttered, "Shit, shit," like he didn't know what to say because he'd finally run out of words. He struck his fist into the mound of dirt by his shoe and pounded it flat until his knuckles bled. "That's why, Eli. I can never forgive myself for driving like that, so out of my mind I couldn't even see the road! Do you understand?"

I stared at him, unable to answer, and turned, hearing the screen door open from the kitchen. My mother must have gone inside when she overheard us, but came charging out after she'd seen us through the kitchen window. Our shovels cast aside had been only one hint that something had gone wrong; we were all used to farm accidents. She carried the first-aid kit we kept on the hook beneath the match safe in the kitchen.

"What's happened?" she asked, looking down on Levi's bloody knuckles.

He stood, wiping the blood on his pants.

"Nothing, Mrs. Yoder. I'm fine."

"Here. Take this to clean your wounds."

Levi glanced at the first-aid kit and made a strange, sad laugh, the same laugh that I had first heard when I'd met him at the bishop's house so many years ago. He shook his hands, palms facing my mother, refusing her help. "It's too late for that," he said, then walked away from our farm for the last time, leaving me to wonder if he'd ever heal.

SEVEN

I WALKED TO EMMA'S house that night, alone, in the dark, with no flash-light or lantern. I needed the air and the stars and glimmer of the moon to light my way, and to prove that I could move through the darkness again. The Amish are taught to grieve in private, and so I took my heart out into the night to practice. There in the privacy of the single-lane road that connected our farm to the bishop's, I allowed myself to cry for Levi, and for the love Hanna had refused from him. She had taught me to read the sky in the summer of 1976, but I wished she had taught Levi to do the same. I wish she could have told him what she had come to believe about the sky, that God hung a star for everyone to guide them in their darkest hours. I wanted to tell him what I had not believed until then, that there were more stars in the sky than trouble in people's hearts, and that Levi was never alone in his despair. I was sorry that it had taken me this long to know it myself.

Emma was expecting me, but not what I would tell her. We sat on the small couch in her room and I tried my best to explain what I knew about Levi. I was worried about his future more than I was worried about my own.

"How can he live so alone like that?'

"When he's ready, he'll join us. Trust his process. Just like I've trusted yours."

She handed me a brush, and I took it and brushed her hair in silence. It was an odd reaction to the news I'd shared, but Emma was Amish and knew the wisdom of moving on gracefully. "You can't change his past any more than you can change your own," she said, her gaze soft in the flicker of the dying candle on the wall above us. "You can only let it go."

I felt my throat tremble.

"It's hard," I whispered.

"Holding on is harder."

"I don't want him to suffer," I said.

"Then stop suffering yourself."

I don't know if her words were meant as a threat or a dare. Emma stared at me, her half-believing eyes wandering, swooping low to my hands. "You still think they're ugly, don't you?"

I flinched, feeling the sting of her accusation. I lowered my gaze to the braided rug on the floor by the couch, wishing that all the secrets I had ever kept could be woven into it, and walked on, and worn out.

"They're not ugly, Eli. That boy was wrong."

I clenched my jaw and closed my eyes, wanting so hard to believe she was right. She sighed and slapped the back of the couch. There was no getting around Emma's hard stare. I did not look away.

"Leroy was wrong," I said.

Emma recoiled, struck by my words. I continued.

"I don't need a camera to see beauty when I have my own eyes. I'm looking at you, right?"

Emma nodded and swallowed. I wanted to reach out and rub smooth the lump in her long white throat, then unfurrow her brow. She looked so concerned there and completely disarmed by my honesty, and I'll admit, I liked this small sense of power I discovered by speaking the truth to her. But just as quickly, she flipped the table back on my lap.

"You're the beautiful one, Eli."

"What?"

"And I want you to hold me."

"Where? Why?" I panicked.

She stared at me waiting. I scratched my neck and turned, hoping that the door would be open so that I could get up and walk, stretch my legs, and breathe. Emma Beiler wanted me to hold her and I had every inner demon in the world advising me against it. The voice in my heart had always been louder and it shouted just then and I dropped the brush and pulled Emma toward me. I cannot say at sixteen whether or not it was passion or love that moved me, I only knew it was working. I wrapped my hands around her waist and her body went limp in my embrace. I had never touched another person like this and the more I held her, the closer I wanted to be. I buried my face into her neck and breathed in her sweetness and rocked her, as I would have liked to rock my sister, and myself, and anyone else who had ever resisted embracing their own beauty.

I don't know how long we held each other. The candle burned down to a stub and we sat in the darkness with the moonlight, content in our silence, listening to the rise and fall of our own breaths. Later, I watched Emma move her hands closer to my own, but rather than hold them, she leaned forward and grazed my wrist with her lips. It was the last thing I remembered before we fell asleep.

We woke the next morning with her father's hand between us, lulling us both out of our reverie. I blinked open an eye, seeing the bishop hovering over us with a pot of coffee and a plate of scrambled eggs and two forks. I turned my head, feeling a pinch in my neck, but I was no more stiff than Emma whose head was resting on my stomach.

"Time for milking," he said, and laughed, even though we all knew it was far from milking. There were no shadows at his feet. I figured it was past noon. I got up quickly, embarrassed, scrambling to replace the cushion between us.

"Slow down, you're early," he said, looking straight at me. Emma was trying to redo her hair and pin it back.

"We missed the morning," I said.

"We stayed up late talking, Datt."

"That's okay. The meeting doesn't start until noon."

I stared at him, curious. It was Thursday. There were no holy services performed among the Amish on Thursday.

"I meet candidates for baptism today," he said and reached out and squeezed my shoulder. "Emma knows I love surprises. And this is one of the best."

I did not want to disappoint Bishop Beiler, or Emma, but I didn't want to lie to them either. I had no more intention of kneeling for baptism in the fall than I did going back to shave beards at the barbershop. My life had forced me to become very present that spring and the only plans I had for the immediate future involved paying back my debts to Patton. It seemed unlikely that I would prepare for baptism while I also awaited my court date. It was like training a horse to run when you were planning to send him to the glue factory before he ever got to the track.

There was no point in me getting everyone's hopes up, even though it was too late. Seated at the bishop's kitchen table were about a dozen kids in *rumspringa*, many of whom I recognized as Canaries and Pinecones in their mid-twenties, including Amos. He looked more startled than surprised to see me walking down the stairs behind Emma, whose sleepy eyes and crumpled prayer cap intensified his suspicions, and confirmed everyone else's. It had been two years since Emma had started *rumspringa* and it was as much her family's guess as everyone else's about why she had waited to get baptized. Her father had been careful not to pressure her, but we all know why he was smiling that day. It wasn't just because the Amish community would become larger by a dozen or more members from our district, it's that his only daughter had chosen to join it. She had made it clear to everyone what she was waiting for, too: me.

Emma took the seat on the bench across from Amos and I took the only seat left, the one next to him.

Nobody spoke. Bishop Beiler poured a glass of water for himself, and beamed a smile as wide as his waist. He thanked us for having the wisdom to join the church, and he encouraged us to tell our friends to do the same.

"Our community is that much stronger today than it was yesterday, and any wayward traveler can rest knowing that it has the hands of you all waiting to carry him home, should he chose to turn back and follow your footsteps."

The bishop then told us of our responsibilities and of the course requirements that summer. He reminded us of the most important day, which was not really the third Sunday in September, when the baptisms were scheduled, but the second Saturday, when we had one last chance to turn back.

"Remember. Hidden sins of pride and disobedience, if not confessed, can lead to the Church's defeat. So think about that and consider the weight of these burdens in your hearts. You want to be lighter, to let the light in you."

Everyone nodded but me.

I kept looking at Emma, trying to prepare her for my announcement, hoping she would understand.

"I think there's been a mistake," I said.

"A mistake? Where?" Bishop Beiler looked down at me through his glasses.

"I'm not supposed to be here yet," I said.

I could feel Emma's eyes on me, but I did not dare return her gaze. I focused instead on Amos' tattered copy of the *Confession of Faith*, feeling the heat in my body. Then I lifted my eyes to the bishop.

"I need to tell you something," I said.

"Now?"

I nodded. Bishop Beiler cast his eyes down at the table of candidates. He took a sip of water and pointed to the door and I followed him outside to the barn where nobody could hear us but the chickens and the cows.

"I think I stole my sisters' souls," I said for the third time, feeling relieved, as if the thorn in a part of my heart had been suddenly tweezed out with the truth.

Bishop Beiler took off his glasses. He was near-sighted and leaned closer to look in my eyes when I told him what I had done so long ago. My nose was runny from the hay and I wiped it when I finished.

"Are there really graven images?" I asked.

Rather than give me a straight answer, he led me into the barn. "What is it?" he asked, pointing to the corner.

"A corncrib."

"Are you sure?"

"I can see the husks poking out of it."

I stared at him. He walked over, mashing the hay and lifted the lid.

"Come look," he said.

I followed his path in the hay and stood behind him, peering in. It looked like a corncrib. Wood and wire and lots of dried corn, a few spider webs in the corners. He pulled out a few ears, digging deeper into the bottom of the crib. "Now look and tell me what you see."

I moved closer and looked down, past the rows of dried corn cobs, to what appeared to be a gleaming white leather bag of sorts with the word SPALD-ING in black. "Do you know what it is?" he asked.

I shook my head.

"It's my secret," he said.

I stared at him.

"You're the bishop. You can't have any secrets."

"Oh, but I can, Eli. Because I'm human."

"But why don't we know this?"

"My secret isn't hurting me, or anyone else, nor is it pulling my attention away from God. If anything, it makes me feel closer to him when on the green."

He dug out a few more cobs of corn, pulling out a nine-iron golf club. I stared at him and he smiled, and in his eyes was the same steely twinkle his daughter shared whenever she got excited. I did not know that Bishop Beiler was a golfer. I knew that the Amish in our area had been debating the participation in the sport after several members had taken it up as a hobby recently. It made sense now why our district was not the dissenting voice, and why there had been no hoopla over the golf invitations I had received from other gangs that spring.

"You any good?" I asked.

Bishop Beiler looked over his shoulder. A barn swallow had flown in over us and landed on the rafters.

"I hit an Eagle once."

I nodded, impressed. Two strokes under par. From what I knew about golf from the men at the barbershop, Bishop Beiler had a good chance of playing with them, but probably never would.

"You play a lot?"

"Not so much. Why? You interested in joining me?"

I scratched my head. I couldn't tell if he was luring me into a trap or not. He was the bishop, after all, and I should have trusted his intentions, but he had that look in his eyes and it alarmed me.

"I just want to do the right thing," I said. "That's why I came to you."

The bishop tossed the corn over the Spalding bag and closed the corn crib.

"That camera keeps you up at night doesn't it?"

"Yes. I worry about their souls."

"You might want to worry about your own from now on. Your sisters are in God's hands, Eli. They've been in God's hands since you were a little boy."

I wanted to believe him.

"Let me tell you something about God's hands," he said and moved over to two hay bales and pulled them out to face each other, motioning for me to sit down. "Did you ever know that Jesus golfed?"

I shook my head. I had thought the game was relatively modern and couldn't imagine Jesus worrying about par.

"And Moses," Bishop Beiler added.

I leaned back, straining to see how God's hands played any part in the recreational pursuits of his own son. Bishop Beiler went on to tell me that one day Jesus and Moses were playing golf together. Jesus was supposed to perform a miracle on a leper that morning, but the sky was clear over Jerusalem and Moses pressured him into squeezing in a game. Jesus didn't want to offend Moses. He hadn't seen him in a while and he wanted to show his gratitude for Moses' hospitality. Jesus didn't play a lot of golf, and he wasn't particularly equipped to handle the bags (his back had been hurting lately) but, nevertheless, he agreed to one round of 18 holes, hoping that he'd warm himself up for the miracle he was about to perform later that day. But Jesus was having a tough time. It was hot, his goat skin bota had sprung a leak, he was starting to get dehydrated and his vision was blurred. It was all Jesus could do to focus on the ball, even though Moses was feeling fine in the heat (apparently he'd grown used to fiery weather after standing so close to the burning bush).

To make matters worse, it was a windy day and Jesus was having a hard time controlling the ball in the wind. When it was his turn, Jesus hit the ball hard, thinking that he was hitting it into a headwind, when the wind suddenly shifted into a tailwind, lifting the ball off the fairway, off the course, and over a small rock median into a pond where a frog caught the ball in its mouth just as an eagle was swooping in to pick him up in its talons. The eagle flew back over the course, over the fairway, and the frog, terrified for its life, opened its mouth, aghast. The ball then dropped on the fairway and rolled down the course and into the very hole that Jesus intended to hit.

"You're serious? This is true?"

Bishop Beiler wiped his brow. He was sweating.

"And you know what Moses did?" I shook my head. I couldn't imagine. "He turned to Jesus and said, 'I hate playing with your father.'"

I stared at him a moment, until he couldn't hold it any more and let out a howl. He lifted his hat and swatted my knee with it. I did not know how this had anything to do with my confession. I had stolen a soul, not a golf ball.

"Don't you see? God plays his hand in everything."

I nodded, wanting to believe that there were no accidents. That everything had a purpose, even pain.

"Then why did he take my sisters so soon?"

The Bishop locked eyes with me and I could see that the tears had come, but he staved them off with a deep breath. "That I do not know. I can only trust that their time had come to go to their spiritual home."

"But why did he leave me here?" I said, feeling my bottom lip tremble. It was a question I had thought about but had never had the courage to ask anyone.

"It wasn't your time to go," he said. "You have not done all of your work here yet. Don't you see? God wanted to help Jesus on the golf course so that he could save face with Moses and get on with his day and help the leper."

"I don't understand," I said.

Bishop Beiler sighed. He put on his hat.

"Whatever you think you've done with the camera was all part of a big plan that you might never have the ability to see fully. But if you can trust that all the bumps and ruts along your road have been there because God wanted them to be there, then you will find peace."

I stared at him.

"But Deuteronomy said a photo steals our souls."

The bishop held up his finger. "Yes. And no. I think what he was trying to say is that when most folks look at a photo, all they see is themselves while they turn their attention away from God. That's why we don't like our photos taken. God doesn't want us to forget that when we see a photo of ourselves, we're actually looking at him."

"So I didn't make a mistake?"

Bishop Beiler shook his head and got up.

"The only mistake you made is not seeing God in you."

I cast my eyes at my hands, wondering if maybe God was there, but had been caught somehow in the webbing.

EIGHT

I HAVE BISHOP BEILER to thank for almost everything else that happened that summer. While I did not join him for golf, I met him every week, for eight weeks, along with the rest of the candidates, to prepare for our baptism and memorize the eighteen articles of the *Confession of Faith* to "Conserve the Standards of Faith and Practice" (Article IV). Together, we were preparing to renounce the devil, the world and our flesh and blood, commit ourselves to Jesus and the church, and be obedient and submissive to it for the rest of our lives. For those of us who were young men, the bishop reminded us that by consenting to baptism, we had agreed to serve as leaders if we were ever called upon by the church. In other words, the stakes were about as high as they could get, and everyone was watching us. With Emma's help, I did my best to assure the bishop, and the community, that I would not be "wrecked on the rocks of worldliness."

The summer moved fast. Levi and I had not only built the summer kitchen and finished planting everything in the greenhouse, we had taken on other odd jobs here and there, rebuilding a covered bridge in Bart and making the cabinets for a retired math professor. Levi insisted on sharing the profits equally with me. By the end of August, I was a few thousand bucks short of paying back Patton's medical bills, let alone finance a new camera. To my surprise, my father suggested an auction. Not just any auction, but he asked the fire department at Gordonville if we could hold an additional auction for Patton in September. They did not object as long as we collected, sorted and distributed the donated items and made sure to keep them separate from those whose proceeds would benefit the fire department.

I asked Emma and Levi to help. They agreed enthusiastically. Amos declined for the simple reason that he felt he needed to prepare for baptism, even though he had been prepared for eight months. I think he couldn't stomach seeing Emma and me together, or admit to any of us that he had started to date a Beachy Amish woman from Leacock and had changed his clothes accordingly to earn her approval this time.

Emma and her mother had always participated in the auctions at Gordonville and were among the veteran cooks. Each year, their job was to lead nearly a hundred other Amish women to help make 3,120 donuts and Long Johns (the pastry, not the pajamas), 3,000 hoagies (subs to anyone not living near Philadelphia), 1,500 ham and cheese sandwiches, 300 egg sandwiches, 1,500 barbeque sandwiches, 3,800 hot dogs, 5,000 sodas and water, 1,300 boxed drinks, enough hot chocolate and coffee to fill our pond, and nearly 900 pounds of chicken.

While these figures may sound like an exaggeration, I invite anyone to visit a Gordonville auction and see for themselves how much food is consumed by the roughly 5,000 to 10,000 auction-goers who attend. The reason I mention this is that Emma and her mother had their minds on a lot, and the last thing I expected from them was to pay attention to my father's auction block.

Things had been going relatively smoothly. The auction was off to a strong start. Throngs of English and Amish crowded the huge yellow and white striped horse tent and the fire hall for quilts, while others scrambled into the garage to bid on antique furniture and handcrafts. A group of Amish guys played rounds of corner ball and those too young to play headed into the stubble of neighboring corn fields to play touch football. To date, it was one of the best attended auctions at Gordonville, mainly because of the weather—a crisp, dry, blue sky Saturday in early September, glowing gold and rust from the leaves on the trees. I had just turned seventeen the week before, and my birthday had come and gone with little celebration only because we were focused on the auction. It had required a massive collection that began in late May and included everything from oriental carpets and boat heaters to bed frames and miter saws. We had used the Esh's barn as a collection site and for storage, although we had to hire a moving company to haul everything to Gordonville, the cost of which I'd deduct from any money we earned for Patton.

By noon, we had earned nearly five thousand dollars, a little more than half of what I needed to pay off my debts.

"Thirty-five hundred more bucks and you're free," my father said.

Free, that is, of my debt. Patton had still not pressed charges against me, but he hadn't dropped them either. He knew about the auction, too. We had invited him and his family and my mother made arrangements to meet them for a meal before or after, whichever they preferred. We had not heard back from them, and though I searched the crowds, I saw no sign of Patton all morning. Emma reminded me that his presence was not the point. It was the effort I had put into helping him recover his losses that mattered.

We were in the middle of a bid on a Black & Decker table saw when Emma approached us with the BBQ sandwiches. Instead of handing them to us, or even looking at us, she set the tray aside on the table and walked over to a box of donations that we had received earlier that afternoon but had not had a chance to sort or list. It was a small open box, and my father, after having searched it, decided there was nothing of real value in it.

"No big items. Just junk from someone's garage."

From the look on Emma's face, there was something more than junk in the box. She looked up, locking eyes with me, and gestured for me to see for myself. The table saw was in mint-condition and the bids were rising: $100, $110, $125, $145, $175. I figured it would fetch at least $300. I had a few seconds to spare and walked over to the box to see what was inside. My father was right. Most of the items were junk, but sitting on top of a rusted cheese grater, and between a ceramic table lamp and plastic radio, was a camera. It was a Leica M3, but because I had already seen so many Leicas in Trevrose my heart did not leap. I figured it was probably just another camera, which excited me only because I'd be $1,200 closer to paying off my debts if we sold it that night. Emma nudged me to check the counter. I reached into the box and flipped over the camera and there in the little window was the number one. That's when my heart started to pound and my father called SOLD, but I did not move. I looked up at Emma, whose eyes shifted to the bidders. Everyone, including my father, was waiting for me.

"Eli," he said, but I only watched his mouth move. I did not really hear what he said after that. I held the camera, realizing this was my last chance. I had never swiped anything off my father's auction block and I knew the penalty for such an action would likely result in my suspension from ever working with my father again, but I was not concerned about my future then, only my past.

Had there been a row of faceless Amish dolls on my father's table that night, I would have looked to them again and asked them for permission. I looked to Emma instead, hoping to see any indication in her eyes that what I wanted to do with the camera was the right thing, but she was as stone-faced as everyone else. I had worked so hard that summer to earn her respect and that of the Amish, but I had already made a promise to my sisters.

I took the camera and ran behind my father, too distracted to notice that Patton had come to the auction and was standing in the corner with my mother. She flashed what looked like two halves of a plaster cast, but I didn't stop to collect them or talk. I ran out of the tent and climbed the embankment to Old Leacock Road, crossed the railroad, and ran south and west through the setting sun, past empty corn fields and silos as black as the trees. I ran as fast as my legs would carry me until I was home. I flung the door open and took the Ohio Blue Tips from the match safe on the kitchen wall. Then I ran outside again and down the walkway, behind the barn and sunk to my knees by the pond.

I lifted the camera above the water and studied it in the moonlight. The metal edges caught the light and the lens reflected an eerie vision of myself. Even though it was dusk, there was enough light to expose the film so I clicked it open and pulled out the spool. I struck three matches at once, then set them against the edge of the film and sat there in silence, watching it burn. It surprised me to see how durable the film was and how long it took to melt. It was warm and I took off my shoes. I had used three more matches by the time it was gone, and even though the ashes were hot, I scooped them up in my hands, waded into the pond, and tossed them into the water.

Then something unexplainable happened. As soon as the ashes touched the water, I saw a series of white lights glowing from the edge of the pond. I stood there, frozen, watching them slowly swirl around me. I wanted to touch them and held my hands out, palms up, only to see the lights go through the skin. When I looked up, I realized that each of the lights were moving through my body, and slowly, one by one, dropping back down into the water. I did not want them to go so quickly and plunged my hands into the water, trying to catch the light, but the brilliant beams sunk deeper, between my toes and the rocks beneath them. I don't know how long I stood wading there, plunging my hands into the water, but when the light was gone and I was alone again, I realized that I was washing my own feet.

I can't tell you how long I stayed in the water. I do remember feeling groggy, like I had just awakened from a long dream. What startled me most in that blurry waking state was seeing a trace of light still in my hands, illuminating the fingers locked inside the webbing. I had never seen the bone structure quite like this, as stark and striking. I stood there and laughed, but the laughter coming from me wasn't mine, not exactly, but the booming in my heart, silencing the lies I had told myself about who my hands had made me in this world. I don't know how long I laughed, but I wanted to stay there long enough for my mother to hear the sound God made when he forgave me for my mistake.

I needed to knock on Leroy's door. I needed to knock on a whole lot of doors the next day, including my Uncle Isaac's. I asked him if he would arrange a hot air balloon ride, since I missed my chance when I was sixteen. He stared at me from the potato garden he was hoeing and said, "Thought you were afraid of heights?"

I shook my head and smiled.

"That was last year," I said. "Things have changed."

Uncle Isaac studied me in the morning light. He pointed to the calf that we had birthed the year before. She was poking her pink nose through the fence behind him.

"You're not the only one who grew," he said.

Uncle Isaac agreed to take me up, but only if I could arrange to find four other passengers. He didn't want to waste the fuel on one person. He said this should be a party. No problem, I thought, knowing exactly who to ask.

Leroy nearly nicked his client when I knocked on his door that day. Even though the door was open, he set the electric clippers aside and walked over and stared at me, like he didn't believe what he was seeing or hearing, so I knocked again so loud that I woke up Forklift, who'd drifted off to sleep under a dryer in the back of the shop. I told him, Levi, the bishop and Emma, too, to meet me at dawn in the soy field behind my uncle's barn. My folks weren't into hot air balloon rides and insisted on staying grounded and riding in the chase truck instead, with Ruthanne. I was surprised my father had agreed after the commotion I'd caused at the auction. I have a feeling Emma had a lot to do with the look on his face when he returned to our farm. He had seen me walking up from the pond with the camera and asked, "Is it finally gone?" I didn't know if he meant the film or the lie or the troubles of my past, but I said yes, then told him I would give the camera to Patton. He seemed satisfied and said nothing more about it.

We were moving on, and we were moving up, lifting off the ground in the wicker gondola, moving higher into the pink swirl of dawn. I had never been higher than Bunker Hill but my feet weren't the only ones that hadn't left the ground until then. Levi, Emma, and the bishop grabbed the edges of the basket, eyes as wide as the balloon itself. I'd urged Leroy to bring binoculars and when we floated over our farm, I pointed down to the greenhouse where I had planted more than two thousand violets. He didn't need binoculars to know what it was. It looked like one huge purple square laid into this quilt, just for him. He turned to me and I saw the tightness in his throat. He simply nodded once and lowered the binoculars and looked down again. The earth rotated slowly below us, and the air grew more quiet the higher we soared over our hayfields and homes. I stood beside Emma, seeing what I had not seen when I had returned from the prison that dull gray day in March. No matter which direction we faced, the land rolled out in one continuous patchwork, where everything connected to the rest. Seeing the world from such heights, I realized that there were no separations and no true boundaries. We were all connected to each other, no matter how many differences kept us apart. I saw the glow in Emma's eyes as Uncle Isaac let out some gas and the balloon dipped lower and grazed the treetops. She was thrilled and beamed a smile. Leroy, Levi and the bishop were enjoying the ride, too, but were too focused on the vast world between heaven and earth to notice that I had reached out to Emma and, finally, held her hand in my own.

NINE

IT IS EMMA'S HAND I feel on my shoulder now, nudging me awake and lifting me up off the desk from where I work. "Come to bed, Eli. Tomorrow is a big day." I would like to crawl into our warm bed with her, but something about the stack of pages I have written between dinner and now won't let me go. There is something incomplete in my story and it gnaws at me and keeps me awake at these hours when I should be sleeping.

Though I am drowsy with the memories of our balloon ride years ago, I am aware of Emma's scrutiny. She reaches over the stack of pages and uncrumples those that I've tossed on the floor, salvaging a phrase here and there that might be useful for my first sermon. Nobody has given me much guidance. A year ago, I would have never believed anyone who told me that by preparing for it, I would end up writing a book.

The other ministers instructed me to prepare nothing at all and to trust what the Lord will say through me. But I can't take that chance. I know that tomorrow's sermon bears more significance for me than most others. My oldest daughter, whom I have named Hanna, is joining the Amish community as an adult. Her brother, my oldest son, Gideon, knelt last year, just one month before I was struck with the lot. Terrible timing. I would have preferred he ran around for a few more years in *rumspringa*, which would have eliminated me as a candidate for ordination among the Lancaster County Amish. Of course, I could never tell Emma that. In a way, I was taking her father's place. She has always loved men of faith, and I wonder, at times, if she really knows who she married. Or maybe she has known my fate all along and was waiting for me to catch up with it.

A cool breeze blows through the window and scatters the pages from the top of the stack beside my arm. Emma shuts the window and pulls down the blind, blocking my view from the old walnut tree, as if she knows the only way to make me come to bed and rest is by cutting me off from my past.

I know that she, too, has not slept much tonight, and I can see her tired eyes in the flicker of the kerosene lamp she's carried with her, if not to light her way, to review my work. I can feel her reading my words and it makes me uneasy. I don't know if what I've written will make sense to anyone but myself and I'm afraid to ask her what she thinks. I can't bear the thought of disappointing her.

She thumbs the stack of pages. "Do you think you could write any more?"

I see the glimmer in her eye in the lamp light and it comforts me to know that her sarcasm has always been her way of expressing love. I nod.

"Too bad," she says. "I need you more than these pages do."

With that, she slips her hand into mine and leads me out of my dark room.

◇

I am not hungry at breakfast and push the eggs around my plate. Our other children, years younger than Gideon and Hanna, fidget in their seats, bundles of energy brimming with anticipation and excitement for the ritual they have heard changes lives.

I roll across the floor in my father's old chair and, like him, deposit my dirty coffee mug into the sink. I pause, seeing through the open screen door my mother and Emma in the garden, cutting the last flowers of the summer. I believe they are bringing them for Hanna, but something about their hushed giggles and bent over posture makes me believe they are conspiring about something that I'm not supposed to know.

They are quiet during the ride to the service and only the squeaking struts in our buggy break the silence. When I ask them why they are not speaking, they shrug. I glance sideways from time to time, catching the look they exchange beneath the brim of their black bonnets. I can't decide if they are more nervous about my sermon than excited for Hanna's baptism. I pray that God will speak through me, because I don't quite trust that the words that will come from my mouth will be as mighty. And might is a good thing to have as a minister. Might and courage and faith.

My stomach flip-flops the rest of the ride. I remember to look at the sky, and I see in the cloud cover a hole where the morning sun burns through. They had called for rain, but even my bones know better than to trust the forecast. There is something hopeful in the air, but I can't detect it and think it's a projection of my pride. Yes, I am happy and relieved that Hanna has chosen to join the church. The father in me knows this looks good for me and my family. It feels good, too. But the young minister inside scolds me. How can I be *Hochmut* and give a sermon? It seems ironic and doesn't feel right.

The morning only gets more peculiar when we arrive at the barn where the service will be. We park beside the empty bench wagon, among a row of two dozen unhitched buggies, the horses chewing damp grass in the pasture behind us. When I climb down from the buggy, I notice that the group of men gathered at the fence post stop talking. I recognize them from my youth, a group of Canaries, all grown men, married, fathers now. I am surprised to see they have come for our service. Most of them have moved to other districts. Aside from the auctions, we have not gathered like this for years, and I half expect to see a volleyball net strung between their buggies. They uncoil the circle they have formed and step out of it to greet me with a passing tentative look that only makes me more nervous. Emma notices it and steps closer to me, as if to block any doubt she has sensed coming between me and what I am supposed to do.

I take my place among the bishop, deacon and other ministers of my district and the service goes as planned. For the most part, it is unremarkable in the best of ways. All the candidates have memorized the 18 Articles of Faith, voices bound with conviction. My stomach settles half-way through the service, and the chatter in my head grows quiet.

I can almost hear my heart speak when out of the corner of my eye, I see the flitter of dust motes in the shaft of laser-light that cuts into the barn when the back door opens. I don't know who is startled more, because we all gasp when we see, backlit by the sun rising behind him, Levi Esh, more white-haired than blond now, bearded and a bit stooped from years bent over his carpenter's bench or hiding from us, we will never know. I catch a glance from the Canaries, who share a bench a few rows in front of me, realizing they've been in on the secret all along. Though I have never liked surprises, I am grateful for this one and I drop my chin in the most imperceptible nod of approval.

Levi is the oldest man we know who has dressed like us and lived like us, but has never chosen to join us. Part of me can already hear the excuses he has made for our children: "But Levi Esh waited until he was like 60 to get baptized!"

I try to hold back the laughter that rises from my stomach, realizing that Levi already knows the power of his influence on others, for better or worse, when I see that he is still wearing those sunglasses. They make him look even more modern now and slightly out of place in our service. I guess he wouldn't have it any other way. His very presence begs us to love him and accept him as he is, flaws and all.

He lifts his hat and drops it on the back bench where the youngest children at the service clamor to pick it up. They hold it like the prized possession it is. Levi walks down the aisle, eyes fixed on me with a crooked smile that suggests he is both happy to be here and embarrassed that he has waited so long.

What makes my heart stop, though, is that Levi has not only come to the service, he has come to kneel beside Hanna. She knows our story and holds my gaze as she would my hand, gentle but strong. She possesses her aunt's eyes, and it is all Levi can do to keep his from spilling with water. She reaches out and puts her hand on top of his and he drops his head, closes his eyes, and recites the *Confession of Faith* as if it were a song he has sung every day of his life. Hearing him, I think it's likely he has. It is both a reminder of the mistakes he's made in his past and a bearing for the action of his future. Just by being here, I know he will be fine, and I am thankful that he has joined us.

When it is my turn to give the sermon, I tell our story, trusting God to guide me. The words flow easily, and though it is an unlikely display among the Amish, I see the tears flow into beards and bonnets. When I finish, I know my story is complete and that my service as a minister will be to help people make sense of the events that don't seem to add up at first, and to find meaning in the pain and chaos of their lives. I know now that it is our responsibility to each other, and to God, to bear witness to the things that go unresolved in our hearts.

I catch the smile on Emma's face when I open my eyes. Hanna and the candidates have already filed out of the barn and Levi follows them, retrieving his hat from my youngest daughter, Ruth, who has somehow taken it into her possession. At the threshold, Levi turns and looks back at the congregation, then puts on his hat and leaves.

A bouquet of the last summer flowers from our garden lays across a place setting at our table. I look over at my mother who winks, pulling out the chair for Levi, who joins us for the fellowship meal. I introduce him to my children and they want to know about the time I took their mother to Philadelphia to find the camera. Levi looks up, perplexed, yet covering for me.

"Oh, my. I don't know that story," he says.

They pester him to tell more tales of me at sixteen, and Levi indulges them with one story of the photocopier. I will not get any verbal compliments from him for the sermon I have given that day, but I know the bishop and the ministers are pleased when they send us home with extra pies.

I stand with Emma by the buggy and load sleepy children and sweets.

"I think I'm going to walk home," I say, full of so much.

We step behind the buggy, out of view from the others, and quickly kiss.

"You're going to be a great minister," she says. "My father would be pleased."

I smile, imagining bishop Beiler in heaven, playing golf with Jesus and Leroy and Ruthanne.

"What's so funny?" Emma asks, detecting much more in my smile.

I say, "The way things turn out."

Emma nods and climbs into our buggy. I wave and walk away.

◇

I take a short cut through our neighbor's alfalfa field and arrive at the walnut tree at the edge of our farm. I can see in the distance, across the road, little Ruth, all cheeks and eyes at six years old, running toward me in her purple dress.

"Papa!" she calls through the gravel dust. "Papa, wait for me!"

"Okay," I shout back to her and wave. I want to tell her that I'm not going anywhere. In fact, I've never really left this tree, which is why I've forbidden all of my children to climb it. It occupies too much of me to allow room for any of them to explore. Ruth is the only one who forgets. For as long as I can remember, she has pestered me to climb it, but my list of excuses exhausts her each time: broken arms, broken legs, broken neck. It's been enough to scare her away, but she doesn't seem scared at all the way she's charging toward me.

"Be careful," I say as Ruth nears the edge of the road. She waits for a few cars to pass. Those that know us go by and wave, those who don't slow down and take our picture. Ruth, seeing the camera jutting out of the window, immediately closes her eyes.

"It's okay, Ruthie. They're gone."

She opens her eyes and smiles, looks both ways, then crosses to where I stand, plowing into my leg with her head. She wants me to lift her up so that she can see the world from upside down and continue our on-going game of "What Do You See" that we have taught her to help her learn English. But I am tired and don't have the energy to lift anything, and instead I hold her hand. She seems fine with my decision, already intrigued by the proximity she has to the tree. Then something shifts in her and awakens the desperation. She tugs on my arm.

"I must climb it," she says.

"Oh, really? Why?"

I want to laugh, but Ruth is serious and points to the tree. She kneels at the base of the trunk, imploring. "For you," she says, but I don't know if she means the tree or me.

"Okay, Ruth. Okay," I say, too tired to disagree. "Just this once."

She can hardly contain her excitement and jumps into my arms. I take a deep breath and lift her into the lowest branch. I'm surprised by her balance and the ease with which she settles into the limbs, like she's been there before. She leans her head against a thick branch and, shielding her eyes from the sun, looks up into the tree, beyond the fringe of gold leaves.

"What do you see?" I ask.

She looks down on me and smiles, "What do *you* see, papa?'

I train my eyes on the bark and the trunk and the branches of my youth, and the scar, though healed, that remains. I turn my mind away from the memory and look up at Ruth. After all these years, I can finally say, "I see paradise."

AMISH PLUCKETS
(also called Pull Buns)

1 cake yeast	3 eggs, well beaten
¼ cup lukewarm water	3 ¾ cups flour
1 cup milk, scalded	melted butter
1/3 cup sugar	¾ cup sugar
5 Tbs. butter	½ cup finely chopped
½ tsp. salt	nuts and cinnamon

Dissolve yeast in the ¼ cup water. Set aside. To scalded milk add sugar, butter and salt. Let cool. Add eggs and dissolved yeast and enough flour to make batter stiff. Cover and let rise until mixture doubles in size. Punch down and let rise again until doubled in size. Make small dough balls about ¾ inch in diameter and dip in the melted butter. Then roll balls in a mixture of sugar, nuts and cinnamon. Pile the dough balls loosely in an ungreased angel food cake pan and let rise for 30 minutes. Bake in 400 degree oven for 40 minutes. After first 10 minutes of baking, decrease oven heat to 350 F. Will be golden brown when done. Turn pan upside down and buns will come unstuck in cluster of rolls. Everyone 'plucks' from the hot cluster.

LEROY'S AFFAIR
(otherwise known as Wet-Bottom Shoofly Pie)

1 unbaked 9-inch pie shell	½ tsp. cinnamon
1/3 Tbs. baking soda	1/8 tsp. nutmeg
¾ cup boiling water	1/8 tsp. ground cloves
½ cup or less dark molasses*	½ cup dark brown sugar
1 egg yolk, beaten	2 T shortening
¾ cup flour, sifted	½ tsp. salt

Dissolve soda in the boiling water. Add molasses. Cool. Beat in egg yolk. Pour mixture into pie shell. Top with crumb mixture of the flour, spices, sugar, shortening and salt. Bake in 400 F oven for 10 minutes. Reduce heat to 325 F and bake 30-35 minutes on baking sheet. It is advisable to use less molasses and prevent spillage in the oven. Pie should be firm when done.

ACKNOWLEDGEMENTS

No book ever comes into the world alone. I am grateful for the help, encouragement, faith and guidance of the following people—family, friends, readers, colleagues, in no particular order, who assisted me during and after the writing of this novel. I could write pages in praise of your contributions, but in honor of simplifying the complex, I'm making a list instead: My parents, Ellis and Joan Payne, Michael Carlisle, Ethan Bassoff and Masie Cochran at Inkwell Management, Diane Gedymin, editor Pamela Feinsilber, Todd Koons, George Grenley, Louise Henriksen, Lysa Selfon Puma, Rosanne and David Selfon, Hilary Blake Hamilton, Amy Lanigan, Laura Marquez, Daniel Christian, Holly Shantara Farrow, Dr. Colleen Lenihan, Scott Stender, Julia Violich, Anna Conklin, Adrienne Hall Lindholm, Diane Liu Scallon, Carolyn Hughes, Tom Schlesinger, Donna Laemmlen, Jennifer Chapin, Kathleen Caldwell, Kevin Smokler, Caroline Paul, Rita Payne, Christopher Gortner, Erika Mailman, Cathryn Ramin, Joyce Maynard, Douglas Heikkinen, Lisen Stromberg, Christie O'Toole, Jennifer Chapin, Peter Chandonnet, Jon Chandonnet, David Moore, Tom Barbash, Dr. Connie Kondravy, Candace O'Donnell, Kirsten McFarlane Heikkinen, Brent Mekosh, Lyndsey Sagnette, Thomas Clarke, Jesse James McTigue, Jango Sircus, Daniel Davila, Ryan Hess, Scott Bishop, Amos King, Monica Thomas, Sue Bowser, Mary Ann Heltshe-Steinhauer, Trudi Mancia, The Copy Shop of San Rafael, Minneapolis Book Club, the Skywriter community and the MFA writing students at California College of the Arts. You have taught me. I'm also grateful to Leslie Iorillo of leslie i. design, photographers Holly Stewart and Cindi Kinny, and Dr. Fred Luskin for his work on forgiveness.

I could not have survived the many spells of doubt without Daniel Weaver, my husband and best friend. Thank you for believing in this story, for shining your light, lending a hand (or two), and for showing me how to laugh.

Lastly, thank you to the Marin Arts Council who helped to make this journey possible, and to the Amish and "English" of Lancaster County, Pennsylvania, whose way of life has enriched my own and given me deep roots.

Reading Group Guide

1. What is the nature of forgiveness? What is the difference between acceptance and forgiveness? How long "should" it take and what does it take to reach forgiveness? Do you need to know who harmed you in order to forgive? Is it necessary to know exactly what happened (the whole story) in order to forgive? Do you need an apology or acknowledgement of harm in order to forgive? Do you need to forgive yourself before forgiving another? Did each of these characters actually forgive - the mother? Eli? Levi?

2. What is the connection between compassion, humility, and forgiveness? In the Amish community? In our ("English") society?

3. How is laughter used in this book, in the Amish community? Is it a sign or indication of healing? Forgiveness? What were the times in the story when laughter was a sign of healing? Did Eli avoid laughter because he was afraid of losing his grief? Of distancing himself from his sisters?

4. What is the role of memory in this book? In the Amish culture? Was the role of Eli in this book to be the carrier of memory? How does writing/being the writer serve the role of communal story teller/memory keeper? What are the burdens and the rewards of that responsibility?

5. How does cooking and gardening offer Amish women creative expression that would otherwise go unseen? What is the significance of Eli's mother's garden? How does she use it, or not use it, to cope with her grief? The Amish are known for their baked goods. What was the significance of baking pluckets in Eli's house? In what ways does food play a role in preserving distinct cultural values for new generations?

6. Hair seems to be a theme in the book. What is the significance of hair to the Amish? What is the significance of the mother's cutting the daughters' braids? Why did Eli find his mother's act in cutting his sisters' hair so frightening and wrong? What was the significance of brushing Emma's hair? Why does Leroy shave off all of Eli's hair rather than just give him the haircut he wanted? How did it affect Eli's plans for rumspringa? Did it help or harm Eli in his journey to self-understanding? What about the fact that Eli becomes an expert shaver, specifically of facial hair?

7. Why is Leroy, the person who actually helps Eli the most, an outsider but not considered "English"? What is the difference to the Amish in these distinctions? Why did the Amish trust him and let him in? How did Leroy facilitate Eli's growth and self-acceptance and help him learn about forgiveness? Why did he use the nickname "Big Ugly"? Did that help or hurt Eli?

8. What do you do when you live in a community with very distinct and defined values and you don't believe or practice them all? How do you know what rules you can break and what rules you cannot? How can you learn when there is so much silence? Is it possible to have value differences and still live in such a homogenous community?

9. Was Eli motivated by survivor guilt after the accident? What about his father? How does his father deal with the tragedy? In what ways does he understand Eli's angst and journey? How is 'hiding' a pattern that Eli adopts from his father?

10. The book is called Kingdom of Simplicity. The Amish call themselves "Plain People." What does simplicity really mean to the Amish? Eli's journey seems to be a quest to understand the complexity of this "simple" culture. In what ways is it simple, and in what ways very complex and somewhat incomprehensible to outsiders, "The English"?

11. The idea of rumspringa seems to reflect a great understanding of what adolescents need. What does it accomplish for the Amish? What are the expectations that are placed on kids in rumspringa and the limits they are given? To what extent does it provide freedom and to what extent is it very constrained —for Eli? for his sister Hanna? for Levi and his brother Amos? What are the dangers of rumspringa—for the community? for the individual teens?

12. Cameras seem to be the focus of a great deal of trauma and in many ways the catalyst for much of what happens in this book. How is it the source of both tragedy and growth for Eli? What is the significance of the Amish belief in 'graven images' and photos? What does Eli actually learn about the camera and its power?

13. Grace and divination, though seldom named in the book, play a large role in Eli's fate. In what ways did Eli get in his own way and prevent grace from

happening? What is the ultimate irony in his fate? What is the nature of a true "calling" and why do people often resist receiving it? Is it possible to move toward a higher truth without changing?

14. Discuss the final scene with the tree. What does it mean? How is the scar used as a metaphor? What does it mean for Eli? What has he been able to do?

15. How does the cover image convey the theme of this book? Whose hands are they really? How does the story continue through this image even after the reader finishes the book?

Recommended reading:
Forgive For Good, by Dr. Fredric Luskin, PhD
Rumspringa: To Be or Not to Be Amish by Tom Shachtman
Amish Grace: How Forgiveness Transcended Tragedy by Donald B. Kraybill, Steven M. Nolt, David L. Weaver-Zercher
The Riddle of Amish Culture by Donald B. Kraybill
A History of the Amish by Steven M. Nolt
Amish Society by John A. Hostetler

About the Author

Holly Payne is a novelist, screenwriter and writing coach who assists writers around the country with story development, writing and revision. She is the founder of Skywriter Series writing workshops and private coaching, and Skywriter Ranch, a writing retreat held annually each summer in the Rocky Mountains. An avid traveler, her first two novels were inspired by trips to Turkey, Hungary and Croatia. *The Virgin's Knot*, published in the U.S. by Dutton/ Plume (Penguin) and in nine countries, was chosen as a Contra Costa Times Book Club Pick, a Barnes & Noble Discover Great New Writers Selection, a Border's Original Voices Book and nominated for The First Novelist Award by the Master of Fine Arts in Creative Writing Program of Virginia Commonwealth University. Payne's second novel, *The Sound of Blue* (Dutton/Plume), is set during the Balkan conflict and is based on a true story of a Serbian refugee Payne befriended while teaching English in Hungary. Payne received a MFA from the Master of Professional Writing Program at USC. She is currently working on a new novel of historical fiction set in medieval Europe.

Holly invites readers to keep in touch and share their own story of forgiveness. Please see the website for more information about the book, the 'story behind the story', and more.

Book Clubs are welcome to contact Holly directly
for in-person and phone discussions!

WWW.KINGDOMOFSIMPLICITY.COM

or email Holly at
holly@holly-payne.com

To learn more about Holly's coaching, workshops and retreats:
WWW.SKYWRITERSERIES.COM